BOOK ONE IN THE QUANTOLOGIST SERIES

QUANTOLOGY

DISCOVERY OF AGES PAST

KRIS AULD

Published by Kris Auld Publishing, 2022

ISBN 978-1-7396131-0-5

Cover design by Virtually Possible Designs

FORWARD BY THE AUTHOR

Working on this book has been a labour of love and I'm extremely proud of the result. As a child I never thought this could be an achievable goal due to my dyslexia. I strongly believe that with passion and commitment people can achieve anything.

I would personally like to thank all my friends and family for their support, encouragement and feedback. When I decided to write my first book I was hesitant about my abilities, however when I began to write I found a confidence I never thought I had.

Creating this book has been an extremely fulfilling and creative experience which I have loved doing. I hope this is the start of my creative journey and I continue to write for many more years to come.

PROLOGUE

The course of human history has seldom been easy, throughout humanity's evolution there have been periods of accelerated advancement. The first major acceleration came within the industrial revolution, leading to the golden era of advancement in the twentieth and twenty-first centuries. Now something seismic was about to be discovered, the year of 2347 will be known as the birth of the Quantum age.

Humankind had dramatically changed since the industrial revolution. Gone were the self-obsessed capitalist industries with their large polluting chimneys, churning out filth and waste in the search for profit. Now responsible and social environmental agendas lead the world's economies. War had become extinct and countries actively helped each other to thrive with more advanced societies helping developing nations achieve their goals.

How and why has society changed to a sustainable way of living over the last 250 years compared to a millennia of self-advancement? In 2087, several events occurred that would change the world forever, ensuring humanity's need to evolve.

During the second half of the twenty-first century, global temperatures began to rise, causing many environmental disasters. Forest fires and hurricanes became more common and the melting of the ice caps accelerated.

2087 started off like every other year, with the usual global issues that countries had learnt to manage. Then in June of that year, the freshwater which had been melting into the seas had a dramatic effect on global Thermohaline circulation.

Thermohaline circulation is what allows the ocean's surface to mix with deeper waters. The mixing is due to the different water temperatures within the ocean. The warm and cold currents regulate the planet's temperature helping to support many complex eco-systems. In 2087 these currents slowed causing a global crisis.

Temperatures in the northern hemisphere plummeted as the warm currents from the equator stopped flowing into the Atlantic Ocean, affecting North America and Europe. This cooling caused huge climate impacts with snowstorms and blizzards crippling Northern Europe, Northern America and Russia. Africa, South America, and Australia received less rainfall causing significant droughts which led to the worst global famine in human history. Asia saw an increase in class-five cyclones which caused deep flooding across the continent and the cities of Singapore, Hong Kong, and Osaka were savaged by the largest storms on record, leaving millions dead.

The dramatic events in 2087 took nearly two billion lives and shook the world to its core. Many governments fell and it looked like the world would descend into chaos.

However, the global climate seemed to be resetting itself and in 2088 calmer weather returned. After the dark events in 2087, the nations of the world came together and united to help each other. Out of all the pain and suffering came a real change in attitudes. People began to care for each other and the values of truth, acceptance, and cooperation flourished. In 2090, the United Nations was reformed and became the United Humanity. World leaders signed a new global Magna Carta called The Reawakening which recognised all life as valuable. It eradicated war and reformed global economies to focus on sustainability, acceptance for all, and environmental protection.

By the year 2347, human society was dramatically different to that of 2090. Old fossil fuel power stations were gone, replaced with green renewable energy. Trees, shrubland, and flowers were planted in every spare scrap of land. The rivers and seas became havens for wildlife and nature reserves were found in every country. Recycling and waste management were seen as the highest priority with new technology helping society to become truly sustainable. These changes were celebrated across the world.

The move away from a greed-based economy changed how people interacted, now every nation on earth had evolved and developed into accepting blossoming democracies. In a show of unity, the world came together on the 5th of June to celebrate The Reawakening and to promote environmental awareness.

In the 250 years since The Reawakening, the world had turned to science to help deal with humanity's problems. With no war or focus on profit, science was allowed to excel, huge leaps were made in medical and environmental agendas helping to create a societal utopia.

This science renaissance had benefited the human race in many ways. Weather and the global climate were now regulated by advanced satellites dissipating tornados, hurricanes, or any violent storms. World hunger had completely disappeared and food production had moved away from intense animal farming leaving more land available for homes and nature. Housing had changed too. Everyone was now expected to live in harmony with nature and people had the choice to live wherever they wanted in the world on the condition they protected it. Property was no longer a commodity which people were allowed to own. It was now the responsibility of communities to manage their districts as a commonwealth, with strict jurisdictional measures aligned to the agenda of sharing natural resources.

Finally, medical science advanced to help people live long and happy lives, letting them lead the life they wanted and ensuring everyone had the opportunity to succeed.

As with all great advances and changes to society, there was a minority of people who craved the old ways, focusing on nationalism over unity. Fortunately, people who held these views were rare and whilst some achieved political power, they never really succeeded in changing the direction of society. In the last few years, a resurgence of the old ways had started to gain traction and some turned away from science and back to self-gratification.

Science developed over the centuries to become almost like a religion. Several huge scientific centres of excellence were created. People could share ideas, work on problems together, and benefit humanity. One of these centres was based at Cambridge University. It had an excellent reputation for science throughout its history, during The Reawakening, the institute led several sustainable energy projects which helped to stabilise the world's atmosphere. In the twenty-fourth century, Cambridge had become a magnet for top scientists from around the world. Most importantly over the last five years, the world's foremost physicist and archaeologist had been working on a very special secretive scientific project that they knew would change the world.

It was only recently that the team made an incredible discovery, this discovery could lead to multiple benefits for humanity and help those dissenting voices which craved for the old days to re-evaluate their position. The team itself was made up of four people who had been selected specifically for the project.

The programme was led by Maya Evans, the world's leading quantum physics professor. She grew up in America and moved to teach at Cambridge ten years ago. Maya had been working alongside Marcus Larsson for years, he was a leading professor in the field of archaeology. Marcus was from Sweden and had a passion for utilising science to help bring to life the stories of the past. There were also two PhD students assigned to the project. Both these students were seen as prodigies. Firstly, Kalani Iona, who like Maya, was a quantum physicist and a specialist in nano technology. Secondly, Luke Adams like Marcus was an archaeologist, he had a unique clarity of foresight and excelled in academic writing. Marcus would often say that Luke could picture himself in the civilisations of old, while managing to communicate the past to a modern audience.

It was Luke's clarity of thought which discovered the connection between ideas, science and quantum physics that would change the world. After a lot of testing, counter checking, mathematical equations, and laboratory simulations the research team realised what Luke had discovered, and it would change their lives forever.

CHAPTER ONE

Discovery

The 12th of September was the day a new understanding of humanity's evolution was unveiled. Marcus was confident that his demonstration in all likelihood would be seen as seismic. Today, he along with Maya would give humanity the chance to study its development through the ages, enhancing humanity's historical understanding. No longer would history be told by the victors but by the archaeologists or as from today, the Quantologists.

It was a bright and sunny morning in Cambridge when Marcus woke. The sun had not long been up, and the smell of autumn was in the air. The beautiful day encouraged him to take a walk through the park as he left his apartment, rather than his usual routine of heading straight to the laboratory. Marcus knew today was going to change his team's lives forever, and he thought it would be a good idea to take some time before making the project's final checks.

Marcus casually walked over midsummer common, a favourite spot of his, only briefly stopping to look at his watch. He wanted to make sure he had time for his detour. Marcus smiled as he stared at the watch. It was an antique that had been passed down in his family for generations and was very precious to him. Watches were becoming rarer and rarer these days due to the palm implants everyone now had. But he had an emotional attachment to this one. His father had left it to him in his will, and it still made Marcus feel attached to him. It was only 8:15 a.m. Marcus had plenty of time before the announcement of their new discovery to the scientific community which was scheduled for 10:00 a.m.. He breathed in the fresh air, releasing a slow breath to calm his nerves.

Keep calm today, *you're good at this*, he thought reassuringly.

As Marcus walked through the park, he could hear a mistle thrush singing in the trees which seemed to comfort him. He soon arrived at the river path, it was surprisingly busy and he walked along it until he found a free bench to sit on. He cleared his throat and sat there in silence just staring into the River Cam, focusing on the fast-flowing water as it passed through the hydropower sluice gates. The sun glistened happily as if to congratulate him on his team's amazing discovery. Out of the silence, a high-pitched beep sounded. Marcus jumped, then rolled his eyes.

Can I not get a moment's peace? he thought.

He tapped the palm of his hand and a holographic screen appeared. It was Luke looking agitated.

'Marcus where are you, I have a few more checks I want to make on our calculations before the announcement.'

Luke's eyes darted back and forth as if he was about to explode.

'I'm just having a few moments of reflection, no need to worry Luke I'll be back shortly,' he said firmly in his thick Swedish accent.

'Marcus, I just want to make sure we are ready,' Luke replied.

'We are, take a deep breath and grab a cup of tea, I will be there in fifteen minutes.' With that Marcus tapped his palm again and the screen disappeared.

He took one more deep breath, then got up and headed back to Churchill College.

***

Back at the lab, Luke swore.

How can he be so calm? his mind screamed. *This discovery will change the way we see the world.*

His heart was racing.

Luke Adams was 25, he had spent all his life working to become an archaeologist. He had a passion for telling stories of the past which led him to excel in his studies. Luke was from the county of Suffolk in England. He had been inspired by the stories of Sutton Hoo growing up.

Sutton Hoo was one of the biggest archaeological finds in England in the 1940s. The archaeological dig found an Anglo-Saxon burial ship, which inspired the nation during the dark times of the Second World War. As a child, Luke would spend hours at the British Museum studying everything about that discovery in the hope that one day, he too would find something as important.

Luke had shaggy black hair, deep green eyes and took a lot of pride in his appearance, even though he spent most of the time in the mud. He had a difficult childhood. His mother had suffered from mental health issues and drug addiction, which unfortunately still remained a challenge to society, despite huge progress being made. Even though they both received a lot of support, his mother eventually took her own life. He never knew his father so at the age of sixteen, when his mother passed, he was left on his own.

It was at this time that his school history teacher spotted his talent and introduced him to a friend of his, Marcus, who would soon become his mentor. That was the real turning point in Luke's life, he felt accepted and inspired. It wasn't long before Marcus became like a father to him and now the two of them were inseparable.

Luke had sacrificed much to become Marcus's apprentice. While his friends at university went out partying Luke would be engrossed in his studies. Desperate to please his mentor. Luke was a sensitive caring guy with a desire for romance. However, any potential relationships were quickly ended. His only focus was on his work which was the most important thing in his life.

The Quantology project they both had been working on over the last five years, only made the bond between Marcus and Luke stronger. They were like family and trusted each other implicitly.

Luke was startled as Maya walked into the lab, she took off her suit jacket, hung it up, then grabbed a white lab coat.

She spoke casually, 'Morning Luke how are you feeling today?'

Maya Evans was 54. She had worked in the field of quantum physics since she graduated from Tokyo's prestigious Gekkō science college. Maya was a small petite black lady. She was originally from Atlanta but her work had taken her around the world. Maya had brown hair which was slightly greying at the sides, deep brown eyes, and she always dressed smartly whatever the occasion. She lived close to Churchill college with her husband Richard and her teenage son Charlie. Her husband was an artist who travelled the world exhibiting his work and her son was following in her field, studying physics at the University of Geneva.

'How am I feeling?' he said forcefully. 'Worried as hell, are we really ready to announce this?'

Maya turned to him and smiled. 'Yes we are, don't worry we know what we're doing.'

'Marcus and I have had lots of experience in presenting papers as well as managing difficult stakeholders.'

Her words seemed to calm him a little. 'Maya, please can you just check these calculations one more time, you know maths isn't my strong point.'

'Of course, but you know I have checked them twenty times already,' she smiled. Maya placed her hand over the table and a large holographic 3D screen appeared.

Maya moved the image around and tapped a few sections on the screen which added up the complex equations and turned to him.

'The coordinates look right to me,' she responded, rubbing his shoulder reassuringly.

As if the weight had been lifted, he slumped down into the chair next to the bench. Maya casually walked over to the drink's dispenser. She pressed a few buttons, and a cup of tea appeared.

She carried it back to Luke. 'Drink this it will calm you down, its strong builder's tea as you Brits say.'

He took the drink off her and sipped it slowly. 'You need to trust us Luke, we know how important this discovery is and we know how vital you have been in making it happen.'

She paused.

'I am grateful you are helping us demonstrate it today, but you're no use to us in this state. We have faith in you and your abilities, so you need to as well,' she said reassuringly like a supportive mother.

As Maya was speaking Marcus walked into the lab, and they both turned to look at him.

'I see you have that tea I told you to drink,' he said, smiling at Maya knowing she was already ahead of him.

Marcus Larsson looked like a typical professor despite only being 45, he was dressed in a tweed suit with a matching waistcoat, brown shoes, and an off patterned tie. He had greying curly blond hair, blue eyes, and a mischievous grin which seemed to light up the room. Marcus had been into archaeology since he was a boy. He had followed in his father's footsteps often helping at digs in his native Sweden. Marcus had grown up around Norse mythology and his Father was famous for discovering an intact Viking burial in the small settlement of Marstrand.

This had caused quite the stir in the archaeological community as it was the first major find of a Viking burial in Sweden for two centuries. Marcus loved all archaeology, however, despite his Norse upbring he had a particular interest in ancient Asian cultures. It caused quite the shock within his family when he went to study history at the university of Hội An, instead of taking up his place at Oxford. Marcus had an independent streak, and he followed his heart which didn't always go down well in archaeological circles. Marcus was single, although he'd had many relationships in his past. However, like Luke his focus was firmly on his work and today was the reason why. It would be the start of a revolution in archaeology.

'Have you seen Kalani?' Marcus asked Maya. 'I really want to inspect the prototype with him, I thought he'd be here by now.'

'Not yet but I told him to be here around nine. I can take another look at it now and complete the final checks,' she replied.

Maya walked over to the science bench and waved her hand. The prototype rose from within the desk until it hovered in mid-air. The prototype had a force field surrounding it for protection. She clicked a few buttons and the field disappeared. The device was triangular, a foot long, and completely smooth. As it hung hovering in mid-air, the sunlight reflected off its platinum casing, causing light to bounce all over the lab. Marcus followed her to the bench and studied a holographic monitor which appeared to the side of the device.

'Right let's undertake the diagnostics on QD1,' Maya said eagerly.

QD1 was short for Quantum Droid 1, this was the name they had given the prototype. First, she checked the sensors, these were designed to be able to evaluate all its surroundings, in particular quantum ageing.

'All sensors responding within expected parameters,' she said, and Marcus nodded.

Luke had now joined them and was looking at the screens with Marcus. The second check she conducted was to test its camouflage functionality, she clicked a few buttons and the device completely disappeared. This made Luke jump, it always did. It was not unusual for things to be completely camouflaged, the technology had been around for a while, but Luke spent most of his time digging around in the dirt, so this tech was still something he was not used to. Maya clicked a few more buttons and the device reappeared again.

The third thing she wanted to check was the support crew as she called it. Maya pressed a few more buttons and out popped ten small versions of the prototype, they were called MQD's for short, Mini Quantum Droids. These devices flew around the room and hovered over the lab gathering data. They were designed to go high into the atmosphere to evaluate and scan large areas, these devices were created to help the main prototype locate points of interest and assess distances. Maya clicked away and they disappeared, she tapped the screen again, and the MQD's reappeared.

'Looks like they are working fine,' she declared. 'Final check, Luke please sit on the chair in the corner?'

Luke nodded and walked to a separate part of the lab which had been set up with a large chair connected to all sorts of equipment. Surrounding the head of the chair was a set of mirrors which reflected into each other. Marcus followed, he waved his hand and another holographic screen appeared. As Luke sat down, Marcus initiated the machine, a helmet-shaped device came down from the ceiling and attached itself to Luke.

'OK let's check its quantum core,' Maya said.

She initiated the programme and several lights came out of the helmet reflecting off the mirrors.

'All OK with the cognition lasers, Luke can you focus on bending them please?'

Luke did as he was asked, and the lasers began to bend.

'Very good,' Maya replied. 'I want to check the cranium perception filter.'

There was a long pause, she muttered something under her breath that Luke and Marcus couldn't hear.

'What's wrong?' Marcus asked, noticing her hesitation.

'There seems to be a slight imbalance to the filter, this really should have been detected automatically as it could have impacted Luke,' Maya continued to review the diagnostic tools.

'Do you think it'll be all right?' Marcus asked worriedly, he quickly looked at his watch. 'Should I cancel the demonstration?'

'No, it's fine it's a quick amendment, I'm not sure why it's not triggered an automatic diagnostic investigation.' Maya tapped a few buttons, 'There, all fixed, I will continue to monitor this function throughout the demonstration. I want to have confidence that the HTC will alert us to an issue like this, does that work for you Luke?'

'Yes Maya, I trust you totally and it's not like we haven't done this before. I just want to show the world what we have seen and what we can do.'

It was at that moment that Kalani walked into the Lab, it was 9:15 a.m. and he was looking very unwell.

'I'm so sorry I'm late I feel awful, are we ready?' he asked, coughing.

Kalani Iona was older than Luke at 36, he had brown hair, brown eyes, and was of Hawaiian descent. Kalani had studied Quantum Physics at the Massachusetts Institute of Technology, or MIT as it was better known. He was exceptionally smart and had met Maya when she taught there for a semester, and they instantly clicked. Kalani excelled at building nanotechnology which had helped Maya test several of her scientific theories.

He was from a family of proud Hawaiians, and they often wanted him to return home. Since the move to England Kalani had tried to help his wife settle, but it was no use and resulted in ever escalating disagreements between his wife and 15-year-old daughter. Maya frequently supported Kalani to work flexibly giving him the option to regularly return to Hawaii. This had helped support his family in the short term but she knew he would have to decide his future path soon. Kalani, his wife Ke'ala and his daughter Lani all lived on campus, they had both travelled with him from the states but Ke'ala was finding it increasingly difficult living in the UK. She missed her parents and wanted their daughter to grow up in Hawaii surrounded by their families, but that was not where Kalani's work was based.

'You do look awful, are you sure you're OK to be here?' Maya asked him.

'I have to be, you need me,' he replied.

That was the truth and Maya nodded reluctantly.

Maya gestured for Kalani to follow her out of earshot from the others.

'We had a slight error with the cranium perception filter, but I managed to fix it. It looks like you did not realign the sensors after we last used the device and for some reason, the safety controls were switched off. I'm not sure why that would happen. I've realigned the device and switched the safety controls back on. It's been corrected now and I will be paying close attention to this during our demonstration,' Maya stated with concern.

Kalani looked shocked, he nodded and went straight over to the holographic screens to check the diagnostics himself. 'I'm not sure what went wrong Maya, I'm so sorry. The realignment could have been dangerous.'

Maya thought for a moment.

'You know as much as I about the risks of our work, the last thing we want is for the lab to be pulled back in time and for us to be stranded. That's why I built-in these controls, to protect Luke and to protect us,' she stared at Kalani waiting for a response.

'I'm sorry Maya, I'll do better.'

'It's okay, we always do our pre-checks before each mission and I'm sure you would have caught it like me.' She gave him a comforting squeeze, knowing he would be upset by this mistake.

'We had better get ready for the demonstration, Luke let's get you out of that chair and tidy the lab,' Marcus said loudly breaking the tension between Kalani and Maya.

***

Over the next half hour, the lab was tidied and the equipment readied, ensuring that they displayed the best impression possible. All the prestigious, distinguished, and respected academics in the archaeological and quantum physics communities had been invited to this event. To the surprise of them all, the top academics accepted their invitation. This was a testament to the respect and trust that both Marcus and Maya commanded in their respective fields of expertise. In truth, their peers were eager to see what they had discovered.

At five minutes to ten Maya gathered the team around. 'This is the discovery of our lifetime, so let's put our best foot forward. As discussed, Marcus and I will present to our colleagues and once my presentation of our quantum theory is complete, I'll join Kalani in monitoring the vortex and the readings from QD1. Marcus will continue to present the demonstration while Luke activates the Quantum field allowing the Droid to go to its destination.'

Maya paused for breath and asked, 'Are you all clear on your roles?'

They nodded, Luke and Kalani took their places and Maya turned to Marcus, gripping his hand tight.

'You're the best presenter I've ever seen so make us proud.'

She smiled and gave him a hug, then returned to her station to make a few final checks. Maya glanced once more at Marcus, smiled and pressed her control panel. As if by magic, the laboratory wall turned into glass, revealing a packed auditorium of waiting dignitaries eager for information.

CHAPTER TWO

The Future of Archaeology

Marcus calmed himself in preparation for his opening remarks. His eyes flickered across the room and he noticed some of the most respected academics in their fields. In the front row to his right was a female professor called Sakura Fukuda, she was in her mid-sixties although she could easily pass for a younger woman. Sakura was of Japanese heritage and had been Marcus's mentor, she had helped him develop his knowledge and passion for archaeology, particularly fostering his love for Asia. There was no doubt in his mind that she had been a major reason why several other archaeological professors were at the presentation. A few rows behind Sakura, he noticed Amari and Janet Kimathi, they were colleagues and good friends he had made during his time teaching in Sydney. They were married and Marcus had been Amari's best man at their wedding, however he had not seen them in sometime. He was glad to see how happy they were, they held each other's hands tightly smiling proudly at him.

To the left of the room, he spotted Flynn Garcia, it was fair to say that Marcus detested this man. Through their long careers they had many differing opinions. Flynn took great pride in deriding Marcus's achievements, and he made it known to all that he did not approve of Marcus's methods.

***

Maya had also been scanning the room, she had spotted some of her friends and colleagues, in particular, she noticed Sofía Sánchez, they had been friends since her time in Tokyo. Sofía had worked with Maya on many of her early quantum experiments and was well respected among the scientific community. To Maya's surprise, she spotted Charlie in the front row. She had told her son about the important announcement she was making today but had no idea he would be here. He must have caught an early aerosphere from Geneva that morning. Seeing him in the audience lifted her spirits and made her more determined to succeed.

The final gentleman she spotted was Dhruv Mahal, the Minister for Global Science. He was the brightest mind of his age and had quickly risen to the most powerful scientific position in the World Council. It was Dhruv who had secured the funding to support Maya's project, he had huge faith in Maya's abilities, mainly due to her support helping to setup the Europa colony. This gave her an immense amount of freedom to choose her team and to research whatever she wanted.

***

Marcus cleared his throat, then clicked his fingers. A large 3D holographic screen appeared behind him, illuminated with the languages of old scriptures and images of the greatest historical ruins such as the Parthenon, Machu Picchu, The Great Wall of China, and the United States Capitol Building.

'Ever wondered what it would be like to see the pyramids in their full glory, glittering in gold? Or to see the Spanish Armada arriving over the horizon on the English Channel as they approached the shores of Cornwall?'

Marcus was in his element, he had no need for notes, he knew their work would inspire and enthuse the audience. 'Today we are unveiling a new way to study the past. Quantology. Quantology is a new form of archaeology. It will change our understanding of historical events. No longer will the history books be written by the victors, they will be based on fact and tell the true story of humanity. This new study will allow us to see what really happened in the past, it will rewrite the history of humanity's evolution and advance our understanding of historical events.'

There was a deep intake of breath, he could tell excitement was building, except for Flynn Garcia who rolled his eyes at Marcus's enthusiasm. 'Maya and our team have been working on a way to open a portal that can transport a probe into the past, this will enable us to observe and record the events of our ancestors.'

At that point, Maya stepped forward and started to talk. 'Over the last three years, our team has been working on colliding beams of high-energy protons together at the speed of light to create an antimatter field. The team have created and developed the new experimental field of cognitive physics. This new scientific development studies our understanding of the human brain. In particular, the power of imagination, desire, and emotion. Our research has discovered that when the human mind reacts to new possibilities or feels something deeply, it causes a disturbance in subspace. This change in subspace creates a micro gravitational pull and ignites dark matter, creating intense energy which was currently unknown to us.'

Maya paused so that the audience could reflect, from her observation she could tell the scientists were captivated.

'The best way to describe what happens, is that for each idea we generate, or emotion we feel, we create a subspace event like a miniature Big Bang. These thoughts of creation and feelings of intense emotion create immense power at the sub-space level. The team have found a way to harness this hidden power.'

Maya stopped and observed the room, noticing complete silence. 'Our research has combined this thought power with the antimatter field, enabling us to create the first stable time portal in existence. Our robust calculations and new scientific processes allow us to transport probes to any time period.'

There was a sound of astonishment from the audience, and she continued. 'The team have developed a set of Quantum principles which allows us to calculate where the portal can open, to the exact minute, anywhere in time. We analysed a multitude of factors including the movement and orbit of the earth, the movement of tectonic plates, along with the fluctuation in spacetime. To create these calculations, the team have developed new mathematic formulas to bring all the complicated variables and assumptions together.'

Maya paused again and sipped some water from a glass on the table next to her. Despite her vast experience she was nervous presenting these findings to the world, *what if they didn't believe the evidence, or what if they declared their work an abomination*, she thought.

Marcus took over the presentation. 'As you can imagine, this discovery could have huge ramifications for humanity and it must be protected. This power, if used in the wrong hands, could cause the destruction of our timeline. People could manipulate historical events for their own gain or make unintended changes to the timeline. Just imagine for a moment if Hitler was persuaded not to invade Russia, or if the invention of the printing press, or God forbid the wheel, was delayed or repressed. It could rewrite our history.'

There was a mumble of concern in the room.

'That being said, we have a duty to understand our past and to use this technology responsibly. Today we will be safely demonstrating to you this new form of archaeology. We will be using Kalani's newly developed geophysical droid, which will be camouflaged and has many backup features to prevent any catastrophic time corruption. This droid will allow us to collect data, scan the terrain, understand environmental conditions, and to observe and record historical events discreetly,' Marcus finished with a huge smile.

Maya had returned to her station and on Marcus's final words she entered a code into her panel. The droid descended from the ceiling, contained within its force field. The triangular platinum device shone brightly, the beams of light from the force field enveloping the object, bouncing rainbow rays of light across the lab and into the auditorium. A sense of excitement fell across the room as the watching academics were enthralled by what was being presented.

Maya signalled Luke to initiate the Hadron Thought Collider. The HTC, as she called it, was Maya's crowning glory. She had spent years refining it and was very proud of her breakthrough research. Strangely, only Luke had been able to get it to work as designed. Maya had spent months with him in the lab working through variations of tests to ensure it was safe and effective. She would never forget the day when he was first able to bend the red beams, it gave her such a thrill to know her lifelong theories were true. Not long after that, Kalani helped her create the stable antimatter and they began to experiment with both technologies until eventually, she formed the first stable vortex.

Luke closed his eyes, his hands tightly gripping the arms of the chair. He was nervous but knew he had to keep calm. The key to the success of the HTC was to keep his emotions under control, or the beams would dissipate like a quiet voice in a crowded bar and the experiment would fail.

The pressure had always been on Luke, ever since Maya realised that he was the only member of the team who could sustain the mental clarity needed to create the time vortex. Luke had always been a calm and thoughtful man. His kind nature came from his challenging upbringing. Luke's passion for history helped him focus and control his emotions. In the early days after his mother's passing, he would sit in silence at ancient sites, taking in all his surroundings as if he could feel the footprints of the ancestors. When Luke first successfully managed to create and control a subspace vortex, Maya was amazed by the composure and clarity of thought from such a young man. Maya, Marcus, and Kalani had all tried to replicate Luke's breakthrough with the HTC, but it was only him who was able to create and maintain the stable portal.

Luke started to breathe deeply, he began to slow his mind and focus his thoughts. Suddenly, the lasers began to bounce off the mirrors surrounding his head and as he continued to focus, the beams of light moved faster and faster.

Kalani triggered the particle accelerator creating the stable antimatter field above Luke's head. After a few minutes, a loud bang sounded, followed by a bright blue orb that appeared over his head.

'Luke, bend the HTC beams,' Maya instructed calmly.

He began to move the millions of bouncing red lasers together until one large beam suddenly pointed up and smashed into the glowing blue orb. The orb collapsed in on itself and formed a purple rotating vortex that expanded until it was a meter wide. It hovered in the middle of the lab above Luke's head. The vortex caused a small tornado, whipping up papers and other loose lab material. There was a smash of glass as several beakers crashed to the floor.

Maya worked furiously at her workstation and the vortex began to stabilise.

'I've connected to our designated location,' she said loudly over the portal's humming.

Marcus turned to the academics. 'Are you ready to see history?'

Some of the academics seem scared, others were elated but not Dhruv. He just sat there, calmly taking in all the information and staring deeply at the rotating purple vortex. Marcus looked over to Kalani and nodded. On his instruction, Kalani remotely guided QD1 into the waiting portal. As the droid entered the vortex, there was a bright flash of green light and it was sucked through subspace into a different time.

***

The lights flickered and the building shook as the vortex admitted a shockwave after the droid entered. The room was buzzing with excitement. Maya focused on her station, making sure the portal was stable. Luke remained calm and controlled. His mind clear on the goal of maintaining the hovering vortex.

Marcus touched his palm and his holographic screen appeared. He gestured, and the screen enlarged a hundred times so that the audience could see what he was transmitting.

'The team have undertaken eight test flights into the past ranging from 10,000BC up to 1805AD. All these test flights were done using our quantum droids. We scan the vicinity first, making sure no one is present to prevent any accidental contamination. Once safe to do so, the droids entered the designated time frame camouflaged, ready to commence their mission. The droids scan the area and record the vegetation, local environment, and the local settlements.'

Marcus then flashed different images and videos onto the screen, showing a prehistoric European village, followed by a Greek temple with worshipers kneeling, an Aztec pyramid with villagers farming, and finally a 16th century Spanish port with fishing vessels and a patrolling warship. The crowd gasped again at what they were seeing. As the academics looked closely, they could clearly see the clothes the people were wearing, the face paint used, and the exquisite buildings.

Marcus continued, 'Luke is able to hold the portal open for about an hour, we are refining this technology to see if we can keep it open longer. This is a one-way trip, as we are yet to understand how to create a return portal. We believe there needs to be an antimatter and HTC vortex on both sides to make a two-sided gateway. Without the option to have our droids return, we instruct the droid to self-destruct, vaporising all components once our scans and observations are complete. This ensures we avoid any contamination to the timeline.'

Marcus took a deep breath and a sip of water before continuing. 'In our demonstration today, we're going to take this one step further. You have just witnessed us send the most advanced droid we have ever created through to one of humanity's key historical moments. The team have been working on this Quantology dig for quite some time. The calculation we have completed today will enable you to witness the exact moment that Mount Vesuvius erupted.'

Excited murmurs came from the crowd.

Suddenly Flynn called out, 'How do we know this isn't fake, or that you haven't used CGI?'

'Flynn we are happy to share all our data and research with you, including the unique sub-space timestamp that comes from every incursion,' Maya responded firmly.

Marcus was furious at Flynn's accusation, but pressed on with the presentation. 'Today we're going to be observing one of the defining moments of the Roman era. We will be observing how the destruction of Pompeii really unfolded.'

There was a shriek of excitement from one of the academics. Marcus tapped his hand and the large screen lit up with the image of the Gulf of Naples, which looked calm. Amari and Janet Kimathi's eagerness got the better of them and they moved to stand next to the glass panel, desperate to get a closer look at what was happening in the Lab.

'What is the local date and time at the droid's location?' Marcus asked Kalani.

'The time is 14:13 on August the 24th 79AD. The droid is working within expected parameters,' he replied calmly.

Amari turned to Janet and said eagerly, 'I always thought the eruption took place around noon.'

Before she had chance to reply, Maya instructed, 'Release the MQDs.'

Kalani clicked a few buttons and ten mini probes shot into the air at lightning speed. They separated over fifty miles, acting as a sensor net to capture every bit of information, whilst the main droid stayed hovering above the bay of Naples, focusing on Mount Vesuvius and ensuring that it did not miss a moment.

The project team continued to gather information. Luke stayed in the chair holding his focus to keep the portal open. The audience just held their breath patiently. At exactly 14:27, a huge explosion took place. The shock wave took about three minutes to reach the main droid. When it did, it shook so violently that the MQDs were knocked out of position, however their stabilisers were able to readjust quickly.

The bellowing ash clouds began to block out the sun, plunging everything into darkness, and violent tremors caused buildings to collapse everywhere.

'Have you seen this Marcus?' Maya asked, pointing at the screen.

Marcus had been observing the data at another monitoring station and he turned to the audience. 'That explosion was 120,000 times larger than the atomic bomb dropped on Hiroshima in the Second World War. That's 20,000 times more powerful than we thought,' he said smiling and thrilled at the new discovery.

Over the next hour, the main droid continued to observe the exploding volcano while ten new screens appeared. All showing the MQDs points of view, as the smaller droids zoomed around the site. MQD3 was observing the volcano's rim, it got close to the molten lava erupting from the cracks in the breaking mountain. MQD7 was exploring Pompeii itself, observing the ash falling on the city and the panic of the citizens running for cover. MQD1 had moved to Herculaneum, observing the people that were running towards the coast in search of rescue, but the rough seas made escape by water impossible. MQD1 paid particular attention to the boats and ships in the port, watching them smash into the docks and coast. MQD1 captured boats sinking, and the audience saw people dying, in fact, on most of the screens lighting up the lab, people were dying.

Marcus's smiling face changed as the realisation he was witnessing a humanitarian disaster started to sink in. His focus shifted to recording the data, he wanted to make sure that the archaeological community understood what really happened in the first hour Vesuvius erupted.

At 15:10, Maya declared, 'Time to vaporise the droids.'

One by one, the MQDs' screens went blank until only QD1's screen was receiving images. Maya looked at Marcus, who nodded back at her as she initiated the final vaporisation order and the screen went blank. Luke, who was sweating vigorously, broke the connection between the vortex and the portal collapsed.

Maya looked over at Kalani, his face was white. It was like all the blood had drained out of him. She then looked at Luke, Marcus was helping him out of the HTC, but he was weak and exhausted. It took a great deal of mental strength to keep the portal open. Maya wiped her glasses and turned her attention back to the audience. She noticed the hushed silence in the room, and as she looked over at their esteemed guests. Maya observed that some of them were in shock, others in tears, and realised the real impact that seeing humanity's past would have on the world.

CHAPTER THREE

The World Council

After the vortex closed, Maya turned to address the audience. 'You have just witnessed the first live observation of one of humanity's historic events. As you can see, this technology has great potential, but we all have a duty of care to respect the past.'

Maya paused.

'Seeing the plight of our poor ancestors really demonstrates the responsibility of our discovery.'

Marcus stepped in, 'Although this may have been difficult to watch, the understanding we can gain from observing events such as this is huge. We have an opportunity to learn and it is our responsibility to tell humanity's past.'

Several of the academics started to clap, which triggered the rest of the audience to break into applause.

'Join us in the room next door to learn more about the process and about our plans for the future,' Marcus finished and gestured to the now open door.

As the audience left the auditorium, Kalani turned to Maya and whispered, 'That was difficult to watch, do you think we're doing the right thing looking into our past?'

Maya responded kindly, 'New technologies and breakthroughs always come with risk, do I think we are doing the right thing?'

She pondered for a moment. 'To be honest, I'm not sure, but do I think we should continue to explore the possibilities of this new technology, yes I do.'

Kalani nodded hesitantly.

Marcus was talking to Luke, 'You did great today, the data and observation we have discovered will give us months of investigatory work. It will be exciting to present to the world the facts about what happened during the eruption of Mount Vesuvius.'

Luke was struggling to speak, 'It does take it out of me Marcus, I need to work with Maya and Kalani to make it a bit more stable before we try that again.'

'Of course, your health is my number one priority,' Marcus touched Luke's shoulder gently but continued to speak eagerly. 'Did you see the reaction from the audience?'

His smile faded as he pondered.

'It does worry me the effect bringing archaeology to life could have on the world,' he said genuinely concerned.

'I know what you mean, but the opportunity to understand historical events and comprehend human evolution is too important to miss. Remember, these events happened whether we study them or not.'

As always, Luke's logical words calmed Marcus's anxiety. He was always amazed at Luke's great clarity of thought and his calm understanding of the facts. Marcus knew that these mental skills were why he could control the HTC. Luke's clarity of mind continually gave Marcus a refreshing sense of perspective, which he valued deeply.

'You're right as ever,' Marcus said smiling.

'Okay team, it's time to face the Lion's Den,' Maya called out. They followed her into the reception room and to the waiting academics.

***

The room was like any other scientific symposium that the academics had been to. In the centre of the room was coffee, tea, and an array of lunch options. Maya had designed it like this to help the academics feel relaxed. She wanted them to understand that, despite the gravity of their new discovery, it was just another scientific demonstration. However, there were no tables to sit down at, this was to be a working lunch and she expected the professors to engage. The plan was for Maya and Kalani to hold discussions with the scientific scholars and for Marcus and Luke to take questions from the archaeological academics. As they entered the room, they noticed the professors were busy helping themselves to food and discussing the demonstration intently.

All four of them were too nervous to eat. Maya and Kalani headed to the right of the long conference room. It was set up with a holographic screen detailing the scientific theories. Marcus and Luke headed to the left of the room which was again set up with screens ready for him to update the academics. The mood in the room was still uneasy, however the curiosity of the scholars soon got the better of them and they started to head over.

First to approach Maya was her young son Charlie, who gave her a huge hug and beamed with pride.

'Mum that was amazing, you never told me you managed to create a stable time portal,' he said eagerly. 'I want to know everything.'

'Well, I didn't want to tell anyone until we had proved its success. We still have a lot more research to do and of course I will tell you all about it,' she replied lovingly.

Charlie stayed close to his mother, asking her lots of questions.

Maya and Kalani were then joined by a group of colleagues from Oxford, MIT, and Tokyo universities. Sofía joined a little later with Dhruv, whom she had been deep in conversation with. Maya noticed he was clearly excited about the discovery, Dhruv respected Sofía and Maya knew he would always seek her opinion on new technology. Maya started to explain how the portal worked, being careful to leave out certain mechanical engineering details. She didn't want anyone to try and replicate her discovery, not yet anyway. She explained how she developed the interface to create the HTC and how it connected to Luke's unique ability to control his thoughts. Kalani explained to several interested colleagues about the droids and the nano engineering skills he had used to develop his probe technology. There seemed to be a buzz of excitement from the group, but it was Dhruv who asked the question that was on most of the academics' minds.

'Maya, very impressive demonstration today but what I want to know is what are the other applications of this technology? It's great that it can be used for historical insights, but what are the practical uses for us in the present?' he asked sternly as if he was frustrated that the scientific element of the work was taking a backseat.

'It's a good question Dhruv, and to be fair our research and development could have only succeeded with help from our archaeological partners,' Maya made a point of saying.

Dhruv had always been focused on the future, he had very little interest in the past.

Maya continued, 'It was thanks to Marcus that I was able to link many of the theories, he would talk to me about the symbiosis of species and how working together for self-preservation both species would thrive and survive. I know it sounds odd, but it was that inspiration that helped me to connect the HTC and antimatter together.'

Maya smiled happily remembering those late-night conversations with Marcus before continuing.

'As for practical uses for today's world, this device has many potential applications but it's still early days. Luke is still the only person who can maintain an open portal. We need to undertake a lot more research to make sure it's stable.'

She now looked directly at Dhruv. It was clear she respected him, but she was not the kind of woman to be intimidated.

'However, just for you Dhruv, here is one of my thoughts. A potential use for this technology could be to transport goods or even people in an instant across the globe. We could encode the time delay for minutes or even seconds which could create a stable vortex to transport anything.'

There was a pause as Dhruv let that suggestion sink in.

'That is interesting Maya, very interesting. What about transporting goods to our bases on Mars, Europa and Enceladus?' he asked quietly but clearly, so everyone knew what he desired.

'It is certainly theoretically possible, but we have not researched or completed any calculations for creating portals across the solar system or on different worlds. The coordinates and spatial positioning would need to be understood.'

She paused again, this time looking at the other scholars. 'I see lots of opportunities to remove travel time either on earth or in space, with more research we will be able to confirm this with evidence,' she replied smiling.

'Interesting, I think we need to discuss more about this technology,' he said in a tone which was evident his request was not optional.

Across the room, Marcus was in full flow. He was enthusiastically explaining the benefits of this new way of studying history.

'Quantology will change our profession, when we discover an ancient ruin or burial, we can now go back in time to visit it for real and document what it actually looked like, not just hypothesise, the possibilities for this technology are endless.'

'Marcus, what you have shown us today is going to change our field of study, but how do we know it's safe? How can we be sure we don't impact the timeline?' asked his mentor and friend Sakura.

'It's a good question, but we have put many controls in place including the camouflage and the vaporisation protocols. There are safeties that Kalani has programmed into the droids, if they start to malfunction or if someone gets too close, they vaporise. The purpose of this work is to leave no sign or trace of us, we will be observing the footprints of our ancestors.' He chuckled at his words.

'What right do you have to make this decision? There are global implications here that must be considered, and the World Council needs to approve this research,' Flynn Garcia said angrily, there was a hint of jealousy present in his words.

'We *do* have permission to test this prototype Flynn.' Marcus wanted to stop that kind of allegation in its tracks.

'Our demonstration has proven that this kind of research will provide an immense amount of data, the potential for understanding our history is huge.'

Marcus pulled up the data and images from Mount Vesuvius. He made a point to highlight the new findings from the demonstration.

'Marcus, how soon can this technology be available? I have half a dozen digs I'm working on where this could really help,' Janet asked eagerly, brushing off Flynn's intervention.

'I don't know yet Janet, as Flynn mentioned, there are wider implications that need to be worked through. For now, only Luke can create a stable portal.'

Marcus put his arm around his apprentice and smiled. 'Maya will need to work on helping us create a more stable field, its important to identify others who can initiate the HTC. I also expect she'll need to get approval from the World Council about how we use this new technology. We need to understand what protections need to be in place, but the possibilities are endless.'

Over the next few hours, the academics bombarded the team with questions, hypotheses, and requests to join the research. Marcus and Maya both took their time explaining what they could while Luke and Kalani took notes. They were all keen to engage with their audience and to make sure that their peers, friends, and colleagues were supportive of their discovery. By late afternoon, the discussions ended, and the research team could finally get some well-deserved rest. Little did they know what the next twelve months would bring, or how their discovery would change the world forever.

***

A few days after the demonstration, one of the archaeological professors leaked some footage that they had been secretly filming of the Mount Vesuvius project online. The footage was a sensation, it went viral, and the world became obsessed with understanding this new technology. They wanted to know everything about it and craved more content.

The World Council summoned both Maya and Marcus to their global headquarters in Jakarta to discuss what to do next. Intercontinental travel had radically changed since the days of gas-guzzling airplanes. People now travelled by aerosphere, they were small silver spherical capsules, each was self-sustainable and used kinetic energy caused by the movement of the earth to power themselves. The spheres were fully automated and could fit around ten people. They utilised the earth's global wind patterns to enhance their speed, this slipstream technology often helped the spheres reach over two thousand miles an hour. In the past, travelling at this speed was often disrupted due to the sonic boom created by travelling faster than the speed of sound, but due to the slipstream technology, the noise from a sonic boom was now able to be dissipated.

Maya and Marcus arrived in Jakarta within a few hours. Jakarta had become a modern marvel and its contemporary architecture gleamed in the afternoon sun. Jakarta had been at the forefront of new housing initiatives since the Reawakening. A particularly successful development was that of large skyscrapers that could defy gravity. These new skyscrapers could move between continents, urgently supporting housing needs. They had helped to transform how the world dealt with natural disasters. The Graviton towers, as they were known, had a permanent base of twenty storeys which were fixed to the ground, a further twenty to sixty storeys could be connected to bases anywhere in the world. Depending on housing needs, floors could be effortlessly added or taken away. The buildings were easily fabricated and had been designed to be carbon neutral. Different cladding designs existed to help match local architecture, however the construction and connection points remain the same. This allowed the buildings to be easily upgraded and maintained to support any new scientific discoveries.

Marcus and Maya were picked up from the aerosphere port and headed straight to the World Council to present their research. Maya spent a lot of time explaining the potential of their project to support human self-discovery. She told the World Council about the opportunities that the discovery could have on modern technology, and it didn't take long to gain the backing they needed.

The World Council formally voted in favour of continued support of their research. However they went further, confirming that the team would be given every resource they needed to continue the development of Quantology. The Council also confirmed that they could recruit any experts they needed, and their team would have the full support of the global scientific community. No doubt, the global popularity of the images from Mount

Vesuvius had played a big part in this decision. However, Maya knew Dhruv had been canvassing support due to the future potential that the technology offered. He had been at Maya's side all the time while she was presenting and backed her fully. He spoke to the Council in detail, highlighting how this technology could be used to advance human society as well as its archaeological benefits.

Maya and Marcus's visit to the World Council was a huge success. They returned back to Cambridge in triumph and got to work planning their new research projects and future time excavations.

Such was the public support the World Council declared that the Global Broadcasting Corporation or GBC would lead the documenting of the archaeological work. It was ordered that Marcus was to present a monthly programme to the world unveiling the latest findings.

These archaeological programmes reached such popularity that the research team now had daily visits from world dignities, heads of state, and royalty. The research team had now grown to a total of a hundred scientists and at Dhruv's request they were moved to the biggest lab at the Churchill campus. Thirty were working on the archaeological calculations whilst the remaining seventy were working on new ideas for the application of the technology. This was a specific condition to get the funding and support from Dhruv. Maya had asked Sofía to help her lead the investigations around the modern uses. Sofía was the only colleague Maya had really trusted, she was her closest friend and they had shared many past secrets together.

Kalani supported both areas of study, his main scientific focus was leading a new field of development in nanotechnology. His expertise in building the probes allowed him the financial support to develop new forms of droid, these robots would be able to better adapt to the different environmental conditions that might be needed. He had developed droids which could operate in space, underwater in deep pressure and ones which could stand the harsh conditions of the atmospheres of Jupiter or Saturn. This was a huge scientific breakthrough.

Marcus was now leading the archaeological investigation. His team of thirty archaeologists worked with Maya's scientists in helping to define which historical events they could observe. It was their job to outline what benefits a Quantology dig could bring to humanity. He had been petitioned by every major university in the world asking to use his technology. He would sort through each of the requests and with his panel of experts ascertain the best potential Quantology excavations.

It was vital that Marcus limited the number of digs to one a month. Luke was still the only person able to operate the HTC, despite over a thousand people trying. Maya had her theories why and was working on a breakthrough, however in the meantime, she had stabilised the device, so it was less onerous on Luke. She had also been able to extend the operating time to three hours and had reduced the mental strain the device caused.

***

Since Quantology's unveiling to the world, the research team had worked on four digs. Each had to be approved and sanctioned by the World Council. The team would have a month to prepare, investigate, observe, and report back. A new terminology was created and the Quantology digs were classed as quantum time trenches. The team would have three hours to observe events, if they needed more time a petition was required from the World Council for a secondary quantum time trench. There needed to be a significant time-lapse difference to the previous Trench preventing any cross-contamination.

The Council instructed that a new prime control for the technology had to be implemented. They declared that no multiple time incursions could happen at a point in history. This control was to prevent any potential time collision or technology contamination within a Quantology dig.

The first three digs had been a huge success, they revealed to the world the historical events that no one had ever seen. The first dig focused on the death of President Kennedy. It wasn't long before the droids helped to discover who really killed Kennedy, putting to bed many historical ideas and conspiracy theories.

The second dig focused on the failed invasion by the Spanish Armada, this was a particular favourite of Marcus. The observations were able to see how the English used fireships to drive the Spanish Fleet onto the rocks and the images brought back inspired the world.

The third dig observed the battle of Thermopylae. This battle had been a legend for thousands of years and to see how the ancient Greeks held off the huge Persian army was of great interest. This dig inspired a new understanding of ancient Greek history and Marcus found himself presenting a lecture on the subject to the children of the world.

The fourth and most surprising dig was not focused on human history specifically, it focused on palaeontology. The team had located a special site they could date accurately where dinosaurs could be observed. They were able to open a quantum trench around 67 million years into humanity's past, which was a huge achievement. Maya and her team had calculated the correct timing and location of a particularly dense field of dinosaur bones. Luke was able to open a quantum trench above a grassy plain full of roaming dinosaurs.

The observations obtained from this dig changed the way the world saw the dinosaurs. The ability for the world to see real-life dinosaurs, the colours of the animals, the way they walked, what they ate, and how they acted sent the world into a frenzy. The image of a mother triceratops with her hatchlings had become ingrained in the public's imagination.

2347 would be known as the year the world got to see what a dinosaur really looked like. Quantology had awoken humanity to historical enlightenment and nothing would ever be the same again.

CHAPTER FOUR

Leap Year

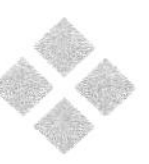

It was around two in the afternoon and Marcus was making the final preparations for the fifth Quantology dig. It was just under six months since Quantology was unveiled to the world and he had never been busier. Today was special, it was the 29th of February 2348, a leap year. He had timed the latest dig to happen on this particular date as he wanted to make it special. The team would be exploring one of his all-time favourite periods in history. Marcus had been obsessed with the culture of the Khmer Empire since he was a boy. Today he was going to see the ancient temples in their full glory.

'When will it be ready Marcus, the network has been waiting for this episode for weeks and the public is getting impatient,' a voice shouted from across the laboratory.

Brett Marshall the head of the Global Broadcasting Corporation came into the lab and marched straight up to him, ignoring a couple of protesting scientists.

Marcus had been lost in his thoughts and was taken completely by surprise by the rude entrance. Brett was a small fat man, around 45, he had shallow grey eyes that seemed to lack any sense of compassion.

Brett had been assigned to work with Marcus since the World Council agreed to the project. He had taken Marcus's life's work and turned it into a reality tv entertainment programme, aimed at getting ratings. This programme style was something Marcus loathed. The sensationalising of Quantology had created deep conflict between them. Marcus wanted to focus on the historical findings and present the facts, while Brett fixated on showing all the gory details which created a macabre fascination from the public. Marcus commented to Luke he thought that Brett's programmes attracted viewers for entertainment, no matter the human suffering. Like the crowds who used to watch public executions, or attended gladiator battles in the ancient colosseums. However, Marcus did have some power. He had become a celebrity in his own right, he hosted the show and could insist on the archaeological content. But it was Brett's production staff who edited it together, often focusing on the sensational images.

'We have a new dig scheduled for today, I told you that Brett. It's vital our calculations are correct and that we are ready to gather the information needed. If we don't put the archaeological work in, your programme will not have the right content,' Marcus said frustratedly.

He didn't have time for this man today.

'I wanted to make sure we are ready to go' he demanded. 'You know the public is waiting for the latest update, it's already a month late, when will the footage be ready?'

'The dig is this evening, once we have gathered our observations and analysed the results, I'll send you the footage in about a week. I'm sure you're love the material we'll bring back,' Marcus replied smiling sarcastically.

'Can you tell me any more about the latest dig, maybe I can release a trailer that could build up some interest?'

'No, not right now, best not to build up any anticipation just encase it doesn't go to plan.'

'You're right of course, no point disappointing the audience.'

And with that, Brett turned and walked away shaking his head.

***

The fifth dig was scheduled for seven that evening. Marcus always liked to conduct an excavation in the evening as the lab seemed much calmer and quieter. He was keen that only key scientists and archaeologists were present. Marcus wanted to ensure there were no unintended distractions for Luke and to give him space to prepare.

At around five, they had a surprise visitor. Dhruv dropped in for a chat with Maya and Kalani. It was not unusual for him to stop by, he was obsessed with the work Maya and Kalani were researching. It was clear to all he had very little interest in archaeological content despite its global popularity.

‘Kalani, can you come with me please I want to discuss the improvements to the droids,’ Dhruv instructed.

As they walked away Maya lifted her head from her console and for a moment, she thought she saw Dhruv give him something. She dismissed it, assuming it was yet another request for more information.

Dhruv had been relentless. He was demanding daily updates on their research and the progress they were making. Maya had a distinct impression that Dhruv was up to something. Although she knew she had his backing, the secretive workings of the Ministry of Science eluded her.

When Kalani returned from chatting to Dhruv he looked flustered, he busied himself with a few tasks when suddenly, an alarm sounded.

Maya rushed over to his station, ‘What’s going on?’

She looked at the flashing monitor and quickly corrected Kalani’s mistake. ‘You decoupled the collider. That could have caused the antimatter to break free of its force field.’

She studied the controls intently making sure everything was secure before turning to him. ‘What’s going on? You don’t make mistakes like this.’

‘I’m sorry Maya…’

There was a short pause. ‘It’s just, well, Dhruv needs my new droids ready to launch next week. He wants to test them in Jupiter’s atmosphere, there’s so much I need to do.’

‘We’re launching the fifth dig tonight, it’s important you are fully concentrating on this project. You need to ensure we protect our team and focus on our research. Do I make myself clear?'

Kalani nodded, 'Yes, sorry, I'll do better.'

Maya's tone softened. 'I will speak to Dhruv tomorrow, I can't have him distracting you from our work, it's too important.'

Kalani just nodded again, he looked into her eyes knowing she had always looked out for him, fearing deeply of becoming a great disappointment.

***

As seven approached, Marcus gathered everyone together. The usual team were joined by Karen Rostov and Simon Miller, both experienced archaeologists of the Khmer Empire. They were there to observe and advise.

A team of scientists were stationed in the observation room outside the lab monitoring several instruments and gathering data.

Marcus was beaming. 'Team, I'm excited about tonight, we will be heading to 1189, to the great Khmer Empire. The droids will be exploring the magnificent temples of Angkor Wat and Angkor Thom.'

'We have an opportunity to explore one of the outstanding ancient cities of the world. Little is known about this period in history except for the incredible ruins made famous by Henri Mouhot in the 1860s. Today we'll observe this culture at the height of its success, under the rule of King Jayavarman VII. It's known as the golden era and I am very, very excited to explore the districts of Angkor.'

Marcus's enthusiasm was infectious, and he looked over at his two friends and expert colleagues, who smiled back emphatically.

'As usual, Maya will be monitoring the HTC while Luke opens the portal. Kalani will operate the droids and I will instruct where to scan and what to observe. Karen and Simon, you will study the data being received from the various probes. I want you to advise of specific areas or buildings we should explore.'

They both gave an excitedly thumbs up.

'Okay, time to go team,' Marcus said, and they all went to their respective positions.

Maya pressed a few buttons and the suspended antimatter field lowered until it was above Luke's head. She entered more instructions into the system and the machine came alive. The red beams started to bounce off the mirrors. A few moments later Luke was bending a single beam towards the suspended antimatter.

'Ready, Maya called out.'

Marcus put his thumb up smiling and she initiated the connection, the room shook and within moments the vortex was formed. Maya steadied the pulsating shockwaves caused by the subspace wake and looked over at Kalani. He nodded, understanding her instruction. His new and improved QD6 droid sprang to life and took off from its dedicated plinth. It hovered for a moment as Kalani tested its sensors and then headed to the portal, as it entered the vortex there was the familiar flash of green light and it was sucked through time.

Maya checked a few screens at her station and confirmed that the QD6 had entered the designated destination at the desire time. She worked away furiously until an image appeared on the large holographic screen in the centre of the laboratory. Maya confirmed the droid had camouflaged itself and it had begun to scan the area. Marcus studied the screen intently which showed a lush green forest dotted with many wooden huts. There were streams and sluices everywhere regulating the water and as the droid turned, it caught sight of the most amazing view, a part of the temple of Angkor Wat. Slowly the temple came into full sight, the setting sun's rays bounced off the golden-capped towers and the great Khmer city was unveiled in all its glory.

Marcus took a deep intake of breath.

'It's more beautiful than I imagined,' he paused to take in the view. 'Kalani, release the MQDs so we can scan the area.'

There was no response to Marcus's instruction, he turned around and noticed Kalani had moved away from his console.

'Are you okay?' Maya asked, seeing the distressed look on her apprentice's face.

'I can't do this anymore. The secrets of our ancestors should remain with them. We dishonour their memories and violate their rights by invading their time.'

Kalani pressed the palm of his hand and a holographic screen appeared. He input instructions and the lab doors locked.

'Kalani, calm down, we're just observing,' Marcus said while Luke continued to focus on keeping the portal open.

'I don't believe you and neither does Dhruv,' he spat at Marcus. 'Dhruv believed you would want to bring back artefacts next. I can't allow that violation.'

Kalani pulled out of his pocket a device. 'Dhruv gave this to me, it's a portable antimatter generator which can connect to the transmitting signal. It makes the vortex a two-way portal.'

Maya looked on in amazement. 'He wanted me to test it, however only Luke can maintain a stable portal. He instructed me to bring back an artifact on today's mission by using one of the mini droids.'

There was a sharp intake of breath from Maya.

Kalani continued, 'He wants to create vortexes for instant travel and sell it to the highest bidder.'

Kalani was now walking slowly around the lab and was getting close to Luke. 'I decided to make my own adjustments to his design. I attached a device like this to one of the MQDs. But I've programmed it to re-polarise the beam and destroy the connection for good.'

His eyes were wild, and his heart was pounding.

'Once I press this button—' He pointed at the holographic screen coming out of his palm. '—it will destroy the HTC.'

'You can't,' shouted Maya, 'That will kill Luke.'

‘I’m afraid it has to happen, to preserve our history. Luke is the only person who has been able to establish the connection. I can’t allow the continued dishonour of our ancestors…’

He paused. ‘Or let that greedy vile man sell this technology.’

‘You can’t do this Kalani, we’re friends, we’ve worked together for years,’ Marcus pleaded.

‘It doesn’t matter, I must protect the past from our interference.’

At that point, Maya and Marcus both lunged to tackle him. They fell onto each other and wrestled trying to deactivate the screen. Maya was pulling at Kalani’s arm to deactivate the screen while Marcus tried to pin him to the floor. Kalani swung his hand, hitting Maya in the face and knocking her into Luke who was still trying to keep the portal stable.

Luke couldn’t risk breaking his concentration as he needed to make sure that the vaporise order was sent to the QD6. He didn’t know if Kalani had sabotaged anything else and was fearful that the technology could fall into a local’s hands, or worse, cause a huge explosion as it crashed.

Marcus finally managed to force Kalani to the floor, but he was still trying to close the screen. Maya had scrambled back to her feet and was heading back over to Kalani. However, it was too late. He managed to break a hand free and with all his might he pressed the button on the floating screen. The MQD was released from the main droid. It shot up in the air and turned to face the open portal, firing a bright red beam directly towards the antimatter vortex.

The beam of light transmitted out from the mini droid hit the portal with a loud bang. It interacted with the tear in subspace and a large yellow ball of light appeared in the skies over Angkor, causing the locals to stare up.

In the laboratory, Luke let out a yell. Marcus elbowed Kalani in the face and scrabbled to his feet, Maya had rushed over to Luke and was frantically trying to get him out of the HTC. She was soon joined by Marcus who pulled at Luke to uncouple him from the device. It was too late and the HTC would not disengage. The beam coming from 1189 had started a cascade failure and without warning, a huge green light enveloped the room causing an electronic magnetic pulse, which rippled through the laboratory. A few moments later, all the electronic equipment exploded. Karen and Simon scrambled behind a metal panel and after what seemed like ages, the explosions stopped, and the lab fell silent. The archaeologists cautiously got up from where they had been cowering desperate to see what had happened. The thick smoke began to clear and they noticed a huge circular void. About a foot of concrete was missing from the floor along with all the team's equipment.

Karen and Simon searched frantically around the room looking for the Quantology research team. They found no bodies or body parts. Nothing was left. No equipment and no signs of the team. Just the lingering smell of burnt electrical wires and an eerie silence.

CHAPTER FIVE

Picking Up the Pieces

It was pitch dark when Marcus came to. He rubbed his head and began to focus on getting his bearings. He tapped his hand and his holographic screen lit up, enabling him to see his surroundings. Marcus slowly assessed the situation and as he paused, he felt the warm night air caress his skin. It was at that point that he realised he was no longer in Cambridge, just as the smell of nature permeated his senses. Marcus scanned the surroundings and noticed thick foliage, trees, and a rocky ground. He looked deeper into the undergrowth just as his mind seemed too catch-up, he realised he was in the Jungle. Marcus's consciousness awoke like a lightning bolt. It was suddenly clear what had happened. He was in the jungles of Angkor.

Marcus scrambled to his feet. He looked around and noticed broken concrete and damaged lab equipment scattered all over the jungle floor.

A sense of panic suddenly hit him as his mind screamed *Luke.*

He began to search frantically for the others, and it wasn't long before he found Maya. She was unconscious. A large piece of metal console lay on her. Marcus pushed with all his might to move it and finally, the metal object fell to the floor with a clatter. He checked her pulse nervously, fearful she may be dead, but thankfully he felt her heart beating. Marcus activated his palm screen and scanned her for a full medical report. The results came back quickly and confirmed that she had a few cuts and bruises but nothing serious. Knowing she was safe to move, he picked her up and carried her to a nearby clearing, placing her gently next to a large tree.

Marcus then began his search for the others. The equipment was scattered over about a mile radius strewn in the thick jungle and searching was difficult. It took him another twenty minutes before he located Kalani, he was also unconscious. Kalani was hunched over a tree. Marcus noticed a large piece of metal lodged deep into Kalani's leg.

A conflict suddenly arose within him. He had considered this guy a friend until today, he would have done anything for him. However, the situation was now different, Kalani had tried to kill Luke. Could he bring himself to help this traitor, the man who had stranded them in the past. Marcus thought about leaving him for a moment, but his sense of morality soon returned. He initiated a scan. It identified that apart from the metal object protruding out of Kalani's leg, he had a concussion. Marcus pulled him over his shoulder, carrying him back to where he had left Maya. Marcus then ripped some cable from a nearby damaged console and tied Kalani tightly to a tree, just to be safe. Marcus then made a tourniquet to tie around Kalani's bleeding leg.

He paused nervously, before ripping a sleeve from his shirt. Marcus stared at Kalani, trying to build up the courage to pull out the large piece of metal from his leg. He took a deep breath, then pulled the metal object hard until it came loose. Quickly tying the makeshift bandage around the bleeding leg and backed away.

Marcus was now sweating heavily. The humidity was stifling and he took another breath to calm and control his emotions. A flash of panic suddenly hit him.

Luke, his mind screamed, and he knew there was no time to waste.

Just as he was turning to leave Maya woke. She rubbed her head and called out to Marcus.

Without thinking he instinctively put his hand up. 'No time to talk, keep an eye on him.' Marcus gestured at the tied-up Kalani. 'I need to find Luke.'

He left without another word.

Maya's head was pounding, she wiped her forehead with the back of her hand and as she pulled it away, she could see it was covered in blood. Maya hauled herself to her feet wiping her blood-soaked hand onto her clothes. She began to look around the area and realised instantly what had happened, she knew they were in big trouble. Maya activated her palm reader and scanned the area, however, for some reason it couldn't get an accurate reading. She scanned Kalani, and the device registered his injuries, she tended to him but noticed that Marcus had already treated his wounds. Maya sighed. She was relieved he was okay.

She stood up and started to pace, desperately thinking about what to do next. Maya's mind raged at how this could have happened. She moved to examine what remained of the lab equipment. Maya rummaged in the wreckage trying to find anything that could be of use. Suddenly behind her came a yell of pain, she looked around quickly, seeing Kalani struggle against his bonds.

Maya rushed over without hesitation. 'Keep still, you're injured. Marcus has slowed the bleeding in your leg but if you keep struggling it'll make it worse.'

Kalani just looked at her.

'What happened?' he asked, confused, but didn't wait for an answer. 'The lab should have been vaporised by the antimatter beam?'

'It's clear you didn't calculate all the variables. As I don't know what your device contained, I cannot be sure what happened. If I had to theorise, then your re-polarised beam reacted with the vortex. This reaction caused the portal to expand and suck everything within a few meters into it.'

Maya paused but couldn't help herself. 'Your reckless actions have put us all in danger, how could you betray us? How could you betray me? We've worked together for years. I considered you to be family.'

Tears were forming in her eyes as her emotions built.

Kalani looked away broken by the reaction of his mentor, but Maya continued to stare intensely at him. He slowly turned to look at her with tears streaming down his face.

'Can you not see what we were doing was wrong, entering the past and violating those who have come before us?'

He stopped, choosing his words carefully. 'We should be looking to the future to support humanity, not trying to peer into our past for entertainment, it violates our ancestors' memory.'

'I understand you may have had issues with the morality of what we were doing, but to try and murder Luke. How could you?' she responded bitterly. 'You could have raised your concerns with me, and you should have told me what Dhruv was doing. What you have done could have far greater impacts on humanity than our study of historical events.'

Maya threw her hands in the air. 'Do you not appreciate the reasons why Marcus has such a desire to understand history? He was helping us to comprehend our past, helping us learn to not make the same mistakes, to show the world how our actions have consequences. 'Look around you, what impact do you think we'll have to the timeline being a thousand years in our past. If that is even where we are. It's you that dishonours our ancestors, and it's you that could impact how our future unfolds.'

Those words hit Kalani hard, he held his head in his hands as his thoughts swirled around uncontrollably. Kalani realised that his actions could have larger implications for humanity than he had ever considered, and he knew he had to make it right.

***

Deep in the undergrowth, Marcus continued to search for Luke. He held up his hand to scan the area once more.

'Why aren't you working properly?' he whispered, as interference continued to block his scans.

Suddenly a red dot appeared on his holographic screen. Marcus scrambled quickly through the foliage following the trail., He wasn't looking where he was going and fell face-first into a muddy pool. Marcus swore, he pulled himself up and pressed on with his search. A little while later he saw something, a reflection of a metallic silver object caused by the light his holographic screen was admitting. Marcus raced forward, he came into a small clearing and he could see Luke. It was a sickening sight. Luke was still strapped in the HTC chair with the helmet still firmly connected to his head.

Marcus approached nervously. He hesitantly checked his apprentice's pulse. Finding no response he began to panic. Marcus urgently cleared jungle debris from Luke, then activated his palm scanner to check his medical status. To his relief, the report confirmed Luke was still breathing, as he looked closer at the medical report something was worrying. Luke's brain patterns were erratic, and the readings seemed to be jumping all over the place. Marcus continued to study the report. Apart from the irregular brain patterns, Luke seemed fine. *The HTC chair must have protected him,* he thought.

Marcus pulled at the helmet, but it wouldn't budge, it was like it had fused with Luke's head and Marcus was becoming more anxious. Eventually, he gave up trying to remove it and instead worked on releasing Luke from the chair. Marcus was more successful at this. It didn't take long before the seat belts were released, and Luke was freed from the device. Marcus hoisted him over his shoulder. However, after a few steps, he staggered and fell to the floor, Marcus was exhausted. His tiredness had taken hold and then all of a sudden, the energy left his body.

I have to do this, he thought to himself as he lay crumpled on the floor.

Marcus somehow managed to find the strength to pull himself up. He hoisted Luke onto his shoulder and started to carry him back to the others.

***

In the meantime, Maya had managed to start a fire by the tree next to Kalani to keep him warm. Once it was burning well her attention turned to searching the debris, and she began to look for anything of use.

'Perfect. This will help, it's the medical kit from the lab,' she said to Kalani.

Maya rummaged through the box finding a hypo-spray. She administered pain killers and antibiotics to Kalani to prevent infection. Maya searched through the kit further and found a dermal regenerator. She slowly undid the makeshift bandage that Marcus had placed on Kalani and began to wave it over his wound. It wasn't long before the wound began to congeal, the bleeding stopped, and the skin knitted back together.

'This will help,' she said calmly.

The trees suddenly rustled loudly causing Maya to jump. She looked around quickly as Marcus entered the clearing carrying an unconscious Luke. She rushed to her feet and hurried over to help. It was clear Marcus was struggling and when she reached him, she helped take Luke's weight.

'Thank goodness he's okay,' she said relieved.

Marcus looked at her, 'I'm not sure he is. I need you to examine him, his brain patterns are acting erratically.'

Marcus lifted his head and noticed Kalani was awake, he gave him a contemptuous stare.

They carried Luke to the base of another tree a little distance from Kalani.

'Has he said anything?' Marcus asked.

'Only the same as in the lab, he did it for the ancestors and to stop us violating history.' Maya put her hand on Marcus's shoulder. 'I'm sorry it's all my fault, I should have realised he was having issues with the project.'

Tears were now forming in her eyes again.

'It was his choice Maya, no one else's,' he responded. 'Anyway, we have more pressing matters right now. The blame can wait. Can you take a look at these readings? I'm not sure what they mean, and I can't get this damn helmet off him.'

Maya activated her palm screen and transferred the data from Marcus.

'This is unusual but it could be due to the intense impact of the re-polarised beam, all his other vitals seem okay,' she said reassuringly. 'We'll need to let him rest and allow his brain to readjust, I'll continue to monitor him closely.'

'Okay but how do we get this bloody helmet off?' Marcus asked exasperated.

Maya completed another scan. 'It's fused itself to the base of his neck, it's a safety control I installed to make sure the helmet didn't come off during the middle of a dig.'

She pulled his head forward and pointed at the metal clamp digging into Luke's skin. 'I think I can loosen it with these.'

She held up some medical pliers and a micro laser she retrieved from the medical kit. 'It will take me some time to remove it.'

Marcus nodded in acknowledgement. 'Go get some rest, I've already gathered food and water over by the fire.'

'It's my fault Luke's in this condition, is there anything further I can do to help?'

'No, rest, it's both our faults for not protecting our students,' Maya replied.

She looked over at Kalani who had drifted off to sleep, she had given him a sedative with the painkillers.

Marcus got up hesitantly, he stumbled again but pulled himself back up and headed over to the fire. He crumpled at the base of the tree and cupped his hand into a broken lab sink that Maya had found. She had used it to collect water from a nearby stream and he drank to quench his thirst. Marcus stared up into the dark canopy, the beauty of the jungle was incredible, stars twinkled between the drifting leaves, if only the circumstances were different. He picked up a piece of dragon fruit that Maya had managed to find and ate it slowly. His emotions were getting the better of him and he began to scowl darkly at the sleeping Kalani, wondering why his former friend could have betrayed them.

***

An hour later, Kalani woke with a start. He had been having that nightmare, the same one he'd been having for the last year, it always ended the same with Kalani being held responsible for the violation of nature. He always saw the same, the Mo'o water guardians dancing on the shores of Kauai creating a swell in the ocean. A tsunami would then consume the beach sweeping his village out to sea.

Marcus looked up seeing Kalani's sweat-laden face, noticing his heavy breathing.

'What's the matter, your conscious catching up with you?' Marcus said sarcastically.

Kalani looked away avoiding any kind of eye contact. 'Can't you see what you've done? Look at Luke, he was your friend and you tried to kill him.'

His emotions were rising again. 'If you didn't agree with the project why help us, why develop your droids?

You are as much a part of creating this technology as we are. Now look what you have done, you've stranded us in the past, our lives are over. We now run the risk of contaminating the timeline, so much for dishonouring our ancestors, you may have killed them.'

Kalani looked crestfallen at those words, he replied quietly, 'What do you mean?'

'We have worked on this subject for the last five years. We put in protocols to protect the timeline and you say you don't know.' Marcus's anger was building. 'The Quantum Butterfly Effect, if you had ever read the documentation I sent you then you would understand. A tiny or insignificant event can influence the way complex societies evolve. Think about it, if you go back and alter the past even slightly a different future could evolve. What do you think is going to happen now we're here, if we accidentally step on a bug that would have stopped a despot from coming to power, or if we influence a culture in any way, then the future we know could be forfeit.'

Marcus's anger exploded. 'You said in the lab that I wanted to bring back artefacts or to influence history, well that was plainly wrong. My only ambition was to learn from the past to help make humanity better. It is you who have put our future in danger, you who have broken the World Council's directive of non-interference, and it's you who dishonour your family.'

Kalani looked away, tears began to flow again, and it was like his nightmare was coming true.

All he could hear in his head was '*I have angered the guardians.*'

'Marcus, I've got it, come here,' Maya shouted.

He rushed over crouching at Luke's side.

'Okay, hold his neck still,' she instructed.

Marcus nodded and Maya began to pull, with a little force the helmet finally came off.

Maya checked a few more readings before saying, 'Looks like he'll be fine, his brain patterns have stabilised, but I'll continue to keep a close eye on him.'

Marcus pulled Luke close and cradled him in his arms,

'You know he's like a son to me, don't you?' he said.

'I do and you're like a brother to me,' she replied reassuringly and reached out to touch his hand. 'Come, let's get him close to the fire, we all need rest. Tomorrow we'll work out what to do.'

They both carried Luke over to the fire and sat down exhausted.

'What are we going to do Maya?' Marcus asked desperately.

'I don't know, but at least for the moment we're safe,' she replied with a strained smile.

***

It had only been a few hours since they decided to get some rest and as dawn broke neither of them had managed to sleep. Marcus had been checking on Luke every fifteen minutes, while Maya had been thinking through a multitude of options in her mind.

As the sun began to rise, the jungle came alive with noises. It was very unsettling for academics used to sterile laboratory conditions. Maya had gone through the medical pack and given each of them several injections from the emergency hypo-spray. She was keen to protect them from as many historic diseases as possible, but that did not stop the mosquitoes from biting. Marcus was suffering the most, his white European skin seemed to attract them more than the others.

'Bloody things,' he muttered to himself, slapping the back of his neck.

Marcus pulled himself to his feet to check on Luke once more, as he passed Maya she spoke calmly. 'Marcus I've been thinking, the best thing we can do is to keep a low profile in this timeframe.'

She hesitated carefully watching Marcus's reactions. 'We're not going to be able to get back home with this equipment.'

She pointed at the broken items on the floor.

'You mean we're truly stuck here?'

'I'm afraid so, there's no way back unless we open a portal by creating an antimatter field, which I can't do without the right equipment.' She sighed, 'There's another problem, it is only Luke who can open the portal and I have no idea what that beam did to him.'

She fell silent, letting her words sink in.

'I need to be honest, trying to get everything we need in this timeframe to recreate our experiment is very unlikely.'

A huge sense of sadness filled the air as Marcus realised what she was saying. His exhaustion set in and he stared at Luke, then looked back at Maya.

'What about Charlie and Richard?' he asked sombrely.

Maya looked away to hide her emotions.

'There's not much I can do.' She paused trying to find the words. 'All I can do is try to protect their future, the best way to do that is to remove ourselves from this timeframe. There are two ways to do this, end our lives or try and find a secluded place, to live out our remaining years where we can't interfere.'

She thought carefully for a moment. 'I, for one, am not ready to end my life today, even though my head is telling me it's the best thing we can do to protect our future.'

Marcus was stunned by her words.

'I can't ask Luke or Kalani to end their lives,' he said, shaking his head.

Maya nodded in agreement. 'Well, what we need to do is to find what remains of our equipment and hide it, do you agree?'

Marcus nodded.

'Okay, well that's the mission for today. In the meantime what should we do with Kalani, we can't just keep him tied up?'

'Let me chat with him again. From his reactions to our situation I think he realises the mistakes he's made. I'm sure he'll help us eventually, whatever happens, we all have to stick together.' Marcus hesitated. 'However, I'll never trust that man again.'

Maya gave him a knowing look.

As they finished talking, a cry came from Luke who had started to wake and Marcus rushed over.

'Stay still,' he ordered, Luke just waved him off.

'My head's pounding,' he said clutching his forehead. 'Where are we and what's happened?'

Marcus spent the next half an hour explaining their situation, while Maya searched for more food. Kalani was still unconscious and tied to the tree, every now and again Luke would shoot scornful looks at him.

'You really mean he wanted to kill me?' he asked Marcus one more time.

'I'm afraid so, but don't worry about that now, just rest.' He gave Luke some more fruit that Maya had found. 'Eat, Maya and I have some work to do.'

Luke nodded, feeling too weak to move.

Over the next couple of hours, Marcus and Maya scoured the jungle, trying to find any equipment they could. Marcus made a makeshift shovel and dug a large pit to put the broken lab equipment in. It seemed like an unending task, a lot of equipment had followed them through the portal and even though they were using their hand scanners to locate it, Marcus was worried they would miss something. Luke eventually gained enough strength and joined them in the search for the remaining items. As they hunted through the jungle, the realisation of their predicament began to sink in. It was clear to them all the danger they now faced.

Kalani, who had woken a little while ago, watched them closely. Marcus scanned the area one more time to ensure he hadn't missed any other equipment. He looked around and noticed Kalani staring. Marcus had been thinking about speaking to him, but seemed to be delaying the confrontation. He finally built up enough courage, Marcus took a sip of water from a lab cup he found during his search and walked over to Kalani.

'How are you feeling?'

'Humiliated and ashamed,' Kalani replied darkly.

'Well, I can't make you feel any better, you have let us all down and put our future in jeopardy,' Marcus replied unsympathetically. 'However, I need to explain our situation.'

Kalani nodded.

'It looks like we are stuck in this time period, based on the equipment we've found there's no way home.'

He paused for a moment to let that message take root. 'We have two options to protect the future. Firstly, we end our lives now, or secondly, we try and find a secluded place to live our lives away from any civilisations that we could harm.'

'You really think there's no way back,' Marcus just nodded. 'I knew I might not survive the explosion in the lab. But I never thought we'd be pulled through time and I wouldn't be able to see my family again.'

He began to cry and Marcus touched his shoulder giving him a small reassuring squeeze.

'I need your help. We must make sure our equipment doesn't fall into the wrong hands, can you help vaporise or hide it?'

'I'd need to see what we have left, untie me and I promise I'll help. I know I've betrayed your trust, but it was all to protect the future, to protect my family and it's still my duty to do that.'

Marcus thought carefully, finally agreeing and untied his bonds..

Kalani began to sift through the damaged equipment while Marcus watched closely, it wasn't long before he found something that could help. 'I can't vaporise it, but I can distort the surrounding area to make the undergrowth and trees thicker, it will camouflage the damaged equipment. If I use this small solar panel from the console, it should sustain the protective camouflage for a long time, I can't guarantee protection forever, but it will give the forest chance to envelop the equipment.'

'Great, let's do that,' Marcus replied and Kalani got to work.

***

Luke had been searching for Maya for some time, he finally found her in a small clearing. She was taking a break by a large tree and was staring at the ground. He coughed quietly to avoid startling her, she looked up and when she saw him, she suddenly broke down.

'I'm so sorry Luke I didn't know he would ever betray us. I can't believe he tried to kill you, it's all my fault,' she sobbed.

Luke put his arms around Maya and gave her a supportive hug, this act of kindness seemed to make her break down further. It was like all the stress, pressure and guilt was pouring out of her.

'It's not your fault, we undertook this project together and none of us knew he would do this.'

'I should have spotted something, now we're all stranded,' she continued to sob.

Luke was also starting to get emotional. He never knew how to handle women or girls crying, in fact, his experience with women was limited.

'There's nothing we can do except make the best of our situation,' he replied, his own emotions continued to build. 'I'm so sorry you'll never see your son again,' tears were now running down his face. 'I can't imagine what that's like.'

They both held on to each other in an embrace trying to come to terms with their situation. Luke and Maya had become close, they had spent a lot of time together building the HTC and she valued his company immensely.

After what seemed like ages, they returned to the mission and continued to search the undergrowth, only finding a few more broken bits of metal. Maya suggested they call it a day and make their way back to their makeshift camp. Luke agreed, he was tired of searching.

Back at the camp, Kalani was showing Marcus how to activate the camouflage filter with his palm implant. Marcus clicked the filter on and off a couple of times hiding the large trench they had filled with debris. Happy with the outcome, Marcus smiled back at Kalani in appreciation. He gathered a few useful bits of technology such as the medical kit, a remote scanner, and a few tools. He placed the items into Luke's backpack which was pulled through the portal. It was placed next to him in the lab before the chaotic events of that evening.

Maya and Luke returned to the clearing. Luke noticed that Kalani was smiling and tinkering with some technology, it was like nothing had happened and his emotions boiled over. Luke ran straight over to him, pushing him hard against a nearby tree.

'How dare you try to kill me? We were friends, how many times have we had dinner together, how many times have we drank and laughed together, and you tried to kill me?'

Luke's eyes were raging, and tears were streaming down his face.

Marcus rushed behind Luke and held him back. 'Get off me, he deserves this, think what he's done to all of us, Maya will never see her family again.'

He then turned directly to Kalani, 'Think about Ke'ala and Lani, where is their husband and father?'

'You think you're all so special don't you,' Kalani replied spitefully. 'It was all three of you who decided to play God and go back in time, didn't you ever think there would be consequences?'

'You know we did,' Luke spat back. 'That's why we designed all the safety controls, it was you who disabled them, you who tried to kill me, kill us.'

Luke broke free from Marcus and launched himself at Kalani, wrestling him to the floor. Neither of them were particularly skilled fighters, so they tumbled around on the floor, pulling at each other.

'Stop it both of you, this isn't going to help,' Maya pleaded.

Suddenly the sound of rustling and voices were all around them, Marcus looked at Maya in panic. He managed to pull Luke off Kalani. Marcus tapped a few controls on his palm screen to activate the camouflage protection.

Maya went to help Kalani, as she pulled him to his feet, he pushed her away. She stumbled which caused her to fall back and hit her head on a nearby rock. Seeing Maya injured on the floor, Kalani hesitated. He looked around and noticed Luke being held back by Marcus, he was in a rage. Kalani turned quickly and fled into the jungle.

Maya scrambled to her feet, however blood trickled down her neck, she had cut herself in the fall and she felt dizzy. Maya tried to run after Kalani, but Marcus pulled her back, it was too late. He held his finger to his lips signalling to them both to be quiet.

'Who's there? show yourself now,' a strange voice called out in an unusual language.

Even though this language was strange and old they understood the words being spoken. The palm implants acted as a translator within their brains. It was a remarkable bit of technology and most people in the future had the implants installed. The translator within the palm implant connected directly to the brain, it enabled everyone to understand and speak the languages of the world. It was a remarkable piece of technology that broke down barriers.

'You have thirty seconds to respond or we'll open fire', the unknown speaker said again.

Marcus grabbed the bag filled with equipment and looked at Maya.

He shouted back towards where the voice was coming from, 'We're Norman traders from the land of Christendom, we are on a trading mission and come in peace.'

CHAPTER SIX
A Khmer Welcome

A group of fifty men suddenly came into the clearing with their bows pulled back and their golden spears raised. Marcus's assumption was that they were soldiers from Angkor. The men were barefoot and wearing robes that Marcus knew as a sompot. The robes resembled that of loose breeches held up by a rectangular piece of cloth wrapped around the waist. Each of the men had smooth bronzed muscled torsos, which complimented their purple robes. Their clothes were embossed with golden thread and embroidered animal patterns. All the men had gold ankle and arm bracelets along with thin gold bands around their necks. One of the men stepped forward. Marcus could only assume he was their leader. His hands were covered in golden rings all decorated with dazzling gems, which shone in the afternoon sun.

His upper body was covered in golden armour and around his neck was a fine golden lattice chain. At the centre of the web like neckless was a deep purple amethyst. The leader wore a golden lotus crown which was covered in more amethyst stones. The crown was also studded with diamonds, which glistened in the sunshine.

Marcus couldn't stop his thoughts turning to archaeology. He had never seen anyone dressed like this and he stared with fascination at the soldiers before him. Marcus noticed the detailed carvings on the men's weapons. These men were not mere soldiers, they were a kind of elite guard.

Luke was also mesmerised by what he was seeing, he had studied history his whole life and now he could see the wonders of the past. However, he was more cautious. Luke understood that this was now the present, not the past, which made him very uneasy. He shuffled uncomfortably as he continued to stare at the man standing in front of him. Luke knew enough to understand this leader must be a prince. There was more, the man in front of him radiated a timeless beauty, he was about thirty and tall, much taller than Luke expected to see from someone of south Asian heritage. Luke's eyes darted over the man's body. Noticing his deep bronze chest radiating in the sunlight.

Luke's eyes focused on the man's face. It was painted with black war makeup, but he could tell the man was kind-hearted. There was something in his expression that Luke could read and he felt safe. The prince had piercing hazel-coloured eyes and he exuded power. It was clear for all to see that his men worshiped him. Luke's eyes connected with the prince's and something strange happened. It was like a spark had ignited. Luke knew he had a deep connection to this stranger.

Their eyes remained fixed, and they held each other's gaze, no words needed to be spoken between them to understand the attraction.

Luke couldn't explain this feeling, he had never felt anything like this before. He had been gay all his life and his sexuality was never a problem. It wasn't for anyone in his time. Luke had had a few partners while studying at university, but this feeling was different. Deep inside him, there was an inner voice calling out that something was special. The silence remained as Luke sensed the man in front of him look deeply into his soul.

A long and uncomfortable silence hung in the clearing until the prince finally spoke. 'I'm Srindrakumaraputra, but the locals call me Prince Srindra. Who are you, and what are you doing on our land?'

As he made these demands, he didn't take his eyes off Luke.

There was a further pause until Marcus plucked up enough courage to speak. 'My name is Marcus Larsson. I am a lord of Götaland. We come as traders to your land to learn more about your culture and trade our merchandise.'

Prince Srindra looked around, he saw no trading carts or merchandise. Marcus could read his mind and quickly spoke again, 'We travelled down the Silk Road from our homes in Europe. We had heard stories of your great city and we followed many trade routes through India and Indochina. After speaking to traders we found the road to your great city.'

Marcus paused for a moment, suddenly finding his throat dry. 'However, we were betrayed by one of our servants who made a pact with a band of mercenaries we met in Lavo. Those mercenaries stole our goods and brought us to this clearing to kill us. I thank you Prince

Srindra for scaring them away and saving our lives, we're forever in your debt.'

Marcus bowed deeply, Maya and Luke followed his actions.

Prince Srindra looked confused and even a bit amused. 'You made it all the way from Northern Europe, then were robbed close to our city?'

He looked at his men who broke out in laughter. 'Here I am thinking you were a Cham invasion force, how have you made it this far, where are your weapons and what are you wearing?'

He continued to laugh.

'Our weapons were stolen Your Majesty and as for our clothes, they're a little worn after all our travelling,' Marcus replied, trying to smile.

'Come with us' the prince declared. 'We'll help you. I have to admit we have not had visitors from Europe for some time and I'm keen to hear more about your culture. Firstly, are any of you hurt?'

'We have a few cuts and bruises but thankfully we're okay, thanks to you,' Marcus replied and bowed again.

'Come' he gestured to them.

Marcus looked at Maya, their eyes connected knowing they had no choice but to follow.

'What about the mercenaries Your Majesty, we would like to capture our servant, he has stolen items very valuable to us.'

'I'll send my men to search for them, but the jungle is thick and bandits can hide easily.' Prince Srindra spoke to his soldiers and about ten of them disappeared into the deep jungle.

'Can I ask you something, did you see that yellow light in the sky last night?'

Marcus shuffled uncomfortably.

'Yes Your Majesty, that was one of the new fireworks we hoped to trade with you. It was set off accidentally when we were attacked,' Marcus responded, trying to dismiss the prince's concern and make the light in the sky seem nothing to worry about.

'That was you, my Father thought it was a sign from the gods and he wanted me to investigate. You'll have to show us how you make such a bright light.'

The prince turned to Maya. 'May I ask about yourself? my understanding is that people from Europe tend to be pale skinned. I have never seen a person from Europe with such a dark complexion.'

Maya looked at Marcus not knowing what to say or how to address the strange comment.

'I'm a scholar and I've worked with Marcus for many years. I come from a region in Southern Europe. My name is Maya and I thank you Your Majesty for saving us,' trying to sound grateful.

Prince Srindra looked at her. 'A scholar you say, I'm sure my mother will want to meet you. The queen's obsessed with natural philosophy, and always trying to expand her understanding of the world.'

He then turned to Luke who was walking behind Marcus trying to avoid any interaction.

'What's your name?' Prince Srindra demanded.

'It's Luke Your Majesty,' he said hesitantly. 'Luke Adams.'

'Welcome Luke,' Prince Srindra replied looking him up and down. 'I've never seen bright green eyes on a person before, you certainly are a strange group of people.'

He chuckled to himself and they were escorted towards the city. Maya briefly looked over her shoulder scouring the jungle desperate to see any signs of Kalani, but it was to no avail, he had vanished.

***

Kalani ran like his life depended on it, while successfully avoiding the royal guards. He forced his way through the jungle foliage, intent on being as far away as possible from his former colleagues. Kalani's emotions had been building and as he ran, he couldn't stop from striking the trees in anger. After what seemed like an hour, he fell upon a clearing by a crystal-clear pool of water and collapsed under a nearby tree. He wiped the dirt from his forehead and breathed heavily thinking hard about what to do next. It was then his situation dawned on him, he didn't know where to go and for the first time he realised he was truly alone.

Time moved quickly as Kalani spent the next few hours resting and reflecting. He managed to forage for fruit and found a cluster of palm trees which brought back memories of Hawaii. He paced around, soon locating a number of fallen coconuts. He picked one up smashing it open with a nearby rock desperate to drink the liquid inside. Kalani breathed deeply with relief then slumped down at the base of a tree. He looked down at himself, in his rush to get away all he had with him was the clothes he wore, a dirty torn lab coat, ripped blood-stained jeans and a simple black T-shirt.

His mind raced. *How am I going to survive like this?*

Kalani activated his palm screen using it to scan the local area, a few seconds later a map appeared in front of him.

I'll head for the lake and shelter there for now, at least there will be food and water, he thought to himself.

Kalani looked at the map for a few more minutes working out the best route to the lake. Finally, he stood up, brushed himself down and set off for Tonlé Sap.

***

An hour after, Marcus, Luke and Maya had met the soldiers they reached the outskirts of Angkor. There were little huts dotted over the landscape joined together by lagoons, the houses seem to float effortlessly between the pools of water. The sight was stunning, with waterwheels and aqueducts connecting the streams as local people fished next to their homes. The elite guard walked past the villagers and the people bowed to the prince, he fondly smiled back at them. It was clear he was a popular man and as they continued the numbers of villagers began to grow. A sense of excitement built as the people were keen to get a glimpse of the prince, his elite guard and the strange foreigners.

The group soon reached the walls of the city. Marcus and Luke looked at each other marvelling at the sight before them, they could see the buildings in their full colourful glory and it was something they had only dreamed of. The huge gates opened, they walked through and crossed a stone bridge that stretched over a large canal. The bridge was adorned with figures from Khmer mythology and the archaeologist's excitement continued to rise, despite their current situation. They were experiencing real-life historical events and the chance to see history was intoxicating. A twinge of guilt suddenly hit Marcus. He knew they shouldn't be in the city but his excitement of seeing Angkor for real, and at the height of its glory made him beam.

They passed through yet another set of protective gates just as the setting sun shone brightly off the many temples. The soldiers turned down an avenue and unexpectedly the great temple of Angkor Wat came into view. It was at that moment Marcus's heart leapt, causing him to trip and fall to the floor in wonder. He had visited the ruins of Angkor many times spending days studying the intricate carvings. But seeing the temple in all its glory made tears come to his eyes and he couldn't stop his emotions from giving way.

Prince Srindra came to a stop, he stared at the reactions of this strange man, *something seems very off with these traders* he thought. However, the prince had not met people from Europe and maybe this is how they reacted.

Marcus managed to compose himself as Luke helped him to his feet, Maya then took his arm for reassurance. He looked ahead at the long straight road which led directly to the temple, the road turned into bridges crossing the large moat which teamed with life. Marcus could see beautiful lotus flowers floating on the water and there were monkeys playing on the nearby bank. *What an incredible sight*, he thought to himself.

Marcus couldn't stop himself, he turned to Prince Srindra and said, 'Your city is truly amazing. Would you allow me to visit the temple Your Majesty?'

'I'm not sure, only the king can approve access to our sacred site.' Prince Srindra gave him a perplexed look and was intrigued by the strangers' reaction.

He turned to Luke, 'Don't you have anything like this back where you're from?'

'No Your Majesty, your city is truly unique and very beautiful,' he replied gently. 'Like Marcus, I would love to see more if you allow, we've heard so many stories about your great city.'

Prince Srindra reacted kindly to those words.

'You'll be my guests while you're here, you may not have items to trade but I would love to hear more from your homeland. Maybe you can share insights into your culture.'

'I would love to Your Majesty,' Luke replied a bit too keenly.

They soon arrived at Srindra's compound, the sun had now set but it had left a faint golden haze in the air, reflecting the light of the many lakes and pools. Like much of the city Srindra's estate was intertwined with water all bursting with life. The lotus flowers were a mixture of white, pinks, yellows and deep reds all dotted between the huge lily pads. The gardens blended in seamlessly with the buildings and were linked by flower beds which were interwoven with paths. The bright gold, red, and blue colours from the buildings reflected brightly on the water, and with all the foliage it made a truly idyllic sight.

Prince Srindra showed them around the compound and when he finished he escorted them all to a nearby guest house.

'You'll join us for dinner and we can talk about our people,' he excitedly declared. 'I'll instruct my servants to provide you with some more appropriate clothing, but in the meantime get some rest.'

He bowed his head and left.

Once out of earshot Maya spoke panicked, 'What are we going to do?'

She looked at them both for help. It was clear she was completely out of her depth. Give her a science problem and she'd excel, but having to act or present on a subject she didn't know, made her extremely anxious. Maya lacked knowledge of ancient cultures, beliefs, and rituals, and she feared her inexperience would cause her to make mistakes.

'Maya we have no choice but to be his guests, there's no option where we can leave without causing suspicion or worse creating conflict,' Marcus said.

'But what about Kalani? He's out there on his own, there's no telling the damage he could do.'

'We have no choice. We'll try and find him but first, we need to work out how.'

Marcus sighed. He rubbed his head which was overwhelmed. 'We have to try and limit the damage we can cause. Let's stick to the trader story and hopefully, we can work out how to leave the city without causing a scene.'

Maya nodded in agreement.

Marcus then continued, 'Let's take this opportunity to clean up and get some rest.'

There was a knock at the door and a number of servants arrived with fresh water to wash and some pleasant-smelling oils. Over the next few hours, they all bathed and rested trying to calm their nerves. They needed to prepare to feast with the Prince of Angkor.

***

As night fell the servants returned, they came ladened with a variety of clothing. The head servant instructed them to strip so he could dress them appropriately to see the prince, the academics nervously took off their clothes until they were just in their underwear. There was a giggle from the servants who noticed the pair of strange colourful boxer shorts Marcus wore. Marcus, however, did not find any of this funny, his embarrassment was only compounded by the servants insisting that they remove all their clothing until they were naked. Eventually all three of them followed the instructions too much embarrassment.

When naked, the three guests were covered in cleansing oils which smelt of jasmine. The servants dried them and began to dress the academics more appropriately for a royal dinner. Maya was placed in a blue and green robe with intricate animal patterns all sewn with silver thread, it had a matching shawl in case she felt cold. Both Luke and Marcus were dressed in similar robes to that of the prince, but were not allowed to wear anything over their chest which made the northern Europeans very uncomfortable.

The servants finished dressing them with golden bangles and elaborate jewellery. Maya had her hair combed and sleeked back secured by a golden clasp. A golden necklace was placed around her neck which had a bright sapphire stone at the heart of it. Marcus's robes were green in colour, they had a red waistband tightly adjusted to keep his robes in place. Thick chains of gold were then placed around his neck with a red ruby jewel hanging down in the centre of his chest, which only seemed to highlight his pale white skin. Finally, Luke was dressed in purple robes. Like Marcus he was adorned with golden chains and had a purple amethyst stone hanging in the centre of his chest. Just like the one Prince Srindra wore. There was a murmur of excitement from the servants as they placed the jewel onto Luke, which made them all a little nervous.

Now dressed they were led out of the guest house and guided through the gardens. The path was lit by flaming torches leading to a large, beautiful pagoda positioned next to the small lake. The servants laid out a large intricate rug on the floor under a beautiful Banyan tree. Scattered over the rug was many different coloured cushions and in the centre was a roaring firepit hanging from one of the banyan tree's branches.

The three of them looked around, there were many nobles in attendance, all dressed exquisitely. They carefully found a space where the three of them could sit together. The servants handed them a freshly open coconut. They all drank nervously. The liquid was very refreshing however Marcus could tell it was alcoholic, it had an unknown kick to it. A few minutes later, Prince Srindra arrived with his entourage all in joyous conversation. As he entered the pagoda all the nobles rose as a mark of respect and the academics followed suit. Prince Srindra was dressed in a similar outfit to Luke, although he was adorned with much more elaborate golden jewellery. Additionally, he now wore a larger golden crown which had golden leaves positioned like that of the lotus flower. In the centre of the crown was a large purple oval amethyst. Prince Srindra sat next to his foreign guests, more accurately next to Luke. The rest of his entourage followed his lead and sat around Maya and Marcus.

Prince Srindra was given a drink by a servant and spoke, 'Welcome my friends, we are pleased to have esteemed guests from Europe with us tonight, they will share in our hospitality in the hope we can better understand our two peoples.'

He turned and spoke to them directly, 'I understand it's been a long and difficult journey for you to reach our city. All though I understand you may not have treasures to trade, I'm sure we can share stories,' he finished with a smile.

Marcus then spoke and unusually for him he was nervous, 'Thank you Your Majesty, we're humbled and grateful for the kindness you have shown us, anything we can do to return that kindness we will do.'

Prince Srindra nodded his head.

'Time to feast,' he signalled his servants and the food began to arrive.

Over the next hour, they ate, drank and chatted. Prince Srindra introduced them to his closest companions Samang Chon and Vannak Ros. They were both very interested in European history. Marcus shared stories relating to that time period taking great pains to keep them as vague as possible. The Khmer were fascinated by the two Caucasian men in front of them, white men were not something many Khmer people had ever seen before. Prince Srindra spent time chatting to Maya, her way of speaking intrigued him and reminded him of his mother. He introduced her to Nearidei Seang and Kesor Khim both favourite female students of the queen. After a while Maya seemed to relax, these women were bright and articulate and she enjoyed their company immensely.

Marcus's nerves seemed to ease, whatever was in the coconut drink had helped and he took the opportunity to understand more about Khmer culture. He was curious about the colour the prince wore, this was never in the texts he had read and he wanted to understand more about its symbolism.

Marcus approached the topic gently, 'Your Majesty, why are your men dressed in purple?'

Prince Srindra seemed surprised by the comment.

'That's a question no one would usually ask, but you're from foreign lands,' he smiled. 'The colours are linked to our court and signal our power. As heir to the throne, my colour is purple and at the age of eighteen, the king gave me permission to form my own elite guard. It's a tradition to help the heir build up strong connections with future commanders and the forces he'll control. I have a thousand men who've committed to fight by my side and fight for the king.'

The prince said proudly, he then stopped and thought carefully for a moment. 'My father, the king, has a personal battalion of twenty thousand men in total, if you count the various battalions around the empire, we have over a hundred thousand men ready to protect our people, either in our active army or in reserve.'

Marcus looked at him amazed, that was much larger than he thought the Khmer army had during this period.

The prince picked up on his reaction and continued proudly, 'My father's men wear his colours of orange and gold and they fight under his banner.'

'Tell me more' Marcus pressed, his enthusiasm taking over.

Prince Srindra smiled.

'My mother has a unique position in our court. It's very unusual for a woman to have her own force except for their personal protection. However, my father values the queen's insight and her influence is of great use to him. Her services to the empire have earned her a private battalion of five thousand men. They mainly support with her scientific endeavours as well as her diplomatic work. Many great minds have come to work in Angkor under her protection, while others have come to fight for her due to the relationships she has built with our allies,' he said with great respect.

'My mother is much revered across the empire. Her forces and scientists wear her colours of blue and silver,' the prince paused again.

'I have two siblings. My sister and brother have small personal guards of around five hundred men all sworn to protect their safety. My sister's men are dressed in green while my brother chose black and red for some reason.' There was a hint of irritation in Prince Srindra's voice.

'Colours are important in our court and trust me, you're already being assessed where you'll fit in.' He suddenly broke into a smile, making his remarks seem like he was joking. But what the prince said was no joke.

Srindra continued to tease Marcus about the way the court worked and Marcus listened intently. The evening seemed to fly by. Marcus was immersed in the culture and enthusiastically chatted to most of the guests, he was obsessed in understanding Khmer society. He took yet another drink from his replenished coconut then looked over at Maya and smiled. She was deep in conversation trying to understand the role of women in this culture, she was equally impressed by the people of Angkor.

Luke on the other hand had remained quiet, usually he would have been as fascinated by the culture as Marcus was. But the events of the last few days had hit him hard. His friend's betrayal weighed heavily on his mind, not to mention the intense headache he hadn't been able to shake. Prince Srindra had been watching Luke closely and noticed something was wrong.

He put his hand onto Luke's shoulder and asked quietly, 'Would you take a walk with me?'

'I guess so,' Luke replied hesitantly. He looked around noticing both Maya and Marcus in full conversation.

He sensed the prince's interest in him and it was clear the prince had sensed Luke's attraction also.

'No need to be frightened,' Prince Srindra said with a smile.

They both got up, Luke adjusting his new Khmer outfit, unsure how to wear it. Srindra led Luke to a nearby path which wove around the lake.

'Something's been bothering me.' He paused looking Luke right in his eyes and placed a hand on his waist.

'Ever since we met, there's been a connection between us. I know you felt it, I could see it in your face,' he said gently. 'This kind of connection is not something that happens very often, and it's never happened to me until today.'

Luke took a nervous inhale, as he did he could smell the familiar scent of the lotus flowers mixed with jasmine which only seemed to heighten his senses.

'Umm, I don't know what to say, I really don't know your culture and what's acceptable.'

He paused.

'I'm keen not to offend you Your Majesty,' Luke replied rather messily.

'You may notice that we are wearing the same colour, in my culture that is the way I can express my interest in someone. I've been given huge freedoms by my father to live how I want and to be with who I want. I know that many different cultures have different views of acceptable relationships but we are an open and progressive people. I knew who you were deep down the moment we met.'

He smiled at Luke with intense warmth.

This kindness made Luke's heart beat faster and Prince Srindra knew it. 'All I ask is let's get to know each other, no agenda and no pressure.'

He took Luke's hand. 'You know you have very soft hands for a trader.'

Prince Srindra smiled at him again as if he could see right through the lie that they'd been telling. 'What is this, may I ask?'

Luke coughed nervously when he noticed what the prince was referring to. It was a ring on his right hand which was a gift from Marcus on his 21st Birthday. The ring was made out of Tungsten, not something available in the current time period.

'Oh, that's just a ring Marcus gave me to celebrate my birthday.'

Prince Srindra seemed a bit taken aback, 'Is Marcus someone special to you?'

Luke could see what the prince was thinking and chuckled. 'Well yes, but not what you're thinking, he's been like a father to me.'

A wave of relief filled the prince's face. 'Well, it's clear you are special to many people.'

Prince Srindra then placed his hand onto Luke's torso, pressing the purple amethyst hard against Luke's chest. 'We both have a destiny to fulfil, and I hope we can explore it together.'

He spoke as if he knew the thoughts running through Luke's mind, it was clear the attraction between them was very strong. 'Let's continue our walk. Why don't you tell me more about where you're from and what you're interested in?'

The remainder of the night flew by. Luke and Prince Srindra spent hours walking around the gardens. Luke was careful what he said about home, and he pulled on his extensive knowledge of early British history to help manage the questions he was asked. When they both re-joined the main group, Maya and Marcus looked at each other concerned. They noticed Luke leave with the prince earlier and could see the connection between them.

Marcus breathed deeply when he noticed their hands touching, he was fearful this might be the start of something that could put the future in danger.

CHAPTER SEVEN

A Modern Perspective

The feast finished in the early hours of the morning. It was hard to know what the exact time was, but Marcus knew it was past midnight. Prince Srindra's court was enthralled by the visitors, and they wanted to know everything about Europe. It was only when the prince declared the feast was over that the courtiers began to leave. Marcus, Maya and Luke were all escorted back to the guest house by servants. They were tended to and dressed in some more comfortable clothing and the servants then left.

As soon as the door shut Marcus turned to Luke,

'Whatever do you think you're doing?' he said furiously at his apprentice.

'What do you mean,' Luke replied taken aback by Marcus's words.

'You know what I mean, it was clear to us all what Srindra was looking for. It doesn't matter what feelings you may have for this man, we have to protect the timeline,' Marcus responded a little bit more sensitively.

'Both of you chatted to him as well, what could I do? The prince wanted to spend time with me, I couldn't say no. What if I had offended him?' Luke was becoming emotional. 'I have no idea what the prince or his guards would have done to us.'

Marcus got up and started to pace around the room, he knew Luke had a point but just stared at him. 'Marcus, if we are going to find Kalani and seek somewhere to hide, we will need help. The prince has already shown great kindness and I trust him. I don't know why but I do. This culture has much more of an enlightened sense of morality than I initially understood. I know you see it as well.'

'Luke's right Marcus,' Maya interjected. 'We need to find Kalani, and we need help to do that, who knows the damage that will be done to the future if we don't find him.'

'You're both right, of course,' Marcus said, holding his head in his hands. 'We just need to be careful, the more we integrate the more we'll make mistakes, there's no telling the damage we've already caused.'

'I know,' Maya said, sitting down next to him and taking his hand. 'But we have to try and survive, all we can do is limit our damage.'

Maya then got up and walked to the window, looking out over the calm waters. 'I've arranged for us to have a tour of the city tomorrow with Nearidei and Kesor. They promised to show us their great western baray, you know that huge reservoir you always talk about.'

She looked back at Marcus knowing that would irritate him, 'For now, let's build trust with them in the hope they will help us.'

Marcus nodded.

'You're right, let's get to sleep we're all exhausted,' he ordered, and they all agreed.

***

It was nine in the morning when there was a loud bang at the door. Luke, who had been looking at his palm screen scanning for Kalani quickly closed it down. Servants entered the room with water for them to wash and fresh clothing. They were cleaned and dressed in the same style as the night before.

'I have orders to take you to Nearidei,' the young servant said hesitantly.

'Thank you, what's your name?' Maya asked the young man.

Completely taken aback by the question, he stood in silence for a moment before replying, 'My name's Atith.'

'Nice to meet you Atith, please take us to Nearidei, I'm keen to see more of your great city.'

He bowed and gestured for them to leave.

Atith guided the three academics out of the prince's compound and onto the streets. Locals stopped and stared at the foreigners which made them all nervous. Marcus's mood seemed to brighten. He was in his element as they passed so many of the ancient sites he had obsessed over as a young archaeologist. He had studied the ruins of these buildings all his life and now he was seeing them being used as intended.

The group arrived at the entrance of Angkor Thom, they all stared with wonder at the amazing half-built monument. Angkor Thom glimmered in the sunshine. It had masons working on huge, magnificent stone carvings. The grey, white, and pink stone seemed to sparkle brightly and the sound of stones being chiselled filled the air. They crossed the bridge by the east gate and were met by Nearidei and Kesor, both seem very excited to see them. As they approached, they greeted their guests with joyful enthusiasm.

Maya spoke, 'Thank you for allowing us to see your beautiful city. To have you as our personal guides is very gratifying and will be very insightful, you're both kind for offering us this tour.'

'You're welcome, Maya. We are pleased to have a fellow natural philosopher among us,' Nearidei said with a smile. 'After our discussion yesterday, you wanted to see how our water management system works and to look at the way our irrigation system is connected, particularly the baray, dykes, and the connecting canals. It does intrigue me that with all the great wonders in this city you want to look at the water system.'

'Your Khmer Hydraulic system is an acien—' Marcus stopped himself and coughed uncomfortably before continuing. 'It is a modern marvel that we in the west have all heard about, it's something your people should be rightly proud of,' he commented and smiled kindly.

Kesor looked him up and down, giving him a quizzical look.

'Let's get going then,' she said finally. 'It's a bit of a walk to the baray and knowing how Nearidei likes to chat, it's going to take us ages.'

She gave her friend a gentle prod.

'Very funny,' she responded, and they set off.

Nearidei was in full flow, she spoke about how they interlock the water system through the canals and overflows were diverted to lakes and dykes. She continued to speak about the need to store water from the rainy season to help with the droughts of the summer months, this policy ensured the city had enough water to prosper.

'Kesor, I notice these statues of multi-headed cobras next to the canals and lakes, some are small and some are larger, is this in relation to Naga?' Luke asked.

'Yes, how did you know that?' she enquired smiling.

'I've heard about Naga on my travels and it always fascinated my mentor.' He looked at Marcus, who smiled back.

Kesor picked up on the look straight away.

'Marcus you seem to have a fascination with our city, I'm not sure how you know so much about us but whatever I can do to explain things further I will,' she said eagerly. 'Naga is very important to our people, she guards our water and in turn allows our city to thrive, without water this city would struggle to exist. Naga protects us, you'll see her statue next to our most special places such as the great baray. She guards our most treasured possessions.'

Kesor smiled and pointed to Luke's chain where a small statue of Naga was attached to the purple amethyst.

He looked down, saw the statue then looked up and smiled, However Marcus did not.

As they approached the western baray, the three foreigners stood astounded, it was huge. Marcus had studied it for years and knew it was the largest hand-cut manmade lake ever created. It was an incredible sight in his time, but seeing it as it was designed to be used was breath-taking. They looked around and could see an elaborate temple in the centre of the great baray with offerings adorning the shrines. Around the shores stood many six-foot statues of Naga protecting the water just as Kesor had said.

Nearidei led them to a special viewing platform where they could appreciate the baray in its full glory.

She turned to Maya, 'This is one of our greatest achievements, it has taken us centuries to create. We have slowly increased the size to meet our population needs resulting in what you see today.'

Maya was in her element, this science and engineering creativity was what she loved, she could see how the people of Angkor had developed the elaborate system which now supported the largest city on earth in this time period. She was fascinated how they had embraced the natural elements of the landscape to help achieve it.

Maya curiously asked, 'How do you maintain the flow of water and the build-up of silt?'

'It's a good question,' Nearidei replied, intrigued that Maya knew so much. 'To be honest, it's a real problem, there are many times we have had to abandon previous reservoirs due to the silt build-up. As the western baray has been expanded over time, it's allowed us to overcome some of the build-ups, we hope now that the force of the water will wash most of the silt away.'

Maya chatted freely not really thinking, 'A few friends of mine spoke about some solutions, have you heard of dead storage or silt traps? This inactive storage solution allows sediment and debris to settle avoiding the need to remove it. The solution also improves water quality and creates an area for fish at low levels. I know this option has proven cheaper than other options in the long run. Another possibility is something called a sediment bypass, this design creates a bypass channel which helps to remove the silt before the water reaches the stagnant region of the dam. Obviously, dredging and dry excavation are standard ways of trying to manage the issues but it is time-consuming and usually only extends the life of the dam for a limited period. Best to invest in solutions while constructing, that's what I say.'

Marcus was staring at her in amazement and like lightning, it hit her what she had just done.

'Obviously, I'm no expert these are just my thoughts, but your engineers seem to have it all in hand,' she said quickly trying to make them forget her suggestions.

'Maya, you never told us you knew so much about water management, I really must introduce you to Chakra, he will be so interested in your thoughts,' Nearidei enthusiastically responded.

'No, it's fine, I don't really know anything. It was just something I overheard, I wouldn't want to waste anyone's time,' she said, desperately trying to change the subject. 'Can you tell me more about those plants growing in the water, I recognise the Lotus leaves but what are those?'

The change of subject seemed to distract Nearidei and she started to talk about the local plants and wildlife.

They spent the next few hours exploring temples around the baray and discussed local customs. Both Luke and Marcus were enjoying themselves so much that for a moment they forgot about their predicament. Around midday, when the sun was highest in the sky Kesor declared it was time for lunch and she took them back to the city. They walked for about forty minutes heading back to the Bayon temple, all the way they continued to chat about the local people and architecture.

Just as they approached the temple there was a huge scream and sounds of stone crashing to the ground, the five of them rushed to see what had happened. They raced around the corner of the temple and were greeted by a screaming man lying under a huge piece of stone. He'd been carving it when it had fallen on him, pinning him to the ground. Maya instantly rushed over, as well as her degrees in physics she had studied medicine and was fully versed in how to triage injuries. As she approached the other masons were desperately trying to lift the large bit of stone off him, they pulled at the large rock, it eventually gave way. Maya rushed forward and she knelt down to examine him, the workers looked on in bewilderment.

She quickly assessed the man's medical condition. His leg was broken, and he had a very deep gash on his chest coursed by a sharp flint of stone that had stabbed deep into him. The cut was bleeding heavily. She ripped a bit of her robe off and pressed it against his wound.

'Hold here,' she ordered.

Another worker didn't know what to do, but followed her orders. She then set about examining his leg, the bone had broken in a few places. Maya ordered another worker to retrieve pieces off a bamboo scaffold which was nearby. Maya created a makeshift splint attaching it with some nearby string they used to construct the scaffold.

'Does anyone have a stretcher we need to get this man out of the sun?' Maya shouted.

Nearidei ordered a couple of men to find one as Maya continued to tend to the injured man.

While she worked Kesor turned to Marcus.

'What's she doing?' she asked in amazement.

'Maya is a healer back home as well as a natural philosopher,' he answered hesitantly.

Marcus was afraid, he knew she shouldn't be helping, it was against what they had agreed.

The men soon returned with a makeshift stretcher, 'Is there anywhere we can take him? I'd like to examine him further,' Maya asked.

Nearidei stepped forward and pointed her to a nearby building, the workers carried the man over to it and as they entered the injured man was placed on a bed.

'I'll need privacy to examine him, if this is okay with you?' she asked Nearidei, who nodded in return.

It was clear the Nearidei's status gave her power over the masons.

'Of course Maya, can I help in anyway?' she asked shakily as she ordered the men to leave.

'Please can you get me some freshly boiled water? I'll also need some more cloth for bandages?' Maya instructed. 'Marcus, can you stay with me to help please?'

She then turned to everyone else. 'Please give me space to work, I'll let you know when it's safe to come back in.'

They all agreed and left leaving just Marcus and Maya alone together.

Marcus turned to her, 'What are you doing?'

'I can't just let this man die when I know I can help, I just can't do that Marcus and before you say anything, yes I know the consequences.'

She activated her palm screen and scanned the man. 'He has multiple fractures in his leg, two broken ribs and…'

She paused for a moment looking at the screen. 'Damn, a punctured lung. I can still help him, Marcus, pass me my bag.'

He did as he was told, he knew better than to argue with her. Maya searched the bag for the medical devices from the first aid kit, she took them out and transferred the scan results from her palm reader to the more capable medical device. It lit up and she waved it over the affected area, the device beeped, and a tube quickly jolted out and inserted itself through the man's skin and into his lung. It began to inflate helping the man to breathe.

Suddenly the mason woke.

'Shit,' Maya panicked. She gave him a sedative and he passed out.

The device beeped again indicating the lung was now stable, the instrument had repaired the hole and the tube retracted back into the medical device. Maya decided she couldn't risk using the dermal regenerator to seal the wound so had to think of another way to stop the bleeding.

She turned to Marcus, 'I'll need to cauterise the injury, can you ask them to get me a hot poker or sword so I can stop him bleeding out.'

Marcus nodded and left without further discussion.

***

It had taken just over a day for Kalani to reach the shores of the lake, it was hard work navigating the thick jungle and he spent time avoiding contact with the few locals he encountered. Kalani had set his palm scanner up to beep a warning if any person came within a hundred meters of him.

The sun had already begun to set as he reached the shores of the lake, he stopped and breathed in the evening air staring at the golden sky as the sun quickly disappeared. He looked over the lake and it was huge, if he was not aware of his location, he would have thought it was the sea. Kalani then felt a strong cool breeze blowing off the water and a sudden wave of contentment came over him, it brought back memories of his home in Hawaii. He crouched down, cupped his hands slowly and approached the lake's edge, he needed to drink.

His mind flashed a warning. *Is this safe?*

However, he knew he had little choice other than to drink.

Kalani's mind spoke again, *I need to find safe shelter for the night.*

He scanned the area around him noticing a few settlements at the lake shores, they were a couple of miles away to his right.

Left it is then, he thought and began to walk fast, knowing he had little light remaining to find somewhere safe to rest.

About thirty minutes later, as the last rays of light disappeared, he approached a small secluded inlet. It had a slightly elevated bank and was surrounded by trees. The inlet had access to the lake and was secluded enough to avoid any locals. Kalani began to clear a small area in between the trees, he hunted around for anything he could use to build a shelter. It was then his mind had time to think, images of his family appeared in his mind, causing an intense sense of grief to hit him. Kalani slumped to the floor and rubbed his eyes, he tapped his palm reader and projected a holographic image of Ke'ala and Lani which illuminated the jungle. He stared at the picture for ages.

How could I have misjudged this so badly.

His mind then turned to his former colleagues. *Please, please let them be okay.*

Another wave of guilt hit him, making his emotions turn black. *What had he done to his friends, how could he have left them to the mercy of these savages? How could he have left them to die?*

***

Maya worked furiously to save the mason, Marcus had retrieved a molten hot sword and she used it to stop the bleeding. The news of her intervention had travelled widely, and a crowd began to gather around the hut. Maya finally finished and the man was stable. His family had gathered and was asking to see him, but Srindra's soldiers now stood guard around the hut on the orders of Kesor. Maya ventured out, seeing the scene before her. She instructed the guards that the family of the man could enter. Kesor was waiting as she exited, she insisted that Maya had done all she could for the man, and it was important that she return to the compound with the rest of the group without delay. Marcus agreed and reluctantly Maya was escorted out of the clearing.

As Maya entered the street, she noticed a large crowd and turned to Marcus, 'Why are these people here?'

'It seems that the news of your medical help has travelled fast, some people are here to see what happened, while others have come to seek help for sick family members,' he said, concerned.

'Oh no, let's get out of here.' She turned to Kesor, who nodded and managed to carve a way through the crowd with some help from a few of Srindra's soldiers.

Nearidei stayed behind to speak to the crowd and reassure them about what had just happened, the rest of them left quickly. They soon arrived back at Prince Srindra's compound being escorted by his men. Kesor thanked them and led the foreigners back to the guest house where they had been staying.

As they entered the hut Kesor spoke quietly. 'News has spread fast about your healing power Maya.'

She paused for a moment not sure what to say. 'Tell me more about how you were treating the worker. I've seen many injuries like that result in death.'

'It's just some medical procedures I picked up from our many travels, I guess he was lucky, and his injuries were not that bad,' she said, trying to make it seem normal.

Luke looked at Maya, understanding the inner struggle she was going through.

'But the way you just went to the aid of someone you've never met, why did you do that?' Kesor asked.

'In our culture, it is important that we help others in need, and I could see no other healer around,' she replied calmly.

Nearidei suddenly burst into the room a little panicked. 'The worker is awake and he seems well except his broken leg.'

She seemed a bit shaken but continued hesitantly, 'He's claiming you used magic on him, he said you inserted a snake into his body.'

Kesor breathed in deeply.

'Maya what is all this about? He is claiming you have used witchcraft on him,' Nearidei said generally concerned.

'Witchcraft!' Maya said loudly and panicked.

Marcus stepped forward, 'All Maya did was help, she used the cloth and tools you provided, I am sure the pain the worker was in must have made him hallucinate.'

'That's the problem Marcus he's saying he felt no pain,' Nearidei responded.

'It must be in his imagination,' Marcus replied. 'Maya is a skilled healer in our community and although she is an expert, she cannot magically heal wounds or stop pain. Look at his leg and the wound on his chest.'

A commotion sounded from outside and they all turned to face the door. Prince Srindra suddenly entered the hut with a few of his personal guard.

He spoke firmly, 'What's happened today? The people are saying you used witchcraft, this news has already reached the king.'

Maya began to panic but calmed her nerves enough to speak. 'Your Majesty I used my healing knowledge to help the man who was hurt, it may seem different to the ways your healers work but I wanted to help. I couldn't see any other healer around and if I did not treat the man he would have died.'

She paused and her voice wobbled, 'Rest assured, it is not witchcraft just the treatments my people use to help the injured.'

Prince Srindra looked at her and turned to Luke. 'Is this true?'

'Yes, Your Majesty, Maya is one of our most skilled healers,' he said reassuringly.

Srindra turned back to her.

'I guess you have more to trade than just stories,' he paused and rubbed his head as if he was thinking about what to do. 'The king has ordered me to bring you to him, he wants to meet you. He wants to understand what's happened today and to dismiss the rumours of witchcraft.'

His tone softened after seeing their reactions. 'Get some rest for now, my servants will be back later to prepare you to see the king. They will make sure you're dressed appropriately.'

Prince Srindra looked at Luke directly, 'I trust you, although I'm not sure why. However, make no mistake, I'll protect my city and my people at any cost, do you understand?'

'Yes Your Majesty,' he replied. 'We are no threat to you, I promise.'

Prince Srindra nodded, then turned and walked out of the hut, flanked by his guards. Both Nearidei and Kesor gave Maya a nervous reassuring smile and followed the prince leaving the three academics in silence and afraid.

After what seemed like ages Maya spoke, 'What are we going to do?'

'Let's stick to the same story,' Marcus responded. 'However, to be on the safe side, let's hide the medical equipment.'

Maya agreed and they dismantled the devices into smaller parts and hid them around the hut.

'Get some rest before we meet the king, remember we need to tread lightly and be vague,' he said, then paused.

'It seems impossible for us not to interfere with the people here,' shaking his head and slumping down on a nearby bed. 'All we can do is our best, lets be as open and honest as we can. Promise me one thing, we stick together no matter what?'

'We promise,' they both replied without hesitation.

CHAPTER EIGHT

King Jayavarman VII

Dusk had set in by the time the servants returned to the guest house. There was a gentle scent of flowers drifting through the early evening air which only served to heighten the academics anxiety. The servants brought more elaborate clothing for them to wear all in the same colours they had been dressed in since they had arrived. It seemed that Prince Srindra had settled on what their status would be in court. They were soon dressed, and the servants led them to meet the prince. He had been waiting patiently for them at the entrance to his compound with Nearidei and Kesor along with about ten of his elite guards.

They nervously approached and Srindra spoke forcefully.

'When you meet the king, remember to speak only when spoken to and to answer truthfully. My father can tell when people are being dishonest. The queen will also be present.'

He turned to Maya, 'She'll ask you questions about the treatment you gave the mason. My mother is one of the wisest women in our kingdom and my Father has entrusted her to lead our scientific and social improvements.'

He paused. 'She's also one of the shrewdest people I know, treat her with respect or you will live to regret it.'

'Your Majesty, can I ask you a question?' Maya enquired.

'Yes of course,' he responded.

'What was the name of the mason?'

She paused for a moment seeing his reaction but pressed on.

'I really don't like referring to him as just a mason, it seems demeaning,' she said carefully.

A little taken aback he responded, 'Rachana Voan.'

'Thank you Your Majesty,' Maya replied kindly.

He gestured for them to follow him. The group began the walk towards Angkor Thom and to the Royal Palace at Phimeanakas.

The city seemed to glow in the dusky light with the temple's dark shadows contrasting with the pink sky. Maya noticed Luke. She could see his nerves were starting to get the better of him. Seeing his anxiety worried her, what was going to happen to him and what had she gotten them all into. As they walked, a cool breeze blew through the jungle, the evening heat was still stifling so the cool air was very much welcome.

Luke finally built up enough courage to ask what had been running through his mind. 'Your Majesty, what's going to happen to us?'

'I'm not sure. Father is kind and Mother is wise, but they will protect our people at any cost,' he said, which only served to make Luke more uneasy.

'What happens if he doesn't like what he hears?' Luke responded hesitantly.

Prince Srindra put his arm around Luke's shoulder.

Marcus gave Maya another worried glance. 'It'll be fine, you and your friends have only ever been respectful, kind and compassionate and he will see that.'

They approached the king's palace and crossed into the east gate of Angkor Thom for the second time that day.

Prince Srindra walked them to the king's private compound and spoke. 'Wait here while I confirm our entry.'

The guards took up position by the main gate which gave Marcus the opportunity to speak to Luke and Maya privately.

'Remember to remain calm, try to keep things ambiguous. From what we know Jayavarman VII had a good reputation, he was seen as a reformer who valued and loved his people. The texts tell us he helped them strive to achieve spiritual enlightenment. After regaining the crown from the Cham, the king built temples, schools and hospitals which led to a golden age for the Khmer people, it's why we wanted to study this period,' Marcus smiled.

Maya rolled her eyes. 'While I appreciate the information Marcus, it's no time for a history lesson. Let's just hope we keep focused and keep out of trouble.'

Prince Srindra returned and gestured for them to follow him, which they did dutifully.

The group entered the inner sanctum of Angkor Thom and were led through a number of hallways, all the walls had intricate carvings on. Marcus stopped and slowly reached out to touch a carving of a horse which was bursting out of the stone and galloping into battle. Prince Srindra noticed his reaction and looked at him with astonishment, he had never seen someone so interested in his culture and someone who seemed so connected to it.

The prince thought to himself, *Why does this man feel close to us? It's like he's been here before.*

'Marcus come, we can't keep the king waiting,' Srindra said kindly but forcefully.

These words shook Marcus awake and he quickly regained his composure and followed the prince into a great open courtyard. The courtyard was surrounded by high carved walls connected to stone towers. At the centre stood an elaborate stone platform adorned with exquisite animal carvings. In the middle of the platform were stone steps, again intricately carved, leading up to two stone thrones which sat the King and Queen of Angkor.

King Jayavarman was in his late sixties. He was thin and fit, much fitter than Marcus was expecting. The king had a warm loving face which exuded confidence, he was dressed in deep golden robes with a large golden lotus crown like Prince Srindra's, but much bigger and more impressive. The crown was adorned with a number of deep purple amethyst stones and diamonds which sparkled brightly in the dusky light. The King wore many golden chains, bracelets and rings radiating power, it was clear to all that this man was revered.

Queen Indradevi was in her mid-fifties, she, like her husband, had a warm smile, however, there was something different about her, there was a sense of knowledge and insight. The way she held herself reminded Marcus of his favourite teacher Miss Dahlström from his time at school, he remembered fondly that although Miss Dahlström managed to be strict she was also compassionate. As Marcus reflected on his past, he recalled that Queen Indradevi was widely credited for helping Jayavarman succeed. It was like the fable said, behind every great man there is a great woman. This woman's deep scientific insight and intelligence were seen as a key stabilising force. The queen was dressed in electric blue embroidered robes, she wore a small lotus silver crown and was adorned in silver jewellery covered in zircons and sapphires. A particular striking item of jewellery was that of a silver snake wrapped around her left arm, it was studded with bright blue sapphires. She was a powerful presence and the court looked to her for inspiration and guidance.

Standing to the right of the king was Prince Virakumara, he was about the same age as Luke, around twenty-five. Virakumara, although young, had his mother's determined look but seemed to lack the compassion. He appeared to have a permanent scowl on his face. Virakumara was dressed in black and red robes and adorned with golden jewellery, all inlaid with polished obsidian stones which were only enhanced by the Red

Ruby chain that hung around his neck. The court and his family addressed the prince as Virak, it was a name which had stayed with him since he was a child.

To the left of Queen Indradevi was Princess Bopha, she was around the age of thirty-five, older than her brothers but with a youthful smile. It was clear she was excited to see the foreigners and wanted to hear more about where they were from. Princess Bopha was dressed in bright green robes, her jewellery like her mother's was silver and embossed with peridot and aquamarine precious gems, Marcus was sure that the gems had specific meanings but at this moment it eluded him.

Prince Srindra stepped forward. 'May I present to you all my guests from Europe. They travelled far to trade with us, however, as they arrived in our lands, they were betrayed by one of their servants who with a band of barbarians stole their goods. I rescued them with my elite guard as I searched for the cause of the bright light we saw two days ago.'

The prince gestured for them to come forward and as they did they all bowed respectfully to the king.

King Jayavarman looked them up and down, paying close attention to Luke and the way he was dressed, in particular the purple amethyst he wore.

He then turned back to his son. 'Why were they not brought to me upon arrival Sri?'

'I was keen to understand what had happened in the jungle first Father. I also wanted to know their culture and ways before bringing them in front of you,' he said respectfully.

The king looked over to the queen who gave him a concerned look.

'Before we get to the miracle healing of the mason what have you learned about the light, I have been waiting for an update,' he said impatiently.

Maya stepped forward and hesitantly answered, 'Your Majesty, the light was caused by one of our fireworks, we were looking to trade them with you when we arrived, unfortunately, it was accidentally set off when we were attacked, we apologise for any upset this may have caused.'

The queen was now staring deeply at Maya, glaring at the similarly aged woman in front of her.

The queen finally spoke. 'I've never seen a firework that can maintain that brightness for such a long period. It didn't explode which seems a poor way to celebrate, are you sure it was a firework?'

Seeing Maya struggling Marcus stepped in, 'Your Majesty, maybe firework is the wrong word. Our people have developed a way of lighting up the sky for a small period of time. It's useful to help bring light to dark places over a large area when needed.'

The queen's attention now focused on Marcus, 'tell me, for individuals who claim not to know much about our people you seem to speak our language excellently.'

She continued to stare waiting for an answer.

'We met some travellers on our long journey, and they taught us. We are all experts in linguistics and have a natural talent for picking up languages,' Marcus responded desperately.

'So, the three of you are here with no goods, no money, no clothing other than what we've given you. You're totally helpless. Yet there was a miracle at the temple today, can you explain this to me?' she asked calmly, her voice clear to all.

Maya again spoke, 'I'm very well practised in healing within our society and I helped the mason Rachana Voan. His injuries were not as severe as some may think, I could see he needed help, so I offered my services. I managed to stop the bleeding and stabilise his condition thankfully.'

The queen looked at her deeply, looking for any signs of deception. 'What about his claims of witchcraft and this tale of a snake entering him?'

She touched her bracelet unconsciously.

'It must have been a hallucination. He was in a lot of pain.' Maya looked at the king and then back to the queen. 'Your Majesties, all I wanted to do was help one of your subjects with my healing knowledge. I'm sorry if I acted inappropriately but I can't see anyone suffer, particularly when I know I can help. I believe he is okay now, isn't he?'

'That he is,' the Queen replied calmly. 'I'm keen to understand more about this healing knowledge you mention, I'm also interested in this night light we have seen in our skies. In fact, I am keen to know much more about your people, your culture and the goods you were going to trade.'

She turned and looked at the King.

The queen's look seemed to spark the king into action. 'You'll join us for the celebration feast tonight, we'll be unveiling our latest achievement, that way we can get to know you better.'

He smiled widely. 'We already have the Chinese and Lavo ambassadors in attendance so a few more foreign friends are welcome.'

The king rose to his feet. 'Speaking of the events later, I need to get ready.'

Everyone bowed and he left with his entourage without saying another word.

The queen stayed where she was and spoke again, 'Sri, I expect you to look after our guests and to take extra care of them, I need to understand their culture much more.'

'Yes Mother,' he replied hesitantly.

She then rose and left the courtyard with Prince Virak and Princess Bopha.

Prince Srindra turned to them. 'That went better than expected. I thought Father was going to scold me much more for not bringing you to him sooner. Come let's go and rest, I have a private residence here where we can wait until tonight's feast. I'll take the opportunity to update you on the guests who will be attending.'

He guided a very nervous Luke, Marcus and Maya out of the courtyard.

***

The stars now shone brightly as Prince Srindra led them via torch light to the most beautiful pagoda, like most parts of Angkor it was connected to a small pond intersecting with a stream which flowed over rocks making a peaceful trickling sound. The pond was filled with many types of fish, none of the academics knew anything about fish so it was hard to tell what they were.

'Maya you did really well with the Queen,' Nearidei said. 'She is notoriously perceptive and has a reputation for getting the answers she wants from others, but I think she could tell how much you cared.'

'I'm just relieved, I really don't want to offend anyone,' she said and looked at Marcus. 'I actually think we should start planning for the long trip back home, with no items to trade I feel we are imposing. Do you agree Marcus?'

Marcus was about to speak when Prince Srindra bellowed from across the room.

'Nonsense, you're my guests and you intrigue me, plus how are you to travel home with no money or possessions?'

That seemed to stump Maya.

'My mother will want to know more about you and your culture, we can trade your knowledge for items to help you get home,' he said proudly.

Maya flinched at that statement, that was not the reaction she expected.

'You don't seem very happy about my proposal,' Srindra said disappointedly.

Marcus stepped in, 'You Majesty I don't want to offend you, but we are really not supposed to trade our knowledge, it's a breach of our most sacred laws. It's also important that we find Kalani the man that betrayed us, we need to settle that dishonour and try at least to recover some of our goods.'

'I can understand why you wouldn't want to share your knowledge, but my mother can be very persuasive. We have helped you for nothing and in return, your knowledge has saved one of our people. You have shown great respect to us.'

Prince Srindra paused for a moment. 'I'm not sure if you realise but our gemstones have a meaning, for example, our purple amethyst means authority, as I am inline to take over the throne, I can use my influence to seek this traitor of yours and help return your goods, how does that sound?'

'That would be amazing Your Majesty,' Marcus replied.

'I do have some conditions, firstly you will remain under my protection at my compound. All I ask is you share your culture with my family while my men seek your betrayer,' Marcus bowed cautiously. 'Secondly, I ask for time with Luke, as you may have noticed I have a great interest in him, there is a connection that runs deep between us which I can't explain. I believe Buddha would want me to explore this.'

Marcus looked at Luke who was a little lost for words, but he spoke softly, 'It would be my honour to spend time with you Your Majesty.'

Luke knew this would anger Marcus, but he didn't care. Prince Srindra was right there was a connection and he wanted to understand it as much as the prince.

'Great that's settled,' Prince Srindra replied reaching for Luke's hand. 'I will set my spies to task in the morning and as soon as they find any information, you can join me on the hunt to find this Kalani, do you agree?'

Marcus and Maya both nodded and thanked the prince for his kindness.

Prince Srindra reclined onto a large day bed and then cleared his throat, 'The feast tonight is important and you'll need to know a few things. There will be a lot of ambassadors and dignitaries present. I fear Maya that the stories of your healing may have reached them. I worry that some of our neighbours and enemies may take advantage. Nearidei and Kesor, I order you to look after Maya, make sure she spends time with the Queen tonight, but protect her—'

He paused. 'You know the usual troublemakers. Marcus, I'll introduce you to my Sister Princess Bopha, she is very special to me, and I trust her deeply. I believe you will enjoy her company. From what I've seen you share the same fascination with the arts as she does.'

He smiled at Marcus.

'Luke you will be by my side tonight, I expect the king might want to speak to me.'

His eyes lingered on the amethyst stone on Luke's chest, then continued nervously, 'I may have caused a bit of a problem dressing you in those colours.'

Nearidei laughed. 'Sri you always push it, and you knew exactly what you were doing. The king is loving and supportive but you seem to get away with so much.'

She grinned and said, 'Your brother will be fuming.'

He gave her a massive smile.

'As mentioned, the ambassadors from China and Lavo are here, but there are representatives from many other provinces even the treacherous Champa, who would like nothing more than to see my father deposed. Beware the ambassador from China, Jiang Liwei, he's a small balding man and intensely clever, he and Father have become friends but his focus, as ever, is to get information about our city, armies, and wealth so his people can exploit us. The other ambassador to know is from Lavo, his name is Sunya Prinya, he and I have been friends since children and his family helped my Father against the Chams. I trust him but he is…'

Srindra thought for a moment, '…fallible, he likes the rice wine too much if you know what I mean.'

The prince sighed before speaking. 'Luke, he may not like the way I've dressed you, so please tread carefully around him.'

He looked at Kesor who knew instantly what he meant but Sri spoke no more.

Luke was suddenly anxious by the Prince's comments, he seemed to be making a clear statement about his intentions and Luke was not really sure why, or if he was even ready for this kind of attention.

'One more thing, my friends and family call me Sri and I ask that you do as well, I really hate this "Your Majesty" title, it's so cumbersome.'

There were sounds of acknowledgement as servants entered carrying drinks. Over the next hour, they relaxed with their new friends until it was time for the feast.

***

The sound of music echoed through the palace. Sri stood up and declared it was time to leave. The group were guided through a labyrinth of corridors. The prince's elite guard led the way and soon arrived in another part of the royal palace. To Marcus's surprise, it was the newly constructed terraces of the elephants. Marcus had studied this site since he was a young man, and seeing it in its full glory made his heart leap, and his senses soar. Marcus knew that the long terrace would be used as a giant parade stand, it was his understanding that it was used for public ceremonies and served as a place where the king gathered large audiences, but none of this had even happened yet.

Five outworks were extending towards the centre square and in the middle section was a retaining wall decorated with many of the Khmer cultures' deities. At the end of each of the terraces there were huge elephant carvings complete with their Khmer riders. Marcus breathed deeply as they were brought closer, he looked at Luke who smiled back at him knowing his excitement.

Around the terrace were large wooden structures and servants were cooking all types of food, to the right were thirty spit-roasted pigs and to the left hundreds of chickens were being barbecued over a huge open fire. Servants were also preparing all kinds of exotic drinks and a carnival atmosphere swept over the monument. They walked through the milling throng with people everywhere, however many of the local Khmers stopped at the sight of the foreigners. The smells coming from the cooking feast seemed to disperse the crowds allowing Sri to lead them to the front of the terrace.

'I must leave you here for a moment and join my father,' Prince Srindra said.

As they looked around, Marcus noticed there were thousands of people gathered at the expansive terrace, it seemed they were all there to celebrate the unveiling of this new Khmer masterpiece.

A horn sounded and King Jayavarman appeared at the centre of the elephant terrace followed by the rest of the royal family, who stood around him in support.

The king then spoke loudly, 'My friends, welcome to the opening of our new national monument. This terrace will be a place where we can welcome our heroic soldiers home from our glorious battles and where we can gather our people together to celebrate.'

The king paused for breath, 'I was reminded today that all our people share in our society's successes. The master craftsmen deserve our huge gratitude and thanks for their incredible creations, their remarkable skills are such an asset to our people. It's important to remember the prosperity of all our citizens is of the upmost significance. Friends, enjoy tonight and make sure you spend time admiring this amazing piece of artistry. The craftsmen who created it are here tonight, please thank them personally for their amazing work.'

The king then signalled to about two hundred masons standing at the centre of the monument.

The crowd erupted with applause and the terrace exploded with fireworks. Luke and Marcus looked at each other not believing what they had just witnessed. Tears started to run down both their faces. When had any archaeologist been able to witness an event like this in history and they were so grateful for the privilege.

The feast soon got into full flow, Nearidei and Kesor stole Maya away to meet many influential Khmer women and began to discuss science, engineering, and philosophy. Prince Srindra re-joined Marcus and Luke this time bringing Princess Bopha with him whom he introduced fondly.

'Gentlemen, this is my dear sister, as I mentioned Marcus, she has a passion for art. I know you'll enjoy spending time with her.'

'Nice to meet you Marcus,' she said shyly. 'Sri's told me how interested you are in our culture and I would love to show you more.'

'That would be amazing Your Majesty,' he replied a little too eagerly, totally enthralled by the opportunity.

'Why don't I show you some of my favourite carvings in the Bayon tomorrow. I'm sure we can spend time looking at what our master masons have been creating on the walls of our new temple.'

Marcus turned to Sri for approval.

'No need to ask my permission,' he said laughing.

'Why don't we go and have a drink and let my brother spend some time with Luke,' Princess Bopha said, holding out her hand.

Marcus took it hesitantly. Turning back to look at Luke, he knew he had no choice but to accompany the princess to a nearby table, however, they both quickly fell into a deep conversation.

'Finally, we have some private time at last,' Sri said.

'Yes Your Majesty,' Luke replied nervously.

'Call me Sri like I asked you to, we're friends now, well I hope so anyway.'

'Yes Your… sorry yes Sri,' he said smiling.

'Why so shy Luke? I can't understand how someone whose travelled all over the known world can be so timid.'

Sri reached out his hand to touch Luke's face gently, which took him by surprise. 'You're a complete mystery to me and that's why you're so interesting, of course, your stunning appearance helps.'

Luke was encapsulated by the power and presence of this attractive man and he couldn't seem to find the words to respond.

Sri then leaned in to kiss him, but, at that moment, the king called out causing them to break apart quickly.

'Sri are you going to introduce this young man to me properly?'

This made Luke shrink with fear.

'Yes Father, this is Luke, he is Marcus's ward and apprentice. He's been studying trade diplomacy, languages, and different cultures for years,' he said fondly. 'As you can see, we seem to have a connection. Albeit why we connect remains a complete mystery to us both, it's like lightning has struck between us.'

'I see, well you know I am free-spirited and celebrate all Buddha's precious blessings. I must ask that you be careful not to give our enemies cause to attack you,' he replied reassuringly resting his hand on his son's shoulder.

'They won't Father, I'm much stronger than anyone realises,' Sri responded.

'I know, I know but I do worry, and I want you to be careful.'

He squeezed Sri's shoulder tightly. 'It's not all about strength Sri, it's about politics and alliances. I love you and you know that but don't risk everything for someone you've just met.'

The king turned to Luke. 'Young man, I don't know you so forgive my rudeness. However, I know my son and he has an uncanny way of finding special people.'

The king looked deep into Luke's eyes. 'You certainly are different from us. I'm not sure how someone so…'

He thought for a moment, '…*delicate* has survived the travel from your homeland.'

Luke was a bit taken aback and a little offended.

Delicate, he thought to himself, knowing the King had no idea about his inner strength.

'Listen to me both of you, whatever happens, protect each other. Make sure you focus on what you really want including what is important to you, but most vitally what is important to our people.'

The king then turned directly to Sri. 'These guests from Europe are your responsibility, you know the forces out there who are trying to attack us. Promise me you will protect our reputation as well as protecting them, it's clear they have no idea of our politics or the potential dangers they could encounter.'

Sri nodded. He was so amazed by his father's support that he couldn't help but hug him tightly.

They slowly broke apart and the king took Luke's hand.

'I ask you to protect my boy, just as he'll protect you,' amazingly the king took Luke's hand and kissed it.

He gave Luke's hand one final squeeze and left the two of them in stunned silence.

CHAPTER NINE

Queen Indradevi

The night of the feast was one of the most amazing events that any of the academics had experienced. Marcus spent the majority of the evening enthralled by Princess Bopha. She took great delight in talking about her culture, the artistry of her people and the scientific breakthroughs her mother had inspired. For Marcus speaking to the people who built and influenced the great Khmer empire, was the highlight of his career so far. It made him forget the situation he now found himself in. Marcus delighted in the princess's company, enthralled by one of the most intellectual women of her age. She talked passionately about the city and culture he adored and it felt truly surreal.

Maya spent the evening with Nearidei and Kesor. They had taken great delight in introducing her to many of the influential women in Khmer society. It culminated with all the ladies gathering around Queen Indradevi, discussing social issues intently. Maya, like Marcus, was fascinated by the situation. It seemed that within this culture women had a lot of social freedoms, something she never expected to see. They seemed well educated and in Maya's mind, this was in no small part due to the queen, after all, she was such a powerful presence. The queen spent the rest of the evening quizzing Maya about her medical practices and asking more about her scientific experience. It was clear that Kesor had told her about Maya's interest in the western Baray and she seemed to be testing her. The queen appeared to be trying to work out what this intelligent exotic foreigner was doing in her city. Maya was enjoying the attention. She was in her element discussing science. Even more she was inspired by the strong women in this ancient culture, who seemed to embrace it.

Sri made sure that both Marcus and Maya would be occupied all night, so he could spend time with Luke, and it was working perfectly. He introduced Luke to his closest friends, and they spent most of the evening chatting and laughing. Luke had never experienced attention like this from anyone, the geeky often muddy archaeologist avoided socialising and dating. Sri had worked hard to make Luke feel comfortable and although he was nervous, he trusted Sri deeply, yet he had no idea why.

Being in Sri's presence was refreshing, the prince seemed to care little what others thought and he had decided to focus all of his attention on this foreigner. Although the king's words about diplomacy and protecting his legacy had made him think. However, the guy in front of him was all Sri cared about at that moment. Late into the night Luke continued to drink the rice wine and was soon talking about his past. Even in his increasingly drunken state, he was careful not to make any historical mistakes, but he felt at ease talking about his love of history and in particular his passion for archaeology. This word confused Sri initially, but when Luke explained it was about learning from the ancestors of the past, he seemed to understand.

At around midnight a large gong rang out, it sounded the end of the feast, and the guests all began to leave. Marcus held Princess Bopha's arm escorting her back to the Queen. She was listening intently to a conversation between Maya and Kesor. They were both deep in discussion about women's rights, agreeing strongly together about how women should have the choice to choose their own paths. Marcus couldn't help but smile as he heard the passion coming from his friend, she had always been at the forefront of equality.

'What's so amusing?' Queen Indradevi asked seeing Marcus's reaction.

All the Khmer women looked up at Marcus, Maya also glared at him closely.

He felt very uncomfortable and replied hesitantly, 'Your Majesty I meant no offence, it's just nice to see my friend speak with such passion. We've often had heated debates usually resulting in a friend brokering the peace, then us having a drink together to make up.'

He smiled.

The queen looked him up and down giving him a dismissive stare, she turned to Maya. 'You'll join me tomorrow. I would like to continue some of the conversations we've had tonight, then take you personally on a walk around our city.'

It was clear this was not optional, and the invite was only aimed at Maya.

Princess Bopha spoke breaking an awkward silence, 'Marcus, since Maya will be busy with my mother, and I'm guessing Luke will be occupied with my brother,' she looked over at Sri who was still deep in conversation with Luke. 'Why don't you join me for a tour of the city also. I'll arrange for us to have special access to the great temple at Angkor Wat and we're explore its artistry.'

He looked deep into Princess Bopha's eyes. 'This is a great honour Your Majesty, but we really need to find the traitor who stole our goods.'

'That's already in hand,' the queen interrupted. 'My son engaged the imperial guard this afternoon, they left at once to seek the man you described.'

She again looked at him, trying to gauge his reactions. 'There's nothing you can do that our soldiers can't do better. Why not take the time to understand our culture, that's why you're here isn't it?'

Marcus cleared his throat and replied, 'You're very kind Your Majesty and I would like nothing better than to explore your great temple with the princess. However, if I can be of help to your soldiers, I would like to offer my services.'

The queen laughed.

'My dear you couldn't keep up with our guard, they are fully trained in elite combat and have the stamina of a great bull elephant. I'm afraid you'll only slow them down.'

She turned to the princess. 'I will ask my guards to accompany you both on your tour tomorrow.'

She gave Marcus a wary look, it was clear she didn't trust him. 'Maya, I'll see you tomorrow, my servants will collect you from my son's compound just after sunrise.'

Without any further comments, she got up and left.

'It'll be great Marcus, don't worry about that traitor, we'll find him, that is if he is still alive,' Princess Bopha responded. 'Let's go and speak to my Brother, I want to know what he has planned for tomorrow.'

She rose from her seat. The Khmer women bowed, the princess gestured for them to follow her and they walked over to her brother.

'Sri, Mother has declared that Maya will join her in the morning for further discussions. I'll take Marcus on a cultural tour of the city.'

She looked at him knowing this news would make him happy.

'Are you okay looking after Luke? I'm sure he won't want to come with either of us.'

Actually Luke did want to see the city, but his pull to Sri was stronger than any other desire.

'I'm always happy to look after Luke,' he replied smiling. Not hiding his feelings which made both Marcus and Maya nervous again. 'I'd love to spend more time with Luke anyway, I'm keen to get to know him better and enhance my knowledge of European culture.'

His eyes flickered towards Marcus briefly. 'I'll let you know if we have any news on this Kalani, that's his name isn't it?'

Marcus nodded back at the prince.

'It's unlikely he could have survived long in the deep depths of the jungle. If the snakes don't get him, I'm sure the tigers will,' he said yawning. 'It's time to retire back to my compound. Bo, you're welcome to join us to avoid the need to get up early tomorrow.'

'Perfect, always thinking ahead as ever little brother. I assume my usual room is made up?' she asked, reaching over and pulling him to his feet.

'It always is, as you well know.'

The princess took Marcus's arm as several servants joined them. They were all dressed in night cloaks for the walk back to the compound, the servants lit torches and began to guide the way. The prince and princess fell back so they could speak out of earshot of their guests.

'I'll keep Marcus busy and find out more, I really like him, I don't see how he can be a spy,' Bopha said smiling. 'I know Mother is keen to spend time with Maya. She's convinced that the stories these strangers are telling us don't make sense. Despite these concerns, I believe there is no danger from them, they don't seem to have the skills to be spies. In fact, something is pulling me to trust them. I'm sure it's a sign from Buddha.'

'Bo, I know what you mean I can feel it too. If anything I think. they need protecting. I sense they're completely out of their depth. I'm sure Mother will figure out what's happening, you know she has her ways. In the meantime, thanks for helping me to spend more time with Luke, he's the one you foretold of, I know it.'

The princess squeezed his hand and rushed up to join Marcus linking her arm with his, Sri followed her lead and did the same with Luke.

They arrived back at the compound after a short walk and Marcus, Maya and Luke were escorted back to the guest house. Bo kissed Marcus's forehead while Sri kissed Luke gently on the lips, leaving Maya feeling very uncomfortable. The royals wished their guests good night and Sri escorted his sister to his private accommodation, leaving the academics in a sense of bewilderment.

They entered the room and silence, a sense of exhaustion, as well as worry, radiated from them all. In the morning they were to be separated. This would be the first time they'd be truly on their own in this time period, and none of them knew what would happen.

***

It was early when Maya woke, she could see both Luke and Marcus still sleeping. She got up carefully not making a noise and poured herself some water from a nearby jug. Maya was not a great sleeper when things were less complicated, let alone now. She slipped out of the hut to sit in peace on the veranda. The sun was yet to rise and the humid heat was still ever-present. Mist rose off the shimmering lake as the birds sang loudly. Maya carefully looked around to see if anyone was nearby, realising she was on her own she activated her implant. She projected a small screen and swiped through files until she found a specific image. It was a holo photo of Richard playing with Charlie as a small boy on the beach in Greece. It was one of her fondest memories. Tears began to trickle down her face, the realisation that she would never see them again began to truly sink in. All she could hope for now was that they would live full and healthy lives.

She wiped her eyes with the sleeve from her robe and closed the screen down, her eyes lingered for a moment where the image had been as her mind relived the memories. Maya stared back out into the lake, trying to collect her thoughts and work out what to do next. She watched the storks at the edge of the water diving for fish in the dawn haze. The calmness of the scene in front of her seemed to help steady her emotions. She heard a quiet noise behind her and turned around noticing Marcus standing there. He sat next to her, placing his hand on hers as if he could read her mind.

'It will be all right, they'll be all right,' he said comfortingly.

She smiled back at him squeezing his hand in return. 'Not much I can do now other than try and protect the future, not that we're doing a great job on that front.'

Marcus's head dropped and they both sat peacefully for a while staring into the calm lake.

Marcus broke the silence, 'What are we going to do about Luke?'

'Not much we can do. We just need to try and steer him as much as we can to make the right choices.' Maya paused thinking carefully about what to say next.

'You're the only father he has ever known. If his feelings are real and it's what he desires, you'll need to support him. But who knows how it will impact the future, however it still may be possible to find a way to limit the impact.'

'I can't help who he falls in love with,' Marcus said worriedly.

'None of us can. This is just another lesson our children need to learn on their own,' she responded kindly but with a tinge of sadness as she thought back to Charlie.

Marcus suddenly noticed a figure walking up the path to their hut, it was one of the queen's servants, he recognised her from the events yesterday. Maya had also noticed the young lady walking towards them.

'Looks like I'm being summoned. Queen Indradevi is not what I imagined, she seems wise and exceptionally clever.'

Marcus pulled his thoughts together for a moment, 'I know I don't need to say this but be careful.'

'Of that, I have no doubt. Marcus I see the way Bopha was looking at you, she's very attracted to you, it was clear to everyone. These people are not shy in hiding their feelings, so tread carefully.'

He thought for a moment then spoke quietly, 'I would love to have got to know her better, if only we had met under different circumstances.'

His head dropped as if his emotions were about to betray him.

'Do what you need to survive,' Maya replied as she pulled herself to her feet, she kissed him on his cheek.

'Wish me luck my friend,' she said, entering the hut to get ready.

Marcus was left alone in his thoughts, staring out into the tranquil water.

***

The young servant who arrived to help Maya was called Phary, she dressed Maya in her assigned robes of blue with the matching silver jewellery. It was obvious that the colours meant something but she, like Marcus was yet to understand what and was fearful to ask. Thankfully the colours chosen complemented her complexion.

Phary led Maya from Prince Srindra's compound and escorted her through the city streets and to the palace. Maya's nerves were building, she knew she needed to be cautious of the queen, yet she respected her and the way that the women in the Khmer empire lived.

They approached the east gates of Angkor Thom just as the sun was rising. Maya was searched before being permitted to enter the palace and was led to the Queen's chambers. She passed through several corridors which opened into a small courtyard, like many of the buildings in the city it had an ornamental pool with lilies and lotus plants flowering. Next to the pool sat the queen, she was dressed in her fine blue robes with her silver lotus crown shining in the dawn sun. The queen sat under an elaborate canopy that like her robes were blue and adorned with exquisite embroidered wild animals.

Phary escorted Maya over to the queen, she bowed and was about to leave as Maya spoke.

'Thank you Phary for your help today, it was much appreciated.'

Embarrassed and not knowing what to do the servant bowed and made a quick exit.

The queen looked at Maya curiously, 'It's unusual to know the names of our servants let alone thank them for doing their duty.'

Maya seemed unfazed by this question and responded gently. 'In my culture Your Majesty, we like to get to know all the people that work for us and to thank them for their service'

'Interesting,' the queen replied. 'I've met a few people from Europe in my time and they were very different to the three of you.'

'It's a big continent Your Majesty, with many different cultures and languages,' Maya said hesitantly.

'Today I would like to know you better Maya, there are some questions I have, and I'm keen to understand more about how your culture values certain beliefs.'

The queen continued. 'Today we'll visit a temple, school, farm, and hospital. I'm keen to know how your people worship, teach, grow food and care for others.'

Maya thought carefully before responding, 'I'll do my best Your Majesty, some of what you ask might be better explained by Marcus.'

'That's okay, I would prefer to hear it from a woman's perspective. In particular I'd like to know your personal thoughts. Before we leave, let's have some breakfast.'

Without any words, her servants brought some freshly brewed tea and fruit. The tea was served in fine cups. Maya knew Marcus would have understood better, but it looked like the ceramics were from China. The servants finished pouring the tea into the intricately decorated cups and Maya waited for the queen to drink first. She began to sip the tea as Maya watched on attentively, keen to mimic her behaviours.

Maya picked up the cup and sipped on the hot tea, she was taken by surprise when an all too familiar flavour hit her mouth.

'Jasmine,' she said inadvertently and with pleasure.

The taste reminded her of her lab, she always drank jasmine tea in the afternoon.

'Have you tasted it before my dear?' the queen asked.

'Oh yes Your Majesty. I've tried it on our travels,' she replied carefully.

The queen studied Maya for any signs of pretence, 'You must have wealthy friends, the tea is usually reserved for royalty.'

'I didn't know that, it was a gift from a trader in Lavo,' she replied.

The queen ignored the comment, knowing she was hiding something.

'So Maya, tell me about what you do back in your home country?'

'I'm a teacher and natural philosopher. I study nature to help my people.'

The queen continued to stare deeply at Maya. 'Interesting, so why did you decide to travel all this way to find our people?'

Maya reflected for a moment, 'Marcus thought it would be beneficial for us to explore other cultures. To help improve our knowledge of the world.'

'With very little protection it seems. I'm surprised your people let you leave,' the queen replied.

'They were keen that we explore the world, our society is not as advanced as yours Your Majesty. We need to travel to understand how to improve ourselves and the life of our citizens.'

Over the next hour, the queen chatted about the culture in Europe, where Maya lived and about the different countries. Maya felt like she was being interrogated but kept calm and replied to all the questions the best she could. It wasn't long until the queen seemed to lose interest in asking questions and suggested they started their tour. The servants were summoned, and breakfast was cleared away. The queen was helped to her feet, and they were both led out of the palace flanked by the queen's personal guard. Maya noticed that the queen's guard included both male and female soldiers all wearing blue uniforms matching the queen's colours.

After about half an hour of walking, they arrived at the temple called Thommanon. Maya had listened to Marcus talk about Angkor for years and she recognised that although the temple was dedicated to Buddha, she noticed many Hindu statues and deities. He told her how the Khmer culture had often worshipped both the Hindu and Buddhist religions. The temple itself was breath-taking, and the detailed carvings along the walls of the structure were hugely impressive, making it a true sight to behold. The queen was led into the inner sanctum and they were met by the head monks. They bowed in respect to the Queen. Inside the temple it was dark except for faint candlelight which illuminated the inner walls, the smell of incense hung in the air and Maya noticed the offerings of flowers, fruit and coconut juice arranged lovingly in front of the Buddha idol.

'So Maya, tell me what you think of this temple?' the queen asked

'It's incredible,' she replied. 'Such beauty and dedication to Buddha, the monks are a true credit to your people.'

The queen looked at her again looking for any signs of duplicity but saw nothing. 'Tell me about your religion, I think I've heard of it, it's called Christianity isn't it.'

Maya paused for a moment, she had to be careful how to respond. She respected people's beliefs but she was an atheist, and was keen to avoid discussing that topic for fear of not being understood.

'There are many religions from my part of the world, the Greek, Egyptians, and Roman peoples worshipped many deities. The Celts worshipped gods linked to the natural world. Christianity and Judaism worship a single deity. All these religions have built incredible monuments to their faiths. I have had the honour to visit many of them and to watch people worship,' Maya commented like a history teacher.

'And what about you Maya, who do you worship?' the queen asked directly.

'I um, well,' Maya stumbled. 'I'm more into natural philosophy. I don't worship any particular god at the moment.'

'Is that right?' The queen stared.

'It doesn't prevent me from respecting and valuing other people's beliefs,' Maya said.

'I understand,' the queen replied, the honesty from Maya seemed to connect with her. 'There are many things we don't know and I believe it is foolish not to study different beliefs.'

'That's my view too Your Majesty, everyone has a right to believe in what they like as long as everyone respects others,' Maya said happily, comforted with the queen's liberal response.

The queen looked at Maya again before speaking, 'Shall we go and see a local school?'

'I would love that Your Majesty, that's where I feel most comfortable,' Maya replied.

They both thanked the monks and the queen's entourage lead the way. They walked to a nearby large hall off one of the adjacent streets.

As they entered, they were met by the teacher, he was young for his age and bowed deeply. 'This school was set up by the King after our recapture of the capital, one of his first actions was to create schools to educate all the children.'

'That's very wise Your Majesty, I've always found educated people add a great deal to society.'

While in the school Maya was shown many different lessons, she listened into a writing class with the queen, then was guided to look at some of the paintings the children had been creating. Maya felt much more comfortable in this environment and the queen could tell. The children were also intrigue by the stranger. They asked all kinds of questions about Maya's homeland as the queen looked on.

Soon it was time to leave, and they headed to a nearby farm, the farmer showed Maya how he used the irrigation systems to fill his rice paddies. The queen told Maya that the fields were the backbone of the Khmer cities allowing a consistent food supply, along with the fruit from the jungle the people were well supported through the changing seasons. The farmer showed Maya that within the rice paddies he had released fish so they could eat the pests, when they were large enough, he told her he would farm the fish also. It made Maya proud to see sustainable farming in use. Maya explained to the queen that back in Europe it was very different, the weather did not allow for rice to be grown easily. She spoke about farming being focused on wheat to make bread, she talked about the different types of fruit and vegetables that were grown back home to what can be grown in Angkor.

The queen was very interested in the different agricultural methods. However it was time to move on to the last stop, the hospital.

As they arrived the queen said, 'I am most proud about our hospitals in Angkor, the King has worked so hard to help our people. Making sure they live long, and healthy lives will ensure that our society can prosper.'

'I couldn't agree more,' Maya replied. 'It's really great to see that you're investing in public health.'

The queen showed her around the hospital, Maya was conscious not to compare it against modern-day standards, after all at this time there was no real understanding of medicine. Her observations highlighted that the main aim of the hospital was to help people with small injuries heal. Maya toured the facility offering a few suggestions to healers about making the splints more effective to help broken bones heal straight. The queen watched her intently, she noticed how Maya flinched when she saw people in pain. She could tell Maya was not used to seeing people in pain despite being a healer.

The queen explained that for contagious diseases people were moved outside of the city walls to avoid mass infection. She described that those who were not contagious but were likely to die were returned to their family to spend their last days together. Maya was impressed by the facilities that the queen had shown her, she had never expected that the medical situation would be this compassionate.

With the last visit completed, Queen Indradevi escorted Maya back to the palace. She had been observing

Maya all day and was very impressed with the woman in front of her. It was clear that Maya was capable and from a society which was very different to hers. The queen observed that Maya had little fear of men and her empathy was something she had not seen often in her long life. It didn't take long for them to arrived back in the queen's private rooms. More tea had been laid out for them. The queen gestured for Maya to sit next to her and she obediently obliged.

The queen picked up a cup and spoke directly to her. 'Now my dear let me ask you a question, who are you really and where do you come from?'

CHAPTER TEN

Princess Bopha

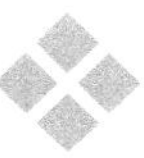

Marcus watched as Maya left to meet the queen, as she disappeared out of the compound, he pulled himself to his feet. Marcus gazed back over the lake watching the rising mist one more time then turned and entered the hut. Luke was still sleeping. He had been asleep solidly since they returned from the feast. Marcus knew Luke was exhausted.

Luke had not spoken much to him since the accident and Marcus understood why. Afterall Kalani had tried to kill him, plus the effect of the reversed polarisation beam from the Hadron Thought Collider had taken a lot out of him. On top of that, the events of the last few days had only compounded his exhaustion and confusion.

Marcus sat down on a nearby bed and looked over at his friend, he felt a sudden sense of guilt.

Friend. He's like a son to me and I think friend and now I've trapped him here.

Marcus sat still just staring at Luke worried about what the future held for them all. Unexpectedly there was a gentle knock on the door. Marcus got up quietly trying not to wake Luke and opened the door where Princess Bopha was waiting.

'Good morning Marcus,' she said brightly.

'Shhh,' he said bringing his fingers to his lips and slipped out of the hut shutting the door quietly. 'Morning Your Majesty. Sorry Luke's still sleeping, he's been through a lot lately and I'm keen he rests. I hope you don't mind.'

'He means a lot to you, doesn't he?' she asked, gesturing for him to sit with her on the veranda.

'He's like a son to me. It's all my fault for getting him into this,' he said uncontrollably.

For some reason, he felt he could open up to the princess.

'It's nice you care so deeply for someone, I've never had a relationship outside my family,' the princess said unexpectedly. 'My Father tried to match me with some suitors, usually connected to his key allies but none of them were what I was looking for in a man.'

She paused for a moment.

'Thankfully my mother ensured I was protected. She made certain I was not forced to be married to someone I didn't want to be with,' she spoke with a deep sense of sorrow. 'It would have been nice to have had the chance to meet someone who cared for me, like you do for the others.'

'Your Majesty I've never had a family of my own either, I became Luke's mentor and naturally looked after him knowing he had no one else in his life.'

'Sounds like we've got a lot in common. Marcus, please call me Bo,' she replied reaching out to touch his hand. 'Will you join me on the tour of Angkor Wat today? I would very much like to spend time with you. The monks have already approved my request for special access if you're still keen to come?'

He looked up and his eyes connected with hers, 'Yes very much Bo, but can we wait until Luke wakes up? I'd like to make sure he's feeling ok before we leave.'

'Of course,' she replied.

They spent the next hour sitting together on the veranda chatting about recent Khmer battles, Bo explained how the King had created an alliance to retake the city. Marcus enjoyed hearing about the historical events he knew so well, and listening to a first-hand account of the battle from the princess was mesmerising.

The door to the hut opened and Luke walked out, making them both jump, he looked much more rested and seemed to be more relaxed. Luke, like Marcus, was still in his night robes, but he was holding a plate of fruit that he had picked up from a table inside, it must have been left there by the servants. He offered both of them some of the food while drinking some fresh juice.

'Good to see you up Luke, are you feeling Okay?' the princess asked.

'Yes, thank you Your Majesty, all the excitement seems to have worn me out,' he replied managing a smile.

'I know my brother has a full day of activities planned for you both, so it's great you're feeling better. I think he wants to take you out of the city,' she responded and then looked at Marcus. 'Why don't you dress my dear and we can go?'

'Yes, Your…' He smiled.

'Bo,' Marcus said and got up, returning to the hut to wash and change, leaving the princess and Luke alone.

'You're a mystery to me Luke,' she paused, thinking for a moment. 'My brother has always been a considered man. He never acts on impulse, yet you seem to have enchanted him, it's very intriguing. Not to mention how Marcus looks at you, he seems to care a great deal. It's very interesting how you've had such an impact on people.'

Luke didn't really know how to respond. 'Um, thank you Your Majesty.'

'I'm not sure it's a compliment, all I ask is you treat my brother with respect. His attraction to you could bring a great deal of danger to him, and to my family,' she replied firmly.

'I'm not sure I know what you mean,' he responded sharply. Luke realised he had spoken a little too forcefully to the princess and he quickly corrected himself. 'Your Majesty.'

The Princess pondered for a moment before responding, 'Once my father dies, my brother will become king. To fulfil his duties he will need to marry, he will need to take a wife from one of my father's closest allies and he will need to produce an heir. If he doesn't, then we will all be in danger. Our alliances could split, and war could come to the Khmer Empire, this is just what the Cham want.'

Those words hit Luke hard, he already felt something very deep for Prince Srindra and what the Princess was saying seemed to shatter his feelings. Not to mention it woke him to the realisation that he could impact the timeline.

Marcus appeared at the door as Luke was deep in thought, he was dressed in the fine green robes that he had been given yesterday albeit they were a bit askew. They seemed to match the robes of the princess. It was like Srindra had planned it. Bo laughed and moved to straighten his clothes. She adjusted the jewellery he was wearing placing her hand affectionately on the red ruby stone.

'Shall we go?'

'Yes, I'm so looking forward to seeing your amazing temple Bo.' He turned and looked at Luke, 'Have fun today but be careful. Remember don't push yourself, your brain's still recovering. If you need more rest ask the prince to bring you back.'

Luke sighed. Marcus was treating him like a child, but he nodded back in acknowledgement. Bo led Marcus by the arm and out of the compound.

***

Over the last day, Kalani had been sheltering in his discrete hiding place, he had managed to build a makeshift shelter from the jungle trees. He created tools he had fashioned out of sharp stones he found on the shore of the lake. Kalani had managed to craft a spear so he could hunt fish. It was also his only means of protection if needed, it seemed the knowledge of his ancestors that had been passed down was really helping him to survive.

Kalani gathered a number of different fruits from the nearby trees. He had scanned them all to make sure they weren't poisonous and safe to eat. All his hard work was paying off, he camouflaged the hut with the jungle material and was able to discreetly observe any passing native boats without being spotted.

He did still have a few challenges. His clothing was not made for the humid environment in Cambodia, he was struggling with the biting mosquitoes and the intense heat. Kalani also had no blankets or material he could use to protect himself if the weather changed. He knew he would eventually have to venture into one of the local villages, possibly in the next few days to seek help. However, his main priority was to work out what to trade. Currently he had no money or items he could exchange which would cause suspicion. For now, he was going to sit tight and use his engineering skills to find a solution. He was determined to create something he could trade.

***

It was about a half an hour walk to the temple, Marcus and Bo were escorted by a few of the queen's guards. They were there on her orders to ensure the protection of the princess. The princess and her foreign guest attracted a lot of attention. They were stopped numerous times by locals keen to get a glimpse of the very pale white man. When they finally arrived at the great temple of Angkor Wat Marcus was captivated, he turned to Bo in excitement.

'Thanks so much for this incredible honour.'

'I'm still not clear why you're so interested in our culture and in our city,' she said smiling at his reaction.

'It's just so unique, and being able to see it in all its glory is such a privilege.'

Bo patted his shoulder and guided him gently to the west entrance of the temple. They approached the sandstone bridge and Marcus stopped to take in the breath-taking view.

Bo looked at him and said in a considered tone, 'Father's been trying to rebuild the temple since we took the city back. As part of our victory, Father decreed we pray to Buddha. He believes that Buddha's teachings are more aligned to our people, however that does cause some tension across the city,' she said with a sense of worry in her voice.

'We used to follow the Hindu gods but after our defeats, Father felt they had little interest in us and our people.'

She paused for a moment, thinking carefully. 'I worry though, some of our people are still deeply connected to the Hindu gods and I fear for him. I do hope he can inspire our people through Buddha's life lessons and teachings.'

Marcus could see she was fearful for her father, and he put his arm around her for comfort. 'The king's a great man and I'm sure he will rule for years to come. He seems to value his people and I'm sure they see that,' he said kindly.

'Thank you Marcus.'

Bo guided him across the great sandstone causeway, something he had done himself in his youth so many times before. They walked arm in arm pausing periodically to look at the carvings on the bridge and to take in the wildlife. They eventually reached the entrance to the temple. They were both met by the head priest who was waiting for them patiently, he greeted the princess warmly.

'This is Tamalinda, but we just call him Tamal,' Bo said, smiling at the priest. 'Tamal is responsible for our great temple and has a deep understanding of our Buddhist faith.'

Marcus looked at the man, he was young for his age and had bright eyes, he composed himself with a sense of serenity.

'He's also my dear brother,' Bo said beaming. 'He chose the spiritual path, one of contemplation rather than war.'

Bo brought her hands together and bowed respectfully which was reciprocated by Tamal, who then gave his sister a playful hug.

Tamal spoke to Marcus, 'Welcome to one of our most important temples, my sister has told me of your deep interest in our artistry and culture, which I find fascinating.'

'Thank you for the opportunity to see this amazing temple, I've heard wonderful stories about it throughout my long journey.'

'You're welcome Marcus, I appreciate you showing us respect, please treat our temple with the courtesy it deserves.' He looked at Bo, 'I'm sure my sister will help you with our rules and rituals.'

She bowed again.

Bo thanked her brother and they parted. She led Marcus into the western gallery.

When out of earshot Bo spoke quietly, 'My brother had a difficult upbringing, he saw a lot of pain and sorrow during the campaigns against the Cham. It was a difficult time for him, so he decided to join the monks with the support of my parents. He spent ten years studying and when we finally retook the city, he joined us to help spread the word of Buddha.'

Marcus looked at Bo, it was clear there was more to this but she didn't seem eager to discuss it further, so he asked no more questions. They soon reached the centre of the temple and he looked around in wonder. The stone carvings were so detailed and crisp, very different to the carvings he studied as a youth which had been eroded by time.

Bo spoke proudly, 'Angkor Wat is a miniature replica of our universe, the temple represents the cosmic world.'

She smiled clearly enjoying telling the story and pointed, 'The central tower rises from this building, it symbolises our mythical mountain, Meru. For our people this mountain is situated at the centre of the universe.'

Bo turned around, 'Can you see the five towers? This corresponds to the peaks of Meru.'

She smiled widely. 'The temple was built about seventy years ago by Suryavarman II who ruled our people. He was a cousin of my grandfather and died fighting the Chams, since we retook the city, my Father has been working intently to restore it and preserve his memory.'

Marcus looked around, his eyes enchanted by the astonishing scene, 'It's truly amazing Bo, we have nothing like this at home.'

'Come, let's explore. I want to show you my favourite carvings, they really come to life,' she said excitedly and led him by the hand pulling him deeper into the temple.

They explored the chambers extensively and lost total track of time, Bo was excited, and she took Marcus to all her favourite places keen to share them. After a while, she led him into the sacred shrine where they both bowed with respect. Bo offered to Buddha a small bottle of perfume. Marcus suddenly felt self-conscious, he didn't have anything to offer, Bo noticed and gave him a golden band from her wrist. Marcus thanked her and offered the band to Buddha, he bowed again, and they both left.

Bo decided to finish their tour at her favourite place and took him to a secluded part of the temple.

She wanted to show him one last carving. 'This is my favourite piece, can you see the elephant carrying one of my ancestors, it's so intricate.'

Marcus nodded and unconsciously touch her shoulder affectionately. Without warning, she pushed him against the wall and kissed him passionately.

'I've never met anyone like you, no one's shared the love I have for art like you have.'

Marcus's feelings took over him, he couldn't stop himself, he pulled her close and spoke, 'Bo I know just what you mean.'

Then without hesitation he kissed her back lovingly.

'Come back to mine?' she asked him, her eyes wide.

All Marcus could do was kiss her again, he couldn't speak, and they headed for the exit. Bo quickly led him through the temple taking every shortcut she could. They left as fast as they could by the west entrance. As they left, she quickly thanked her brother for his hospitality and called for the queen's guards. Soon they were escorted back to the princess's private residence, they both walked as quickly as possible, keen not to draw any unwanted attention.

They soon arrived at Princess Bo's compound. It was much like Prince Srindra's, except it was smaller and she had stone carvings adorning her grounds. Like the prince, she had lakes and water channels linking the buildings. The princess dismissed the guards as they entered the compound and quickly guided Marcus to her private residence, she ordered the servants to leave who obeyed without question and turned to kiss him again. He put his hand on the back of her neck and caressed her beautiful face. Marcus kissed her forehead, then her neck, slowly moving down to her chest causing her to exhale with pleasure.

Bo pulled a string on her robes causing them to fall to the floor leaving her naked, she stood there in just her glittering gems and silver jewellery. The aquamarine and peridot necklace sparkled while her silver lotus crown looked like a halo.

She looks like a goddess, Marcus thought.

Bo looked at him with her deep hazel eyes, 'Come with me,' she insisted.

Marcus, who seemed enchanted by her, reached out his hand and she led him to her bedchamber.

***

It was a few hours later when Marcus exited the bedchamber, he was wearing an emerald night robe that Bo had lent him. Marcus was glowing. This woman had enchanted him. He felt incredible after the passionate love he had just made to the beautiful princess of Angkor. Bo excited him like no other, he had never experienced any emotions like what he felt now. Marcus smiled with contentment as he reached for a jug of water from a nearby table. He poured a cup for himself while looking around the room, as he sipped, he studied the amazing artworks on Bo's walls. He was fascinated by the images in front of him and wanted to know who had created them. In his passion, he had not seen any of these works when he entered. The vibrant landscapes and portraits of the Khmer people were strikingly beautiful.

He heard a subtle cough and Marcus turned around to see Bo staring at him with a wide grin.

'I see you like my private collection.'

'They're amazing Bo, who painted them?'

'I did,' she said. 'Painting has been a love of mine for as long as I can remember.'

'Do your talents never end.'

'You have only seen a few of my talents,' she replied flirtatiously.

Bo walked over and took the water out of his hand and kissed him once more.

Marcus held her in the sensual embrace before slowly pulling away. 'What are we going to do? We can't tell any of our friends about this can we?'

'I don't know.' She looked away staring at one of her water landscapes and said, 'All I know is that after many years of searching for someone I can connect with, I've found him. I'll not give that up for anyone.'

She turned back to him and looked him straight in the eyes, 'What about you Marcus, what do you want?'

He breathed heavily, still holding her tightly.

'It's complicated Bo, there are things you don't know about us and we will have to leave at some point,' he said sadly.

She pulled away on hearing his reply, 'But why, what do you have to go back for? You told me you had no family.'

Marcus looked away.

'Tell me what's bothering you, it's obvious to us all there are things you three are hiding. My mother has tasked us all to find out what.'

Marcus was a bit taken aback by the revelation and moved away, 'Bo I can't, please don't ask me too. I need you to trust me when I say we're decent caring people. None of us are here to hurt anyone.'

'Of that I am sure,' she replied pulling him back into a loving embrace once more.

All of a sudden one of the princess's guards entered the room, he stopped quickly taken aback by seeing the princess in a compromised position.

He averted his eyes as they both broke apart swiftly and Bo shouted, 'What's the meaning of this intrusion?'

'Sorry Your Majesty, the queen has ordered that you both be brought to her at once,' he declared.

'But why enter my room without waiting for me to grant you access?' she shouted.

'The queen feared you might be in danger and ordered me to come for you straight away.'

'But why would I be in danger from Marcus, he is my friend and so are his companions?'

'I don't know Your Majesty, but the Queen was very clear on her orders and she wants you both at the palace now, she said this was an order,' the guard said hesitantly.

'You'll wait outside while Marcus and I dress for the queen, leave now or you'll be punished,' she said furiously.

'But I am not allowed to…'

'Out *now*,' she screamed, and the guard wobbled.

'Yes Your Majesty, I'll just be outside if you need me,' he said and quickly left.

'What's going on,' Marcus said fearfully looking at Bo intensely.

'I've no idea, but I expect it relates to what you're hiding and why your friends are here. Tell me now before we leave for the Queen. If you don't I can't protect you, or Maya and Luke' she replied honestly.

Fear had gripped Marcus. He was afraid for his friend's safety and a wave of emotion hit him.

Marcus stuttered, for some reason he knew he could trust Bo totally and whispered, 'We're from the future.'

CHAPTER ELEVEN

Prince Srindra

Luke returned to the guest house after Marcus left, in truth he was still feeling pretty exhausted. It was as if he still had the vibrations of the pulse from the HTC ringing in his head. Luke hoped the effects from the destabilising beam would have worn off by now. But it was uncharted territory and he had no idea what impact the repolarised beam would have on him.

Luke slumped onto the bed and held his head in his hands. *What I'd give for some paracetamol.* He calmed his mind and it wandered to the prince. *Why is he so interested in me and why am I so interested in him?*

There was a knock at the door, Luke pulled himself up to answer it, he opened the door and smiled, it was Prince Srindra.

'You look tired Luke, maybe some of mother's rejuvenation tonic will pick you up,' he said, walking into the hut without waiting for an invitation.

Sri grabbed a cup off the table and yanked a flask out of his belt. He pulled the cork out then poured thick green sludge into it and forced it into Luke's hand.

'Drink, it will make you feel better,' he insisted.

Luke not wanting to offend took the green sludge and drank it slowly.

'Ah that's horrid,' he gaged. 'Sorry, Your Majesty.'

'I told you to call me Sri and yes, it is, but it will make you feel better. Trust me Luke,' he replied kindly.

After a few minutes, amazingly Luke did start to feel better.

What's in that stuff? he thought to himself as the prince discussed the day ahead.

'I'll get dressed and we can leave Sri, what do you have planned for us today?'

Sri moved close to Luke and kissed him sensually. It took him completely by surprise and they fell back on the bed.

He felt Luke's heart beating fast and pulled him close, 'I think you know what I'd like to do today.'

Luke breathed in the sweet scent coming from the powerful man and kissed him back, 'Are you sure this is wise, you heard your father last night?'

'Yes, I'm sure,' Sri said smiling. 'Let me help get you dressed. I love choosing what you wear. I'm not sure about the clothes you wear back in Europe, but you don't seem to manage to dress in our clothing very well.'

He laughed and Luke smiled back, he acknowledged the truth in Sri's words.

It didn't take long before Luke was dressed as Sri wanted. He was dressed in his familiar purple robes with the large amethyst prominently placed on his chest to match the prince's. Sri sprayed a sweet-smelling scent over them both then took his hand. He guided Luke out of the guest house, his pale white chest reflected in the sun and he was directed towards the stables. They entered the impressive building. It was full of beautiful horses in all colours. Suddenly to Luke's surprise he spotted a number of large elephants. They were striking, intricately dressed in golden chains with studded gems, covered in purple banners and adorned with golden armour.

'This ones ours,' Sri gestured to the animal. It had a huge Amethyst stone on its head making it clear to all this was the prince's personal elephant. 'My friends Samang and Vannak will be riding with us today.'

He pointed to the two friends Luke met the other night, they were already climbing onto an elephant. 'I'd like to take you to a special secluded place deep into the jungle. It's my favourite retreat where I can relax with my friends. It's away from our people and away from my family,' he looked at Vannak and smiled.

The prince's elephant was soon prepared and the servants helped them climb onto the animal. A few minutes later they left the compound with the elephants in all their splendour walking proudly through the streets of Angkor. The prince beamed and waved at his people as they passed, it was clear from the reception he was getting they loved him. Flanking the elephants were the prince's royal guards, about fifty of them on horseback with spears and bows raised. *What a sight to behold*, Luke thought to himself, he couldn't believe he was part of something so breath-taking and something so grand.

He looked at Sri's smiling face who just stared back. Without any words Sri reached out and squeezed Luke's hand for reassurance. The entourage continued its procession out of the city and as they approached the jungle Luke was still in wonderment of his situation. He turned back to look at the city. His eyes fixated on the remarkable skyline behind him. Luke was captivated, he was experiencing history unfold and seeing things archaeologists had never imagined.

***

Once they left Angkor they journeyed through the jungle, it was a unique experience travelling by elephant. As they trekked Sri took time to point out the different types of birds and plant life. He enjoyed showing Luke the beauty and scenery of his country. An hour after they left the city they arrived at a secluded location. The elephants hiked up a narrow steep rocky path soon approaching a levelled clearing. Luke looked around and he could see for miles. The hill was only small but it gave a great vantage point of the jungle, as well as the large city in the distance. The party continued on, and it wasn't long before Luke spotted a small settlement. As they approached the buildings the surrounding jungle came to life, screeching monkey's and bird song filled the air. The settlement was the private retreat called Kar Trasa Doeng. After Angkor was retaken, the king created a hide away for his family deep in the Koulen mountains. It was far enough away from the city to ensure complete privacy. The entourage passed through a large fortified gate. A path led them to several wooden buildings. At the centre of the settlement was a large lake. The houses surrounded it and in the middle of the water stood a beautiful carved five-storey pagoda. Its roof was bright gold and its walls were painted a brilliant white. The doors and windows to the pagoda were vivid red, adorned with gold decorations. The compound was larger than Luke initially thought, and he noticed that connected to the large lake were numerous small pools, linking all the guest houses. Each hut had its own jetty with a bright red boat covered in shimmering golden decorations.

Sri looked at Luke's expression. 'We're safe here. We can be ourselves without fear of others watching.'

He looked over at Samang, who was helping Vannak descend from the elephant, 'My friends are like us too, they've been together for the past ten years under my protection.'

Luke turned to look, he could see the connection between the two men, there was a gentleness between them which reminded him of his close friends back in Cambridge. In the 24th Century sexual choice and freedom of individuality was available to all. Society had an evolved sense of personal freedom that enabled everyone to live their lives how they wanted, to be with who they desired and to choose the identity they preferred. It was hearing the prince's words, *Under my protection,* that Luke realised his life had changed. The man he was back in Cambridge had to be suppressed, he needed to fit in with the societal restrictions he now faced and this was a sobering thought. Luke had studied much about the historic persecution of LGBTQ communities, but had never seen or experienced prejudice back home. Nor had he faced it here, well at least not for now, after all he was under the prince's protection.

Servants helped them both dismount the elephant, while the elite guards rode to the stables.

'Don't worry, we're safe here,' Sri commented.

The four of them were led into one of the main reception areas. The prince's trusted servants removed all their travel clothes leaving them naked, which made Luke very uncomfortable. Each of the guests were led away by an individual servant to a cleansing pool and washed in sweet-smelling oils. Luke flinched as he was bathed, he was extremely embarrassed by this situation, he was not used to attention like this, let alone being naked in front of strangers. The servant attending to him ignored his reactions and continued with the ritual. He averted his eye trying to ignore the awkwardness but as he looked up, he noticed all the other men were smooth and manicured, he had observed the smoothness of their chests but didn't realise they were shaved all over.

It must be a culture thing he thought.

Luke was now feeling very self-conscious, he instinctively moved his hand to cover his modesty, the unkept hair on his body made him feel very out of place.

Sri chuckled as he saw Luke's reaction to the servants.

'You Westerners, so prudish,' he laughed standing there proudly, letting the servants do their job like it was the most natural thing in the world.

Sri turned to his personal aid Charya, 'Please see to Luke and make sure he has your full treatment, looks like he needs it.'

The servant bowed lowly and took Luke's hand leading him away from the cleansing pool.

Luke looked back nervously and asked, 'What's going on, what's he going to do?'

'My servant is going to clean and prepare your body, it's clear you're not used to our customs and our ways of grooming. Don't be afraid, he knows what he's doing.'

'No, I'm fine honestly,' he replied desperately, trying to get out of the situation.

'Luke, you are in my court and under my protection, you will do as I ask,' he said jokingly. But it was clear this was an order. 'I'll meet you after Charya has fulfilled his duties.'

Not sure how to respond, Luke just nodded and followed the servant into a nearby chamber. Charya got to work, he started by cutting Luke's hair, he carefully tidied up the shaggy black hair styling it to match the prince's. To Luke's surprise Charya then pulled out a large sharp knife and began to shave him all over, the fragrant oils helped to lubricate his skin enabling Charya to shave extremely close. This was an emasculating experience. Luke had never been treated like this which made him feel very vulnerable and totally controlled. Charya finished his work and bathed

Luke once more. He followed by applying yet more oils making his skin extremely soft. Luke was turned around a few times, Charya wanted to make sure he had done his job properly. Luke was given a small loincloth and then led back to the prince. Sri was relaxing with his friends by the lake, he was sitting on cushions drinking out of a fresh coconut. As Luke approached, he looked at the scene not really sure what to make of it, he was feeling so out of his depth. He had never been in a situation like this. He had never been very confident around strong self-assured men, he found history far more interesting than complex relationships.

'Join me.' The prince gestured and Luke shyly obliged. 'Here, drink this, it's quite refreshing but has a bit of a kick.'

Sri handed Luke his coconut and he began to drink. He coughed as the liquid hit his mouth, the taste surprised him, he wasn't expecting the strong alcohol taste that had exploded in his mouth.

Luke's nerves got the better of him, he took another sip to calm himself, Luke tasted coconut milk but noticed something else.

A hint of mango, he thought. *And maybe some of the local rice wine.*

'What do you think?' Sri asked watching Luke's reactions carefully.

'It's nice, I like the flavours but it's a bit strong for me,' he replied smiling. 'Are you trying to get me drunk?'

'Ah, course not, don't be a Cham,' the prince said, slapping Luke's shoulder and laughing. 'Today's all about us getting to know each other and having a bit of fun, how about a dip?'

Luke nodded hesitantly. Sri got up and walked along the lake side showing off. Both Vannak and Samang laughed at his antics and then cockily Sri jumped into the cool water. There was a large splash followed by the noise of birds taking flight, frightened by the sound. The jungle seemed to come alive again full of squawking and shrieking.

'Come on Lukie it's lovely,' he called out playfully.

Luke got to his feet still hesitant, but also excited, there was something about this man he couldn't put his finger on. Luke walked to the water's edge and looked over the picturesque scene in front of him, he smiled seeing the lotus flowers blooming and the water lilies floating.

It's so romantic, the thought turned his attention to Sri, he looked deep into his hazel eyes, smiled and jumped in eagerly.

The cool water heightened Luke senses, Sri swam over splashing playfully and Luke splashed back, his heart was racing. They laughed and joked pushing each other back and forth when suddenly Luke decided to swim as fast as he could. He teased Sri to follow him, Luke was a strong swimmer, something he had loved to do at university and it took Sri by surprise. He chased gleefully following Luke around the shallow lake, and it didn't take long until he had Luke cornered. Luke tried to escape but was trapped close to the pagoda, Sri smiled as a nearby Bayan tree bathed him in dappled shade, only enhancing

Luke's attractive features. Sri knew he had him cornered and with one large thrust, he pinned Luke against the pagoda wall holding him tightly. Sri looked into Luke's sparkling green eyes. He leaned forward forcefully and kissed him, pushing him hard against the wall.

It was a kiss Luke would remember for the rest of his life, his emotions began to build and there seemed to be a small tremor which shook the pagoda. Sri looked up in surprise, but the sound was nothing to worry about and turned back kissing Luke once more. It was clear they had an affinity together. Sri held the back of Luke's head. He had wanted to do this ever since he saw Luke for the first time in the forest, yet had no idea why and kissed him once more. Luke kissed back. Sri knew they felt the same magnetic connection which only enhanced their infatuation. Their embrace broke down any barriers or shyness that existed before.

Sri took Luke's hand and guided him to some stone steps by the edge of the lake, they were met by one of the prince's trusted servants who helped to dry them. Sri looked across the lake seeing his friends smiling back at him, he had known them both since a child. Vannak had never seen him so taken by someone. It was he who had pushed Sri to pursue the young foreigner. Vannak was Sri's cousin, they grew up together and as kids were inseparable, he thought of Vannak more like a brother. Much more than his actual brother Virak, who in truth he loathed. Virak's lack of compassion, desire for the old ways and complete absence of a sense of humour was of constant irritation.

Sri gave Vannak a wink and turned back to Luke who was still being dried off. He put his arm around Luke and escorted him to his nearby private quarters. The chamber was thick with fog as they entered, their senses overwhelmed by the sweet-smelling incense that filled the room. Luke looked around and noticed such beautiful artwork adorning the walls. The room was filled with decorative sculptures and colourful paintings.

'My sister's work,' Sri commented, pulling Luke close for another embrace making Luke's heart beam once more.

Sri closed the door to give them privacy and gestured to the bed. Luke eagerly followed noticing the many orchids adorning the room. He approached the bed and on the crisp white sheets were exquisite flower petals arranged in an elaborate pattern. On a nearby table were fresh fruit and more drinks. It was clear Sri had planned this, arranging all the details with his servants before they arrived. He was keen to make their time together special.

Sri held Luke from behind hugging him tightly, he slowly turned him around kissing him again. He was totally infatuated with this stranger and had no idea why. Somehow, he knew Luke needed his protection and that they were meant to be together. It was like the world seemed to be telling them something.

Sri's hand touched Luke's face slowly caressing his skin, his hand moved sensually down the side of his neck and onto his pale body. Sri looked deep into Luke's eyes. Neither of them could wait any longer and like wild animals, they embraced each other passionately. Sri pushed

Luke onto the bed, he climbed on top of him until they were face to face.

'Fates brought us together. I don't know why, but I know you're meant to be mine.'

***

Luke woke a few hours later. He was still held tightly by the man he'd just made love with and couldn't move. He felt so protected by this man, the prince of Angkor.

Who is he? he thought to himself. *And why do I connect with him so much?*

His heart beamed as the realisation he was in love sank in. The last few hours had been the most amazing and incredible experience of his life. His mind was in pure ecstasy. Luke lay there in a haze of happiness, listening to Sri's gentle breathing as he slept, he could feel Sri's beating heart against his skin which only made his feelings more intense.

Suddenly a loud scream came from outside and they both jumped with a startle. Sri leapt up out of the bed, he grabbed his golden bow which he had placed nearby.

'Wait here and don't move, I'll protect you,' he said without hesitation and left the room, shutting the door behind him.

Luke was terrified, he didn't know what to do, he was naked except for the loincloth he had and the bed sheets, he felt so vulnerable. Luke heard yet more screams and he crept towards a nearby window, he held the bed sheet around him and peered out. He was presented with a scene of panic with servants and soldiers running for cover.

Thud. Luke turned his head to the direction of the pagoda on hearing the terrifying sound. He saw a strange looking man fall from the pagoda and hit the floor hard. The man was dressed in black robes with deep black striped markings across his face. It was a colour and style he had not seen in the city. Luke looked closely at the man. He could see an arrow sticking out of his chest. Dark red blood began to appear seeping onto the stone path beneath him.

Luke recoiled at the sight and fell back onto the floor. He crawled behind the bed completely terrified. He had never seen anything like this. Violence didn't really exist in his world and seeing a man murdered in front of him shocked him to his core.

Luke peered over the bed when suddenly, a man dressed in the same black robes smashed through the door and entered the room. Luke noticed the man was holding a large sword in his hand. The attacker's mad eyes searched the room for any inhabitants and soon found Luke. The man rushed forward pulling Luke up by his neck and forcing him against the wall.

'What are you?' he shouted looking at the white skinny man, unsure what was before him.

The man continued to grip Luke's throat tightly, then forced the sword up against his neck.

'Answer me,' the man ordered.

Luke was so petrified he couldn't speak, the attacker lifted Luke higher by the throat, causing him to choke and his feet to dangle helplessly.

This is it, Luke thought.

He could feel his breath leaving him and his consciousness slipping away.

I didn't think I'd die like this, he thought and closed his eyes.

'No! a voice shouted from behind as Sri ran into the room.

There was a *thud*, and an arrow burst through the man's chest centimetres from Luke's heart. Blood splattered all over Luke's semi-naked body and he fell to the floor. The man that was so focused on killing him crumpled into a heap, dead. Sri dropped his bow impulsively and rushed to help Luke.

'Are you ok?' he asked desperately and all Luke could muster was a nod as he rubbed his throat.

'We're under attack from the Cham, they've sent one of their assassin squads to kill me. We need to get out of here,' he demanded, but Luke couldn't move.

Sri tried to lift him up but as he did another Cham assassin entered the room, catching them both by surprise.

The assassin shouted, 'For Champa' and raised his sword ready to strike.

Without thinking, Luke activated his palm implant which created a bright holographic screen. It showed a photo image of the smiling Quantology team back in the lab at Cambridge. In the confusion the assassin hesitated, Sri grabbed his jewel encrusted dagger from his quiver and in an instant, he plunged the knife deep into the assassin's chest, and the man fell to the floor.

'What the hell was that?' Sri screamed, trying to comprehend what he had seen. Luke remained silent. He was in total shock and couldn't speak.

Sri came over and shook him hard, 'Get yourself together we need to move.'

Luke stuttered and pulled himself to his feet, they crept to the door. Sri spotted Major Rithy Keo, the head of his elite guard fighting. Keo cut down a large assassin then he sighted Sri and rushed over.

'Your Majesty half the guard are dead along with Samang and Vannak, these bastards crept into the compound and slit their throat while they slept. I've managed to get the rest of the guard together and we're holding them off, we have horses waiting to get you out of here, come.'

'Keo how did they get into our compound and how did they know I was here?' he shouted.

'I don't know Your Majesty. Only a few people in court knew we were coming here.'

'We'll need to find the spy that sold us out,' Sri replied.

'What about him?' Keo pointed to Luke. 'He stays here, we don't know anything about him or his people. These Cham scum could be in league with them and I can't risk your safety, I don't trust him.'

Sri pinned Keo against a wall.

'Luke saved my life and I trust him. Do you understand? I'm not letting him out of my sight, he's important to me and important to our people' Sri roared with anger.

'Yes Your Majesty, sorry I didn't mean to question you,' he said bowing his head.

Sri released the major from his grip, his attitude softened and he held his friend's hand.

'Trust me I'm telling you Luke and his people are special. The gods have sent them to us and I expect you to protect him with your life, do I make myself clear?' he demanded.

'Yes Your Majesty,' Keo responded without hesitation.

They rushed through the compound stopping only to grab robes to dress. As they moved fast, they passed a number of servants and guards lying dead. Sri saw Charya was among them. Sri looked at the dead servant feeling an immense sense of loss, he had been with him since a boy. Luke glanced to his left and saw more of the elite guards fighting the black assassins, Keo gestured to his men and more guards came to protect the prince. They passed the pagoda and headed towards the stables and towards the exit. Prince Sri looked over the lake where he saw the blood-stained bodies of his closest friends lying motionless. His feelings erupted and he punched a nearby building. The prince stopped for a moment and grabbed his bow, he crouched down and shot an arrow expertly into an assassin scaling the pagoda and watched as the man fell into the lake.

Keo pulled Sri up, he had to force the prince out of the compound. A number of men had to fight him from going back in.

'You have to leave,' Keo insisted.

Sri was guided past the elephants who were screaming in distress. Luke noticed they had arrows embedded into their thick hides and he could see their screams of suffering, which made him recall with horror. Yet more soldiers joined to protect the prince and they finally reached the stables where horses had been readied.

Keo handed Luke the reins to a horse and tried to force him up.

'I can't ride,' he shouted in panic. Keo looked at him amazed along with the guards protecting him.

In the commotion, Sri yelled, 'No time to discuss that now.' Sri hoisted himself onto a horse and rode over to Luke. He gestured at Keo who lifted Luke onto the Prince's horse. Luke was placed in front of Sri who held him tightly from behind. About ten of the royal guards mounted horses and surrounded the prince in a protective formation.

Keo came close and reached out for the prince's hand and they gripped each other's wrists. He bowed his head and said, 'We'll take care of the rest of these scum. Get back to the city, there could be further attacks and your father will want to know you're safe.'

He paused and looked around, 'My men will look after you, ride now and stop for nothing.'

He slapped the prince's horse which reared into the air and the protective formation began to gallop.

Luke looked over his shoulder, he could see the remaining guards re-entering the compound as smoke rose from the burning pagoda. Sri gripped onto Luke tightly and road furiously towards Angkor.

What's going to happen to us,? Luke's mind raged, *Will Sri understand, will he ever trust me again?*

CHAPTER TWELVE

Re-Group

Marcus entered the Queen's residence with Princess Bopha and Maya rushed over to him. She embraced him and he could see in her face she was concerned. The Queen called the Princess over to her leaving them both surrounded by guards.

'What's going on?' Marcus mouthed to her.

'I don't know,' she whispered back. 'There's been a lot of commotion since the queen and I returned. Her private guards have been watching me closely, I don't like this Marcus I don't like it one bit. Do you know where Luke is?'

'No, I left him back at the hut when I went to the temple with Bo,' he said concerned. 'All I know is he was meeting Prince Srindra.'

They both looked over at the queen who had now been joined by her youngest son Prince Virak. The queen had her back to them and was looking down at a map on the table, she was surrounded by her advisors and was in deep conversation.

Maya whispered desperately, 'Do you have any idea what's happening? You must know if anything significant happened around this timeframe, it's your profession after all.'

'It's not that easy,' he sighed. 'There's very little known about this period in history, there are basic lineages of the monarchs but not much detail except for the carvings on the walls and a few records kept by travellers. It's reported that there was a lot of conflict between the Khmers and the Chams around this time. It resulted in a lot of fighting which I've studied on the carvings.'

'Bring them here,' the queen ordered to her guards. Maya and Marcus were pushed forward.

'Who are you people?' she said looking at them closely.

'We've already told you Your Majesty,' Marcus responded in a calm tone glancing at the princess.

'I don't believe you, either of you,' the queen said calmly and coldly. 'Since you've arrived strange things have happened, that light in the sky, the miracle healing and now one of our main water aqueducts to the city has run dry. You were interested in our water systems were you not?'

The queen didn't wait for a response. 'When I look at you, your clothing, your manicured skin and the way you speak our language, how can I believe you are here as traders with no goods to sell.'

She paused for a moment and looked directly at her daughter scowling, Bo had already tried to plead their case, the Queen turned back to them.

'It's clear you've bewitched two of my children, which only makes me more concerned about your motives.'

'Don't be foolish Mother, how can you think that?' Bo interrupted.

'How can I think that?' the Queen said exasperated. 'Look at you, you're infatuated with the man. My dear you've not shown interest in finding a partner for years and now I see you swoon every time you're with him.'

The princess looked away only confirming the queen's suspicions.

A guard suddenly burst into the room.

'Your Majesty,' he shouted breathlessly. 'As requested, my men and I followed the aqueduct trying to find the source of the blockage.'

'Tell me what you found,' the queen said impatiently.

'It was sabotage, the Cham have destroyed a part of the Aqueduct, we're under attack.'

***

Sri was still holding Luke tightly as they rode rapidly through the forest flanked by his protection. They descended down the hill and onto the main road back to Angkor, they picked up pace on the level ground galloping intensely.

'Who are you?' Sri whispered into Luke's ear. 'Some kind of wizard, a celestial being?'

He paused then said quietly, 'A god?'

Luke placed his hand on Sri's arm that was wrapped around his waist. He gripped it tightly, then spoke gently.

'I'm none of those things and I am from Europe. Just like I told you. I can't explain, but we mean you no harm, I promise you that. Please believe me.'

'I do Luke, but I need more, what was that thing that came out of your hand,' he whispered.

'It's just a tool Sri, it's something you may not have seen before, we kept it secret so as not to scare anyone.'

'Do you mean the others have this tool?'

'Umm yes,' Luke responded. realising he shouldn't have said anything.

'What does it do? Why is it in you and how does it display things? Sri demanded. 'Is it magic?'

'It's not magic and it's hard to explain, I really shouldn't be talking about it. Please don't make me, at least not here,' he replied desperately clinging onto the horse.

'You're right it can wait, but I need answers,' Sri said dominantly, and all Luke could do was nod.

***

At the palace the Queen walked up to Marcus flanked by her guards, 'you better not have anything to do with this attack,' she declared. 'If I find out you do, you'll wish you had never come to my city. Take them to the cells for interrogation.'

'Wait, Mother you can't, please I know he's not involved and I know he's kind, please don't do this,' the princess pleaded.

'Bo, I must do as the queen asks, please don't get in the middle,' Marcus replied, worried for the princess.

Bo ignored him and ran to him pushing the guards out the way, she grabbed his head looking him straight in the eyes.

'You don't understand what she means by interrogation, she'll torture you,' she then grabbed Maya's hand. 'She'll torture you both, and when Luke gets here, she will do the same to him.'

Maya took a huge intake of breath and gripped Marcus's shoulder. The tension in the room was reaching breaking point. It was then that another soldier came rushing into the room.

'Your Majesty the guard has been mobilised and the king is ready to see you,' he said.

'I'll be there in a moment, take them,' she ordered her guards.

'Your Majesty there's another matter the General Thorn wanted me to tell you, more Chams have been spotted at the Kar Trasa Doeng retreat. It seems like an organised attack and at present we don't have a lot of details. The General believes it's not a full-scale invasion as our other outposts have not reported attacks.'

She looked at him. 'That's where my son is, Sri was going to Kar Trasa Doeng today, have we heard from him?'

'No Your Majesty,' he bowed, slightly fearful of her reaction.

The queen turned to her daughter. 'How do we know they're not involved Bo. We're under attack, for Buddha's sake I hope your brother is alive.'

Prince Virak interrupted impatiently, 'Mother take them now, why are they still in our presence, let the royal inquisitor get answers out of them.'

The princess put her body in front of them both.

'Don't be foolish Brother.' she looked at the queen. 'We've been under attack many times Mother you know this, the Chams are always trying to get revenge on us, either by trying to assassinate Father or…'

She paused. 'Sri.'

The queen breathed heavily and began to pace.

'How would they know where he was?' she asked herself.

'You know as well as I do there are spies in this city, trust me Mother, these people are special. They had no information where Sri would be and they're not part of any Cham plot,' Bo insisted.

'What makes you so sure Bo, I don't understand why you're being so protective. If you don't tell me I will take them for interrogation. I need to protect the city, to protect our people,' the queen replied sternly.

Bo looked back at Marcus who like Maya was completely terrified by their situation, her eyes darted back to her mother and she took a deep intake of breath. 'They are from the future.'

Maya looked at Marcus whose head dropped in shame. Maya couldn't stop her outburst. 'You told her? What about the consequences you're always going on about? What about the butterfly effect? What about the future? What about my family?'

***

Prince Srindra entered the city at pace, his horse galloped up the main promenade flanked by his protection. He reached the palace stables in no time and jumped off his horse handing a servant the reins. His attention turned to Luke, whom he helped to dismount.

'I need you to follow me, do you understand?' he asked.

Luke nodded. Sri rushed through a side door which led into the palace followed closely by Luke. They raced through a number of rooms until they arrived at the King's chamber. As they entered Luke saw the King sitting in his throne watching. Srindra looked over and saw his mother, sister and brother along with a number of generals and colonels in full discussion which seemed heated. In the corner of the room were Maya and Marcus who seemed to be under guard and petrified.

'Sri,' the queen cried, rushing over to embrace him.

'What happened?' she asked as they broke apart.

'We were attacked by an assassin party, very similar to the one that attacked Father last year, I think they were aiming for me. Samang and Vannak are dead, along with a number of our soldiers.'

'Oh no, Vannak,' the queen responded genuinely upset. 'What am I going to tell his mother?'

'What's going on here?' He looked around, seeing the frightened looks on Maya's and Marcus's faces.

'It's a long story, guards put him with the others,' the queen ordered, pointing at Luke.

Sri put his body in front of the approaching soldiers and drew his sword.

'You will not touch him!' Sri shouted. 'I'd be dead if Luke hadn't saved my life.'

His heart was beating fast.

'They're not who they appear to be,' the Queen said delicately, knowing how her son felt about the man he was protecting.

'I know that Mother.' He looked back at a frightened Luke. 'But I know they're good and I know they mean us no harm.'

'Stop this disobedience all of you, I will ask the questions here!' the king shouted, finally losing his patience. 'Sri I'm happy to see you're safe, General Thorn has informed me that the Cham have either been killed, captured or are in retreat and that's our main priority. The general has initiated an investigation and is seeking out the traitors who told them of your whereabouts.'

The king's tone softened. 'I know you and your sister have vouched for these strangers, but I need to understand what they are doing in our city and the dangers they may pose to our people. Guards, put Luke with the others. Indradevi, join me to question the foreigners.'

The king pointed to the Queen's throne. 'The rest of you may stay and listen to what our visitors have to say but it will be under my discretion. If there are any more outbursts from any of you, I will have you removed from this room. Do I make myself clear?' he demanded.

A chorus of *Yes Your Majesty,* rang out and Sri, knowing he could not disobey his father, stepped aside, letting the guards take Luke.

The queen took her throne and turned to her husband, 'Let me do the questioning my dear.'

'As you wish my love,' he replied, happy to let her cross-examine.

'My daughter tells us you have come from the future,' the queen said.

Luke shot a desperate look at Marcus and Maya, who looked back unable to say anything, their eyes were wide and frightened. Luke turned and saw Sri looking at him with his mouth open, trying to take in what his mother had just said.

The queen continued.

'If it's true, prove it,' she ordered.

All three of them stood in silence not responding, they really didn't know what to say or do.

Sri turned to her.

'They're from the future,' he said astounded.

'That's what your sister claims, although I see little evidence of that, I suspect deception,' she said coldly.

'There's no deception,' Sri said. 'Look at the evidence, we found them in the forest alone with nothing, look at the clothes they were wearing and the way they act, it's clearly nothing we've seen before.'

His Mother looked at him understanding his logic. Sri then walked over to Luke and pulled out his hand.

'And there's this,' he said touching Luke's palm gently, causing the holographic screen to appear in the chamber.

There was a huge gasp from everyone in attendance and whispers of *magic* and *devil worship*. The king jumped but stared intently at Luke who was visibly shaking. The pressure was getting to him and as he stood there the vibrations from the HTC returned to his head, for a moment it looked like he was going to collapse. Maya quickly rushed to his side knocking the prince's hand away and she closed the holographic screen, she caught Luke just before he fell.

'What's that?' the king demanded.

They all stood there in silence with Maya holding Luke closely protecting him just as a mother would.

'I'll not ask again,' the king stated.

Marcus took a deep breath. He didn't know what to say or how to undo the damage. It was then he decided to open up, they had no choice. After all, even if they kept quiet, they would be tortured and none of them could hold out against such pain.

He walked forward putting his hand on Maya's shoulder reassuringly and said, 'Your Majesty, it's true we are from the future. The yellow light you saw two nights ago was a portal from our time. My team and I were studying your culture when one of our colleagues sabotaged our work, this caused an explosion which pulled us into the past. Since the accident, we've been stranded here and are desperate to find and stop Kalani, the man who betrayed us. We need to stop him before he causes any more damage,' Marcus stopped and looked up at the king.

'Study our culture, why?' the queen asked.

'The legacy, buildings, and artistry that the Khmer civilisation left have been a marvel to the world. However little is known about how you lived and worshipped. In the future, different civilisations have learned to live together peacefully. Learning from our history helps our evolution and strengthens our knowledge and understanding of each other,' Marcus responded.

The queen had moved to the edge of her seat.

Now we're getting somewhere she thought.

'When are you from and what do you do there?' she questioned further.

'I'm the lead archaeologist. This is someone who studies the past and Luke is my apprentice. Maya is our lead scientist. She creates advanced technology to help improve our people's advancement and was supported by her apprentice Kalani. It was our work that created a new way to observe the past.'

Marcus paused for a moment, his eyes darting across the room.

'We're from over a thousand years in your future, we really shouldn't be here, it was a huge mistake,' he said and finished by shaking his head.

'Why should you not be here?' the queen pressed.

'Our work was only to observe our history, being here puts that all at risk, we are interfering in the past which could affect our future, and we could change the timeline. Every action we take while being here could affect our future, causing changes in the timeline and creating a different future to the one we've come from.'

He looked at Luke and Maya. 'It was clear we were not ready to use this technology.'

He chose his words carefully. 'When we were pulled into the past we vowed not to interfere in your culture, to go and hide somewhere, but we've all failed miserably at that. I guess it's human nature to interact and we cannot deny who we are.'

Princess Bopha jumped in. 'So that's why you're so interested in our temples and our carvings. It's why you seemed to know so much about our city?'

'Yes Bo, I've been studying the ruins of Angkor since I was a child.'

'Ruins!,' Sri gasped.

Marcus sighed. 'That's my point, many things have happened between now and our time. We can't change that and we shouldn't be sharing any of this.'

The queen addressed Maya. 'You lead this thing called science? I would like to know more. Are there many women leaders where you're from?'

Maya looked at Marcus and spoke hesitantly, 'Yes Your Majesty I lead a number of scientific areas of research. In our time men and women are equal at all levels and everyone has the ability to be whom they want, it doesn't matter around gender, wealth, race, or sexuality.'

'Interesting, very interesting,' she replied. 'I can see your predicament and it's quite a story. I'm still not sure I believe it, but you have given me a lot to think about.'

Suddenly Prince Virak shouted causing them all to jump.

'You believe all this crap Mother? Can't you see they are tricksters here to steal are wealth and secrets? I really can't believe you are all listening to this. Sister, you're a fool, how could you fall for this man.'

He pointed at Marcus.

'As for you Brother, you've always let that,' he pointed at Sri's crotch. 'Make your decisions for you. 'Mother have you gone mad, we should kill them and kill them now.'

Both Princess Bopha and Prince Srindra stepped in front of them.

'I'll kill you Brother, don't think I won't,' Sri spat.

'Stop it now,' the king shouted. 'You're acting like children. You never look at the bigger picture.'

The queen spoke loudly, 'Virak don't be an idiot, have you not seen these strange things with your own eyes. As much as I doubt this situation, I have seen these individuals be kind to our people and respectful of our culture. Sometimes I worry about your judgement, always jumping to violence.'

She turned to Sri.

'I thought better of you, kill your own Brother? You'll need to do much better than that before inheriting the throne,' the Queen said, shaking her head.

'Sri you will take them back to your compound, but I am putting them under my protective guard,' the king ordered. 'Your mother and I will consult our advisors further on this matter, that is my decree.'

'But Father, you can't.'

'Virak you're crossing a line, I will not have you speak to your father like this,' the queen interjected. 'Sri, go now and take them back to your compound. Bo, you can go with them too. Virak, leave our presence now, I'll visit with you later.'

'Wait,' Marcus pleaded to the king. 'I implore you to keep who we are and where we're from a secret, we must protect the future it is of the utmost importance.'

The king sighed. 'Very well, I will limit the knowledge to a few trusted advisors and I declare that anyone who shares this information will face death.'

Sri ushered the foreigners out of the throne room, giving Virak a contemptuous stare. Bo followed her Brother closely and they left flanked by the King's personal guard.

Sri leaned to speak to Luke.

'From the future, I guess there's a lot more I need to know about you,' he said with a smile that calmed Luke's anxiety a little.

Maya turned to Marcus as they walked, she was still gripping Luke closely.

'We're in a right mess, what are we going to do, and what about Kalani he's still out there?' she said exasperated.

'All we can do is trust the people that have been kind to us, I really don't know what other options we have.'

He gave her a strained smile and they left the palace for Prince Srindra's compound.

CHAPTER THIRTEEN

Prince Virakumara

The chamber was dark, it was filled with thick smoke emanating from the burning incense. Only a few candles lit the room causing ominous shadows to form, they reflected off the red and black tapestries hanging from the walls. The intricate tapestries had violent depictions of historic Khmer battles from the ages. Prince Virak was an avid collector of this art and often studied it in detail. The room was full of dark bamboo furniture and in the middle stood a large daybed covered in cushions, which were scattered untidily. Upon the bed lay a woman. She had dark black hair with deep brown cloudy eyes, she was young, around the age of twenty. Unlike most of the people of the region she had a pale complexion, although it was clear she applied chalk paste to enhance her pale skin. She was dressed in black robes and had golden jewellery studded with red rubies. The woman's name was Chantrea Mas, she lay on her front staring at the door smoking a local herb, waiting for her master to return.

The door slammed open and Prince Virak entered in a furious mood.

He looked at the woman lying on the bed and ordered, 'help me out of these clothes.'

'Yes Your Majesty,' she replied, getting up and slowly moving towards him.

'Chantrea, you know what to do,' he ordered.

She started to remove all of his clothing leaving the prince naked, except for his jewellery. She then began to cleanse him, washing every part of the prince's body making sure to do a proper job as he watched on scowling. She dried him delicately and applied sweet smelling oils careful to make sure the prince was fully covered. Chantrea then dressed him in fresh robes, she spent time adjusting them making sure they were hanging correctly. She arranged his jewellery, bringing to the front the large black obsidian stone and adjusted its golden chain, which was studied with rubies. She made sure it was placed prominently on his chest, just as he liked it. Chantrea then rested her hand on the large obsidian stone. She knew how particular Virak was about his jewels and his status.

'Is that better Your Majesty?' she asked carefully.

'Much, I needed to get the stench of my brother away from me, I really can't believe my family, they are so weak,' he said bitterly. 'The way my brother throws his weight around is vile, just because he's the heir. I can't believe my parents stand for it, or let him get away with his perversions.'

Chantrea put her arm around him and guided him to the nearby bed.

'Tell me what happened, what are they going to do with these strangers?' she enquired delicately.

'I don't know, they didn't listen to me as usual,' he replied frustratedly. 'All I know is they are now under the protection of the king. My brother is charged with their guard and they are at his compound, with my sister.'

'What about your plans Your Majesty?' Chantrea asked.

'They will have to wait. These strangers have changed everything.'

He paused for a moment then muttered under his breath, 'From the future, what a load of rubbish.'

Chantrea put her hand on his, she then began to stroke his arm, she knew this calmed him down and made him more pliable.

'Is that what they said, that they're from the future?'

'Yes, and my family believed it. My sister stood up to my mother to defend them, I've not seen her make a stand on anything. She's always been self-centred, she wouldn't marry to strengthen the family, such a selfish woman always putting herself first.'

He got up and started to pace. 'Father lets her get away with anything, I certainly wouldn't if I was king. She'd be married to whomever I decided was best, she'd support the family, no matter the cost.'

He breathed in some of the incense smoke, then took a drag of the herb Chantrea had been smoking, he coughed a little then spoke again.

'And there's my brother, he's always put his personal needs and desires first. He's obsessed with this young stranger and would've done anything for him.' Virak took another drag and turned to Chantrea. 'He even pulled his sword on me.'

She gasped.

'Both of then stood in front of my Father defending these strangers, but what I can't understand is the reaction from Mother, it was like she believed them. I had to listen to the crap these charlatans spoke.'

His temper spiked.

'Can't she see through their deception? Can't she see this is a plot from my brother,' Virak shouted exasperated and collapsed back onto the bed.

'The queen is wise, she's always looked after you Your Majesty,' Chantrea said, trying to calm him.

'I know that,' he spat back at her and pushed her away. She flinched instinctively, 'I don't need you to tell me what my Mother is.'

Virak got up and started to pace around the room again, muttering to himself.

'How did those assassins miss? If only they'd killed him, I would be next in line.'

'You will my lord, it's only a matter of time until your father realises that Prince Srindra is not fit to lead our people.'

'Father's a fool. He dotes on my brother despite the risks his actions bring us. My brother has the army behind him also, it seems that he has all the support. If only the assassination would have worked,' he said again.

'You managed to burn all the correspondence didn't you? General Thorn is searching for traitors and you know how ruthless he is.'

'Yes my lord, it's all gone, nothing can be traced back to us from the Chams. I made sure our correspondence was sent through local dissidents,' she replied making her way to his side.

She pulled his face to hers.

'At least some of his closest allies are dead,' she said, kissing him trying to improve his mood.

The prince kissed her back, then pushed her onto the bed and forcefully climbed on top of her.

'You're right, we have had a small victory,' he declared, pinning her to the bed. 'I will be king one day and you'll be by my side.'

He put his hand on her throat and began to kiss her, he was going to take what he wanted no matter the cost.

***

It had been about two days since Kalani had set up his camp. He had formed a camouflaged projection net using the power from his scanner which created the reflective cover. It was of basic design but based on the camouflage technology he used to create the QCDs. He was desperate not to attract attention, however things had changed and his need for help had become urgent. Since early evening he had begun to vomit and he couldn't stop, he coughed once more noticing blood in his phlegm and spat it onto the jungle floor. Kalani assumed that the water from the lake had caused him to become sick. Although his palm scanner confirmed it was safe, it was the only thing he could think of that could have caused him to become ill. Kalani had become dehydrated and was now frightened to drink, which was making him weak. His anxiety levels were high and he was fearful of his situation.

The sun had just set and there was a bright blue moon in the sky. To Kalani's surprise, he heard noises coming from the jungle and the sounds were close. He stayed deadly quiet listening intently. He could hear shouts from people, the sounds were getting louder. Angry cries seemed to come ever closer. Kalani managed to pull himself up, fearful it was soldiers searching for him, he staggered behind a large banyan tree. He suspected that his camouflage technology would protect him but fear still drove him to hide. Kalani watched as a number of men dressed fully in black rushed past in silence, they were running to the lake. Their faces were covered in black markings and were carrying large swords, he noticed they were very different to the locals he had been observing from the shores of his camp.

He kept still as the men passed, however, he thought he heard one of the men say to another, '*We failed, the prince lives.*'

Which made Kalani shudder, the scientist was out of his depth. History was not his subject. He had no idea what had happened during this timeframe which made him very uneasy.

More loud shouts came and Kalani saw several soldiers pass in a hurry, this time they were dressed in the traditional golden outfits of the Angkor forces. He recognised their uniform straight away as the soldiers were dressed like the men that captured his peers in the clearing. Except these men, were dressed in an orange and golden uniform. Guilt hit him when he thought of his former colleagues, he hoped they were still alive. His feelings of guilt caused a sudden weakness in him and he fell to the floor, as he hit the undergrowth the sound of twigs breaking echoed off the trees.

A soldier stopped and called out, 'Who's there?'

This made Kalani jump but he kept very still and quiet.

'I can hear you, show yourself,' the soldier shouted. He began to approach Kalani's hidden camp.

As the soldier reached the camouflage barrier an electric spark shot out, it caused the man to let out a shriek.

'What the hell, I've been stung!' the soldier yelled.

Kalani had rigged the barrier to emit a low electrical charge which would give anyone who approached a small electric shock.

Soon another soldier approached and received a similar jolt, they both backed off. 'I think there's a nest of wasps here, let's move on. There's no point in getting hurt, the noise must have been an animal. I think I saw those Cham bastards head towards the lake.'

The soldier gestured to the left of Kalani's camp. The men turned and marched towards the lake following the trail of the black assassins who had passed a few minutes before.

Kalani breathed a sigh of relief and pulled himself to his feet.

It's no good he thought. *I'll have to seek help. I need fresh water and some food or I'll end up dead. I'll wait until morning, no point leaving at night and risking meeting the soldiers.*

Kalani them collapsed onto his makeshift bed, desperate to get some rest before setting off to the nearby fishing village.

***

It was pitch dark when the Queen arrived at Prince Virak's compound, she had made the unusual decision to visit her son even though the hour was late. His reactions and behaviour at court had worried her immensely, in particular, his deep dislike of his own brother troubled her immensely. The queen knew of the rivalry between them, that was normal, but the animosity and hatred that seemed to be growing could ruined their dynasty. Indradevi was a smart woman and knew her children's emotions well. Virak's body language all through the meeting worried her, he was hiding something, and she wanted to know what.

When the queen arrived, she took the prince's servants by complete surprise. She entered the compound forcefully, ignoring their pleas to wait. They desperately tried to delay her so they could alert the prince. The queen just continued walking to his private quarters waving them off, she forced the door open and walked straight in. As she entered the room the prince was in the middle of having sex with Chantrea.

'What's the meaning of this disturbance? I'll have your heads,' he shouted and looked around.

He let out a yell when he realised it was his mother. He dragged himself up from the bed, quickly retrieving a robe to cover his modesty.

'Leave us,' the queen ordered Chantrea, who got up from the bed naked and bowed.

She slowly put on her robe and left the room.

'So, this is what you do, whore around with the touched,' the Queen said firmly.

'Mother what's the meaning of this?' Virak asked abruptly.

'I wanted to speak to my son after the fool he made of himself in front of the king,' she said forcefully.

'*I* made a fool of myself?' he said in disbelief. 'It was my siblings who made themselves look foolish, they're putting strangers before our kingdom, those people are a threat to us.'

The queen walked around the room pacing for a moment, this gave her time to choose her words carefully.

'My son you're hot-headed. You don't think things through and jump to conclusions, you seem happy to sentence others to pain and death at ease.'

Her tone took him by surprise, she had never spoken to him like this.

'How can you stand there in front of me and say that your brother and sister acted selfishly, they were trying to save the lives of the strangers.'

She paused, now looking him directly in his eyes. 'You seem to be focused on yourself no matter who gets in the way, do you think our people will respect you for that?'

She stood there in silence, waiting for him to answer.

'All I want,' he stumbled. 'Is for our people to be safe and to prevent any future Cham invasions.'

'Do you really think these foreigners had anything to do with the latest assassination attempt?' she probed.

'Yes, I do,' he replied coldly.

'Then you're either a fool or a liar,' she said vehemently. 'These strangers may not be telling the truth but it's clear to me they have no idea about our politics or our culture. If you would listen and observe more you would know this.'

The prince shuffled uncomfortably.

'I've taught you many things my son and listening was one of the most important lessons. Don't take me for a fool, there was a reason you jumped to the assumption that the foreigners were involved. It was like blaming these strangers was convenient,' she stopped, waiting for an answer and there was another long silence until he responded.

'I could see that my brother and sister had been taken in by them and I was convinced they were up to something. Even if they weren't behind the Cham attack at least we would have gotten answers in the interrogation,' he said uncomfortably.

'Is that so?' the queen replied. 'In my view, this was either you being vindictive to make your siblings suffer, for people they have expressed a fondness for.'

The queen paused.

'Or you had an alternative reason and let me think what that could be,' she said sarcastically, then walked up to him pushing Virak against the wall. 'If I find out you had anything to do with the assassination attempt on your brother today, I will make you suffer a fate worse than death, even if you are my son, is that clear?'

'Why would you think that mother,' he said in surprise.

'The hatred you have for your brother is no secret, I hear things and know of your ambition. Listen to me and listen carefully, your behaviour, your focus on the dark rituals, and your lack of compassion will not be tolerated. You'll respect your father, you'll respect your brother, and you'll work to help our people, or you'll not live very long.'

'What are you saying Mother?'

She ignored him and walked towards the door turning back to look at him one last time, 'I brought you up better than this. If you don't change your ways, I'll ensure you're taken out of the line of succession altogether. One more thing, if I have any further suspicions about your loyalty, I will make sure you're interrogated by my personal inquisitor to find the truth, do I make myself clear?'

'But I haven't don…' the prince tried to say before he was interrupted.

'Do I make myself clear?' The queen repeated.

'Yes Mother,' he said finally.

'Good, I want you to see me tomorrow morning, it's clear you require some further schooling. I expect you at the palace by ten.'

She left the prince's quarters and headed for her horse and the short ride back to the palace. As she walked through the compound, she passed Chantrea and gave her a scornful look. The queen had never liked her, she was the daughter of an old rival and despite the fact that Chantrea's mother had died giving birth, she still carried this bitterness towards her daughter.

Chantrea had been brought up in the royal court but was considered touched. She had suffered from delusions and hallucinations when she was young which the court feared. During her youth Chantrea's speech had also been muddled and her behaviour strange, which only cemented her peculiarity. Many members of the court had shunned her but not Prince Virak, he had a fascination with the woman which only infuriated his mother further.

Chantrea watched the queen leave, quickly returning back to Virak, desperate to hear what had happened. As she entered the room it was clear it had not gone well. He was throwing bowls at the walls and smashing the furniture, he could never control his temper.

'What happened Your Majesty?' she asked carefully.

'My mother seems to know everything, it's like she can read minds,' he said desperately.

Chantrea rushed over trying to calm him down. 'Does she know about us, and what you ordered?'

'No, but she's not stupid, she suspects, and she can see how much I hate my brother. *Argh.*' Virak lifted the bed and threw it.

'Now she wants to tutor me again, she wants me to support him better, I can't do this,' he shouted as his emotions continued to build.

'You must my dear, for your sake and for mine.' She started to stroke his arm again trying to calm him down.'

'Get off of me,' he said angrily, pushing her away. 'Don't you ever tell me what to do.'

He raised his hand and slapped her across the face causing Chantrea to fall to the floor.

She looked up at him with tears rolling down her swollen face and the familiar voices returned.

Kill him, he deserves it, kill him now.

Chantrea managed to shake those thoughts from her mind, she had become well versed at controlling them.

She pulled herself up once again putting her hands around him. 'Calm down, it's okay I'm here. We'll be fine my love and one day you'll get everything you desire.'

Chantrea's words seemed to sink in and Virak fell to the floor with his head in his hands.

She pulled him to her chest and said, 'Patience, your time will come.'

CHAPTER FOURTEEN

The Search

Prince Srindra ordered his personal guard to accompany the king's men, boosting their protection as they walked back to his compound. Everyone walked in silence. Maya, Marcus, and Luke huddled together fearing what would happen to them, after all, they were just academics. They were not leaders, not warriors, and not diplomats. Princess Bopha walked closely behind them, she too was worried about the situation and gave Marcus a strained smile, trying to hide her true concerns.

They arrived back at the compound in the late evening. Although the sky was dark, the bright moon lit their way. There was a freshness to the night. A gentle breeze blew cold air across the lake and bright stars sparkled on the water. The servants had prepared for their arrival with a large fire in the central courtyard, an impressive feast and musical entertainment for them all to enjoy. When they arrived the fire was burning brightly, the flames seemed to move in time with the joyful native music playing in the background. The prince's compound was in a celebratory mood and it was clear from the servants smiling demeanour they had no idea of the events that had just occurred.

The prince quickly summoned his head servant, he told him to dispense with any activities and instructed that only the princess, Marcus, Maya and Luke would dine tonight and no one else was allowed in the compound. Sri called the captain from the king's guards and captain Heng Phon from his own elite force to his side. He instructed the king's men to patrol outside the compound and Captain Phon to patrol the interior. Sri was keen that his own forces guarded him and his companions. He only wanted his trusted men close to protect against Cham assassins or other malcontents. Both the commanders bowed acknowledging his orders and left to take control of their respective units. The rest of them were alone for the first time since the foreigners' true origins were revealed.

Sri sighed heavily, not knowing where to start.

After a short pause he spoke. 'You all need to eat. You must be hungry. It's been a traumatic day and you need to build your strength. We must maintain our wits, there are dangers out there you're not aware of.'

Marcus looked at the prince and nodded, he moved forward hesitantly to eat, and the others followed. In truth, they were famished, they hadn't eaten since breakfast and it was upon seeing the food that they realised how hungry they really were. After they gathered food, Bo gestured for them to sit down under the same Bayan tree that they had on their first night. There was a sombre atmosphere hanging in the air and they all took their seats in silence. Luke sat close to Marcus, he was dreading what was to come and the questions Sri was going to ask. He liked him, more than he had liked anyone else and yet he knew the feelings between them were wrong. A sense of shame hit him, followed by an intense fear as he thought about their situation. Suddenly the vibrations returned to his head. It was like someone was drilling into his skull, the vibrations were much worse this time.

Luke dropped his plate which smashed when it hit the floor. He fell forward and clutched his head with both hands. Sri instinctively rushed over to help.

'What's wrong?' he asked desperately.

'Vibrations, HTC,' he stuttered still gripping his head.

There was a sudden rumble of thunder from above, making everyone look up, yet there were no clouds in the sky.

Maya looked over at Luke, he was now lying on his back, gripping his head and yelling. She rushed over and pushed Sri out of the way, this behaviour was something he was not used to, but he backed off as he was concerned for Luke.

Maya quickly looked around checking it was still the five of them and said, 'I must examine him, he was suffering from temporal tremors when we arrived, but I thought they'd passed.'

Luke gripped her hand tight and managed to force out, 'It'—been—happening—since—we—got—'

He couldn't say any more and pointed to the ground indicating since they arrived

'Why didn't you tell me?'

He again forced the words out.

'It—happens—stressed,' he said breathlessly. Luke looked like he was going to pass out.

Maya turned to Bo and Sri, 'You've both seen this already so please don't be alarmed.'

She activated her palm implant and the holographic screen appeared. Maya clicked a few buttons, and a scan was activated. A red beam enveloped Luke, and after about thirty seconds a holographic image of his brain appeared.

Bo gasped and gripped her brother.

'What is this magic?'

'It's not magic Bo, it's just a tool. Leave Maya so she can work,' Marcus interjected putting his arm around her, trying to calm her down.

Maya continued to review the readings and her expression changed to one of concern.

'Prince Srindra, do you still have my bag in our hut?' she asked.

'Yes, I've ordered my men not to touch anything,' he replied.

'Go and get it, I need to give Luke something for the pain.' Without responding he left at once to retrieve it.

Maya continued to scan and then turned to Marcus. 'I can't determine what's wrong, but the polarised beam seems to have activated a dormant part of his brain.'

She enlarged the scan and showed Marcus the affected area on the left side of Luke's brain.

Marcus studied the readings carefully, 'What does it mean? What does this part of the brain control?'

'The left side of the brain is mainly connected with mathematics, reasoning and scientific understanding.'

Maya paused. She studied the readings once more. 'The left side is also the main part of the brain that is connected to language. It's where our palm readers transmit the language algorithm. That's what helps us assemble words and sentence structures for all the different languages without translation delays.'

Sri came running down the path and handed Maya the bag. She rummaged around and soon found the hyper-spray, she injected Luke and within an instant, he started to regain control. A few moments later he slowly sat up.

'What was that you gave me?' he asked croakily.

'Just a mild sedative to calm your nerves, it seems when you get worked up or stressed it triggers a powerful pulse in your brain causing these tremors.'

Maya pulled up the scan and pointed to the area of concern. 'I don't know exactly what's happening, but there seems to be a synaptic loop which vibrates on a certain wavelength. I'm sure it's linked to the beam that Kalani shot through the vortex, it must be the cause of this temporal tremor. I'll need to keep a close eye on you, we have no knowledge of the potential side effects from time travel, please wear this.'

Maya held up a small round metal pin and placed it at the base of Luke's neck. She pushed it in firmly.

'Ouch,' he said as a spike penetrated his skin.

'Sorry Luke, this will alert me to any changes and it'll record data if another tremor happens again,' Maya replied.

'Your technology is incredible,' Bo said, making them both jump.

'I'm sure your tools would have looked just as incredible to people a thousand years ago,' Marcus replied kindly.

Bo pondered for a moment, reflecting on his comments.

'So, it's really true, you're from the future?' Sri asked.

Luke looked at the ground and responded hesitantly, 'Yes, I'm sorry, you must understand we aren't supposed to be here. I'm not allowed to discuss anything about where we're from.'

He slowly looked up at Sri, 'As much as I may want too.'

Now Luke's seemed to be stable an urgent thought suddenly struck Marcus, he seemed to lose his composure as he realised the situation.

'Prince Srindra, we really need to find Kalani. I'm desperately worried about what he's been up too, he's dangerous. Kalani possesses technology and skills that could be very damaging in the wrong hands.'

Sri replied, 'My men are out searching, he couldn't have gotten far. My men tell me that Major Keo is returning from Kar Trasa Doeng, now he's cleared the area of Cham. I'll put him in command to find this Kalani, trust me, we'll get him.'

'Please just capture him, don't hurt him. He's as frightened as us,' Maya interjected. 'Your Majesty, our scanners may be able to pick up his trail more effectively, please let us help with the search?' she asked.

'Let's eat and get some rest first, I'll consider your request in the morning. I can't do anything until we have light. There's no point searching the jungle at night, it'll only put us in more danger.'

They all reluctantly agreed and they began to eat as silence fell across the group again. When they had eaten enough, Sri suggested they all retire. The three foreigners were then escorted back to their hut by the prince's guards.

***

The sun was slowly rising over the large expanse of water, and the sounds of the birds grew louder, signalling the start of the day. Kalani had not slept well, he woke regularly due to the intense stomach cramps he was experiencing, and he knew he needed help. Kalani eased his body up and shuffled to a nearby tree to steady himself.

It's only a few miles to the nearest village, he thought.

Kalani struggled down the lakeside, stumbling over uprooted trees and boulders stopping often to catch his breath. After what seemed like hours, he came upon a group of villagers who were working on their fishing boat.

They looked at him in surprise and backed away, they had never seen a man who looked like Kalani.

'Who are you?' the lead fisherman shouted, raising his rusty spear.

'Help me,' Kalani pleaded desperately.

He moved forward and the fishermen backed away.

'Help me,' he said again and then collapsed.

***

Marcus, Maya, and Luke didn't get much sleep, they each took turns to rest while one of them kept guard, constantly checking the door and windows. All night they observed the prince's men pacing the compound. Outside their hut stood two soldiers standing guard which only heightened their feelings of being trapped.

Maya reassembled a specialist medical scanner as soon as they got back to the hut. She had initially dismantled it when she saved the mason, conscious of it being discovered. However since Luke's condition worsened, she retrieved it so she could check him regularly. She examined him through the night, Luke's health was her top priority. Maya made a point to scan his readings every hour, constantly checking for any abnormal brain activity, this only made Luke more anxious. Maya was very concerned, after all it was her invention that had created his condition and she felt an immense guilt about the situation they were now in. Her mind was full of remorse. She personally selected Kalani as her apprentice and actively encouraged him to support the new field of Quantology. But it was him that betrayed them and betrayed the future.

Maya completed her latest scan as the dawn light shone through the window. Marcus looked at her, the morning sun sparkled off her black skin and he smiled wearily. Suddenly there was a knock at the door which startled them all. Marcus opened the door and it was Bo with some servants carrying an array of fruits and juices.

'I thought you might like breakfast,' she said as she walked in.

The servants placed the items on the table, bowed to the princess, and promptly left.

Bo turned to face them, 'Sri and I have been talking, we think you're right, we should look for this Kalani. With your technology, he poses a danger to our people.'

She paused, choosing her words carefully. 'We're also worried that if your technology got into the hands of our enemy, it could be devastating for our people. Sri left earlier this morning to explain the situation to the king. Before he departed, he ordered Major Keo to ride ahead to find the forces that he'd already sent out searching. However, Sri needs to seek the king's permission for you to join us, this is now a matter of state security and protecting our kingdom is our highest priority.'

'Thank you Bo,' Marcus said with a relieved smile.

She reached out for his hands, 'I don't know where this leaves us, but you know my feelings.'

Her big eyes looked into his.

Marcus shifted uncomfortably. He had only met this woman a few days ago, but he already had strong feelings for her. Marcus looked around the room and noticed Maya and Luke watching him.

'Bo I don't know either, to be honest, I don't know what any of us are going to do, all I can focus on at the moment is finding Kalani and preventing more damage.'

'I understand,' she said, looking away. 'It's just I've never met anyone who felt the way I do about art and culture. Let alone someone I can connect with.'

'Whatever happens, we'll be friends and we'll explore the cultural things we love, if your father allows that is.' He turned to the others. 'We all need to find a way of living here and at the moment I don't know what that means. There's no way we can return home to our time, we can't recreate the technology that brought us here.'

Maya sighed and spoke, 'Let's just take one step at a time shall we. Come on all of you eat something, I'm keen we're ready to leave with Prince Srindra when he returns.'

The others agreed.

They had just finished breakfast when there was another knock at the door. Bo rushed over to open it, revealing Sri standing before them. He entered, not waiting for an invite and was followed by a stern-looking man around fifty. He was dressed in robes in the same blue colours of the queen's court. Marcus recognised him from the meeting with the king yesterday, he was part of the queen's battalion. The man was in good shape for his age, he was tall and dressed in intricate silver chained armour. It was similar to the golden armour they had seen Prince Srindra wearing when they first met. His silver armour was studded with sapphires which symbolised his rank and allegiance to the queen.

'This is Colonel Piseth Myan, he commands the Queen's Battalion under my mother's orders. I trust him implicitly; he has been my mentor and is one of my mother's most faithful advisors.' Sri cleared his throat. 'The king and queen agreed that we should search for this Kalani. The queen insisted Myan command the mission and the king has ordered we take with us appropriate protection.'

Maya looked at Myan, he had a hardened look on his face like he had been fighting all his life. However, it was clear from his manner that he was suspicious of the foreigners.

Myan stepped forward. 'I don't know you, or trust you, but both Prince Srindra and Princess Bopha have attested to your characters, and I respect their judgment. It's clear that this Kalani presents a threat to our Kingdom and finding him is of the utmost importance.'

He stared at them intently.

'I'm undecided what threat the three of you pose. The queen has asked me to lead this mission and report back to General Thorn, he commands all of the Empire's forces. This mission is now under a complete information blackout. No one outside this room is to know our true plans or where you come from.'

Myan pushed the breakfast plates aside on the table and laid out a detailed map.

'This is where the prince found you,' Myan pointed at the map and got straight to the point. 'The traitor couldn't have gone this way. My men would've found him.'

He gestured towards a garrison marker on the map. 'This way is predominantly marshland, which is very hard to navigate, it's full of dangerous animals. I doubt he would have headed that way, if he did he is likely to be dead. In my view he's headed towards lake Tonlé Sap, probably in this area…'

Myan pointed to the shoreline of the lake.

'There is water and food there and it's where I would've headed. There is one problem, locals have reported sightings of Cham activity, we expect their assassins used the lake to get close to Kar Trasa Doeng disguised as fishermen. I have my men searching the area to hunt down these traitors, that gives us an advantage. They have been instructed to look for signs of this Kalani. This mission will be dangerous and you need to understand the threat. But, your technology could be helpful in tracking down the fugitive faster.'

The colonel turned to the prince. 'As you know Your Majesty, I've expressed my concerns about putting you in more danger. Nevertheless, the king supports your choice to join the search and of course I will respect his orders.'

He turned to Bo. 'Princess you'll stay here, protected by my men.'

'I will not, I'm coming with you' Bo replied firmly.

Myan sighed, 'I cannot risk taking you, I don't know what dangers are still out there.

'I'm not staying here. I want to accompany Marcus and be of help.'

'This is not up for debate. Your father has declared you will stay behind. No more arguing, it's the king's wish and he will not change his mind.'

'Bo it's not safe, I need you to stay here,' Sri interrupted before she could speak. 'I can't protect you and our friends at the same time, it's too much of a risk. I need you to stay here and be my eyes and ears in court, you know why.'

Bo knew there was no use arguing and remained silent.

'Okay, we set off in an hour. Be ready outside the compound,' Myan ordered. 'I've arranged for a legion of my men to accompany us, there will be no mercy for any traitors we find,' He nodded to the prince and left.

'Bo, I know what you're going to say but there's no way father would let you go.' He then turned to Luke, 'I'm not sure you should go in your condition.'

Maya interjected, 'Luke comes with us. I need him close to me in case of any further tremors.'

'Very well, get ready and I will meet you outside,' Sri left quickly to prepare, followed closely by Bo who continued to protest.

***

The fisherman looked down at the man who had collapsed in front of them, they had never seen someone like this before.

'Devi, what shall we do with him? He looks in a bad way?' another fisherman asked.

'I don't know Sopath, but we can't just leave him here, let's carry him back to the village. Thom will know what to do.'

Devi picked up the strange man placing him over his shoulder and they carried him back to the village, flanked by the other fisherman.

They arrived at the settlement and Sopath rushed to get the village elder Thom. After a few minutes Thom rushed out of his nearby hut.

'Devi, who is this?' he asked.

'I don't know, he came for help and collapsed.'

'He looks very poorly.' Thom turned to a local female villager.

'Please get some boiled water and my special herbs, I'll see what I can do to help him,' Thom instructed. 'Devi, carry him over to the temple and place him on the floor in front of the shrine.'

The woman quickly returned carrying water, a cloth and a basket containing Thom's special herbs.

As he began to examine Kalani, Thom gently poured the water into Kalani's mouth causing him to cough. Kalani's eyes opened and he looked terrified.

'Where am I?' Kalani stuttered.

'It's okay, you're safe, I've seen this disease before, stay still and drink this.'

Thom mixed the herbs into a cup of water and instructed Kalani to drink it. 'Devi, keep an eye on our guest and get some food, Sopath come with me.'

They both moved away from Kalani so he couldn't hear them. 'Soldiers from Angkor were here earlier looking for Cham assassins. This man doesn't look like one of them but they need to know we've found a stranger. Go find some of the soldiers and bring them back. I'll make sure we hold him here until they return.'

Sopath nodded, he picked up his spear and a bag with some supplies. He asked a few of the villagers in which direction the soldiers went and then left.

Thom quickly returned to care for the stranger, who's fever had caused him to pass out once more.

CHAPTER FIFTEEN

Found

Bo led Marcus, Maya and Luke out of the prince's compound an hour later. As they walked, Luke noticed the early morning mist rising slowly off the decorative ponds. The ponds were connected by several carefully designed channels, which meant there was always flowing water. For some reason, the sound of the water seemed to calm his nerves. The group passed the intricately designed gates at the front of the compound and arrived at a formal parade ground. They were met by an amazing sight which only increased Luke's anxiety further.

Five hundred soldiers stood before them dressed in decorative blue robes, their silver armour sparkling like diamonds in the sunlight. The men carried long silver spears and each of the infantry had a bow and quiver secured tightly to their backs. Supporting the troops were about fifty cavalry, the soldiers on horseback wore the same bright silver armour, although they had two sapphires embedded in their chest plates. In addition to the cavalry, ten war elephants stood before the group.

Marcus had seen carvings of elephants like this, however he never expected to see it in real life, he stared at one elephant, noticing its regal stance. The animal was adorned with elaborate silver armour which stretched from its head all the way down its trunk. Marcus looked closer and he noticed that the armour had sharp silver spikes ready to strike at the enemy. His eyes moved up the impressive trunk and he was drawn to the centre of the elephant's head. The silver headpiece had a large bright sapphire embossed in the centre which oozed power. Marcus gulped still trying to take in every detail before him, he noticed one final thing. The elephant had bright golden caps which were attached to its tusks, they were about three feet long and were as sharp as the finest swords.

Colonel Myan rode proudly on a white horse. He was an imposing man, he was bald, had bright eyes and a chiselled chin. He had a large build and he road back and forth inspecting the legion barking orders. He was flanked by Prince Srindra who was the only soldier not dressed in blue, he wore his familiar purple robes and golden jewellery that they had all become accustomed too. The prince like the colonel looked immensely powerful.

Maya was also taken aback by the sight in front of her, she noticed that in addition to the soldiers, cavalry and elephants there were a number of supply carts being pulled by larger horses. The carts were laden with food, additional weapons and were protected by archers positioned on top of the wagons. They were painted blue and adorned with silver protective armour and again intricately decorated.

Once the men were readied, they were formed into ranks, Prince Srindra rode over to the commanders, there were five captains each in charge of around a hundred men and one captain in charge of the fifty cavalry. Overseeing the unit was Major Sovann Moat, he was one of ten majors the queen had in her battalion all managed by Myan. Major Moat would command the five hundred and fifty-strong unit including the elephant division. However, on this sensitive mission, the queen had personally asked Colonel Myan to join and be responsible for Prince Srindra, Marcus, Maya, and Luke safety. Myan had gathered his officers together and was deep in conversation when the prince joined him. The officers fell silent and bowed, many of them had known him all their lives and were keen to hear what the prince had to say.

Sri spoke. 'Yesterday I sent five of my elite cavalry units to scout ahead, these were led by five of my most trusted captains, and each of them had orders to focus on different parts of the lake. My men are searching for traitors whether that be Cham invaders or collaborators within our ranks. The queen has ordered that you, her top unit lead the expedition to find a man named Kalani, he is a betrayer of our guests.'

Sri pointed to the three strangers standing with the princess at the edge of the parade ground.

'This is a matter of national security and we must capture this man alive, do I make myself clear?' he ordered.

'Yes sir,' they all responded.

Sri bowed his head to the queen's commanders and rode back to the princess with the colonel following.

He stopped directly in front of them looking down from his horse. 'You three will be travelling on that elephant.'

He pointed to the largest and most elegant elephant. 'This is to be a difficult journey, don't mistake the beast for a comfortable ride, it will be long and hard but we'll find your traitor.'

He turned to his sister, 'Bo, head back to court, go and protect our position.'

His expression softened.

'I need you there, be my eyes and ears,' he said gently.

'Yes Brother,' she said sarcastically and bowed. 'I'll go there directly. My own guards will accompany me, no need for any additional protection.'

She pointed to a few of her men who were waiting by the supply carts.

'May Buddha be with you,' she said, bowing to them. She then walked confidently passed the soldiers on the parade ground and headed out of sight.

Sri turned to Maya. 'Can your technology pick up any trail of this Kalani?'

Maya beckoned Sri and Myan forward and she turned her back from the parade ground so only the five of them could see, she clicked a few buttons on her hand and a small screen appeared. The horses that the prince and Colonel were riding reared and snorted at the sight of this strange image, but they were soon brought back under control.

'The device can only scan a twenty-mile radius, but it is detecting something unusual in that direction,' Maya pointed to the west. 'It's detecting an electronic field of some kind. That can only come from someone who uses our technology, so it must be from Kalani.'

'That's the direction I suggested when we reviewed the map,' Colonel Myan said smugly and turned to Prince Srindra. 'Your Majesty, I'll ready the men.'

He bowed and rode off.

'No time to waste, come let's go,' Sri ordered and led them to the elephant.

A few soldiers helped Marcus, Maya, and Luke onto the large intimidating animal. Once they were secured the rider grabbed the reins of the elephant and on the colonel's order, the battalion moved out, taking the most direct road towards the lake. The parade of soldiers marched through the city with locals cheering them on. The reactions from the people took Maya, Marcus, and Luke by surprise making them smile, it was crazy they were part of anything like this. The queen's battalion marched quickly, they soon reached the edge of the city and onto the main road heading towards lake Tonlé Sap.

Maya breathed the air in deeply and looked over at Luke. 'How are you feeling, any more pains or anxiety?' she asked. She smiled, knowing how ridiculous the question was.

Luke returned the smile and said, 'Nervous, but I'll be okay.'

He paused, trying to pluck up some courage to ask the question that had been bothering him. 'What do you thinks happening to me?'

Maya sighed, she knew he wanted her to give him the answers, but she didn't have them, all she could try to do was reassure him.

'I'm not sure Luke, just try to keep calm. The only theory I have at present is that the tremors could be an echo from the beam that Kalani triggered. It could have created some kind of temporal connection with your brain.' She put her hand on his shoulder and tried to smile reassuringly. 'I'm sure it will fade in time but without my lab equipment it's hard to say.'

'I can see things… things I haven't told you about,' Luke replied hesitantly.

'What do you mean?' Marcus asked, he had been listening carefully to their discussion but couldn't stop himself from interrupting.

'When the vibrations happen, it's like I can see patterns. I recognise some of these patterns as numbers from your calculations,' he paused thinking carefully about how to continue. 'I've not been able to control these numbers or change the pattens, but it feels like our first experiments. You know, when I was able to bend the beams and create the stable portal. I'm not sure what I'm saying, but I can control the calculations and I think I understand the numbers. I think subspace is trying to tell me something.'

Luke froze for a moment. 'I feel that my mind has been freed. It's like a force of some kind is flowing out of me and I think it can be controlled.'

Maya looked at him with concern.

'It could just be the stress of our situation, try and put it to one side for now,' she said, carefully trying to hide her real emotions. 'We've all been through so much and we need to focus on what's ahead.'

'I know, but there something there, I can feel it. However, you're right we must focus on what's ahead,' he replied.

Luke's mind pondered for a moment while Maya and Marcus gave each other a look of concern.

'I'm not sure what I'll do when I see Kalani again,' Luke said darkly.

'I know the feeling,' Marcus replied trying to change the subject. 'Maya what about you? He's caused us all so much damage, but he's betrayed you the most.'

She considered his question carefully before replying.

'I know he has, but I still care for him,' she chose her words carefully sensitive of Luke's state of mind. 'What about his family? Yes he's made mistakes, he's betrayed us, but I can't stop thinking about Lani and Ke'ala.'

She sensed their objections but continued. 'He made a terrible mistake, but I still need to help him if I can.'

Luke looked away staring into the jungle.

'He tried to kill me,' he said in a tone that was calm and matter of fact.

'I know, I know, and he needs to be punished for that. But we can't abandon our beliefs and principles of justice.'

'We're in a dangerous situation. Do you think we can rely on our Khmer friends to apply our sense of morality, or our sense of justice?' Marcus asked.

'I trust Sri,' Luke replied. 'And you're right Maya he needs to go to trial and be judged fairly for his crimes. I'll make a case to Sri and maybe the king or queen can act as arbitrator.'

Luke thought before continuing. 'We must insist on no death penalty for his crimes, even if that is the law here, it's not ours.'

Maya looked directly at Luke and took his hand, 'I think sticking to our values is of the upmost importance despite our situation, let's find him first and we can go from there.'

They all agreed, and they continued their journey to the lake not knowing what they may encounter.

***

The legion had been on the road for a few hours when a warning horn sounded. Tensions began to rise, and several of the infantrymen pulled their bows back ready to fire. Another large horn sounded coming from the road ahead and the atmosphere changed. The soldiers put their weapons down and the group of men riding horses approached fast, they were dressed in Prince Srindra's colours. The prince rode out to meet them, and he embraced the lead rider, Luke could see they were talking but couldn't make out what was being said.

The prince turned and rode back with his captain at his side, and they approached Colonel Myan. Sri gestured for the three of them to join him. They descended the elephant helped down by a few soldiers and headed over.

'Great news, we've found this Kalani, one of the local villages raised concerns about a man they found. Captain Nisey's men are guarding the village, but this Kalani is unwell. They're not sure if he will survive the night, they believe he has water sickness.

Maya took a deep intake of breath, 'Can I see him? Maybe I can help.'

'We'll head there now but remember he's an enemy of the state as far as we're concerned,' Sri replied.

'Let me help him, he hasn't hurt your people, but he does need to pay for his crimes against us,' Maya pleaded.

Sri walked over to her, 'I get it, Maya, let's find him first. It will take us a few hours to get to the village but at least we know where we're heading.'

She nodded acknowledging his comments.

The procession of soldiers made good time arriving in the small fishing village ahead of schedule, just as it was starting to get dark. Maya didn't wait for approval, she jumped down off the elephant as soon as she could and rushed up to Sri. The others followed as quickly as they could.

'Take me to him,' she ordered.

'Who do you think you are?' Colonel Myan stepped in front of the prince.

'It's okay Colonel, they're not used to our ways,' Prince Srindra looked at the colonel trying to explain. 'Maya he's this way, come with me.'

They were led by a frightened village elder into a temple by the lake. As they entered, they saw Kalani unconscious laying on a bed of straw. A fire had been lit and there were a few locals attending to him with herbs, while soldiers dressed in the prince's colours stood guard.

Maya rushed over to him touching his forehead and turned to the prince. 'I need the area cleared, you and Myan can stay but I think it would be best if only a few of us are present, if you know what I mean.'

Maya tapped her hand and the prince picked up on her signal.

'Everyone out now except Luke, Marcus, Maya, and Colonel Myan,' Sri ordered.

The soldiers and locals bowed to him and left the temple without any comment.

Wasting no time at all, Maya pulled the medical scanner she had been carrying and began to assess his condition.

'He's weak, looks like he has typhoid,' she continued to study him.

The prince walked over to Luke and Marcus.

'What's typhoid?' he asked.

Luke spoke quietly knowing he shouldn't explain but he couldn't help himself, 'It's a type of fever that can spread throughout the body, affecting many organs. Without being treated quickly it can be fatal. I'm sure you've seen it before. It's usually spread by bad water. Sometimes the water has nasty things in it which attacks the body. The disease does not exist in our time, we have medicines which cure it and the world's water is continuously monitored. Our governments make sure the water is safe for both humans and nature.'

Maya reached into her bag and pulled out the hyper-spray and clicked a few buttons injecting Kalani. 'This should stabilise him, but I need blankets, food and some sterile water, boiled water will be fine.'

'We have supplies in the wagons,' Colonel Myan replied. 'I think it's best we keep the temple sealed off to just us. I don't want anyone seeing this technology, they won't understand, and it could cause panic.'

He looked at Marcus. 'Come with me, we'll get the supplies.'

Marcus nodded and they left.

Maya continued to scan and treat the unconscious Kalani while Luke looked at him with contempt.

Sri picked up on his attitude and asked, 'What did this man do?'

'He sabotaged our work and caused us to be pulled into the past,' Luke replied coldly.

'Yes, you've mentioned that, but how did he do it and why?' Sri pressed subtly for answers.

'He activated one of our probes to direct a feedback beam into the vortex we created, the beam was directed towards me. Kalani wanted to break our ability to observe the past by killing me.'

Luke turned and looked straight into Sri's eyes with his emotions building. 'I'm the only person who can open these portals at the moment. We developed this technology together and this man was my friend. I ate with his family, we socialised together, we were good friends and yet he tried to kill me.'

'But why would he do this?' Sri asked gently putting a hand on Luke's shoulder noticing his volatile state.

'He claimed that we were messing with history, disrespecting the past and the gods from his culture. But it was he who has affected the past and he who risks the future.'

Frustrated tears started to roll down Luke's cheeks and he turned away from Sri trying to hide his feelings.

Sri just pulled Luke close into his arms to comfort him, he held him tightly not saying another word as Luke's emotions poured out.

***

Myan and Marcus exited the temple and headed directly to a few of the colonel's men.

'Is the area secure Captain Tola?' Myan asked a young strong man to his right.

'Yes sir, the men have taken up defensive positions and we have sent scouts out to search the area, to make sure it's clear of enemies,' Captain Tola replied. 'The light is fading fast so I've arranged for a number of lanterns to be lit around the village.'

'Good thinking Captain, bring the supply carts to me, we need some items?' Myan ordered.

The captain bowed and raced off to carry out his orders. A few minutes later the carts were pulled up outside the temple.

'I need blankets, food and water' Myan demanded from one of his men.

'Yes sir.'

A soldier started to rummage through the supplies, however, he suddenly let out a huge yell and a high-pitched scream came from another. Myan rushed into the cart, he dragged the soldier out of the way and investigated. Myan soon realised what the issue was, he pulled Princess Bopha out of the cart, she had been hiding underneath a pile of blankets.

'Your Majesty, what in Buddha's name are you doing here?' he asked, exasperated. 'The king and queen will be worried sick and they'll have my head for this.'

'I had to come,' she said getting out of the cart and brushing herself down.

She moved to Marcus and hugged him. 'I couldn't stay, I needed to know what was going on and I didn't want to leave my brother or Marcus.'

Myan threw his hands up in the air and frustratedly muttered under his breath.

'Captain Tola,' he then shouted.

The commander rushed over to him, 'Yes sir?'

'I need you to ride back to the city and inform the king that the princess is with us, they'll be extremely worried by now and will have sent out search parties. She'll need to stay with us for now as it's not safe to send her back, especially at night. You know this road well, so get back to the city quickly, take five of your best men with you and stop for nothing, that's an order.'

'Yes sir,' the captain looked at the princess and Marcus was sure he picked up a sense of contempt in the captain's eyes. However Tola bowed to them both and rushed off.

'I want to see this Kalani, take me to him,' the princess ordered the Colonel.

'As you wish,' he responded frustratedly and led them both back to the temple with the supplies in hand.

'Why did you come? It's far too dangerous for you out here and your father will be furious,' Marcus asked her as they walked back.

'I had to come,' she looked around making sure no one could hear. 'There are traitors here, someone betrayed my brother and I need to be here to help protect him. He trusts people far too much.'

They entered the temple and Bo saw Maya still tending to Kalani.

'Will he be okay?' she asked abruptly.

It made them all jump, Sri turned around and saw Bo. He was furious.

'What's she doing here?' he shouted at Myan.

'She hid in the supply cart Your Majesty,' he replied, irritated. 'I've had to send Captain Tola and five of our best riders back to advise the king, he'll be going crazy.'

'What the hell do you think you're doing?' Sri turned on Bo. 'You've put our men in danger and put our position at risk from our enemies, you have no right to be here?'

'I have every right,' she shouted back. 'I want to protect our people and our…'

'Quiet all of you, I need to concentrate,' Maya shouted back at them. 'I don't care why you're here, but I am trying to save this man, I need to focus.'

Silence fell on the temple as Maya activated her palm reader again. 'His temperature is too high and his blood pressure has dropped. Oh no.'

At that moment Kalani began to go into cardiac arrest and his body began to fit.

'Luke, come here and hold him steady,' Maya ordered.

He instinctively rushed over to help her, Luke held Kalani down looking straight into his rolling eyes until his body went limp, Luke started to feel desperately sorry for the man in front of him.

Maya fumbled through her bag and pulled out two small metal strips, she forced Kalani's shirt open and place them on his heart.

'Clear,' she shouted, and Luke let go of him and an electric pulse shook his body.

A gasp came from the room, however no signs of life from Kalani.

'Clear' Maya shouted again, and a pulse shot through his body while Maya looked at the screen in front of her.

'I have a heartbeat,' she said with a smile.

Luke let out a sigh of relief and Kalani suddenly released a moan. Maya tapped the hyper-spray and injected him with some more antibiotics and a sedative.

She pulled herself to her feet and turned to the others. 'He needs rest, I can't risk moving him yet. We'll need to stay here tonight.'

'We can't move anywhere until the morning anyway,' Myan replied. 'The road's not safe at night, and I want to make sure we have the daylight to take the prince and princess back to the city.'

Myan let out a relieved sigh. 'My men have secured the area so we should be safe for now.'

Maya turned to Marcus. 'Can you sit with Kalani? I need some air.'

He nodded and she left the room.

Bo followed her wanting to understand more, they walked to the village centre where a number of soldiers stood chatting and drinking at the village well.

'How did you do that?' she couldn't help but ask Maya.

'Keep it down, we need to keep this between us, no one else can know about our technology.' Bo nodded in agreement. 'It's just tools, something we have developed over time, it's not magic.'

‘So you keep saying Maya, but it’s incredible to see,’ she said, picking up two cups and filling them with water from a barrel.

Bo gripped Maya’s hand and said, ‘You’re an amazing healer.’

Maya took a sip of water and looked into the jungle trying to ignore the comment. As she stared something caught her eye in the fading night light, a reflection caused by one of the lanterns.

Maya’s eyes adjusted and she asked, ‘Bo who’s over there? It looks like one of your soldiers and some strange people.’

Bo turned around and looked at the men in the undergrowth, she recognised the soldier, it was Captain Tola. Myan had sent him back to the city, she then looked at the other men. They were dressed in black with black war makeup and running toward them. She screamed.

The sound startled everyone and the queen’s soldiers started to fall. Maya pulled Bo to the ground and they both cowered behind the well. Myan rushed out of the temple, drawing his sword and instantly cutting down one of the men in black. Sri followed him and managed to get to Maya and Bo just in time. He drew his sword and began to fight another black-clad assassin who had been charging toward the princess.

‘Run’ he shouted at them.

Bo took Maya’s hand, and they ran back to Luke and Marcus who had exited the temple, they were both sheltering behind a supply cart.

The queen's battalion began to battle the attackers and a number of soldiers joined Myan. The struggle was fierce. The men of the queen's battalion fell as the Cham continually fired arrows from the trees. It was at that moment fifty of the prince's elite guard rode into the village with their purple robes flowing behind them. They fired volleys of arrows into the trees and enemy snipers began to fall to the ground. This distraction gave the queen's cavalry a chance to regroup and they charged at the attacking assassins cutting them down and clearing a path. Myan took this opportunity and signalled his infantry to follow him, he was going after Captain Tola. Myan saw Tola strike down one of his own men, it was clear Tola had betrayed him, and his oath to the queen. Myan was enraged that his apprentice was fighting on the side of the attackers.

With the support of the prince's men Myan skilfully fought his opponents, cutting down man after man until he reached Captain Tola. They were now fighting face to face and Myan's swordsman skills were clearly overwhelming the young captain in front of him. Eventually, Tola's sword was knocked from his hand hitting the stone floor with a clatter. Myan gripped the captain's neck and pushed him against a nearby tree, his face red and full with fury.

'Why have you betrayed us?' he demanded, holding his sword ready to strike his own apprentice.

'I serve another who respects the old ways, no more weakness from the old foolish king and his feeble family,' Captain Tola spat back and reached for a dagger in his belt.

However, Myan was too quick for him and plunged his sword deep into his former mentee's chest and the traitor fell to the floor dead.

Sri and the rest of the colonel's men had dispatched most of the attackers. As Sri looked around he thought to himself, *there's so few Cham assassins, the attack was always going to fail against a defending force this big. So why did they attack?*

Sri paused for a moment trying to think, then it came to him. It must have been a suicide attack with the aim to kill himself, the princess and as many of the queen's commanders as possible. Thankfully Bo had alerted them to the danger.

Bo Sri's mind suddenly screamed, followed by *Luke*. He ran back to the village searching for them frantically.

A few moments later he located them sheltering behind the overturned cart, he let out a sigh of relief seeing them safe. As he passed the village centre something caught his eye, it caused him to scan the surrounding trees. He soon saw what it was, a black assassin holding a bow high up in a tree about to release an arrow.

'No!' he yelled, alerting the others to the danger.

Maya looked up seeing the man who had just fired an arrow towards them, she could see where it was heading. As if in slow motion the arrow was cutting through the air toward the princess. Without a second thought she threw herself in front of Bo. The arrow hit

Maya's chest with a disturbing *thud* and she let out a horrifying cry.

Sri picked up a nearby spear which was laying on the ground and threw it at the archer, it hit him directly in the chest and the assassins twitching body fell from the tree. Sri turned back to the others and Bo was screaming, Marcus was frantically scanning Maya for any signs of life. He rushed over to them, followed by the colonel and a few of his men. They stopped in their tracks as they saw the arrow sticking out from Maya's heart.

Marcus broke down, clutching his friend in his arms.

Luke pulled at him. 'Help her, there must be something you can do.'

Marcus held her tightly in his arms, finally through a mass of tears he said, 'She's dead, there's nothing we can do, not here, not anywhere.'

CHAPTER SIXTEEN

The Queen's Battalion

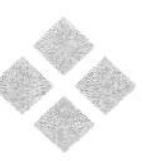

The next few hours were a blur, Colonel Myan took control of the village. He swept it for attackers with some trusted men, while being cautious about others within his unit. After all, it had been his apprentice who had betrayed him, something he now had in common with the late Maya. Prince Srindra's elite scouts continued to arrive at the village. The prince instructed Captain Nisey and his fifty skilled men to take over the protection of Princess Bopha, Luke, Marcus, and the unconscious Kalani. Sri trusted none of the colonel's men, he insisted that only his forces were to be allowed into the village temple.

The princess had been inconsolable since Maya's death. Maya had sacrificed herself to save her, and that guilt laid heavily on her heart. In the commotion after Maya was killed, Sri managed to force them all back into the temple with the help of Captain Nisey. One of the captain's men carried Maya's body back with them. Marcus covered her in a blue sheet that he'd ripped from the overturned cart and then sat in silence. The prince ordered his men to block the entrance to the temple and protect the princess, Luke, Marcus and Kalani at all costs. He made it extremely clear that if anyone entered the temple including the colonel's men, they were to be eliminated. Sri ordered his elite guard not to yield their protective position to anyone but him, and only if he gave them the right password. This was a precautionary measure in case he was captured. If he gave the wrong password, it would alert his men that danger was present. Once Sri had given his orders, he hugged his sister and then turned to the grief-stricken Marcus and Luke.

'I'll get revenge for this betrayal, you have my word,' Sri said sympathetically.

He reached out to Luke gripping his hand and then left quickly to join the waiting colonel.

The prince walked to the centre of the village and saw scenes of chaos, dead soldiers and civilians were scattered around the tiny settlement. The colonel had ordered that the dead attackers be piled up at the edge of the village and their bodies burnt. He noticed Myan dispatching any surviving assassins, his men threw their discarded bodies onto the now burning pyre. When the colonel was sure the village was clear of enemies his attention turned to the dead body of Captain Tola. He took great pleasure in stripping the queens armour and uniform from the dead man. Myan then dragged the traitorous captain's limp corpse across the ground throwing him onto the burning heap of attackers.

Sri on the other hand was searching for survivors from their forces, he found several injured soldiers from his elite guard and the queen's battalion. They were being cared for by some of the locals. It was at that moment a village elder approached the prince and bowed.

'Your Majesty, my name is Thom and I speak for the village, we'll do everything we can to help your soldiers. They protected us without hesitation when the fighting began and we're eternally grateful.'

'You're welcome, I'm just sorry we couldn't save more of your people,' Sri replied sombrely. 'Thank you for protecting my family and serving the empire, your support to us will not be forgotten. There's more work for me to do, any help you can give to our wounded is much appreciated. However, please tell your people to stay clear of the temple until I declare it's safe to enter. The discovery of a traitor in our forces has hit me hard. I've instructed my men to protect the temple and the princess at any cost. If anyone decides to disobey my orders, I guarantee they'll not survive. Do I make myself clear?'

'Yes Your Majesty,' he responded without hesitation and bowed.

Sri nodded back and then walked towards the shores of the lake, he smiled upon seeing his friend Captain Oudom Voan. Voan had been one of the first men to join the prince's elite guard when Sri created it on his eighteenth birthday, and he trusted Voan implicitly. Voan had dark hazelnut skin, which complemented his large dark brown eyes. Voan's most striking feature was his huge smile, which showed off his sparkling white teeth. Voan was known for his humour and was seen as the life of the party, but he was also a ferocious warrior feared by many. What made Voan stand out to the prince, was his exceptional leadership, his men were fiercely loyal and would follow him into fire.

Sri had sent him to scout the western coastline of Tonlé Sap, during this mission, Voan captured an assassin trying to escape after the attack at Kar Trasa Doeng. He interrogated the man and forcefully extracted the planned attack on the village. The captain raced back as quickly as he could. It was his men that arrived just in time to clear the enemy snipers from the trees. During the chaos after the battle, Voan was ordered by the colonel to bury the dead Angkor soldiers. It was a sombre task, but he made sure the soldiers were given a respectful burial.

The prince approached his friend, Voan and his men were still digging makeshift graves in a secluded piece of land by the edge of the lake. The prince watched, not saying a word as his men lay their fallen comrades' bodies gently to their final resting place. The dead were covered in earth followed by a few stones to mark where they lay. A sense of huge sorrow and responsibility hit him, Sri knew this was the price he had to pay to protect his people.

When the time was right the prince coughed, surprising Voan and his men. Sri walked up and embraced Voan like a brother.

'Glad to see you're still alive Your Majesty,' Voan said with a grin.

'I'm going nowhere, despite what my enemies keep trying to do,' he replied smiling. 'What's the strength of our forces and who's able to fight should there be another attack?'

'It's still sketchy but so far I know that the queen's infantry has a hundred and forty dead, including Major Moat. They also have seventy injured which leaves under three hundred fit for battle, but they're badly shaken. The queen's cavalry is still hunting down any attackers, but their position is better. I know ten are dead and that includes Captain Tola. However, five men are missing, they're the riders who went with him back to the city to advise the king about the princess. The ten elephants are fine, it looks like the scum were too cowardly to go near them although we lost two riders to arrows. As for our men, of the five search parties we sent out, four of them have made it to the village. I know we've lost thirteen riders so far including Captain Chhay, it was his riders the Cham attacked first, but he and his men rushed to protect the princess.'

Sri let out a sad sigh. 'Chhay is dead.'

Voan nodded and put his hand on the prince's shoulder.

'I'm afraid so, his men fought with honour,' Voan replied. 'Nisey's men are all accounted for and are guarding the temple on your orders. Major Keo and his men arrived after the battle. The colonel instructed him to take over interrogating the remaining captains in the queen's battalion. Captain Khean's men have not yet returned. Keo said he couldn't find them.'

Suddenly there was a sound of hoofs galloping and they both turned round, Myan had found his horse and was riding over to them.

'It's essential I find out what happened to those five men I sent with Tola,' Myan said forcefully. 'I need to know if they're dead or were part of the betrayal. I must know how far this goes within my forces.'

'I understand your concerns Colonel, I fear for my mother's safety. Voan, his men and I will join you in your search. I also have a scout party missing which I'd like to find. Colonel you can choose fifteen of your cavalry to join us, that's if you still trust any of them.'

Myan was about to speak but Sri held his hand up, 'While we're gone, Captain Nisey and his men will guard the temple with strict orders to kill anyone who enters. Major Keo will lead the remaining Queens Battalion, with Moat dead and the betrayal of Tola we need to be sure about the loyalty of your remaining commanders. Do I make myself clear?'

'Yes Your Majesty,' he responded frustratedly.

'Come, select your riders and let's search for the missing men,' the prince ordered.

Myan nodded and left to select his most trusted remaining cavalry.

A few of Voan's men brought over horses for the captain and prince. Voan blew his horn and mounted his horse, it took a few minutes for his unit to mobilise, and they were ready to move out. Myan rode to join them with his chosen men. It had been a long night of fighting, betrayal, and death. As the dawn began to break the sky glowed an ominous red.

Prince Srindra took a deep breath and raised his sword and shouted, 'Ride with me, ride to find the traitors of our people and ride for the glory of the empire.'

***

Captain Nisey had barricaded the entrance to the temple, he placed his men in strategic positions around the room covering any potential weak points.

Nisey turned to the frightened inhabitants and said, 'Listen to me and listen good, you'll follow every order I say without question, my men and I will protect you until the last man, do you understand?'

They all nodded, tears were still streaming down Bo's face, she reached out to Marcus who grabbed her hand. Her large eyes looked into his, Marcus was no longer crying but his deep sense of loss consumed him. Marcus couldn't help but pull the sobbing Princess close to him, trying to comfort her, but this only made her cry harder.

Luke sat alone in his thoughts. His eyes lingered on the dead body of Maya. It was still covered by the blue sheet Marcus had placed over her. Luke was in shock and his mind raged with anger. He couldn't think clearly and his thoughts were clouded in darkness.

This triggered his temper to rise and his mind exploded.

How could this happen, what about Maya's husband, what about her son?

The vibrations in his brain returned, Luke instinctively clutched his head as the others looked up.

Maya's not here, who can help me with this now and how can I stop it, Luke stumbled forward placing his hands on the temple floor to steady himself.

Suddenly, the temple began to shake.

'It's an earthquake,' one of the guards shouted.

'We remain here at all costs,' Captain Nisey yelled. 'I have my orders, we don't leave.'

Luke hadn't noticed the commotion, his mind was still raging, and his eyes were wide open. Staring at Maya's dead body as the tremors continued to get stronger.

'What's that noise?' a familiar shaky voice shouted behind him.

It was a voice Luke recognised and it broke his focus on Maya's body, he turned around to see Kalani was now awake. The earthquake suddenly stopped to the relief of everyone except Luke, who hadn't noticed it was occurring.

'What's happening? Where am I?' Kalani asked, stumbling to his feet.

He noticed Marcus was clutching a strange woman and gave him a confused look.

Captain Nisey stepped in and pushed Kalani back to the floor. 'You were dying and some kind villagers helped you, they informed us of your presence. Prince Srindra arranged a search party at the request of your friends. Thankfully your colleague Maya helped to treat you, but then our forces were attacked by the Cham.'

'Attacked by who and where's Maya?' he asked shakily, fearful of the powerful man standing over him.

'We were hoping you could tell us who the attackers are, the captain pressed.

'How would I know, I've been hiding in the jungle for the last few days,' he paused, thinking. 'I did see some men dressed in black, they passed my camp muttering something. I'm sure they said, *the mission had failed and the prince lives.* But I didn't know what that meant, I felt so sick and hid until morning, then I sort help.'

There was a moment of silence while everyone digested the words.

Kalani looked around the room and asked again, 'Where's Maya?'

Luke's emotions got the better of him, he rose to his feet and shouted, 'She's dead and it's all your fault.'

He walked over to the sheet on the ground and lifted it, showing Kalani Maya's cold lifeless body.

'She risked everything to save you, she mentored you, always looked out for you, looked out for your family and now look at her.'

He gestured to her lifeless body. 'You did this, you killed her. What are we going to say to Richard and what about Charlie, how are we going to explain how his mother died? Wait we can't, we're stranded here.'

Luke's emotions finally gave way and he burst into tears, slumping to the floor next to Maya. He covered her dead body carefully just as the morning sunlight entered the room.

***

Prince Srindra, Colonel Myan, Captain Voan, and their small force had been riding for about thirty minutes after leaving the village. They had taken the main road back to the capital trying to trace the steps of Captain Tola. A few miles down the road their search party soon found what had happened to the brave riders. They approached a clearing which was at an intersection, there were five paths that led to different towns around the region. The intersection was surrounded by trees and in the middle of the crossroads were the five dead men. They had been killed by the same arrows the Cham used during the attack.

Prince Srindra rode around the intersection constantly looking up at the trees, then at the men lying on the ground.

'They were shot from these trees. Tola must have led them here to be slaughtered.'

Myan jumped off his horse and walked over to one soldier who was face down. He flipped him over and stared deeply into the open eyes of the dead man in front of him.

Myan sighed, he reached out and closed the man's eyes gently. 'This was my brother's son, I encouraged him to join my legion, he was like a son to me.'

He got up and kicked a nearby bush out of frustration. 'These were some of my best men and Tola just led them here to die, what monster would do that?'

'I think we all know that,' Voan said, turning the other men over and checking for signs of life. 'Bourey, arrange the men to dig some graves, let's bury them with respect shall we.'

Voan's soldier nodded, and the men got to work.

The group spent the next hour digging graves and clearing up the area, there were no signs of the dead rider's horses, but the assumption was that the Cham had taken them.

The prince looked around one last time and said, 'Let's get back to the village, I'm keen to get the princess and our visitors back to Angkor as soon as possible.'

Just as they were getting ready to leave, one of the soldiers spotted horses charging toward them and sounded the alarm. Myan and Voan ordered their men to get ready to fight. As the riders came closer, he realised the riders were dressed in golden orange robes, it was men from the king's battalion.

About fifty riders approached at speed and rode straight for the prince and Colonel Myan. The king's battalion was known to be fiercely loyal, many of the men within it had fought with the king during the retaking of Angkor. The king's battalion was like the prince's elite guard made up of faithful men, but much larger and better equipped. Every member of the royal family who was next in line, was allowed to create their own guard at the age of eighteen. Those men and their families serve that royal household, when that heir becomes king, the soldiers could join the new king's inner circle. The existing Kings guard choose to either join the new ruler or go their separate ways, it was a way of creating a bond of brotherhood and trust between the forces. Many of the current king's battalion joined to fight for the king when he was young, however, due to the king's long life many of his ageing soldiers' families had now also joined the king's guard.

Sri rode out to meet the charging riders and as he approached, he realised the importance of their leader. A large man was surrounded by riders, he was dressed in bright orange robes and numerous golden chains all studded with Diamonds. Sri realised it was General Vidyanandana Thorn, or General Thorn as the court called him. Sri had known the general most of his life, he was an exiled prince from Champa and he hated the usurping Cham King Jaya Indravarman, it was he who had slaughtered his family in the succession crisis of 1167. Indravarman put Thorn's family to death so he could take the Champa throne. Loyal servants spirited the boy away and it was the generosity of the Khmer King which had protected him. Thorn joined the king's guard soon rising through the ranks due to his expert military mind. The king valued his strategic thinking more than any other. It was Thorn's audacious plan that retook Angkor back from the Cham and his iron fist that brought the warring factions within the city back together, all pledging loyalty to the king. Thorn was a fierce fiery man who was in his early forties, he was very young to be in charge of the Khmer forces. He had small eyes surrounded by wrinkles and long dark hair which was unkept. The General was a fit and active man and had sole authority over the Khmer army due to the respect the king had for him. Thorn was also Sri's mentor and protector.

'Let me guess, it's the princess,' Sri said as they all came to a stop.

'How did you know Your Majesty?' the general replied angrily. 'Your father has gone crazy. He's been in such a frightful panic since her disappearance and your mother has been inconsolable.'

'We found her hiding in one of our supply carts, she's safe but we were attacked.'

Thorn let out a sigh of relief, 'Thank Buddha.'

'She never thinks things through,' the prince responded. 'However, that can wait for now as I have important news. The queen's battalion and my forces were attacked. We've managed to fight them off, but we lost a number of good men including one of our foreign guests.'

Sri jumped down from his horse and walked over to Thorn, who also dismounted and they embraced like brothers.

'I've made sure the princess is safe, she is under the protection of my men, no one can get to her,' Sri said confidently.

'General I do have important and shocking information,' Myan said joining them. 'We were betrayed by one of my Captains.' He bowed his head in shame. 'After the battle we decided to ride out searching for some of our missing men. I sent them back to inform the king about the princess's whereabouts. Captain Tola led them here where the five riders he commanded were killed by Cham assassins, under his orders.'

General Thorn took in a deep breath and Sri continued, 'It was Tola who betrayed us, his forces tried to kill the princess, the queen's battalion's commanders and myself.'

'That's very concerning, I knew Tola personally and I know his family well,' he replied staring at Myan. There was a natural rivalry between them.

Myan had expected to take over the king's battalion, but it was Thorn the king gave the command to, which surprised everyone.

General Thorn turned back to the prince and continued, 'The empire is on the highest level of alert. All of our units across the empire have been mobilised, we're ready for an attack.'

'That's good news my friend, but there are traitors within our ranks. I don't yet know where they are, or what units they are in, but I know these traitors have leaked privileged information to the Cham. They've threatened both mine and the princess's life,' he said with regret. 'We've finished burying our dead and are planning to return to the village. I'm keen we gather our remaining forces and get back to Angkor by nightfall.'

Sri breathed deeply. 'Can you send some of your fastest riders back to advise the king and queen of the situation?'

'Captain,' Thorn pointed at a splendid rider dressed in golden and orange robes. 'You heard the prince, take your men and ride non-stop.'

The captain bowed and rode to his unit, he communicated the message and they left immediately.

'Your Majesty, my remaining men will join you and with your approval, I'll help Colonel Myan interrogate his unit.'

'I think that's an excellent idea,' Sri responded. 'My men are already interrogating them, but your help is very welcome.'

Happy to support,' Thorn replied looking at Myan who seemed broken by the betrayal of Captain Tola.

'General, I have a further concern, I still have one of my scouting parties missing, I hope they're back at the village when we arrive,' the prince said. 'Come let's go.'

Voan sounded the familiar horn, and the riders formed a line flanking the prince, on Sri's signal they began to charge back to the village.

***

Kalani had plucked up enough courage to walk over to Maya's body, he touched her cold skin and was in disbelief that she was dead. He knelt beside her and gripped her hand. Despite all he had done, he loved this woman, she mentored him, she cared for him and she meant a great deal to his family. Seeing Kalani's reaction, Luke's anger subsided and he realised his feelings were as raw as Kalani's. He could see the impact her death was having on his former colleague and he knelt down beside him. Marcus joined them both and unexpectedly pulled them close.

'We need to look after each other, whatever's happened in the past is now over. Unless we stay together, we'll all end up like Maya,' he pleaded.

Luke looked at Kalani.

Could he ever bring himself to look at his former friend, he thought.

'Marcus I can't trust this man and he needs to take responsibility for his actions.'

'He will Luke, you have my word on that,' Princess Bopha said, joining them all.

Kalani looked up at the beautiful Princess, 'I'll take responsibility for my actions and am ready to be judged, I accept my fate.'

'It'll be a fair trial Kalani, whatever the outcome I'll be there for you, just like Maya was,' Marcus's voice wobbled.

Marcus's kindness was the last straw and Kalani broke down, his emotions erupted and he seemed to melt into a ball on the floor in deep despair while Marcus desperately tried to comfort him. Prince Srindra's elite guard looked on in amazement at the strange behaviour, Khmer men did not behave in such ways.

An hour later there was a knock at the temple door. Prince Srindra gave the appropriate password and entered. He greeted Captain Nisey warmly and then explained the situation. Sri ordered his men to join the interrogation with Colonel Myan and General Thorn. Sri wanted every man interviewed before making the journey back to the city.

Captain Nisey left and Sri turn to Luke, 'So this is the traitor. What do you want me to do with him, after all he tried to kill you?'

'There will be a trial,' Bo interrupted before Luke could answer. 'I've agreed with Marcus it will be a fair trial with no death penalty and Luke has confirmed that is acceptable.'

He glared at her for a moment and then turned back to Luke, 'Is this what you want?'

'Yes Sri,' he replied. 'Our ways are a little different to yours. It was Maya's deepest desire that he face a fair trial and we judge him against our laws, after all, it was us he betrayed.'

'As you wish,' he said turning back to the princess. 'You've caused so much trouble coming with us, I needed you at court to protect our interests. Last night both of us could have been killed. Who would have been left to run the court. Don't answer me, you know this is what he wants?'

He sighed. 'How can I trust you if you won't follow my orders, you're only alive because Maya gave her life for you, Bo you do realise that don't you?'

'Yes I do Sri,' she broke down in tears again as her brother's words hit hard. 'I only wanted to help and protect you.'

'You would've done that better at court and you know it. You wanted to come here to be with him.' He pointed at Marcus. 'Don't lie to me.'

'There's some truth in that,' she replied trying to compose herself. 'But I really did want to help you too.'

Sri approached his sister.

'We're so alike,' he said smiling and gave her a huge hug. 'But we must get back to the city, I'm worried for mother and father.'

Bo nodded and turned to the others.

'Maya will come back with us, she sacrificed herself for my sister and we will mourn her in our own special ways. No one can question your loyalty now.' He turned to Kalani. 'You on the other hand will return to the city in chains, now move.'

Sri instructed them to leave the temple holding a sword behind Kalani. As they exited, he instructed one of his guards to chain the prisoner, Kalani was placed in a transport cart guarded by archers. The others were escorted back to the war elephants where the princess, Marcus and Luke were helped onto a very well-guarded elephant. They took their seats and stared at the soldiers carrying Maya's body carefully to another cart. Bo took both their hands. A deep sense of guilt and sorrow consumed them all and they remained silent.

Prince Srindra walked through the village square to General Thorn who was thoroughly interrogating the remaining captain of the queen's battalion. From his discussions, he hadn't been able to find any further signs of deceit, well for now at least. Thorn signalled to the prince to speak to him privately and they moved out of earshot.

'It's no use doing this here, I need to get back to the city and get my undercover operatives to investigate them all thoroughly, including Myan.'

'Very well General, but I saw how Myan fought he's no traitor,' the prince replied.

'He may want us to think like that, let me worry about the interrogation. I'll launch a full investigation and I will find the truth.' The general turned and looked the prince deep into his eyes. 'The king has specifically asked me to safeguard your right of succession and to protect your legacy. I'm as much your servant as the kings, never forget that.'

Sri reached out and grabbed the general's hand in friendship.

'I think it's about time we move don't you, we've got what we came for and I'm desperate to get back to court,'

'I agree Your Majesty,' and with that, Thorn signalled to the prince's commanders to move out and the horns sounded.

Sri and Thorn mounted their horses and rode to join Myan. Their forces began to move with the prince's purple riders leading the way, the queen's battalion in the middle and the golden riders from the king's battalion guarding the rear.

CHAPTER SEVENTEEN

Forty-Nine Days

The journey back to Angkor was thankfully uneventful. The queen's remaining infantry, cavalry and war elephants including the one carrying the visitors arrived back in the city safely. The troops marched directly to the royal palace at Phimeanakas, where the king and queen waited impatiently for them to arrive

Sri jumped off his horse and greeted his mother warmly.

'Where is she, is she safe?' the queen asked urgently. 'I'm going to kill her.'

'Calm down my love, you know what she's like,' the king responded kindly.

'Bo's safe, she's over there.' Sri pointed to the large elephant just entering the parade ground. 'Before you go to greet her, I need to give you an update.'

He quickly brought them up to speed with the attack. Sri told them of the betrayal from within the queen's battalion and the sacrifice Maya made for Bo. The revelation that Bo had nearly been killed and that Maya had saved her, took the queen by complete surprise.

'It's been an eventful few days,' Sri paused wiping his brow. 'Mother, we need to investigate these traitors in your battalion.'

She nodded a bit shaken by the news.

The prince turned to the king, 'Father, Thorn has agreed to lead the investigation. However I would like representation from the queen's, the princess's, mine, and Virak's forces to take part. I'm worried there's something deeper going on, something that could affect us all. If anyone is betraying us within our inner circle, I want us all to know, do you agree?'

The king gripped Sri's shoulders and smiled widely. 'My son you're becoming more of a leader every day, I agree fully and I will personally oversee the investigation. But it can wait for now, I want to see my daughter.'

The king took the queen's hand and they rushed over to the approaching elephant, flanked by the royal guards.

'Father,' Bo called out as she stepped down running to embrace him.

She turned to the queen, 'I'm so sorry for causing you so much worry.'

Her emotions gave way and she collapsed into their arms.

'I won't say your disobedience is acceptable, but I thank Buddha you're safe,' the queen replied, trying to comfort her only daughter. 'Your brother has told us about the attack and about Maya's death, it's a great loss, she was an exceptional woman.'

'She sacrificed herself for me,' Bo said through tears while her parents consoled her.

Sri rode back to the supply wagons leaving Bo with his parents. He instructed his men to take Kalani to the cells for now, until they could work out what to do with him. He then ordered that Maya's body be taken to the main temple in Angkor to be cleansed. Sri needed to talk to Marcus about how they wished to hold her funeral. When he finished with his men Sri rode over to Luke and Marcus, they seemed lost in the commotion of the parade ground. Sri dismounted his horse and walked over to them. Luke was still dressed in the same purple robes he had been given, while Marcus wore the green colours of the princess. During all the commotion of arriving back at Angkor, Sri had forgotten his responsibility to these men. They both looked broken.

'I know it's been a rough few days but you both need rest. I've instructed my men to take you back to my compound while we work out what to do next,' Sri said kindly. 'I've requested that Maya's body be taken to the main temple at Angkor Wat, we'll hold a formal funeral ceremony in the coming days, if that's what you wish.'

He looked at Marcus.

'I, um.' He paused trying to gather his emotions.

'Yes, I think that's a good idea,' Marcus responded quietly. 'Maya was not a particularly religious person, but she respected people of all faiths, I do appreciate what you're doing Your Majesty.'

'It's my honour Marcus, she saved my sister and protected our people from who knows what.' Sri breathed a sad sigh, 'Come let's go, I know you'll both want to rest, as do I.'

The prince signalled for his guards to join them, he instructed that they be taken back to the guest house.

'I'll join you when I can, I have to brief the king about the attack. It's the second in only a few days and he's put the empire forces on full alert. Remember I'm here for you, no matter what, if you need me send a message with one of my men.'

Luke thanked Sri and the guards escorted them out of the parade ground. The prince then rode back to his father and mother who was still deep in conversation with Bo.

***

'Chantrea!' Virak called out, rushing into his private bed chamber.

'What the hell happened at that village? Can these Cham bastards not do anything right!' he yelled at her.

As usual, the room was filled with smoke and the smell of incense hung heavy in the air. Chantrea was in a daze, she had not long taken a drag from her long pipe, it was filled with the seed of the poppy.

She looked up at him and smiled, 'Your Majesty, would you like some of this to calm your nerves?'

'Give it here,' he snatched the pipe off her.

Virak took a deep drag and collapsed on the bed.

'That's better,' he mumbled. 'What happened in that village? I gave them every chance to kill my brother, plus there was a bonus, my sister was there too. I can't believe Captain Tola failed.'

Virak pondered for a moment, 'I'll miss him though, he's been such a good and loyal friend.'

'He was a great man and he showed me such kindness, our cause will miss him. However, I have taken precautions Your Majesty,' Chantrea said in a calm tone. 'The captain was spotted visiting our compound despite our best efforts.'

'What have you done?' Virak asked urgently.

Chantrea smiled at him and gently took his hand, 'Tola was one of the captains who escorted your mother here the other night. This morning I heard two of your men discussing how they had seen him in your chambers before. I feared that they would connect you to the traitor.'

Chantrea put her hand on Virak's face and kissed his bottom lip, she then pulled back and said, 'To protect you, my love, let's just say a few of your guards had a little accident.'

She took another drag of the pipe. 'We really need to repair the crumbling walls at the back of the compound, it was such a shock to see the wall collapse on your guards as they patrolled.'

'What are you saying woman?' the prince shouted in frustration.

'I've sent your condolences to the families of the men who perished. The accident was such a shock, what a horrible sight for me to witness. How will I ever get that image out of my mind,' she said smiling. 'It was such a coincidence that those were the two men I observed discussing Captain Tola, don't you think?'

Chantrea took another deep drag of the pipe and then put both her hands onto Virak's face. She kissed him, blowing smoke deep into his mouth, they only broke apart when he started to cough.

'I've informed the king about the accident. It was such a nice gesture of him to send you additional funds to repair the compound. I wonder what you could do with that money,' she said, smiling at him once more.

Virak looked at her in amazement. 'Your talents never cease to surprise me.'

He kissed her forcefully pinning her to the bed.

'Let's discuss what to do next, after we've had some fun.'

He kissed her neck tenderly, moving down her body slowly. The smoke-filled room slowly fell into darkness, as the remaining dusky light faded.

***

It was a long hot night and despite their exhaustion, Marcus and Luke couldn't sleep. Sri came to see them late into the evening. He informed them of the plans for Maya's service. The king had granted her the freedom of the city and she was to be given a hero's funeral. He advised them that his servants would dress and ready them for the ceremony in the morning, which only made the situation more finite. Sri left them to their grief and returned to his quarters for the night to rest.

Marcus and Luke didn't get much sleep. As dawn broke they both listened in silence to the bird song which echoed loudly around the compound. Not long after, there was a knock at the door and five servants arrived. They began to clean Marcus and Luke, ensuring that they were prepared properly for the day. Both were dressed in white robes. Marcus knew that colour was symbolic within Buddhist tradition, it was worn by those who were directly related to the person who had died. Wearing white was a sign of respect, something they both felt deeply for Maya. The servants took particular care in dressing them and made sure they wore respectful jewellery. Albeit Sri had insisted that Luke still wore the purple amethyst he had given him. Marcus was presented a large green emerald the princess had gifted him in honour of Maya.

Just as they were dressed, there was a knock at the door and it was Sri. He walked in clothed in his striking purple robes along with his finest golden Jewellery, including the golden lotus leaf crown they had all become so accustomed too.

He smiled kindly and said, 'How are you both feeling? You look shattered.'

'We're bearing up for now, it's a difficult time for us both,' Marcus said and paused. 'We still don't know what you're going to do with us, or with Kalani.'

Sri walked out onto the veranda and gestured for them to follow. He dismissed the servants and sat down by the water's edge looking over the pond.

'I don't know either to be honest, you both have the freedom to go if you wish, we'll not stop you. As for

Kalani that will be determined by the outcome of the trial.' Sri paused choosing his words carefully, 'There's a belief in Buddhism that a person will continue the cycle of birth, life, death and rebirth until they reach nirvana or enlightenment.'

Sri sat thinking for a moment. 'Many Buddhists believe that forty-nine days is the longest length of time that a person's soul can remain in a temporary state. In my culture, the total mourning time often lasts those forty-nine days. My people conduct a prayer for the dead every seven days for seven weeks until the forty-nine days are over. It's my personal belief that those prayers help to support the deceased on their journey into the afterlife.'

Sri paused again, noticing both of them looking at him. 'Here's what I suggest, you need time to mourn Maya and time to think about what to do next. Take the next seven weeks to mourn, go to the temple every day with offerings for Buddha and write prayers every week. After the mourning time is complete, I'm sure your options will become clearer.'

Marcus looked at the prince and said, 'This is not a custom we're used to, but it will allow us some time to mourn and adjust to our new life. What do you think Luke?'

'I'm not sure what to think Marcus. Everything we have ever known is gone and I don't know what we're going to do.' Luke thought for a moment. 'However, some time to reflect would be welcome, but only if you're okay with us remaining here Your Majesty.'

'Of course you can, and Luke you know I want you to stay, as does my sister,' he responded smiling. 'I've told you both before to call me Sri, after all, Maya saved my sister's life and I'm now forever in your debt.'

Sri turned to Luke. 'You know my feelings for you, as does most of the court,' he spoke carefully, trying not to trivialise the situation and turned back to Marcus. 'You'll both always have a place in my court as long as I reign, you have my word.'

As Luke reflected on their situation his mind sparked, 'What about Kalani, when will he face trial?'

'He's done nothing criminal within our kingdom, but he has wronged you, so we will allow you to conduct a trial. My father will oversee events and stand in judgement. However I've declared that the trial can wait, I saw Kalani's reaction to Maya's death. I've permitted him to join you under guard at the funeral to mourn his mentor. After that, he'll be returned to the cells and await trial. The trial will be held after the seven-week mourning period, to give you all time to reflect. He has been stripped of all physical items and any technology we found on him will be returned to you. We have no right to use this equipment, something we'll discuss in more detail at a later date.'

Marcus spoke hesitantly. 'I think sometime for him to reflect is a good thing, but I'll need to deactivate some of the capabilities of his palm implant. I really appreciate you letting him attend the funeral, Maya was of huge importance to him, despite his actions.'

'It seemed the right thing to do,' Sri responded. 'There is one other thing.'

He smiled and went on to say, 'my sister is insisting on seeing you Marcus.'

'We're a right pair,' Marcus replied, looking at Luke. 'We travel back in time over twelve hundred years and we find love…'

He shook his head in disbelief. 'Luke, we're going to have to live our lives the best way we can in this timeframe, let's take the time to mourn and reflect on what to do next.'

Luke nodded his head and turned to Sri, 'Will you show us more of your ways, in particular, more about your religion and how to calm inner thoughts?'

Sri looked at him not sure what Luke's comment was referring to but replied. 'Our monks will be able to help you with the search for inner peace, it will do you both good to reflect. Come, it's time to go, my men are waiting to escort us to the temple to say goodbye to your dear friend.'

Sri got up and began to move, the others followed anxious of the dreaded day that was to come.

***

It was another sunny day, like most days in Angkor. The temperature was warm and humid. The temple at Angkor Wat was looking spectacular. Huge orange and golden flags waved in the wind and the same-coloured banners cascaded down the temple. The beautiful walls adorned with intricate carvings gleamed in the morning sun. The smell of incense was everywhere, and the temple's sacred shrines were surrounded by offerings and candles. At the centre of the temple, Maya's body lay covered in the most spectacular woven blue shroud which depicted the animals of the jungle. The patterns were sewn with silver thread and at the centre of the shroud was the most remarkable woven lotus flower. The queen had instructed her personal seamstresses to work through the night and create something worthy of Maya's sacrifice, to support Maya's journey into her next life.

Sri led Marcus and Luke to the temple. As they entered, they noticed how full it was. The mourners were split distinctively into five different groups, position at the north side of the temple was the king's court. They wore their bright golden and orange robes with their finest gold, diamonds, and amber jewellery. To the west of the temple was the queen's court dressed in beautiful blue robes with their sparkling silver and sapphire jewellery. To the east were Prince Srindra's court, clothed in purple robes with their gold and amethyst jewels glimmering. Finally, to the south were both Prince Virak and Princess Bopha's courts. Virak's court wore black and red robes with golden and ruby jewels. The princess's court wore immaculate green robes and silver jewellery with peridot and aquamarine gems. The sight was something to behold, it was extremely rare that all the courts of Angkor came together. The king insisted that the full court assembled to pay their respects to Maya Evans, the woman who gave her life for the princess and saved his daughter.

Marcus and Luke were overwhelmed by the scenes and sounds as they were led to the centre of the temple. Even through their grief-stricken state, they could see and appreciate the spectacular sight. One of the king's guards brought Kalani up from the cells and he was led to join the others. Kalani was dressed in white just like Marcus and Luke. As he approached, all three of them looked at each other. A sense of deep grief hit them all. The magnitude of the situation in front of them served to intensify their pain. If not for the raw emotions created by the death of their dear friend, Marcus would have been fascinated by the ceremony taking place. Princess Bopha walked from her court's position to join Marcus, she took his hand showing her gratitude and support for him to the crowd. Prince Srindra followed his sister and put his arm around Luke, reaffirming his support for the young frightened man. The sound of a loud bell rang out and the crowd all turned to look at the Body in front of them.

Tamal, the head priest of Angkor and the son of the king and queen stepped forward and began to chant. The crowd joined in with the funeral chanting. It was a humbling sound, full of sorrow. The prayers continued for some time, then a large drum was struck, and the chanting stopped. Tamal gestured for the king to step forward. The king bowed to his son and with the queen on his arm they moved to the centre to speak.

'Welcome, as some of you know our court has had the privilege of being visited by some very special friends from Europe.' He gestured to the three strangers dressed in white. 'These friends helped us repel an invasion from our Cham enemies. In this fight, their, and our, dear friend Maya Evans sacrificed her life to save that of my daughters, Princess Bopha.'

The princess gripped Marcus's hand hard as silent tears fell down her face. 'To sacrifice yourself to save another is the most honourable act a person can give, the Khmer people salute her actions. The queen and I thank Maya for her sacrifice, and we thank her friends for their support. As a people we owe them much gratitude. I now ask them to step forward to say a few words about the brave woman we have lost.'

This took Marcus and Luke by surprise, Marcus looked at his frightened apprentice and squeezed his shoulder reassuringly.

'Leave this to me,' he whispered.

Marcus's experience as a lecturer helped to give him confidence and he stepped forward. He spoke from the heart, 'Maya was an exceptional mind, her abilities have changed the world and inspired many. She lived by the highest standards and always put others first. We've lost a free thinker, a loving and compassionate person, and a true friend to us all. Her family are unable to be here today which only makes me sadder. The Khmer people will be her family today, and together we will all mourn her loss. Maya, you are loved, you are respected, and you will be sorely missed.' In those final words Marcus broke down. Luke and Bo reached out to help him.

Tamal began to chant again, and the crowd joined in. A number of drums and bells sounded. Marcus was given a flaming torch to light the pyre that Maya's body rested on. Luke and Kalani were also given torches and the three of them walked forward together, to light the fire. They looked at each other as one by one they placed their torches onto the wood. Gradually the increasing flames erupted into an intense fire.

They watched her body burn brightly and they let out great sobs of sadness. As the fire continued to burn the mourners left the temple, bowing respectfully as they did. Tamal, Sri, and Bo remained with them for support. They all watched the fire burn for over an hour, until the large pyre had disintegrated into ashes. Maya's remains were then placed into a beautiful golden urn which was adorned with jewels. Tamal had decreed that over the next forty-nine days the urn would remain at the temple. It would stay for mourners to pay their respects to the great Maya and to pray for her rebirth.

***

The next few weeks went quickly. The threat of an imminent Cham invasion seemed to have eased, although the Khmer army was still on the highest level of alert. The king brought together senior investigators to assess members of the court. He gave special powers to General Thorn to examine suspicious behaviour. The king also asked him to personally review all accusations raised about potential Cham collaborators. Thorn to his role seriously and investigated members of the court fiercely, it was causing quite a stir, the court was rattled by the allegations and distrust was rife. The general was ruthless in investigating Captain Tola's friends and family, but it hadn't yielded any further information. Thorn was getting increasingly desperate, often using more forceful methods to find evidence, sometimes overstepping his position. After a particularly difficult day the king had to intervene in an inquisition hearing. A popular member of his own court was on trial due to a financial irregularity, Thorn was trying to use it to force a confession about collusion with the Cham.

The king pulled the general out of the assembly and advised him to regain control. He made it clear the general was to follow due process. He commanded that Thorn seek the queen's council and no longer interrogate the court without evidence of any wrongdoing. The king knew that morale in the city was low and he was becoming fearful of a full-scale revolt by his subjects. The people were afraid and the distrustful environment had the city on edge.

Kalani was returned to his cell after the funeral. He had been patiently waiting out the mourning period until his trial. Kalani had accepted his fate. He knew his actions had caused irreversible damage and would accept any judgement the king decreed. The delay to his trial didn't worry him, it was out of respect for his former mentor and friend, after all, it was his fault that she was dead. From his cell, he could see the great temples of the city and spent much time in deep meditation. When not meditating, he was writing complex equations on the cell walls in chalk, trying to work out a way back home. Marcus was a frequent visitor, on the first visit he reprogrammed

Kalani's palm implant so that only the language translator worked. All other functionality was permanently removed. Marcus made it clear to Kalani that as part of his punishment, he would never be allowed access to any technology from the future. Kalani seemed to accept this and as Marcus's visits continued, they built up a bond, often speaking fondly about the past and about Kalani's family. Marcus took time to understand more about Kalani's concerns which led to his ultimate betrayal. They spoke in length about the morality of Quantology, he was keen to understand all of Kalani's concerns. The discussion about their work helped to bring them closer, which led Marcus to re-evaluate his choices and his own decisions. He went over and over in his mind what he could have done differently, he tortured himself about what he could have done to prevent Kalani from choosing the wrong path.

While Marcus's attention was on Kalani, Luke had taken the time to come to terms with their new life. Sri helped Luke see the possibilities of the life he could now lead and they had become very close. Their connection whatever it was, ran deep.

A month passed since Maya's death and Sri had taught Luke to ride. They would regularly go out together exploring the jungle, forgetting both their worries and to be amongst nature. It seemed yet another thing they had in common. Being in touch with nature seemed to help Luke, it calmed his mind. The vibrations in his head had stopped and he seemed at peace.

Luke's increasing happiness began to cause an inner conflict, he felt so relaxed with Sri, he felt safe, he felt loved and that was something he had never experienced. Yet every day without exception, Luke would visit Maya's ashes at the temple. He would say a prayer for her and pause to remember her family and the life they once shared. Although Luke wasn't as close to Maya as he was to Marcus, he still felt a deep responsibility for her death and he felt guilt about her family's loss. His growing happiness contradicted his feelings and the conflict weighed heavily on his mind.

Sri understood Luke's emotions and did everything he could to support him. He allowed Luke space to process his feelings and gave him time to evaluate what he truly wanted.

It was well known at court that Luke and Sri had become close and it was common knowledge they were in a relationship. Although there were vocal critics, the king had given his full backing to his son and to his relationship.

In the fifth week of mourning Maya's death, Luke seemed to have come to terms with his situation and his attention now turned to Marcus. They had been distant since the funeral, both not knowing what to say to each other. Marcus had shut himself off from the world, only focusing on his visits to Kalani. Luke had become worried, in fact very worried as Marcus had never behaved like this. Marcus also visited Maya's ashes at the temple daily, to say a prayer and reflect. The loss of his friend seemed to dampen his usual infectious zest for life and he appeared to have aged significantly.

Bo was also concerned about Marcus. She tried hard to get him motivated, asking him to visit a new irrigation project commissioned by her father, but he refused. She requested for him to join her to see some new carvings that the skilled stone masons had been working on, but he refused again. He remained at the hut, spending most of his time staring at the lotus flowers in the pond and reflecting.

It was on the sixth week that Bo insisted that Marcus walk with her to see the new carvings, she had to order him to come. Even in his despondent state, he knew he could not refuse an official order from the princess. Bo's private guard accompanied them but kept a respectful distance and she took his hand. They walked from Sri's compound to the Bayon temple.

'Please my love, I know this is hard, but I wanted you to see this,' she sounded incredibly pleased.

They arrived at the temple and the masons were busy working. She led him to the east wall, finally stopping where a mason was carving.

Bo took his arm and they moved forward, 'Look what they've been working on.'

She pointed at the stone images in front of him. It was a scene of the army that marched to the village, the attack of the Chams and then as he looked closer, he could see the image of a woman standing tall protecting a figure on the ground, it was Maya, and she was immortalised in stone.

Marcus reached out and touched the rough surface, it still needed to be finished but he could see the fine image. He looked to the left and he could see the start of another carving, it was showing the army returning to Angkor and Maya's funeral. Marcus's heart pounded fast, and he smiled at Bo, the fact that the Khmer people included Maya's sacrifice in their beautiful work made his heart sing. He continued to study it in amazement when another thought hit him hard.

We're not supposed to interfere, now there are carvings of us on the walls, in one of the greatest temples in history.'

His face dropped.

'What's wrong my love?' Bo asked, noticing this shift.

'This is a most gracious honour Bo, but we can't be on your carvings. We're not supposed to be here and this could affect the future,' he said sadly.

'It's my choice, and my father loves to document our victories. I'm sure it will be fine, there just carvings, no documentation stating who you are and where you're from. Come, walk with me I need to discuss something else.'

'I'd rather head back. I want to visit Kalani and say my prayers for Maya before sunset.'

'Marcus Larsson you will walk with me to the western baray,' she responded curtly.

'I need to tell you something,' she said a little gentler.

They continued to walk for another half an hour still flanked by her private guard, many of the people they passed bowed and they soon arrived at the large viewing platform which looked over the lake.

Marcus took a deep breath. A cool breeze gusted off the water offering relief from yet another stifling day. 'What is it Bo? Why have you brought me here?'

She looked away. Her emotions began to build. Lately, Marcus hadn't shown her the same affection he had when they first met. She was concerned he no longer had feelings for her.

'Before Maya's death we connected like no other, I know you felt it. I have tried to give you some space and to be there for you, but I need to know, do you love me?' she asked.

This question seemed to floor Marcus, he was struggling with the loss of his friend and worried about how he was going to provide for Luke and Kalani.

He paused, 'I care deeply for you Bo, but with Maya's death and all that's happened, I'm not sure what I feel.'

'Marcus, I understand, but you must look after yourself too. Luke and Kalani are worried about you. I am too, I love you, can you not see that?

'Why do you need to know?'

'Maya could see your feelings for me, why can't you say what you feel?' Bo started to cry.

'Why do we need to discuss this now, I need time that's all, please Bo, don't get upset,' he responded gently.

She turned to face him directly with tears rolling down her cheeks. Bo placed her hand on his face and said slowly, 'I'm pregnant.'

'What did you say?'

'I'm pregnant,' she said again and looked away. 'I'm not sure what to do, or who to tell.'

Marcus suddenly realised how he was reacting. He rushed up and held her tightly, 'It's okay Bo, I'm here for you. I love you. I have from the minute we met.'

'What are we going to do?' she asked, looking up at him.

'I don't know, what will the king and queen say?' he asked softly. Marcus was unsure how situations like this were handled in Khmer society.

'I don't know, but nothing will stop me from having my baby,' she looked up at him. '*Our* baby.'

Marcus just stood there, holding Bo tightly, his mind was racing a hundred miles an hour.

'We should tell your brother first, he will offer his support,' Bo nodded and sobbed deeply into his chest. It was as if a huge weight had been lifted from her and she was grateful for Marcus's support.

CHAPTER EIGHTEEN

Trials & Tribulations

It had been fifty days since Maya had passed. The time had come to let her move on to the next life. The king had arranged for an elaborate early morning royal procession, her ashes would be carried on a golden carriage to the great western baray. Marcus had suggested it, thinking it would be a fitting honour to scatter her ashes in one of the greatest man-made engineering projects from the ancient world. That morning Marcus and Luke rose before sunrise, they were met by the king's guard as they left their hut and were led to the parade ground which was situated next to the prince's compound. When they arrived, both Sri and Bo were waiting for them. They bowed to Sri, then they both mounted the horses that had been prepared for them. Sri indicated that the party was ready to set off and they began the short ride to the temple. Angkor Wat gleamed as the sun slowly rose over the magnificent temple with the rays of light illuminating the spires. The scene seemed to calm Marcus, knowing Maya would have loved the picturesque view.

They dismounted their horses as they reached the temple, waiting monks directed them through the corridors to meet the king and queen, who were praying at Maya's shrine.

The king greeted them warmly and said, 'Today we set Maya free, she will travel one last path before taking on a new journey. This journey is for you, her closest friends to say one final farewell. Ride with her and set her free, the queen and I will pray for her here at the temple while you guide her to the next life.'

The king then bowed to them.

'Thank you Your Majesty,' Marcus replied kindly and bowed in return, as he did Kalani entered the shrine.

'Thank you once again for allowing Kalani to join us,' Marcus said, giving Kalani a sympathetic look.

Marcus had spent a lot of time with him since Maya's passing. He understood how lonely and frightened Kalani was. The king agreed that he could accompany Maya on her final journey. Kalani cleared his throat and shuffled uncomfortably, nervous to be in such company. He was dressed like Marcus and Luke in white robes to show their respect for Maya one last time.

'Come, it's a short ride to the western baray, let's say farewell to our dear friend,' Sri declared, breaking the awkward tension.

They were all led out of the temple by Tamal, who carefully carried Maya's ashes. Kalani was guided to a nearby cart, he looked broken, like his soul had been crushed. A guard chained him to a seat while another watched him carefully, they needn't have worried, Kalani would run no more.

Maya's ashes were placed on a bright red and gold carriage, they were surrounded by flowers and offerings that people had left at the temple. Tamal said a prayer and then Sri, Bo, Marcus, and Luke mounted their magnificent horses. They rode to approach the carriage and slowly surrounded it. Leading at the left of the carriage was Marcus followed by Bo, to the right Luke, followed by Sri. The prince gave the signal, and the procession began, it didn't take long before they were riding through the streets of Angkor. The people had gathered early and applauded as they passed. Maya's selfless sacrifice for their princess resonated with the people and many of them wanted to show respect and gratitude. The crowds swelled and the people threw flowers onto the passing carriage. The procession reached the Bayon temple and Prince Srindra noticed Virak watching intently. His brother was standing with that woman Chantrea, he never understood Virak's attraction to her. She was known to be touched and he had no idea why his brother was obsessed with her. Virak stood there coldly, he stared at them as they passed by, not clapping, not offering thanks, he just stared angrily. Sri felt a rage growing inside him and he glared back at his brother, they locked eyes for a moment then Virak turned and walked out of sight.

Within no time at all the procession arrived at the great baray. The entourage dismounted and Maya's ashes were carried to the water's edge. Marcus looked at Bo for reassurance and she smiled back, it was less than a week ago at this very spot he found out she was pregnant. Marcus took her hand and looked into her eyes, they smiled at each other and they walked to join the others. Marcus was nervous about today and nervous about the future. They had decided to wait until after Maya's mourning period was over to tell anyone about Bo's pregnancy. They had no idea how the news would be received and were both fearful of their friends and families' reactions.

Marcus looked around at the picturesque scene and took a deep breath. 'Today we say the final farewell to our dearest friend. Maya, you have inspired many of us and we miss you every day.'

Marcus paused to gather his emotions. 'I hope whatever journey or decisions we take in the future makes you proud.'

Marcus gestured for Luke and Kalani to join him.

'Your passion, commitment and brilliance will be sorely missed.'

All three of them held the urn and they bent down to the water's edge, gently scattering Maya's ashes into the waiting lake. They watched as the water took the ashes far out into the lake. Each of them took a moment to reflect. Marcus's eyes lingered on the floating ashes and tears began to fall.

Goodbye my dear friend, he thought as he felt Bo's hand grip his shoulder.

***

It didn't take long for the procession to return to the city, Kalani was taken back to the cell and the mourners each went their separate ways. Sri had decided to take Luke away from the city for the day, he was keen to distract him from his grief. He was a strong believer of living life to the fullest and was intent on helping Luke to live the same way. During Maya's mourning period they had spent much time getting to know each other, walking through the city, and riding out in the country. After the ceremony in the morning Sri thought that an adventure to explore the temples at Roluos would be a great distraction for Luke. They had both spent much time talking about their passions and Sri knew that Roluos would peak Luke's interest. This journey would be the furthest Luke had ridden but Sri was confident in his abilities. Luke had been building up his riding skills and the adventure today would definitely help distract him.

Sri was right, the adventure to the temple was a great experience, so much so that they had to ride fast back to the city to keep the light. Luke was becoming a great rider, which surprised everyone, he seemed to bond with the horse and riding was quickly becoming one of his favourite pastimes. As they entered the city, they rode confidently flanked by the prince's ever-present guards. Luke reared his horse and began to charge. It was now a race. They carefully avoided the locals as they weaved through the tight streets trying hard to beat each other back to the palace. Luke was leading the race and excitedly arrived at the prince's compound first. He was ecstatic he managed to beat Sri to the stables, who was chasing him fast from behind. Sri cantered up and bowed playfully, acknowledging his defeat. Luke laughed as they both dismounted and headed up the path into the courtyard in need of freshening up. It was at that moment Luke stopped, Sri looked up and he noticed both Marcus and Bo waiting for them. Sri looked at his sister curiously and his playful expression vanished.

'What's going on here?' he asked.

'We have some news to tell you,' Marcus said firmly. 'And I think we need your help.'

His toned softened as his voice began to wobble.

'Brother, I'm pregnant,' Bo blurted out.

There was a silent pause that seemed to last for ages, Sri looked at her amazed.

'Are you sure?' he asked pointedly.

'Yes,' she replied frustratedly. 'I'm not sure what to do and how it will be taken in court.'

Her emotions started to build.

'Come here,' he said, pulling his sister close. 'I assume you're the father Marcus?'

'Yes,' he replied hesitantly. 'I'll do anything to look after Bo and my child, I can promise you that.'

Luke walked over to Marcus and gave him a hug.

'Congratulations, congratulations to you both,' he said, happily turning to the princess smiling.

'It's not that easy,' Marcus replied. 'We're not married and well it's going to cause complications.'

'It's a bit late for that,' Sri replied, still holding his sister. 'We'll need to tell Mother and Father; I'm sure they'll know what to do.'

'What do you think they'll say?' Bo asked tearfully.

'I'm not sure, fathers got a lot going on with the investigation of court and then there's the trial of Kalani. I'll go to Mother first.'

Sri continued to hold his sister. 'It'll be okay. I'll look after you whatever happens.'

Sri pondered for a moment. 'I'll call her here, I don't trust her court and it's important we keep this quiet, at least until we know what to do next.'

He finally let go of Bo.

Sri signalled to one of his guards who came over to them, 'Prak I need you to go to the queen, ask her to visit my compound urgently.'

He unfastened one of his precious amethyst jewels, 'Give her this and tell her it's urgent.'

The guard nodded, he pocketed the jewel and left without delay.

Sri turned back to his sister, 'Get some rest while Luke and I freshen up, I expect it will be an eventful night.'

She nodded, and he turned his attention to Marcus.

'I know you're an honourable man. I expect you to look after my sister and most of all protect her,' as he finished speaking a few drops of rain started to fall.

Marcus gave Sri's shoulder a reassurance squeeze just as the heavens opened and they all left to prepare.

It continued to rain heavily all evening and the city streets turned to mud. Sri feared that the change in weather would deter his mother from visiting but around nine in the evening the queen arrived. It was unusual for her to leave the royal palace late in the evening and even more unusual for her to leave in this weather. Her visit to Sri's compound attracted a lot of attention. The message from Sri had been cryptic, it was very rare for him to act like this so the queen knew what he had to tell her was important. So she came without delay as requested. She entered the prince's compound quickly, her servants following her closely. They had been trying to hold a canopy high above her to stop the rain, but the storm winds made it impossible to shelter her from the weather. It didn't faze her. In truth nothing really did. She just pushed past the servants and headed into the rain towards her son's private residence.

The queen didn't wait to be announced and she entered Sri's main living area. She saw her son, daughter, Marcus, and Luke all looking at her with concern. Her wet windswept hair clung to her face, she pushed the drenched hair to one side and reached for a towel from a servant. The queen dabbed herself and looked up, she could feel the tension in the room and noticed they were nervously drinking. She composed herself, carefully taking off her drenched cloak and handing it to her servant. She was wet, irritable, and keen to get to the point.

'Sri why have you called me here, what's going on?'

Sri got up slowly. 'We would like to talk to you privately.'

His eyes flickered to her servants.

The queen instantly picked up on his signal and dismissed them, Sri handed his mother a goblet of wine.

'What's going on? Tell me *now*.' Her temper was rising as she continued to dry herself.

Bo got up. 'Mother, the issue is me, I'm—'

She paused, finally summoning enough courage to say, 'Pregnant.'

The queen looked deep into her eyes before they darted over to Marcus, 'It's yours I presume?'

'Yes Your Majesty,' he responded hesitantly.

She walked up to her daughter and forcefully placed her hand on her belly. 'How far along are you?'

'About two months,' Bo replied.

The queen took her hand off her daughter and turned away, she walked over to the open door which looked out onto the lake. The heavy rain was buffering the water causing the surface to ripple frantically, just like her mind.

She turned back to Marcus, 'You'll need to marry my daughter, if you do, we can protect her.'

She looked at him directly, 'If you don't, yours and her life will be in danger.'

'I'll do anything for Bo and my child Your Majesty,' he responded.

'Good, good, I have ways I can protect you both.' She then turned to Sri, 'This can't get out, I need you to protect her while I pull a plan together. Only those of us in this room and the king can know.'

'Yes Mother, of course, it's why I sent for you,' he replied, thankful she was here.

'My first grandchild,' the queen said smiling which took them all by surprise.

'I was hoping for an heir from my son, but it looks like you have other priorities,' she stared at Luke. 'The wedding needs to be quick. I'll need seven days to arrange it. I'll speak to the king tonight, we'll need his support and to have a backup plan just encase the news gets out.'

She turned to Marcus. 'What have you done to my family? You've turned our lives upside down'

She shook her head in frustration. 'The king's busy preparing for your trial against this Kalani, are you ready to present your case about his crimes?'

'Yes Your Majesty I'm ready. I believe he'll admit his guilt, so the trial should be quick,' he replied.

'Good, good, let's get that over with. Then we just need to focus on the traitors in our court, the threat of a Cham invasion and the covering up of my daughter's dishonour,' she said with anger building.

The queen walked over to the table, picked up a cup of rice wine and drank it quickly. She paused for a moment with the eyes of the whole room on her. The queen poured herself another drink and took a large mouthful still thinking.

Finally, she looked at them all, 'I need to leave now and start planning. Bo you'll stay here with your brother until I'm sure your compound is safe, do you understand?'

'Yes Mother,' she replied.

'It's important you follow every order I command. I cannot protect you if you don't,' she said threateningly. 'Sri, walk with me, I need to speak to you alone.'

Sri took his mother's arm and they left the room. They exited his home and walked towards his pagoda which looked over the lake. The storm continued to rage. The rain bounced off them frantically as they entered the courtyard. There was a sound of thunder rumbling in the background and a sudden flash of lightning lit up the sky. By the time they reached the shelter of the pagoda, the rain had soaked them both.

'Listen to me carefully, you need to protect Bo with every asset you have, if Virak finds out it could be disastrous. You know how he desires for the old ways and what he's been advocating. It's him I don't trust and he could use this to his advantage,' she sighed and shook her head. 'These strangers have brought us so much trouble, yet for some reason, I trust them. After all, Maya gave her life for Bo.'

She put her hand on his, 'I know how you feel about Luke and I'm happy for you, but tread carefully my son.'

The queen paused and a smile appeared on her face. 'Bo being pregnant could create an opportunity for you. Think about it, if you don't have an heir, you can choose your own successor to the throne. Who better to appoint than your nephew, someone you help raise and train to lead our people.'

Sri looked at his mother, she was always thinking about politics, always thinking about how to protect her family. Ever since he was little she had taught him the dangers of court. She was an expert at surviving and had navigated many political dangers. He knew he had to follow her advice at all costs.

‘I understand mother, we’ll protect her with our lives.’

She pulled him close and hugged him tightly, ‘I love you whatever happens, but your priorities have changed, you protect your sister until I get everything arranged, is that clear?

‘You have my word,’ he replied forcefully.

‘Now make this compound secure, only have your closest allies here. This news can’t get out, do everything you can to lock down your home.’

The queen pulled his face to hers and they touched.

‘Your legacy has a future, don’t lose sight of that,’ she said tenderly and kissed him on the forehead.

The queen pulled back and gave him one last reassuring look. She touched his hand gently then strode off confidently into the raging storm without saying another word.

***

It was still dark when the king awoke, around five in the morning. The heavy rains had come late this year and last night’s downpour had taken everyone by surprise. His eyes took a moment to adjust to the dim light, soon his gaze moved to the bedroom window and although it was still dark, he could see a glint of light rising from the east. The king got out of bed carefully, trying not to wake the queen, or Evi as he called her. He loved his wife deeply, however, Indradevi was not his first wife. The king had been married before to Evi's sister Jayarajadevi, they had married when he was in exile. It was his first wife that inspired him as a young man, she taught him about Buddha and the value of life.

Princess Jayarajadevi or Jaya as she was known was a devout Buddhist and when she came of age, she gave all her royal possessions away to the poor. With the support of her sister, she set up a number of schools to educate and care for young girls. It was Princess Jaya's passion and love of Buddha that eventually inspired the young Khmer Prince to follow the same religion, and it was that faith that ultimately help him retake Angkor. There was great sadness when Jaya suddenly died. The king had been so excited when his wife went into labour with their first child. However, the birth was difficult and sadly Princess Jaya died a few hours after giving birth. The baby boy Raksmei was born prematurely and he soon succumbed to an infection, he only lived for a few days.

After the loss of his beautiful wife and child, the young prince was distraught and turned to her sister for solace. It was in their joint grief that Indradevi and the then prince fell in love. Their support of each other in the most difficult of times brought them closer than they could ever have imagined, eventually leading them to marry in a lavish ceremony. Princess Indradevi had the same fire and passion in her soul as did Jaya, when Indradevi fell pregnant with Srindra, the king feared she would befall the same fate. Thankfully Srindra's birth was free of complications and Queen Indradevi went on to bear the king three more children. When Jayavarman regained the throne, Indradevi made sure all young Khmer girls got a good education. They dedicated the programme to her sister and former Princess Jaya.

He looked at his wife again, he would do anything to protect her, his family and the kingdom. The king walked slowly over to a door which led out onto an ornate balcony. He opened it and entered into the early morning humid air, taking a deep breath. The growing light began to reveal the golden tall spires of the temples in the distance, as the king stared the sky turned vivid pink. Despite the morning light, it was a grey damp start, the ground was still saturated from last night's storm and even though it was early morning humidity was high. The king looked over his city, intrigued by the world in front of him and the streets seemed to burst into life.

The king yawned widely, he was tired, it had been a late night. Evi told him about Bo's pregnancy. He was shocked by the revelation and fearful for his daughter's safety. If the news got out it could have the potential to create negative reactions from court.

The last few years had been difficult, he had asked the people to make many sacrifices since retaking the city. The king worried that the scandal of his daughter's pregnancy, could cause descent. He feared political repercussions and at worst the undermining of their royal position.

He sat down on a nearby bench and breathed in the humid air once more still thinking deeply. The king was feeling particularly anxious today and the weight of his responsibilities weighed heavily, however he needed to be strong, he needed to be a leader. Today he was to stand judgement over the stranger from the future, the stranger who had brought doubt and chaos to his city. The king got up slowly clutching his back as he moved, he looked once more at the now bustling streets and adjusted his night robes.

Time to get ready, he thought and walked back into the palace, willing to face the day.

***

Prince Virak galloped into his compound, he raced passed his guards ignoring their pleas to slow down, causing a number of them to dive out of the way. The prince soon reached the stable, he jumped of his horse and threw his cloak at a nearby servant.

'Get my horse ready to ride in an hour and make sure it's clean,' he barked at the frightened stable hand.

Virak rushed through the compound until he reached his private chambers, he barged into the room, expecting to see his lover in bed, but the room was empty. He looked around furiously and noticed the door to his terrace was open and he rushed through. Chantrea sat in a lounge chair looking over the calm pool of water in front of her.

'Why have you called me here? What's this about? You said come urgently,' Virak shouted.

Chantrea didn't even look at him, 'I've some interesting news that might cheer you up,' she said cryptically.

Chantrea loved to play games with him, even if it did cause her torment and pain in the long run.

'Well spit it out,' he ordered forcefully.

'A little bird in Srindra's compound tells me your mother visited your brother and sister late last night,' she said superiorly.

'What did she go there for? They haven't found a connection between us and the events at the village have they?' he asked worriedly.

'Not that I'm aware of, I hear from my sources your mother only stayed a short while and she left concerned, the rumour is she has instructed the princess to stay under the protection of your brother.'

'What's this all about?' Virak pressed.

'There's more, your brother's ordered a number of his servants to leave, only those who are closest to him may enter his private residence. Unfortunately, my source is not one of them, but I'm working on finding out more information,' she replied confidently.

'What about his guards, has he reduced those as well?'

'I'm told only his most trusted men are to guard him inside the compound, but he has increased his protection around the perimeter,' she paused. 'It seems to me they're protecting a secret, something that could be very useful to us.'

Chantrea flipped her hair back, revealing a dark bruise on her neck, it came from the most recent beating she took from the man in front of her.

‘It means there will be less protection inside his private residence, do you think we could get to him there?’ Virak asked, keen to know what Chantrea had in mind.

‘I have some ideas, but you need to have patience, it’s vital that we understand what they’re hiding.

‘Very well, but make sure I’m told as soon as you know anything, I have some information of my own,’ he said keenly. ‘I’ve finally made contact with a tribe of shinobi. The Chinese ambassador gave me a very useful contact.’

He smiled. ‘I’ve promised the ambassador that once I’m king, I’ll make sure our people trade with the Chinese and in returned for his support, our forces will become a key military ally.’

Chantrea got up slowly and walked over to him, she kissed him gently on the lips and spoke quietly. ‘Tread carefully my love, the Chinese have their own agenda.’

She turned and disappeared into the room leaving him alone on the veranda to consider her words.

***

It was around ten in the morning when the king entered the council chamber. A thick mist had gripped the city and the air hung humid and heavy. The king had summoned his council in readiness for the trial. The council were made up of important men and women from across the empire. The members were the king’s most trusted friends and family whom he turned to for advice and guidance. The council was important in maintaining oversight and control of the empire, it helped to keep the nobility in line and pre-empt any potential rebellion. There were eight strategic roles which made up the ruling council, all overseen by the king.

Minister for the treasury was Nakry Moau, she was an exceptional woman who had a gift for finance. Nakry had been a close ally of the king and queen for many years and she helped them raise the finance to wage war against the Cham occupiers. Since they successfully retook the city a decade ago Nakry had managed to build a large surplus of wealth, which was used to protect and enlighten the Khmer people. Minister of Defence and security was General Thorn, he was the king's most trusted military advisor, he was a great strategist and he fought side by side with the king when they retook Angkor. The queen took up the role of minister of science, she took great pleasure in working to develop new technologies and improve the living standards of her people. Minister for foreign affairs and intelligence was overseen by Prince Srindra. This role did not sit easily with him but the king insisted he fulfil it. The purpose was to build the prince's skills for when he would eventually become king, it was vital that Sri built strong allies. In truth, the queen ran the intelligence network and everyone knew it, however, the king wanted Prince Srindra to learn these skills. Sri spent much time with the queen, absorbing the art of diplomacy and intelligence gathering.

The Ministry of Education was overseen by Princess Bopha, the queen had convinced the king after a lot of persuading to appoint the princess. It was clear she had a passion for education after taking a keen interest in the queen's school programme as a child. The role of minister of agriculture and irrigation was appointed to Prince Virak, although in truth he had little interest in the role. He was responsible for ensuring the empire grew enough food, and most importantly that the water canals were maintained. It was his role to liaise with all the provinces and ensure the security of the empire. The minister of justice was overseen by an old balding man called Phala Sym, he was from one of the oldest and most trusted families in Angkor. Phala helped to shape the new constitution based on their Buddhist beliefs. His role was to oversee and appoint all the judges across the empire, while also supporting the provinces to deal with crime. Phala was wise in many ways and helped the king to make decisions on crimes of state. These crimes carried the death penalty and the king struggled with this responsibility. It was only the king who could sentence people to death and that duty weighed heavily. Minister of religion was of course led by the king's son and most trusted priest Tamal, he oversaw all the empire's religious doctrine and the king's large temple building programme.

The chamber was full of commotion as the council members prepared for the trial. The king finished reading an important letter from the ambassador of Lavo and looked around the room. All his advisors were present except his daughter, there were looks of concern on Sri and Evi's faces but the king chose to act in his usual confident reverence. The queen signalled to a servant who brought her water, it was at that moment the king stood up and began to pace around the room.

'Thank you for coming today friends, this is the first time I have called you here since our visitors arrived.'

'Father, we're not all here, where's Bopha?' Virak interjected.

'She's unwell, I'll cover her duties,' the queen replied coldly.

'Thank you, my love,' the king responded. 'General Thorn, what progress have you made on identifying traitors within the city?'

The king scanned the room.

'I've interrogated Captain Tola's family and from my investigation, they had no knowledge of his treachery. I give you my word on these findings, I was very thorough. I've also investigated all officers within the queen's battalion. With the support of Colonel Myan we questioned every soldier and investigated any suspicious activity.' General Thorn turned to the queen, 'Your Majesty, I'm confident that Tola was a rogue traitor but I have some recommendations I'd like Colonel Myan to implement. They'll improve the security of your battalion if you are in agreement.'

'Thank you General, I'm pleased you've found no further traitors. I'll review all your recommendations with Colonel Myan. I've personally met with all the families of the soldiers who lost their lives in the attack, the state has compensated them for their loss.' She paused and looked over at the king. 'I'm concerned about my force's capabilities. Their duties have been focused on science, not fighting. I'll be looking to reshape the Battalion and seek stronger training.'

'Mother, your men fought with pride,' Prince Srindra interjected.

'That may be so, but we had a traitor amongst us, we lost many good men due to that man and his betrayal,' she replied ruthlessly. 'I've asked Myan to work with your forces my son, it's clear your men have skills mine lack.'

'General, what about traitors within our city?' the king asked.

'We've intercepted many messages, searched everyone entering or leaving the city but found nothing other than goods being smuggled. Phala, I've sent you the details, looks like they were avoiding taxes, I'll let your men deal with that.' Thorn turned to the king. 'Your Majesty I've relaxed my inspections as you requested but my men continue to search for Chams spies across the empire.'

He sighed. 'It seems for now anyway, they've gone to ground, no further attacks have been reported. I'll keep our forces on high alert for now at least.'

'Thank you General, needless to say, keep up the investigation, but do it carefully, I don't want a rebellion on our hands,' the king replied.

'Yes Your Majesty,' Thorn nodded.

'Phala, our attention now turns to our visitors and the capture of this Kalani. I'm not sure what we're to do, he has not committed any crimes in our city. However he has betrayed his companions resulting in the death of

Maya. Marcus also tells us his selfish actions have threatened many other lives, but how can we judge that?'

'I'm not sure I buy this future story,' General Thorn spat.

'How do you explain their technology?' the king asked.

'Illusions, tricks, all designed to confuse us, I still have concerns they were part of the Cham plot,' he rebuffed.

'How can you say that?' The queen snapped back which was very unlike her. 'Maya gave her life to protect Bo, you've heard her testimony.'

General Thorn shrugged.

'I can vouch for them, whether you believe they're from the future or not is no consequence, they're no danger to us,' Prince Srindra said angrily.

'Silence, I have spoken to you all personally about their claims to be from the future. I decreed that none of us would mention where they're from openly. Not between us and not to anyone. It could create unrest and as much as I want to know more, we have a duty to protect our kingdom and to protect the future.'

The room fell silent, they all wanted to discuss the topic further but the king had made up his mind.

'Now what do we do with this Kalani,' the king said once more.

'Banish him,' Thorn replied.

There were sounds of agreement from a few council members.

Tamal gave a quiet cough and spoke. 'I've spent a lot of time with Kalani as requested by the princess. I think I have a suggestion which could help. Kalani is a deeply spiritual man, release him into my order. I'll help him with his inner struggle and his search for enlightenment. You granted me this opportunity to turn my life around Father, let me do the same for Kalani.'

There was a stunned silence at the proposal.

'Do you really want to bring him into your order?' the king asked in disbelief.

'I do. Everyone deserves a second chance,' his son replied kindly.

'If you're sure,' Tamal nodded and the king turned to the guard at the door. 'Bring them in.'

The guard bowed and left to fetch the foreigners. They had been waiting outside patiently for the council to deliberate. Kalani had been silent ever since he left the cells, he waited with his former colleagues expecting to face the death penalty despite Marcus's assurances that wouldn't happen. But he was ready for that outcome, if that was the king's judgement.

Before the guard led them into the chamber Marcus whispered to him, 'Whatever happens, we're both here for you.'

They entered into the presence of the ruling council and Kalani stepped forward.

'I'm ready for my punishment,' he said clearly.

'Kalani, you have committed no crimes in my kingdom. However, you have confessed that you tried to kill Luke. These acts in them self would result in serious punishment, but it's also important to acknowledge that your actions have led to Maya's death.'

Kalani's head fell.

'I've reached a decision. I decree that you join my son's order at the temple, you'll learn our beliefs in the hope you can find inner peace and cure your demons.'

Kalani looked up at him as tears began to trickle down his face.

'Let me make this clear to you, if you don't respect our people and our believes at the temple, I'll give you no mercy in the future, do I make myself clear?'

'Yes Your Majesty,' Kalani replied bowing.

'Tamal you may take him to the monastery, guards remove his chains,' the soldiers released the bonds.

Tamal bowed to the king and went to support the frightened and fragile man who had just been judged. Kalani was led out of the room without any further discussion.

A strange silence fell over the chamber, and Marcus couldn't help but step forward. 'Thank you Your Majesty, both Luke and I appreciate your mercy and your support.'

The king let out a huge sigh. 'Marcus I don't know if what you've told us is the truth, but you're now under my protection. I'll say this however, you both need to decide if you want to become citizens of the Khmer Empire or if you're going to leave. I know you've both become close to my family so I have a vested interest in what you decide. However I can't have confusion unsettling my court. You're under no obligation to stay, but I'd like to know your decision by the end of the day. Do I make myself clear?'

There was a threatening hint in the king's voice and Marcus felt the king's dark eyes penetrating him.

'Yes Your Majesty,' he replied automatically.

'You'll both have dinner with the queen and I tonight, my guards will bring you to the palace,' he ordered.

Marcus bowed. Luke looked subtly at Sri whose eyes flickered towards him. They connected for a moment and Luke knew he was not to speak. The guards ushered them out of the council chamber, they were to be escorted out of the royal palace and back to the prince's compound.

Just as they walked through the palace courtyard Marcus noticed a beautiful woman, she was looking keenly at them. The young woman stood out from the other courtiers as she had dark black hair and pale white skin. She smiled at them as they passed and bowed her head.

What was that about? he thought. He didn't have time to consider it as Sri's guards led them out of the palace quickly and back to the prince's compound.

CHAPTER NINETEEN

Choices

Marcus and Luke soon arrived back to the place they now called home. It was strange for them to think of the little hut as home, but they had been living there for nearly two months. Both had become accustomed to the prince's compound and although they had suffered the loss of Maya, they were still in awe of it, and the incredible surroundings they now lived in. The prince's compound was a large enclosed area, it must have been the size of eight football pitches. There were many buildings, water features, bridges and pagodas positioned to maximise its status. There were fine carvings that adorned the intricately decorated buildings all symbolising Khmer culture and the Buddhist faith. Even the small guest house they were living in was painted exquisitely. It had become their sanctuary in all the chaos that surrounded them. As they walked through the gardens, Marcus gently put his arm around Luke, giving him a reassurance squeeze, like a father would a son. They continued to walk slowly together, both in silence pondering the words of the king. They reached a tranquil spot by the lake and Marcus sat on a small stone wall. He looked out across the water as Luke sat next to him.

There was a short silence before Marcus spoke. 'Luke you're free to make your own decisions, you have no obligation to me.'

He paused and looked at Luke. 'But I can't leave Bo, I just couldn't abandon her in this situation. If only I could've stuck to the rules we laid down when we first got here.'

Luke cleared his throat and responded carefully.

'What options do we really have?' he said calmly. 'Where would we go? Let's face it, we've already made a mess of things here with Maya's death, the princess pregnant, Kalani becoming a monk. The truth is, if we went anywhere else, we would risk further damage.'

Luke pondered his words for a moment and turned away. 'My heart's with Sri.'

He plucked up enough courage to look at Marcus. 'I don't want to go anywhere without him. Like you I want to stay and accept our new lives here.'

Marcus stared at the young man he knew so well.

'Very well, but we need to do better at protecting the timeline, our actions may already have caused an effect. We must do everything we can to prevent contaminating the timeline further. I suggest we bury the technology we have left and deactivate our implants.'

Marcus sighed, 'It's going to be difficult to adapt to life without our technology, but we've come a long way in the past few months.'

Luke agreed and they spent the rest of the afternoon working out what to do and how to integrate into Khmer society.

As the sun was setting, Prince Srindra rode calmly into his compound. He dismounted his horse and looked up at the orange sky smiling before heading to his private residence. He nodded as he passed two guards protecting the entrance, Sri had known them both since they were children. He had made sure it was only his trusted soldiers within his compound walls and his closest friends protecting his home.

'Anything unusual happen today?' he asked them.

The tall guard replied, 'all quiet here Your Majesty, the princess and your foreign friends are waiting for you inside.'

The prince bowed his head in gratitude and entered the room, Bo was sitting on the veranda looking over the lake with Marcus who was studying a small carved statue of Buddha. Across the room, Luke was looking at a manuscript that Sri had lent him detailing the history of his ancestors.

'Have you made your decision, are you going to stay?' he asked, making them all jump as none of them realised he had entered the room.

Marcus rose to his feet and walked over. 'Yes we have, we'd both like to stay, if you will have us that is.'

'I'm very pleased to hear that,' Sri sighed in relief and looked towards Luke, who smiled back.

'There's one problem, we'll need something to do as we can't live off your hospitality for the rest of our lives,' Marcus insisted.

'I'm sure we can find something that two talented archaeologists can do within our great city.'

Luke walked over to Sri and took his hand, 'I've decided already, I want to join your elite guard and to learn how to protect the people I love. I want to explore this great country with you.'

'I'd like that very much. I'll ask Major Keo to start your training.'

'I don't want to be a commander or anything, just a loyal soldier,' Luke replied quickly looking at Marcus's face. 'I promise only to use my skills to defend myself and others, I'll not influence the decisions or actions the commanders make.'

'Luke it's a fine line you're taking, just be careful, although I'm not one to talk.' He turned and looked at Bo.

'Marcus, I've an idea what you can do. Why don't you help me with the education plan I have been working on, you're a professor after all, and well, I'll need some help when the baby arrives,' she said kindly.

Sri walked to the nearby table and poured himself a drink. 'I think that's an excellent idea Bo, however we need to address other matters first. The king's requested that Marcus and Luke join him tonight at a banquet he's laid on for the Lavo Ambassador.'

Sri turned to Bo. 'You need to come as well. Now that Marcus has confirmed he's staying, the king will announce your engagement to him.'

He then turned to face Marcus.

'I need some information from you first, mother is working on the plan, come let's discuss.' They all sat down reviewing the events of the evening that were to come.

***

It had been a long day in the council chamber, the king had wanted to discuss lots of key matters of state and Prince Virak was in a foul mood, he hated these meetings. The king had chastised him for the issues with the eastern Baray, it had begun to silt up again and was causing issues with the city's water supply. Additionally, the large storm the night before had caused extensive flooding to a number of the city streets.

It's not my fault the blasted things keep silting up, nor can I control the weather, he thought as he left the room furious.

Virak rushed down the palace steps and was met by Chantrea who had been waiting for him patiently. 'Come, I want to get out of here, I can't stand being in this place.'

Chantrea took his arm, 'Is my understanding correct that we're to return later for a feast with the Lavo ambassador?'

'Yes, another pointless event. The Lavo are weak,' he looked around making sure no one could hear. 'We should have full autonomy over them, not allowing them to govern themselves. Now we have to eat with them, such a waste of time.'

Chantrea asked cautiously knowing the prince's mood, 'I notice the princess didn't attend the council meeting, any reason why?'

'My mother said she was ill and got irritated when I enquired why, so I asked no more.' He shook his head.

Sensing there was no point asking further Chantrea changed track, 'What happened with the trial of this Kalani?'

'Father declared there was no crime committed on our lands and Tamal insisted that Kalani joined the priesthood, Tamal spoke about forgiveness and respect. Honestly what a waste of breath, I would've had his head on a stick,' he blustered

'I saw the two other foreigners leave earlier, they're strange to look at,' Chantrea interjected.

'They're strange all right and have caused so much damage to our plans. Come let's get out of here,' Virak said as he reached the stables.

He mounted his horse and instructed Chantrea to sit behind him. He set off back to his compound at pace.

***

The palace was alive with music when Prince Srindra, Princess Bopha, Luke and Marcus arrived at the feast, it was a little before eight. Torches directed the guests to a central courtyard full of trees all decorated with floating candles. In the centre of the courtyard was a meticulously carved wooden table, it was huge and could easily fit about fifty guests. The table was laid out with stunning golden place settings which sparkled in the candlelight. The courtyard was full of stone carvings, they were of animals from the jungle and drew Marcus's eye.

The palace was full of guests, including all the council members along with nobles from the city who were already drinking and laughing. The king and queen were yet to arrive as was the custom, the prince noticed some friendly faces and directed the group to Nearidei and Kesor. They were dressed in their finest blue robes reflecting their allegiances to the queen. Prince Srindra wore his familiar purple colours adorned with golden chains and rings decorated with amethyst stones. Princess Bopha was dressed in her vivid green robes. She wore them loosely and tightly fastened a piece of cloth around her waist, to help hide any potentially visible bump. The princess, like her brother, wore her silver jewellery and crown all embossed with aquamarine and peridot gems. Luke was dressed in the same colours as the prince, however, this time he was dressed differently. Luke wore the uniform of the prince's guard, although he still wore the golden and amethyst jewellery the prince had given him. Marcus on the other hand wore the colours of the princess openly and he proudly held her arm as they reached their waiting friends.

'Where have you been and why all the secrecy Your Majesty?' Kesor asked. 'I've missed spending time with you and your guests.'

She looked Marcus up and down. 'Has something happened or is something going to happen?'

Sri just laughed. 'You're always one step ahead Kesor but you'll just have to wait and see.'

She smiled back at him.

'You look radiant this evening Your Majesty,' Nearidei complimented the princess. 'It's like you've found something to light your passion, it reminds me of our days studying and how excited you got when we learnt something new.'

'Thank you,' Bo replied shyly. 'It's been an interesting few months.'

She looked back at Marcus and squeezed his hand.

Just as he began to speak the sound of a large gong rang out, it echoed off the surrounding walls. Everyone looked up as the king and queen dressed in their finest clothes walked onto the high steps with the ambassador of Lavo and his wife.

The king spoke, 'Welcome, we're joined here tonight by our dear friends and allies from Lavo, who like us, have suffered terribly from the Cham aggression and I welcome their friendship.'

The king gestured for the ambassador and his wife to follow him. They walked down the steps to the large table where everyone was gathered. The king signalled for his guests to take their seats. It wasn't long before the food began to arrive, and the table was alive with discussion.

Marcus looked over at the king and queen just as the king let out a huge belly laugh. The ambassador had said something which the king found amusing. It was clear they enjoyed each other's company. His eyes then fell upon the pale white woman with dark black hair he had noticed earlier. She was staring back at him which made him uneasy. He turned his head quickly and noticed Bo about to drink some rice wine.

He subtly put his hand on hers and said, 'My dear, don't drink that it's bad for the baby, trust me I know things which will help keep our child safe.'

Bo put the cup down and called over a servant, she requested some fresh fruit juice, 'I'll follow whatever you say Marcus, I trust you totally.'

The night went fast, the food was delicious and the more they ate the more the servants brought out. Eventually, everyone had had their fill and the plates were cleared away. The guests congregated around large fire pits in the courtyard.

Prince Srindra left to speak to the Lavo ambassador while the princess excused herself to inspect the latest carving from her favourite mason, Kesor and Nearidei joined her leaving Marcus and Luke alone. The queen noticed, she pointed it out to the king and they approached the lone foreigners.

'So, have you made your decision?' the queen asked Luke and Marcus bluntly.

'Yes Your Majesty, we would like to stay if that's okay with you,' Marcus replied.

'Very well, you are now citizens of the Khmer Empire and are under the protection of our people,' the king said smiling. 'You'll follow our rules and live by our code.'

They both nodded and Marcus once again began to speak, 'We would like to contribute to your people

Your Majesty. Luke has requested to join the prince's force and Sri has accepted him into his elite guard.'

'I pledge my service in protecting the city,' Luke said firmly.

'Thank you for your commitment and your loyalty to my son,' the king replied

Luke bowed his head and Marcus spoke again, 'Bo has requested that I help her with her education plan for your people, is that acceptable to you?'

The king smiled widely. 'That sounds like a great idea Marcus.'

The queen interjected, 'You're both very close to my children and they trust you, as do I now. But you need to understand my children are the most precious things to me, and to the empire. It is they who hold the fate of our people in their hands, and it is they who will help our people develop. I expect you to assist them with these difficult tasks.'

They both nodded nervously and the queen turned to the king.

'Now we know their answers it's time to announce,' the king agreed.

He suddenly walked over to the large gong and struck it. 'Friends, gather round and listen, I have a very important announcement to make.'

The invited guest did as they were requested. Sri and Bo re-joined Marcus and Luke. The crowd formed a crescent waiting to hear what the king was about to say.

'Today we celebrate our alliance with our Lavo friends, however, I have another alliance to announce. Our foreign friends were more than the traders that many of you believe, they are in fact allies from afar. I sent out scouts many years ago and have been in correspondence with potential allies from across the world, to strengthen our forces and protect our empire. Marcus is a prince of Svithiod, which is a cold rugged land in the far west. He came here to forge an alliance and brought with him other great scholars to share their knowledge. As some of you may know he was betrayed by traitors within his court who left him to die. Prince Srindra found and rescued our new allies, and they were brought into the city under our protection. These strangers have proven their faith and loyalty to us, Maya their healer helped to save an injured mason. Marcus's apprentice Luke then saved Prince Srindra during the Cham attack in the Koulen mountains. Finally, Maya paid the ultimate price by jumping in front of an arrow which was destined for my dearest Bo. In light of these acts, I would like to strengthen our bond as allies and with my daughter's permission, I have offered her hand in marriage to the prince of Svithiod.'

The king beamed widely, 'And it is with great pleasure that Marcus our friend and ally has accepted.'

There was a cheer from the crowd, followed by Bo and Marcus kissing.

The queen then said, 'To cement our alliance, Marcus will remain here with us, their marriage will take place on the night of the full moon, that's two days from now and we'll be ready.'

The servants brought out more drinks, and then dancers and musicians filled the courtyard playing joyful music. Many of the guests went to congratulate the couple, who everyone could see were very much in love.

Virak, on the other hand, was in no mood for celebrating, he was stunned by this announcement. It threatened all of his potential plans. He had arranged for the princess to be married to the Chinese ambassador. It was part of the deal for his support and now that alliance was in jeopardy.

Virak walked slowly over to Chantrea and whispered in her ear, 'Can you believe this shit? Prince from the west, what a load of crap. What am I to do about the ambassador, this has the potential to ruin us. Make no mistake we need to deal with this.'

Chantrea took a sip of her drink and looked around carefully before answering. 'There could be a reason for this, I expect it has a lot to do with why the princess has been staying at your brothers' compound.'

She took another sip and then turned to face him.

'I need to get closer to them, sorry my love for what I'm about to do.'

She looked him in the eyes seeing his confusion then slapped him hard across the face.

'How dare you say that to me,' she shouted and ran back into the palace which caused everyone to look round.

Virak stood there in shock. He had never been hit before. He rubbed his face and walked out of the courtyard enraged, but also confused at what had just happened.

The party continued despite Virak's interruption and at around midnight Marcus suggested they leave, it was late, and Bo needed her rest. As they were leaving Bo excused herself, she needed to visit the bathroom. She walked into a large room and saw a very visibly upset Chantrea. Bo had never liked this woman, she seemed to leach off her naive younger brother. But she couldn't help but feel sorry for her, seeing how upset she was. Bo walked over to her putting her arms around the sobbing woman.

'What did my brother say to make you so upset Chantrea?'

She continued to sob, she looked at the princess and slowly spoke.

'He demanded I…' She paused. 'I'm not sure I can say.'

'Go on tell me,' I won't judge you.

'He demanded I lay with him again, then spoke vile words to me when I refused, he knew how important it was for me to remain whole until I'm married.'

She sobbed harder.

'He's already forced me to break my vow and now I'm worth nothing,' she whispered through tears. 'I didn't have a choice.'

She broke down again. 'Tonight, when he ordered me to come to him again, I snapped. I couldn't do it. I can't be a woman like that.'

Chantrea pulled down her robe to reveal the many bruises that Virak had inflicted on her.

'I know what many of you think of me,' she said emotionally. 'I've been under his control since we were little and when my family died, he was the only friend I could turn to. But what friend treats you like this, even if he is a prince.'

Fear seemed to strike her as the realisation of her actions sank in.

'I've nowhere to go,' she said panicked. 'He won't take me back after that, I've no family left in this city, what am I to do?'

'You'll come with me for now, I'll help you find somewhere to live,' the princess replied.

Do you mean it?' Chantrea sobbed in desperation. 'But nowhere will be safe in the city from him, he'll get me, he'll force me to lay with him again.'

'He will not, you will be under my protection and the protection of Prince Srindra. Virak will not be able to get to you at his compound,' the princess said angrily.

Bo called out to one of Prince Srindra's guards who was waiting outside the bathroom, she ordered him to not allow anyone to enter until they were ready to leave. The princess helped Chantrea clean herself and when they were both ready, she escorted Chantrea out to join everyone who was waiting.

Sri gave Bo a confused look.

'She's coming with us, don't ask me questions here,' Bo said forcefully.

He got the point and they all set off for his compound.

***

Sri was furious at Bo for bringing Chantrea back, he expressed to her on many occasions the danger this woman could put them in. However, the princess stood her ground, which was very unusual. Bo told Sri it was their responsibility for allowing Virak's abuse to happen and she would protect Chantrea from him at all costs. Sri placed Chantrea in rooms that were furthest away from them all. He made it clear that they would deal with the situation after the wedding. Chantrea herself spent much of her days in tears, trying to convince the watching servants or spies, as she thought of them that her plight was real. Bo had been visiting her every couple of hours, trying to console the broken woman and to help her face the world, but it was no use. Through tears, Chantrea told the princess to focus on her wedding and forget about her for the time being.

The next few days were a blur, there was so much preparation for the wedding that the princess was too busy to deal with any of Virak's problems. Servants looked after Chantrea but kept Bo updated. However, Bo stopped by as often as she could spare. Prince Srindra spent time supporting Marcus, schooling him in the rituals associated with a Khmer wedding ceremony, in readiness for his upcoming union. Luke on the other hand had started his training with Major Keo and was busy learning his fighting skills, he was exhausted. Luke's focus as a child was on learning about archaeology. Now he found so much joy in learning these new combat skills, which excited him, as did the thought of becoming a soldier in the prince's guard.

It was the night before the wedding at around seven that the princess went to see Chantrea, this time Marcus accompanied her. She approached her room and nodded to the guards who were patrolling outside. Bo knocked on her door and she was invited to enter. Chantrea was awake but her hair was a mess and she looked terrible.

'You need to snap out of this spiral of fear. I've instructed my household that you'll join us once we move out of Prince Srindra's compound.'

'Thank you Your Majesty, I appreciate your support. I'm not sure what I would've done without your help.'

Chantrea started to well up again. 'I don't want any of what I told you the other night to be shared wider, I would be horrified if the queen found out about what your brother has done to me.'

'My brother needs to pay for his crimes,' Bo replied.

'No, please don't, I can't have others knowing about what's happened to me, everyone will know I am not whole,' Chantrea responded terrified.

'But you can't let him get away with this, we have laws against it,' Bo said kindly sitting next to her as Marcus watched on uncomfortably.

'It'll scandalise the royal name. I don't want that, it will hurt the king,' Chantrea replied.

Bo thought for a moment and she knew what Chantrea was saying was true. The king had many troubles and he could do without a scandal in his own family.

'I just want to get my life back together and move on,' Chantrea sighed. 'Your Majesty as much as it's great to be under Prince Srindra's protection, why are we in his compound?'

Bo moved uncomfortably before replying, 'With all the Cham attacks my brother wanted me here to ensure my protection, he also wanted me to meet his foreign friends and to form our alliance.'

She turned to Marcus and smiled.

'Are you really from the future?' Chantrea couldn't stop herself from asking. 'Prince Virak told me about you, I know I not supposed to know, but he was convinced it was a lie. I promise not to tell anyone.'

This time Marcus shifted uncomfortably, 'Um, well, yes we are, but the king has sworn that no one is to talk about it, the people will not understand and we must do everything to protect the future.'

'I'm not sure I understand,' Chantrea said slowly.

'But I've never really understood about what goes on at court,' she lied.

'Well put it this way, if I interfere with current events or talk about the future, it could be dangerous,' he replied carefully.

Bo cut Marcus off before he could speak again, 'Anyway enough of that, why don't you come and help me choose my clothes for the wedding tomorrow. I would like you to be there with my ladies in waiting, would you like that too?'

I would be honoured Your Majesty,' Chantrea replied. 'Could you give me some time to clean up, I'll come to the prince's residence once I'm ready.'

'Good, I'll see you there,' the princess said and left with a relieved Marcus.

The invite was just what Chantrea was looking for, to help her gain the princess's trust. She didn't take long to tidy herself and to don the green robes of the princess's house. She made her way to the prince's residence and was directed to the princess's rooms by servants. Bo smiled when she saw her.

'What do you think about this robe?' she asked. 'I've a few different styles but I'll need to change a couple of times in the day.

The robe was a light turquoise colour and had silver thread with a pattern that showed both animal and religious imagery. Next to the robe was the princess's stunning jewellery, all silver with studded gems of aquamarine and peridot, the most spectacular piece was that of her crown, like her brothers in the shape of a lotus flower topped by a large aquamarine gem.

'Thank you once again for letting me join you in this special honour.' Chantrea looked over at Bo's friends whose expressions were fixed, they were trying hard not to give away their true emotions.

'Your very welcome,' Bo replied. 'You already know Kesor and Nearidei.'

Chantrea bowed to them, she knew these two ladies well and to say they were not a fan of her was an understatement. However, the princess had ordered them to help Chantrea and of course they agreed. Bo had asked them to guide her, while also observe her actions encase of any strange behaviour.

Time flew by that evening. The four women went through the gowns, selecting what the princess would wear and what they would also dress in. This was to be the wedding of the year, so the royal seamstresses and jewellers prepared everything. In addition to the wedding preparation, the queen had instructed investigations be done to ensure that both Marcus's and Bo's horoscopes matched, it was a much-revered part of the service and it was particularly useful to ensure that the wedding ceremony was held quickly.

The morning before the wedding was a mad panic, Sri and Luke helped Marcus get ready. Unusually the princess dressed on her own so she could wrap and bind her pregnancy, trying to avoid any visible signs to others. She was soon ready, then met by her three ladies in waiting who helped with her hair and jewellery.

At around midday, the temple at Angkor Wat was starting to fill with the honoured guests. It looked amazing and was covered in the green colours of the princess. A sense of excitement and happiness filled the temple. The king and queen entered and prayed to the statue of Buddha. Not long after, Marcus followed dressed in green robes showing his allegiance to the princess. Luke was at his side dressed in Prince Srindra's uniform, they both bowed to Buddha. Finally, last to enter was the princess looking radiant, as did her three ladies in waiting, they all bowed to Buddha and Bo joined Marcus.

Tamal was overseeing the ceremony and next to him stood Kalani who was acting as his aid. Tamal rang a loud gong, and the crowd came to a silence, he said a prayer out loud and then instructed the couple to light candles, he guided them to place the candles by the large Buddha. Incense filled the air while Marcus and Bo laid more flowers around the statue to give thanks. Tamal began to recite the prayers Vandana, Tisarana, and Pancasila.

Once he finished, Bo turned to her family to say goodbye. It is part of the Buddhist ceremony to say farewell to her family as she moves onto a new path and new family. This was very emotional for Bo and she hugged them tightly. Bo then knelt at the shrine and prayed to her ancestors to give thanks.

Tamal called for them to make their vows and Marcus stepped forward, he was overcome with nerves and shaking a little. To observe an event like this would have been a dream of his, but to actually be the person getting married was overwhelming.

He calmed his nerves and spoke loudly, 'Towards my wife I promise to love and respect her, be kind and considerate, be faithful, let her make her own choices in life while I provide her with security and love.'

Bo replied, 'Towards my husband, I promise to love and cherish our union, to share my kindness with my friends, be faithful, protect and invest in our passions while undertaking my marital responsibilities lovingly and conscientiously.'

Tamal then said a few more prayers and bowed to Buddha before raising his hands up in the air. He declared they were married and the crowd cheered once more. More offerings were left at Buddha's shrine and Bo was ushered to a private chamber. The princess wanted to change into another robe that was more comfortable for travelling in.

This time her ladies and waiting were ready to help. However, she backed away and asked them for privacy while she finished undressing. She came out of her private room in a hurry and asked her friends to attach the final jewels to her robes, of course they all obliged. As Chantrea was helping the princess put on the final piece of jewellery, she noticed a bit of fabric caught in her robe. Chantrea knew what this cloth meant, and everything clicked into place. She continued to dress the princess without saying a word and when ready, Bo re-joined her new husband and they walked out of the gates of the temple to applause from the waiting public. The king led them personally to his favourite elephant. They were both helped onto the large animal looking radiant in the bright sun. Horns sounded and the couple started to parade the city streets with men from the king's, queen's, Srindra's, and Bo's own forces marching proudly. The streets were alive with colour and the newly married couple waived happily to the crowds of Angkor. Tens of thousands of people came out to see the glamorous princess and her new foreign husband.

The parade toured the city with the princess's soldiers leading the way supported by Prince Srindra's elite guard. The couple were in the middle of the parade proudly astride the large elephant draped in Bo's colours, around the elephant were her ladies in waiting and household servants also dressed in her colours. The king's guard and the queen's battalion followed at the rear showing their support for the marriage. Finally, the parade ended at the royal palace where thousands of people had gathered. Bo and Marcus carefully dismounted the elephant. The public cheered and continued to throw flowers many waving furiously to get the attention of the royal couple. Chantrea spotted a man in the crowd that was following the procession. She recognised him instantly even through the disguise he was wearing. She saw an opening in the crowd and she took the opportunity to collect flowers from the excited public, she moved down the line of people carefully thanking the public until she reached the man she knew so well.

Chantrea collected the flowers he was holding and whispered into his ear, 'She's pregnant.'

Virak paused in shock for a moment, he nodded back at her and quickly left.

CHAPTER TWENTY

Deception

Princess Bopha and Marcus's wedding day celebrations went by quickly, their joyful experiences would stay with them forever. It had been a long time since Angkor had seen a royal wedding and the king was delighted with the reaction from his people. He was grateful to have something positive to celebrate and distract from the Cham threat. The king was so pleased with the reception, he declared the day an official holiday, only further exciting his subjects. Huge feasts were held across the city and people toasted to the health of Princess Bopha and Prince Marcus from Svithiod. At the palace, dignitaries gathered from across the empire along with the Royal family's closest friends. The celebrations were dazzling, everyone feasted and danced until the early hours and the city buzzed with excitement.

The party finally ended, and the exhausted couple travelled with Sri and Luke back to his compound. The queen's plan for now, was for the princess to continue to stay at Sri's compound. She would be protected there until the queen could officially announce her pregnancy. Bo would continue to remain under her brother's security, out of sight from the public until the baby was born. Bo's absence would allow the queen some flexibility, avoiding any potential rumours around when the baby was conceived.

Sri had already arranged for Bo and Marcus to have their own permanent residence. He converted one of the old pavilion's not far from his quarters in readiness for them. Since Marcus was now moving in with Bo, Sri requested that Luke moved in with him, rather than being on his own in the small guest house and Luke happily agreed. This was the start of something special, Bo and Marcus would have a chance to grow as a couple while Luke would hone his skills to become a protector.

A few weeks after the royal marriage the queen declared that the princess was pregnant. The announcement caused much jubilation and delight across the Khmer Empire. The Khmer people loved the princess very much. Many had benefited from the educational programmes that she had introduced with the queen. After the official announcement the next few months passed quickly, they were some of the happiest months the four of them had ever experienced.

Bo and Marcus's new home had become a hive of activity, the queen and king visited often. They were excited about their first grandchild. The princess's closest ladies in waiting moved into accommodation nearby and became a great support for her. Chantrea seemed to thrive in this new environment, she became very close to the princess, she seemed to understand her needs perfectly.

Marcus would leave most days to support Bo's education agenda and in truth he loved it. He relished the opportunity to work on something which helped the people. In supporting Bo with the programme, he found himself often representing her at the king's council. Marcus made sure he only discussed Bo's educational plans and not interjected with his own ideas, despite his desire to help. He knew better than to further complicate the timeline.

It was a very happy period, the city was quiet, the people were content and the fear of a Cham invasion had passed. It seemed that all was well in the world.

***

It was an early spring morning as a cool breeze blew over the city. Chantrea left on what had become her usual journey to the market to buy some fresh fruit. The princess had become particularly fond of the foul-smelling durian fruit, to everyone's displeasure. But Chantrea wanted to please and personally sort the ripest crop for her. She browsed a few of the local stalls taking pleasure in her freedom, she seemed to have forgotten Virak for now, she was happy and content serving Bo. Chantrea picked up a beautiful jade necklace and looked at it, the colour reminded her of the robes she now wore. She no longer dressed in the black and red of Virak's court, but that of the new allegiance she had now committed herself to. Like the rest of Srindra's compound, Chantrea was at peace and since the wedding, she had experienced happiness for the first time. She was without the ridged restrictions Virak imposed on her, without the fear of violence she faced daily and without the need to deceive others. Chantrea had begun to shine. After the first month of serving the princess, she swore to herself she would remain loyal to her new house. She would do everything to avoid her former lover and denounced his mission to become king, that she so willingly accepted long ago.

Chantrea placed the necklace down and thanked the seller before moving to buy fruit. She completed her purchase and headed back towards home. Chantrea smiled and nodded at a few people she knew, then turned the corner to walk up to the compound. Suddenly without warning, she was grabbed from behind and a hand put over her mouth, she was then pulled into a nearby cart. She tried to scream but it was no use, the man who snatched her held on tight and tied a gag around her mouth. He then placed a bag over her head, bound her hands and feet and forced her to lay face down. The cart moved fast. She felt every bump and stone in the road. The journey lasted for what seemed like hours, all the while feeling a foot pressing down hard on the back of her neck. The cart stopped abruptly, Chantrea was dragged out and hoisted onto the stranger's shoulder. She sensed the light change as she was carried into a dark room. The stranger that carried her threw her onto the hard floor, not concerned for her welfare. She heard his footsteps depart, leaving her restrained and unable to move.

A little while later she heard footsteps again, this time they approached slowly and stop near to where she was lying. The person pulled down her blindfold and as her eyes adapted to the light, she saw the face of Virak. Her frightened eyes looked up at him fearful of what he was about to do to her.

'First things first.'

He pulled Chantrea towards him, raising his hand high and slapping her hard across the face, so hard she fell back to the floor.

'That's payment with interest for the one you gave me, I've waited far too long to do that,' he said.

Chantrea felt the side of her face redden and could tell her eye had begun to bruise.

'So, my little cuckoo, it's been a long time since you sent me any information, is there a reason for the silence?'

He paused, waiting for an answer, realising she was still gagged he pulled the material out of her mouth allowing her to speak.

Chantrea breathed in deeply catching her breath, she looked up at Virak with deep hatred hidden behind her terrified eyes.

'It would've been foolish for me to try and contact you, Srindra's men have been watching my every move.'

Virak ignored her comment.

'Tell me what's been happening over the last few months,' he demanded.

'I've been getting close to your sister, she trusts me. I'm close to them all which is helping me to find out the truth,' Chantrea had managed to break free of her bonds and pulled her hand to her swollen cheek.

'Your abduction of me isn't going to be easy to explain,' she said, staring at him.

'I'm getting impatient, what have you learnt?' Virak demanded.

He gripped her bound legs so hard it caused her to cry out in pain.

'As I told you, I believe she was pregnant before the wedding, but I have no proof. The queen announced that the princess was pregnant a few weeks after they got married, without proof they conceived before the marriage, it won't help you,' she replied carefully.

Virak continued to inflict pain on her, and she tried with all her might to ignore it. 'What else have you discovered?'

'As I've said, I'm very close to your sister and she trusts me fully. She hasn't shared anything else that would be of use to you yet. One other thing, I expect you already know this, but there is a closeness between this Luke and your brother, that is something we can use.'

'Is that it, everyone knows that,' he said frustratedly but released her legs. 'So, I have missed out on your company for the last few months for very little it seems.'

He snorted, 'This baby, whatever it may be is still a threat. My brother could use the runt to take my throne.'

Virak paused and smiled. 'Luckily I've a plan which suits your skills. When the baby is born you will wait patiently until the time comes for you to take it, you will deliver it to the Cham emperor as a gift from me.'

'I won't do it, how could you do that to your sister, to your kin?' Chantrea cried.

'I'll not have you speak to me like that,' he slapped her across the face again. 'You'll do as I ask or these will fall into my brother's hands.'

He held up hidden correspondence that he found in her room. Chantrea had kept the letters to the Cham from Virak, she was to use them against him as a last resort.

'I see you recognise them,' he said smiling. 'I don't know what plans you had for these, but I'm much happier knowing they're in my hands.'

'Those will incriminate you as much as me,' Chantrea replied desperately.

'Will they indeed,' he said throwing them into a nearby fire. 'Oh, look what I have here, new documents,' he smiled cruelly enjoying himself. 'I wonder what they say. Your deception gave me an idea and our Cham allies helped me to create the evidence, to ensure your loyalty to me. These show your betrayal of our people.'

He sneered at her knowing he had her cornered.

Chantrea looked at him and her head dropped, she knew she had no choice but to follow his orders.

'I will do as you ask, as I always have,' she responded.

'Good girl,' he patted her on the head condescendingly. 'I want to give this child as a gift to the Cham, to show my commitment to our alliance. If you fail or are caught, I'll use these letters to prove your guilt. Then I'll find another way to kill the little brat. If you disobey me again you'll meet a far worse fate. I've got spies everywhere, never forget that.'

A few moments later she was blindfolded and gagged. Chantrea was carried back to the cart by the unknown abductor. The ride this time seemed quicker. She was soon tossed into undergrowth near to where she had been taken. It took her a few tries to get the bindings off, but she managed to pull the gag and the blindfold away. Chantrea heaved herself into a ball and clutched her head sobbing deeply.

What am I going to do? her mind raged.

It took a little while for her to build up enough courage to move, she straighten her clothing and hair then headed back to the compound as Virak's viper in the nest.

***

It had been six months since Kalani joined the temple under Tamal's guidance and he had made a lot of progress. He had always loved to study, whether micro engineering of religious texts he enjoyed being immersed in learning. Tamal had been patient with him, always taking time to explain about the scriptures. In return Kalani would share with the priest about his culture and the believes his people followed. Tamal had become very protective of Kalani, he saw in him some of the same emotions he struggled with as a boy before joining the monastery. Kalani had taken time to reflect on his life, his efforts to understand Buddhism had helped change his way of thinking. He now felt calmer, more in control and better adjusted to deal with the pressures of life.

Marcus and Luke visited him often and strange as it seems all three of them had become close. Kalani loved to hear about what they had both been up to, about the city and the life outside his studies, though he had no desire to leave the temple. He felt safe where he was, happy in his reflections and learning. As much as his mind was calm, he still had moments of regret and moments of shame, which haunted him deeply. His mind would dwell on Maya's death and he would pray for forgiveness often. Kalani knew he was the reason they were all here and that she died because of his actions. It was not just the guilt of Maya he struggled with, his mind would focus on his family and how he had left them alone. Kalani worried that the future he once knew no longer existed, because of his short-sightedness.

Tamal had taught him to meditate, Kalani would do this when his thoughts became negative and he found a way to ease the pain in his mind. Kalani's immersive studies in Buddhism helped to focus him, he found solace in the belief in reincarnation and the cycle of life. He studied the scriptures to understand the Buddhist teachings. He was fascinated in how the way someone lives their life, impacts their soul and their search for enlightenment. He reflected on the religious teachings and understood that the cycle of life applied as much to science as it did Buddhism. Kalani remembered long discussions with Maya about the birth of the universe, how the formation of stars led to the creation of worlds and eventually life. He reflected on what lives, will die and that in death life forms again. The connection between science and reincarnation seemed to call to him and this gave him comfort.

It was on one particular hazy humid day that he took himself deep into the archives at the temple. He stretched hard to grab a scroll on top of a high shelf in the temple's deepest library.

What's this scripture? he thought to himself as he unrolled the paper.

Tamal had suggested it to him, he thought it might help him align his spiritual and scientific beliefs. The scripture was one of the earliest he had seen. It must have been over three hundred years old. He read the beautiful scroll and his mind came alive. The text flowed into his brain and his mind connected with it, something struck him hard and he could see the calculation, the way to get home, back to his family and back to the future.

***

'Bo's gone into labour,' Marcus shouted excitedly to Luke. 'The midwives are attending to her, but I couldn't help it. I used my palm reader to scan Bo and I've checked to see if everything is okay, thankfully it is, but she's carrying twins. This changes everything, I want to get the medical kit just encase anything goes wrong. I know we said not to use our technology, but I can't risk it, Luke I just can't.'

'Calm down,' Luke said giving him a hug. 'I'm sure everything is fine, but if you want to get it as a backup then we can.'

'Tell me where you buried it, I just want it close encase anything happens,' he said with a sigh.

'Come, we'll retrieve it together,' Luke gestured to the door and they rushed to the stable.

Both men mounted horses and charged out of the compound, Luke rode fast, he had become an excellent rider. He was so good that Marcus struggled to keep up. They charged down the streets heading for the western baray. As they reached the water Luke rode to the right soon arriving at Prei Kmeng temple. He jumped down and tied his horse to a nearby tree and disappeared into the jungle. Marcus caught up and dismounted his horse desperately trying to catch him. Thick foliage was everywhere and Luke pulled out his sword, he swung at the branches cutting a path through until he finally came to a halt.

'See I marked X on this tree?' he shouted to Marcus.

'X marks the spot.' Marcus rolled his eyes. 'I guess too many pirate films when you were a kid.'

Luke pulled out a small trowel from his bag and he began to dig into the ground, soon he heard a scraping sound on the top of a metal box. Luke continued to dig out the item finally pulling it up, he opened the clasps on the box revealing the equipment.

'It's here,' he said quickly pulling out the medical kit which included a scanner, hypo-spray, and dermal-regenerator.

Luke fastened the box back up and buried the rest of the items quickly. He got up and brushed himself down.

'Shall we go?' he said excitedly, and Marcus nodded.

They were soon racing back through the streets until they reached the prince's compound. They jumped off their horses tossed the reins to a couple of surprised stable boys and rushed into the grounds. As they entered Luke was moving so fast that he crashed into Sri and they fell to the floor.

'Where have you both been,' Sri said annoyed pulling himself to his feet. 'Bo has been calling for you Marcus, where did you run to, she's in a right state.'

'Sorry Sri, I'm heading there now, I just needed to get something,' Marcus replied, quickly heading for the door.

'What did you need to get that was so urgent you left my sister alone?' Sri shouted, his anger building.

'Just this,' Luke said showing the medical equipment. 'It's just if we need any extra help.'

'Luke, we've spoken about this, no technology from the future, we made a pact, we all did,' he said angrily, looking at Marcus.

'It was my idea, I just needed to have every tool around us encase something goes wrong,' Marcus replied a little too emotionally. 'I won't lose her or my children.'

'We don't have time to talk about this now,' Sri said exasperated. 'Go, she needs you!'

Marcus smiled at him and turned to Luke, he grabbed the medical kit and ran out of the room heading for their quarters. Marcus burst through the door as Bo screamed through another contraction.

'Remember to breathe, don't forget those exercises I taught you,' Marcus said.

'Where have you been,' she screamed at him.

'I just needed to get something, I'm here for you now,' he replied quickly taking her hand.

'Come on, I will do them with you,' he started to breathe and Bo followed his lead.

About an hour later the baby started to crown.

'One more push should do it,' one of the old midwives said.

'Come on my love we can do it together,' Marcus said as Bo gripped his hand tightly.

'Ahhhhhh!' she screamed and the baby was born, the midwife cut the umbilical cord and washed the baby.

After a few tense moments, it began to cry.

'It's a beautiful baby girl,' the midwife said, smiling at them both.

There was a sudden cry from Bo again as another contraction hit her, the midwife gave the baby to a nurse and went to examine Bo.

'Keep pushing, it's twins,' Marcus whispered quietly. 'Hold onto me.'

She looked at him lovingly and pushed again.

'Ahhhh' she screamed and panted, she pushed again. 'Ahhh.'

A few minutes later another baby was born. The midwife cut the cord, she washed it carefully and the baby began to cry.

'It's a boy,' the midwife said with pleasure and handed Bo both her new born babies.

The happy parents looked at each other smiling.

'I'm a father' Marcus said in disbelief.

'A father of twins,' Bo replied wearily.

'It's such a gift to have twins, Buddha must be smiling on us,' she said, knowing Marcus's beliefs didn't extend to hers.

He kissed her forehead. 'My family.'

CHAPTER TWENTY-ONE

Blessings

The birth of healthy twins was hailed as a great gift from Buddha. The king and queen were thrilled and arranged for celebrations to be held across the city. Marcus was just relieved that his new children and wife were doing well. The next few days were a haze, with many dignitaries visiting the couple congratulating them on the birth of the twins. The king and queen visited often, taking great pleasure in holding their new grandchildren.

Tamal and Kalani visited the twins four days after they were born. It is tradition that before the children's blessing ceremony a horoscope is created by the high priest. It details the exact time and date of the children's birth helping to inform the sacred rituals. Tamal advised the anxious parents that their babies' names should begin with the letter J, to align with the horoscope.

'Once you know the names of my niece and nephew I will bless them at the temple, this needs to be done within a month,' Tamal said kindly and smiled.

Kalani excitedly gave Marcus the horoscope that he'd spent many hours creating.

'I'm sure you'll enjoy studying this,' he said, giving both parents a hug. 'There's so much joy in the Buddhist religion.'

It took them the next few days to decide on the names of their babies. They finally agreed that the little girl would be called Jorani, meaning radiant jewel. They gave her the second name of Maya, keen to honour the memory of the woman who had saved Bo. The little boy was to be named Johan. This name meant a lot to Marcus, it was the name of his childhood friend who inspired him to study Asian cultures. They gave Johan the second name of Raksmei, in honour to the king. It was the name of his first son who died shortly after he was born.

It had been over a week since the babies were named. The queen made her way into Sri's compound to visit with her daughter once more. As she entered, she waved the guards to move out the way. She was keen to speak to Bo before the blessing ceremony, which was scheduled for later that day. The queen's demeanour had changed since Bo became pregnant, she became much more connected to her daughter and was in her element. The queen loved having children around her and becoming a grandparent was very exciting.

Bo sat out on the veranda looking into the lake holding Jorani. Chantrea was sitting next to her holding Johan. As the queen walked in she gestured to her to hand her grandson over and Chantrea obliged. She got up and indicated to the queen to take her seat on the veranda. The queen sat down and Johan was placed in her lap. Chantrea bowed to them both and exited.

'My dear, now that you've given birth, don't you think it's about time that you returned to your own compound. You have responsibilities in your own court. I know you like to be close to your brother, but I think it would be best for the children that you make your own home.'

'Are you sure we're safe?' Bo asked. 'I don't want to put my children in any danger.'

'What do you mean danger, it's your court Bo. You decide who and what you do in it. Your father and I have been renovating the buildings while you've lived here, in readiness for you to return with our grandchildren. It'll be the perfect place for you to bring up the future of our line. Plus it's nearer to us,' the queen said smiling. 'Why don't I show you both around after the blessing ceremony?'

'I'd like that, I'm sure Marcus would too,' Bo replied a little hesitantly.

'Great it's settled, this will be a special gift from both of us,' the queen replied. They spent the next few hours looking after the babies and getting ready for the blessing.

At three in the afternoon, the king gathered the dignitaries and specially invited guests at the temple. They were all dressed in their distinctive colours showing their allegiances to their respective houses. The king and queen stood next to Marcus and Bo, while Prince Srindra, Luke, and Prince Virak stood to the right. To the left stood the queen's ladies in waiting, Kesor, Nearidei, and Chantrea.

Tamal walked to the centre of the temple and began to chant from the holy texts. He placed the children on a large mat in front of the statue of Buddha. Around them, monks placed offerings of flowers, candles, and incense all while Tamal continued to bless them. He held out his hand to Kalani who gave him a bowl of holy water which had a lotus flower floating in the centre.

Tamal sprinkled the water on the children and called out, 'Jorani Maya I bless you with the love of Buddha and the love of our people. Johan Raksmei I bless you with the love of Buddha and the love of our people.'

Kalani then stepped forward, he tied around the babies' wrists five different sacred threads which had been woven into one. This was to welcome 'Khwan,' a spirit that would protect the children. The band Kalani tied onto the children was made up of five different coloured threads, to bless the children with wisdom.

The first thread was white which symbolised the transformation from the delusion of ignorance into the wisdom of reality. The second thread was yellow which symbolised the transformation of pride into wisdom of sameness. The third thread was blue which symbolised the transformation of anger into a mirror like wisdom. The fourth thread was red which symbolised the transformation of the delusion of attachment into the wisdom of discernment. The final thread was green which symbolised the transformation of jealousy into the wisdom of accomplishment. The five woven strands represented the strengths of Buddhism. Faith, energy, mindfulness, concentration, and most importantly, wisdom.

Tamal rang a large gong and declared the children blessed, the crowd erupted with applause and the ceremony came to an end. Across the city, bells rang out to give thanks for the new Prince Johan and Princess Jorani. The blessing was over and the guests in the temples started to disperse.

***

'Luke, I need to speak to you!' Kalani shouted, trying to catch his attention before he left the temple.

Luke had changed significantly since they arrived, gone was the skinny shy naive boy who cared only about archaeology. Luke was now a man who had been training to become a warrior. His mind like his body had changed, he seemed stronger, more self-assured and he liked how he felt.

'Luke, wait,' Kalani called out again pushing his way through the crowd.

Luke looked back noticing Kalani calling to him, Kalani stumbled and fell to the ground.

Luke rushed over to him, 'What's all the shouting about?' he asked.

'I need to speak with you about something, it's important. Do you have time now?' he asked quickly. Kalani was excited, he couldn't contain his words.

Luke looked around, he signalled to Sri he was going to talk to Kalani and he would catch him up. Sri nodded in acknowledgement..

'I always have time for you,' he replied. 'What's this all about?'

'Come with me,' Kalani gestured to a door in the temple.

Luke followed him through a number of corridors until they reached the inner sanctum.

'Look, I've found this,' Kalani pulled out a very old text, it was fraying at the edges and extremely delicate. 'It talks about portals to the heavens.'

Kalani pushed the bit of paper into Luke's hands. He looked down and he could see the calculation and he recognised it instantly.

'What is this?' He asked confused. 'These look like the Quantology equations that Maya created.' Luke unexpectedly put up his hand as he examined the document further, 'wait what's this, it's like our study of cognition physics.'

'This document is three hundred years old. I don't know how this kind of information got here,' Kalani said in amazement. 'But there's more, it shows me how to create a portal without antimatter. We just need a high-level surge of electricity to create the stable field, if I set up a circuit like this.'

He pointed to the diagram on the page, 'Luke, we can get home.'

'Kalani we can't, we don't have the lab or tech to do this,' Luke replied in disbelief. 'How would we get the coordinates right? We could be flung anywhere.'

Kalani hesitated.

'Well, I've been out searching where we crash-landed last year and I've found some of our equipment. I managed to salvage some parts and I've also been able to make some components here.'

He showed Luke a number of items under a sheet on a nearby table, there were a few circuit boards connected to a mini quantum droid which seemed to have power. Luke then spotted the familiar helmet he had worn so many times. He walked over to the table and picked up the helmet. Luke stared back at the device that had so nearly killed him.

'It may be crude, but with the power sources from the MQD and these new calculations…' He pointed back at the document. 'I think we can replicate the lab.'

Luke looked at him in amazement, then it hit him. 'Where did these documents come from? Can you really trust them?'

'I don't know Luke, but these calculations are like Maya's, I know it,' Kalani said. 'Look, I have fused these circuits to the HTC helmet, what we need to do is to get a large surge of power to help start it all.'

'How are you going to do that?' Luke asked. 'There's nothing here that can create such a surge.'

'Ah, that's where you're wrong,' Kalani said with a smile. 'We use the weather, well lightning to be more precise. I have set up a lightning rod on one of the towers and trailed a wire to this.'

He held up a small metal object. 'We can store the surge into this quantum battery, Maya used them as a backup to maintain the power levels if the power to the HTC cut out. It's just dead that's all, if we wait for the right storm, we'll have a few days to use it.'

Kalani was beaming with excitement. 'If you bend the beams when I release the power we should be able to trigger a portal.'

'But how do we know where we're going, how do we calibrate the co-ordinates?' Luke asked.

'We use our implants and synchronise them together. That will calculate the correct spatial coordinates to return to. It should be simple, not the complex coordinates we needed to complete in the lab. I really think we can do it,' he grinned widely.

'What about the lives we've built here?' Luke replied sadly. 'What about Marcus and his new family, he won't abandon them to go home.'

'We're still a danger to the timeline just being here, it would be prudent for us to go, but I know it will be everyone's own personal choice.' Kalani paused and looked down at the equipment on the table. 'I want to see my family again. I want to make sure they're okay.'

'I know,' Luke said, putting his hand on Kalani shoulder. 'I'll help, but first I need to understand your plans.'

Kalani smiled and began to explain the calculation and how Luke could establish the portal. The discussions went on late into the night until Luke declared he needed sleep.

He headed back home, *well home for now*. His mind racing about how he would break the news to Sri.

***

The king and queen accompanied Sri, Marcus, and Bo back to the compound. They arrived at Bo's house just as the light was starting to fade. The servants had laid out some light refreshments for them all. The king picked up a goblet of wine and turned to Sri.

'My son, you've done me a great service, you protected your sister with honour, now it's time for her to re-join her own court.'

Bo had already told Sri about the news they were to leave. Sri was nervous, he had always protected his sister ever since she was young. Sri had concerns that the arrival of the twins would put them in greater danger, not less. However, he understood the king and queen's reasoning for Bo's need to get back to her own court. He knew Bo's court had to become strong, it needed to develop its own identity. It was important that her court grew to protect the new Prince and Princess. Sri turned to face his father, straightening his back.

'I've only done my duty. I'll continue to protect Bo and her children wherever she lives.'

'You're becoming wiser every day,' the king replied beaming.

'I've arranged for us to view your new home tonight, it looks beautiful in the candlelight,' the queen said proudly. 'I'm sure your ladies in waiting can look after the children while we explore.'

Bo turned to Chantrea. 'I sent Kesor and Nearidei away to help establish the new school in the village by the lake. Will you be okay to care for my babies on your own?. The guards will still be outside patrolling.'

'Of course Your Majesty. Please go and see your new home, it's so exciting.'

She gave Bo a reassuring smile.

'Very well mother let's go now, while we have at least a little light.'

The queen nodded, she took the king's arm and they left. Sri, Bo and Marcus followed and were met by a number of the king's guards. They were escorted through the compound and towards the waiting carriage which was to take them on their journey.

Chantrea could hear the queen talking about the carvings in their new home, she waited patiently for their voices to disappear out of earshot. She paused looking at the sleeping babies, then put her hand into her robes to pull out a note Virak had given her in the temple. She slowly opened it, her hands trembling. In her heart of hearts she knew what it was going to say.

Bring the boy to the temple tonight he's the danger, kill the girl. I've arranged for transportation out of the city. Be there by eight at the latest, I don't care what you have to do or who you have to kill bring me that boy.

Tears began to fall down Chantrea's face, she looked at the sleeping babies and collapsed to the floor. After a few minutes she slowly began to compose herself, she reached for a piece of paper and quickly wrote a note. She needed to at least try and explain her betrayal. She finished writing the note, gave it a kiss and placed it on the table. Chantrea picked up a sharp dagger which was nearby, she held it high above the sleeping Jorani and paused.

I can't kill a baby, Virak will have to do that himself, her mind screamed.

She threw the dagger to one side and wiped the streaming tears from her eyes. Chantrea now looked down at Johan, he had begun to move and she picked him up to calm him. She cradled the boy carefully until he drifted back to sleep, and then put him under her robes. Chantrea picked the note she had written off the table and placed it where Johan had been sleeping. She left the room quietly and walked confidently across the compound, turning back to take one last look at the house that she had come to call home. Chantrea composed herself and stroked Johan gently under her cloak. *Go now or be discovered*, a voice in her head said. Without another thought she left the compound disappearing into the darkness of the night.

***

The sky was alive with stars as Kalani walked out of the temple, the air was hot and humid, but he felt elated. Telling Luke about his discovery had given him a new sense of purpose and the thought he might see his family again made his spirits soar. Kalani stopped and turned back to look at the incredible temple behind him, even in the dark the golden spires sparkled in the moonlight. He could see the princess's green banners still hanging from the temple walls from the twins' blessing.

He thought to himself, *I'll miss this place, it really is a marvel.*

He smiled and began to cross the western bridge. Kalani wanted to explore the city and take in all its beauty before he started work on their exit plan.

He came to the end of the bridge and spotted something unusual. It was the princess's lady in waiting. She looked agitated, upset even and he sensed he needed to help her.

'Are you okay, Chantrea isn't it,' Kalani called out.

Chantrea turned around in terror, she looked him straight in the eyes and froze.

'Is everything okay? I don't normally see you out this way,' he said as he approached.

It was at that moment he spotted the baby and he looked closer. It was Johan. Kalani could see the band he put on the child that very afternoon.

Chantrea saw his reaction and spoke quickly, 'I couldn't get him to sleep, I thought a walk in the city would help.'

Kalani looked at her strangely.

'But it's not safe, where are the guards and your protection,' he said, confused.

Something felt very wrong. Suddenly Kalani noticed a flash of silver, he felt intense pain and everything went dark.

Little Johan let out a cry. Chantrea gripped him tightly and fell to her knees as tears began to stream down her face. Her eyes fixated on Kalani. She watched helplessly as deep red blood seeped from his neck. His throat had been slit. Slit by the man standing over the crumpled dying body, it was Prince Virak.

Virak looked a Chantrea in disgust.

'Weakness,' he said, staring at her shaking body. 'The horses are ready, go now, go with Bhante quickly.'

Chantrea tried to move but she couldn't, she was paralysed with fear. Suddenly a large man picked her up, she was clutching a screaming Johan tightly as he carried her to a nearby cart. The man placed her down.

'Stay under the covers and keep that brat quiet,' he barked.

The man flung at her a leather pouch. 'Feed him with this milk if needed.'

Then he covered her with blankets. The cart rumbled frantically through the streets and a few of the blankets slipped. Chantrea got one last glimpse of the city she called home, before quickly pulling the blankets back over her head. She knew she could never return. Her life had changed forever.

CHAPTER TWENTY-TWO

To Hell and Cham

'Marcus, I know they've gone over the top, but I have to admit I love the green tiger carvings at the entrance,' Bo said happily as she walked back to Prince Srindra's compound.

'It's so big, do we need that space. I'm happy here close to your brother and Luke,' he replied.

'We need our own home. It's tradition and the people expect it. We're still close enough to our family and my brother will always look out for us,' she responded, knowing full well they couldn't refuse the king.

As Bo walked up the wooden steps to their home she could hear a baby crying, she looked at Marcus and rushed past the guards who bowed to her.

'It's okay my sweet,' she said as she picked up Jorani to comfort her. 'Where's Chantrea?'

Bo looked around. 'More importantly, where's Johan?'

Marcus stared at her worriedly, he rushed around the house trying to find Chantrea. He suddenly heard Bo shouting for the guards and he hurried to see his wife,

'What is it?' he shouted in confusion.

'Look, look,' Bo said thrusting a piece of paper at him, she erupted into deep sobs clinging onto little Jorani who was now screaming.

Marcus opened the note, it was from Chantrea. His eyes glazed over with fury as he read,

I've taken Johan to my masters in Cham. The love and kindness you have both shown me is something I've never experienced. I'm so sorry I've betrayed you. But I have to do this, I have no choice or they will kill me. I promise with every fibre in my body I will protect little Johan. I know you'll never forgive me but I must complete the mission or my life is forfeit. Please know I'll care for him as my own and devote my life to his protection.

-Chantrea

Marcus looked up at Bo in disbelief at what he'd just read. Bo was screaming at the guards who seemed slow to comprehend what had happened. More of Sri's men entered the room.

Bo continued to scream, 'My baby, she's taken my baby!'

A guard ran out and crashed into Major Keo.

'Sir, one of the royal children has been taken,' he said in a panic trying to gather his words.

'What?' Keo said in disbelief. 'We need to lock down the city. Ride to General Thorn as fast as you can, he'll mobilise our forces.'

The guard bowed and rushed to the stables. Keo turned to another soldier.

'You, alert Prince Srindra now,' he ordered and the soldier ran to the prince's residence.

Keo rushed into the princess's home, 'Your Majesty, we're need to close the city down. I'll mobilise the prince's forces straight away.'

He looked at her frightened face.

'Is this the note?'

Marcus nodded. Keo took it and read it quickly, he then looked at them both.

'We'll get him back, I promise you.' Keo bowed to them and rushed out of the room.

***

The next few hours were madness, when the king heard about the abduction of Johan he ordered all forces to mobilise. The king's battalion, queen's battalion and prince's guard were readied. Each force took a section of the city and searched house by house for the new prince. The king sent riders out in all directions to search everyone who'd left the city. In addition he sent out envoys to his allies, asking for help.

The queen was devastated when she heard the news and rushed back to be with her daughter. The princess was a broken woman, she had found true happiness for the first time in her life and it had been ripped away. The queen found Bo sobbing when she arrived. Bo held on tightly to Jorani, not trusting anyone to come near. Servants desperately tried to calm Bo down, but she was inconsolable.

The queen instructed everyone to leave, she sat down next to Bo and said quietly, 'I didn't teach you to be weak in front of the people, we're under attack and you need to be strong.'

'How can I be strong Mother? What are they going to do with him? What if they—' she stopped and burst into tears again.

This time the queen was a bit gentler, 'we'll find him Bo, but right now he needs his mother to be strong, the people expect it.'

The queen pulled her close. 'Give me Jorani, she needs to be changed and fed.'

The princess slowly let go of her daughter and the queen took hold of her, she smiled at the child and called for a servant.

'Please change her for me, do it here where I can see you.'

The scared servant bowed and took the child.

The queen turned back to Bo, 'I need you to be strong, I need you to fight. We need to focus on the search and I'll need your help to do that, now try and compose yourself. Firstly we need to find out why Chantrea would do this.'

At that moment Prince Srindra rushed in with Marcus.

'We found something,' the prince replied.

Sri looked at Marcus knowing the terrible news he was about to reveal.

'Well, what is it,' the queen said impatiently.

'Kalani's dead,' Marcus spat out.

Bo looked at him in disbelief. 'Dead, but how? What's going on tonight.'

'Luke found him, he sent a rider back to us with this note,' Marcus handed it to the queen.

She read it out loud,

'Kalani's dead, his throat was cut. We're not sure if it is linked to Johan's abduction but it's suspicious. Send more men we need to cover all roads out of the city.'

'Oh Marcus,' Bo said starting to lose it again.

He grabbed his wife and held her tight.

'Our only focus is finding Johan, keep strong my love,' he said pulling her close.

Marcus looked over to Sri while comforting his wife.

'I'll ride with you. I must find my son.'

'We're leaving now, I want to find Luke and help with the search,' Sri turned to the queen. 'The king is coordinating the search from the palace. Mother, take Bo and Jorani back there, you'll all be safer within the palace until we know what's going on. Father has sent a number of his personal guards to escort you.'

The queen nodded.

'Thank you Sri,' she replied a bit shakily picking up a now calm Jorani.

She turned to the princess. 'Wipe those tears away and be strong. When we ride to the palace the people need to see their princess is in control, they will be frightened, and we must calm them.'

She turned back to Marcus and Sri. 'Go find my grandson, do whatever you need and whatever the cost.'

Marcus bowed and began to leave. Surprisingly the queen gripped his arm. 'I'm truly sorry about Kalani, I know you were close. Tamal had told me how hard he'd worked to mend his ways.'

Marcus couldn't formulate words to reply, he just nodded again and left with Sri.

A servant appeared with a bowl of water. The young girl sat the princess down and helped to clean her up, she wiped Bo's eyes and straightened her clothes. When ready Bo took Jorani off the queen and they walked out into the dark night.

***

The cart had been moving relatively fast for the last couple of hours. Little Johan had fallen asleep in Chantrea's arms, despite all the commotion. She didn't know what direction she was going in. All Chantrea knew were her orders from Virak, give the baby to King Jaya Indravarman. She knew the leader of the Cham was ruthless. He was responsible for many Khmer deaths including that of her own family. They had died in the battle with the Cham when Angkor was retaken. However, Virak had made a pact with this murderer and nothing would get in the way. He was intent on taking the throne and if that meant killing his own family, well that didn't faze him.

The cart continued to thunder along the road, Chantrea remained quiet, always holding onto Johan tightly. Suddenly she heard men shouting and horses galloping close. The sounds got louder, then she heard a man shout, 'STOP.' The cart came to a slow halt and Chantrea thought she heard about five horses circling the cart. She took a deep intake of breath, but was too scared to release it.

'What's this about, I am taking my wine to Rovieng,' Bhante replied casually.

'We've been ordered to search all people who've left the city tonight, no exceptions,' the soldier said, Chantrea recognised the voice straight away, it was Major Keo.

'It's just me and my wine, I'm happy to give you some if you let me on my way. I don't want to be late or I'll miss my contact and the journey would have been a waste,' Bhante said joyfully.

'I said no exceptions,' suddenly Johan let out a small cry. 'What was that? Men search the car...'

Before Major Keo could finish his sentence Bhante had thrown a dagger directly between his eyes. Major Keo's eyes stare back for an instant, then he slid slowly off his horse dead. Confusion gripped the men over what had just happened. Keo's horse reared in fright jarring them awake just as the blur of another dagger passed by. It hit a young soldier to the right of Keo directly in his chest, he fell off his horse writhing in pain. The remaining men regained control and one fired an arrow hitting Bhante in the arm. Bhante, however, ignored the pain and managed to throw two more knives, one narrowly missed Keo's second in command while the fourth hit the youngest soldier in the leg, he let out a yell and clutched his wound.

The two remaining soldiers charge Bhante, Chantrea heard swords clashing and decided to make a run for it. She quietly slipped out from under the blankets and entered into the forest clutching Johan carefully. She didn't look back, she didn't know if the soldiers saw her or not, Chantrea just ran for her life and the life of the child.

***

Bo managed to keep it together as she rode through the streets to the palace, in the king's own carriage. The people watch her intently as she held her remaining child tightly, it was as if her nightmares were coming true. The queen sat beside her, often nodding and smiling at the people. She was keen to give the impression that they were in control, despite what had happened. Officially no one had been told about the prince's abduction but somehow it got out. The city was tense and the people were worried about another Cham invasion.

The king was busy with his advisors as Bo and the queen entered the throne room. As soon as he noticed them, he signalled they join him. The king greeted them warmly, he gestured to the large table. Around it stood a number of key army colonels along with the king's council, all were there except Prince Srindra, Marcus and Tamal. The queen stared hard at Virak. He looked back at her not reacting to the queen's penetrating glare.

'The army's mobilised,' the king said.

He showed them a large map detailing the search area. The princess noticed several carved figures placed strategically on the map. It indicated the forces that were assigned to each area.

'We're doing all we can, trust me my sweet we'll get him back, whatever the cost.'

The door opened and a major from the king's guard entered, he rushed over to General Thorn and handed him a note. The general opened it and read it carefully before handing it over to the king.

'Father, is it news on the search?' Bo asked forcefully.

'No my dear, it's from the ambassador of Lavo, our allies are pledging their support for us. Lavo province is sending a battalion of men from the governor's personal guard to help with our search.' He paused for a moment, 'And if needed to begin a campaign against the Cham.'

He took a deep breath and began to pace the room. 'Thorn where are my updates from the riders, they're due back, aren't they?'

The king was getting frustrated.

'Yes Your Majesty, I have the reports but so far no news of Johan. Major, go check again for more riders and let us know any update,' Thorn ordered and the major rushed off.

'I need to see Prince Srindra,' the king shouted at Captain Voan, who was representing the prince at the meeting. 'Go find him.'

The king then turned to the queen. 'I want to know about our forces near the Cham border, also what are our spies in the Cham court saying?'

'My dear there has been limited contact with the Cham court, however as you know Indravarman has been planning to kill our line for some time. He wants our lands for his own, this is not new news.' The queen sighed. 'We have been fighting the Cham forever, they win a battle, we win a battle, they kill us, we kill them, however this is a new low.'

'That man has no honour, his deceit and cowardice seem to have no ends,' the king shouted back.

There was a loud noise which startled everyone. Prince Srindra and Captain Voan entered followed by Tamal.

'Father, Major Keo has not returned, it's very peculiar as he always follows protocol. I want to lead a group of men to find him, he was searching the road to Rovieng,' Sri said forcefully.

'My son, I know you want to get our nephew back, but this is dangerous. I can't lose you and my grandson on the same night.' The king's eyes flittered to Bo, knowing those words would cut deep.

'Father, you want me to step up to be a strong ruler, then let me lead. I will take a number of my personal guard with me, Marcus and Luke will also ride with us,' Sri turned to Bo and the queen. 'Mother, with your permission Colonel Myan has requested to join me with his best men, do you consent to this?'

'Yes my son, take what you need and do what you have to do,' she replied

Sri then spoke to Bo. 'There's no way I can stop Marcus from joining me, I'm sure you understand.'

'It's his right to go, as it's mine. I want to come and find my child!' Bo shouted.

Before the king and queen could speak Sri jumped in, 'I can't look after you and search for your son at the same time, you have to stay here and look after Jorani. You need to trust me and your husband, let us do the hard work.'

The prince turned back to the king and his council, 'General Thorn I need you to mobilise the rest of my force along with the queen's battalion, king's guard and any other forces we have, just in case I fail.'

'Sri what are you saying?' the king asked.

'What I'm saying Father, is we must not stand for this terror, we need to retaliate against the Cham for this vile conduct. Whether I survive or not you'll need to invade Champa.'

The king was stunned, he was a man of peace, a man that followed Buddhist teaching closely and only used force as a last resort.

The king turned to his council. 'Well, what do you all think, if we do as my son says then we'll need to formally declare war. All of us need to agree if we're to take that action.'

Nakry spoke first. 'Your Majesty, we have the funds to wage this war.'

She paused. 'If this is not a reason to go to war, I don't know what is.'

'I agree Your Majesty, we need to show our strength, our men are ready. All you have to do is give the order,' General Thorn said forcefully.

'There is precedent in law too Your Majesty,' Phala confirmed. 'But in truth we need to punish the Cham for their crimes whether there is legal precedent or not.'

Prince Virak spoke, 'are you sure it's wise to risk our forces on this, could it not give the Cham an opportunity to counterattack.'

'We're ready for any Cham attack,' General Thorn interrupted.

'If you're sure then you have my backing,' Virak confirmed.

Surprisingly Tamal then spoke, 'I know our religion doesn't condone war and we try hard to live by the Buddhist values. However, the abduction of our young prince and the brutal murder of Kalani within our city.'

Tamal shook his head, 'something needs to be done.' He looked over at his sister then back to his father.

'I'll back any action you decide to take.'

The queen then spoke calmly, 'We have our allies' support, we have the strongest force we've had in twenty years and we have morality on our side.'

She paused and looked at her husband. 'Crush them, spare no mercy on these beasts.'

'My daughter the decision is down to you,' the king said kindly.

'Do whatever you need to get my baby back, I don't care the cost,' she said coldly.

'The decision is made. We mobilise for war. General, call our forces together and we'll gather at Stung Treng. I'll lead the invasion of Champa personally. My son you have permission. Go, ride for Rovieng and stop at nothing to get Johan back.'

CHAPTER TWENTY-THREE

The Dirty Deed

Chantrea had been walking for ages, little Johan was now screaming, she had no food, no water, and no milk for the sobbing baby. She was completely lost. She eventually came upon a small pool of water and cautiously crept to the edge. She drank frantically, then cupped her hand and dripped some water into Johan's mouth. He coughed a little, but thankfully he drank. Chantrea decided to wash him, she removed his dirty clothes and bathed him in the cool water. It was such a relief from the stifling heat that it made him laugh, causing another wave of guilt to hit her.

What am I going to do? she suddenly thought to herself.

Chantrea's mind spiralled and she began to sob loudly. There was a sudden *crack* in the forest, she looked around scanning the foliage but saw nothing. She turned back to Johan and lifted him out of the water cradling him once more. Her eyes were drawn to a moving reflection in the pool, she followed it as it reached the edge of the lake and looked up. Chantrea was confronted by a man dressed in black, pointing an arrow directly at her.

'Stop,' she shouted. 'I'm on a mission to present a gift to King Jaya Indravarman.'

The man didn't move. She heard further noises surrounding her. Chantrea looked around desperately seeing many men dressed in black, pointing yet more arrows at them as she cradled Johan tightly.

***

Sri arrived back at his compound where Luke, Marcus, and Colonel Myan were waiting.

'The king has agreed, we are to ride with our men to search for the prince. Thorn will mobilise our forces for a full invasion.'

Myan looked at him in disbelief. 'The king agreed to a *full* invasion?'

'The whole council agreed, there's no going back from here. As of today, we're at war with the Cham and nothing will stop us until we find Johan, take their capital city, or die trying,' Sri said firmly.

'It's about time Your Majesty, you have my men and my loyalty at your bequest. We'll follow you whatever the cost,' the colonel said bowing his head.

'Marcus. Luke. I know you've both vowed not to interfere in our society. You're under no obligation to come on this mission, it will be dangerous and I cannot guarantee we'll return,' Sri said, looking at them.

'Nothing will get in the way of me finding my child, not the Cham, not you and not the future. I'll ride with you whatever the cost,' Marcus replied sternly.

Luke stepped forward, 'You have my sword, bow, and heart. We'll find the despicable people who took Johan and they'll live to regret it.'

Sri smiled back.

'We ride now to find Major Keo. The queen's authorised you, Colonel, to join us on our hunt along with fifty of your best riders,' Sri said relaying the orders to Myan.

'They'll join with fifty of mine while the rest of our forces join the king's invasion. My plan is simple, we ride for Rovieng and search for Keo. We'll meetup with the king's forces in Stung Treng if we make it in time and join the invasion of Champa.'

There were sounds of agreement. Sri ordered that they meet at the stable in half an hour. They busied themselves preparing their gear, collecting supplies and praying to Buddha. When ready, Sri gave the signal to move out. The officers rode out of the compound to greet the men assembled on the parade ground.

Prince Srindra ordered Captain Voan to ready the men to leave. A short while later they were riding on the east road and out of the city.

***

Chantrea was escorted out of the jungle by the men in black, she soon realised she was back on the road she had fled from. Her eyes adjusted in the bright light as she exited the forest, she blinked and looked up seeing about twenty black riders surrounding the cart she had been travelling in. As she looked closer, she noticed that there were five of the prince's soldiers lying dead on the floor, their purple robes stained with blood. Chantrea heard a painful moan and noticed Bhante, he was slumped against the cart desperately pressing at a wound on his neck, it was oozing dark red blood.

'Major Yom, you've found the crazy bitch,' Bhante said to the leader of the men.

'Yes, she's slowed us down considerably,' Yom replied angrily.

'You'll need to take her and ride for Champa, these men are the prince's force. Srindra's no fool he'll be on his way. Mark my words.'

'We'll leave when I say,' Yom said frustratedly. 'I can't carry any dead weight. I won't allow anything to slow us down.'

He reached into his cloak and brought out a jewel-encrusted dagger. 'You've been a good spy Bhante but we can't carry you and I can't leave you for the enemy to find. You might give up our secrets'

Bhante looked at the man with horror, realising what was about to happen. Yom suddenly plunged the dagger deep in to his chest. Bhante panted hard gasping for breath, he slumped forward and called out in pain. It wasn't long before he fell silent.

'Bring her, she's caused us enough trouble. If I didn't need her to look after that runt, I'd have slit her throat,' Yom said wiping his dagger on one of the dead soldier's purple robes.

Chantrea was lifted onto one of the horses and instructed to cling to its rider. Once secured to the horse, the man she heard Bhante call Yom approached her. He was older than she initially thought and had a long scar down his right cheek.

'We have orders to bring you and the brat back to the king, he wants you both alive. Do exactly as I say, and everything will be fine,' Chantrea gave a scared nod. 'Give the baby this, he needs milk, or he'll not survive the journey.'

Yom gave her a leather drinking pouch.

'Men, we'll ride for Rovieng, then over the Mekong at Stung Treng. We'll need to be cautious. The Khmer forces are on high alert and despite what you've heard, they're still a formidable force. Yom mounted his horse, gave the signal to depart and they rode off at high speed.

***

Prince Srindra and his forces had been riding for hours, they'd not stopped since they set off from Angkor. The prince had dispatched scouts ahead to search for anything unusual, but had heard nothing back from them. Not long after midday the group stopped for water. As they were drinking the sound from a horn rang through the trees, it was the sign of danger. The men quickly mounted their horses and began to ride, more horns sounded and the tension within the group rose. A few minutes passed then a rider was spotted. Sri rode out, flanked by his men to meet the soldier who was galloping fast towards them. Without stopping the scout circled the prince telling him the area ahead was secure. Sri signalled to Marcus and Luke who rode to join him. The riders followed the scout and reached an abandoned cart, which was surrounded by dead bodies.

Sri dismounted his horse and surveyed the scene closely. He could see by the colours of the robes that it was his men lying dead at his feet. Luke and Marcus joined him, and they followed Sri as he scrutinised the scene of death. Sri stopped when he saw Major Keo's body lying motionless. His eyes were still open, with a dagger embedded deep within his skull. Sri put his hand to his friends face and closed Keo's eyes, he pulled out the dagger and tossed it to one side. His hand moved until it was resting tenderly on Keo's chest. Sri looked down at his former friend and there was silence for what felt like hours. Finally, he took a deep breath and turned back to Luke.

'Keo was a good friend and a great soldier, I'll miss him deeply,' he said slamming his fist down on the dry earth.

Sri rose to his feet and his attention turned to the stranger lying dead beside the cart. Colonel Myan joined him assessing the carnage before them all.

Silence hung heavy in the air, only broken by the sound of screaming monkeys nearby.

It was Colonel Myan who spoke first, 'I've seen this man around the palace. I think he was a trader, he met with most of the court. In fact, I think I even brought something off him for my wife.'

'Interesting, looks like he was shot in the neck.'

Sri pointed to an arrow which had been broken off. 'The arrow looks like one of ours, but look here, there's a stab wound in his chest.'

Sri examined closer and Myan crouched down to join him. 'This looks like it's been caused by a dagger, I don't think it could be one of ours, the wound looks too small.'

Sri got up and began to pace around the cart, he jumped into it examining the contents.

'He didn't have many goods to sell, and what's with all these old blankets,' Sri examined closely pulling the blankets back. 'What's this?'

He held up a pouch with what looked like a makeshift teat. Sri smelt the container and threw it at Marcus.

'Milk,' he declared.

Marcus looked at the pouch, gave it a sniff and nodded. Captain Voan appeared behind the colonel, he whispered to him not wanting to disturb the prince while he was examining the scene.

Myan gave Voan a nod, 'Your Majesty, Captain Voan has found tracks, they're riding east, he thinks it's about twenty or thirty horses, we need to continue.'

Sri looked up from the cart and at the colonel. 'Your right, we need to keep focused, nothing can distract us until we find Johan. It's imperative that they're not allowed to leave the kingdom.'

Sri cleared his throat and said, 'Ask a few men to stay behind and bury our friends, but leave this traitor for the tigers, no point wasting time on him.'

The colonel nodded and the group made their way back to their horses. As they mounted Captain Voan rode over to Sri.

'The men are ready and our best trackers are scouting ahead. We can tell by the strides of the horses they're riding fast. We have no time to waste.'

Sri nodded and they set off again riding as fast as they could, it was quite a distance to get to Rovieng. They rode all through the night and by the time they arrived in the trading town of Rovieng the sun was rising. The prince instructed the men to wait at the edge of the town as Marcus, Luke, the officers, and a few guards rode to the temple. They were greeted by the head priest who bowed deeply.

'I'm Prince Srindra, here's my royal seal.' Sri produced a document with the king's mark. 'I need food for my men, water for the horses and we need to rest for a few hours. I also want to see the town's ruling council, now.'

The young priest who was clearly not used to interacting with royalty replied hesitantly. 'Yes Your Majesty, I'll get them right away. I'll ask the monks to find food and water for you all. In the meantime, your men can rest next to the temple. There's a place they can set up camp.'

The priest waved to a few of his colleagues whom he instructed to help.

'I'll find Arun Tep, he's the leader of our town. My fellow monks will be of service to you with whatever you need,' the priest said, then rushed off to find the town's council.

On the instruction of the prince, the men from the queen's battalion and the prince's guard began to set up camp. Sri flanked by his officers walked amongst them.

He shouted, 'We'll stay here for two hours, get some rest and eat what you can before we ride on.'

Sri turned to Marcus who was looking anxious, 'I know what you're going to say, but I must let the men and horses rest otherwise we won't be strong enough to fight.'

'I understand,' Marcus replied calmly. 'It's just how do we know where we're going? I don't know what to do?'

Marcus was exhausted and when he finished those words, he fell to the floor. Luke, who was securing his horse, noticed and rushed to help.

Sri just stood there watching Marcus, he showed no sign of compassion. 'You need to be stronger and show leadership to the men. Get up, take a few breaths and eat something, you're no use to me like this.'

Luke looked at the prince, it was the first time he'd seen this ruthless side of him.

'Don't look at me like that, either of you. We're commanding men who are willing to give their lives for your child. Marcus, you need to show strength and leadership. The men need to know you'll fight and kill for them, as much as you would for your own son.'

Luke bowed to Sri who nodded back, then left to organise the men. Luke helped Marcus to his feet and led him to a nearby fallen tree. He gave his former mentor some bread and water then paused for a moment.

'Sri's right, it's their code. You need to be seen to lead and to show strength. The men need to know that we'll stop at nothing to achieve our goals, while also protecting each other.'

'Luke, I know, I'll do better I promise,' Marcus replied emotionally.

Over the next hour, some men ate while others rested. The officers gathered in the temple and were looking at the potential routes that the enemy could follow. Colonel Myan approached Marcus and Luke who were resting under the shade of a tree.

'The prince has asked that you join him, he's speaking with the town council now, come there's no time to waste.'

Luke and Marcus followed the colonel into the temple, the head priest and the town elders were already sitting. Prince Srindra looked up seeing both enter, the elders gasped, they had never seen anyone from European descent before.

Sri looked back towards the elders, 'Arun, are you telling me the people of Rovieng have seen nobody enter the town in the last few hours. No traders or travellers have passed through, I find that very hard to believe.'

'It's the truth,' Arun replied, completely terrified by the prince's direct questioning.

Sri looked at a few of the other town's people who like Arun were frightened.

Somethings wrong here, he thought to himself and began to pace.

An elderly lady spoke, 'Your Majesty, you're welcome to any of our food or resources to aid in your search. My name is Sonisay Thi. Our town has always been loyal to the king. I think your men will need more nourishment. Would you help me carry more food back to the camp.'

She pointed at Luke.

There was a short-confused silence then Luke replied, 'Yes of course.'

Sri looked at him knowing this was a strange request, he nodded to give his approval.

Luke followed the town elder through the streets, he was flanked by a couple of Sri's guards that had been ordered to protect Luke. She guided him to a small hut.

'Here's some more bread, I made it fresh this morning, she said loudly.

Sonisay then put her fingers to her lips indicating something was wrong.

'My daughter collected this water from our well this morning,' she spoke loudly.

Sonisay then clashed pots together to make loud noises and to simulate she was gathering items to take back to the temple.

While she did this, she signalled Luke to come closer and whispered, 'Men dressed in black have our children as hostages, we've been ordered by their leaders to tell you they haven't passed this way.'

Sonisay then shouted, 'We have some cured meat if you like. I'm sure the prince would enjoy it. I've made it myself and its very good.'

She pulled him close. 'There are two men dressed in black watching our every move, I'll point them out to you when we leave.

Yes, you can take the milk too,' she said again loudly.

'The Cham leader is hiding in the jungle behind the market, they arrived an hour before you did.'

Sonisay paused, before calling out, 'Can you hold this for me.'

She then put a jug of water in his hands and grabbed some food.

'That should do it,' she shouted and led him out of the hut.

Just as they left she said, 'Kill the two men in black, then please save our children.

Luke walked with her back to the temple and replied, 'Thank you for the food Sonisay, the prince really appreciates your kindness.'

As they walked he leaned to her, 'Is there a woman or baby with them?'

Sonisay smiled at him as they walked, she touched his hand and gave him a subtle nod. Luke nodded back and casually scanned the main town square, as he walked past a vegetable stand, he could see the two men who were dressed in black cloaks walking around. Luke's eyes darted back to the elderly woman and she nodded subtly.

They returned to the temple and placed the food on a nearby table. Sonisay called out for the prince's officers to eat, Luke walked over and gave Sri some of Sonisay's bread.

'Johan's here, he's hidden in the jungle,' he whispered. 'The cham are hoping we'll charge off in a different direction so they can slip away. Sri, their spies are watching you most, get their attention until I can arrange for them to be taken out, then we'll surprise their main force in the jungle and get Johan back.'

'How do you know all this?' he whispered back.

Luke nodded over at Sonisay. She was joining in with the discussions the officers were having, but looked completely terrified. 'Act like nothing's changed, we need to take out the spies first. The lives of the town's children are at stake.'

Sri nodded and as Luke walked away, he grabbed his arm, 'I do trust you. I trust you with everything.'

'As I do you,' Luke smiled walking back to the officers casually, trying to avoid attention.

'I need some rest before we ride,' he declared loudly for all to hear and walked back to the camp.

Most of the prince's officers were still at the temple, however as Luke walked back to the makeshift camp, he noticed Captain Voan sitting by a small fire with some of his men.

'Captain,' Luke said as he approached. 'I need to speak to you.'

'Luke, join us, we have a long ride ahead and we need to build our strength.'

'There are other concerns,' Luke sat down and turned to the soldier's present. 'Would you mind giving me a few minutes with your captain?'

The soldiers bowed and walked away. 'I need you to do something for me, but we must be discreet.'

'What do you need,' the captain replied.

'Two of your best bowmen, they'll need to take positions on top of the temple, I need them to kill two men dressed in black, they'll know who.' Luke was careful to look like he was chatting normally, 'I'll give this sign when I need them to fire.'

He held up his hand and clenched his fist. 'These men are the Cham assassins. Their leader is holding hostage the towns children, we need to take these men out before they can make a signal to their forces that we know there here.'

'You can count on me, but what about the rest of their force?'

'I need you to get our men ready and in position in the jungle. The Cham are located in the undergrowth by the market, remember this needs to be done by stealth.'

Luke got up and thanked his friend.

'You know, I think I'll return to eat with the prince after all,' he said, noticing one of the men in black looking at him in the camp.

He nodded to Voan and whispered, 'I'll distract them while you get the men in position.'

Luke walked back to the temple at a steady pace, he soon entered, and Sri looked up concerned.

'I've decided I need more food. It'll help me be ready for the long ride.'

Luke noticed the assassin had followed him back to the temple. He decided to sit down next to Sri, he grabbed some bread and began to eat.

Sri and his officers were reviewing the map and discussing it with the locals.

'Is this the best way to Stung Treng?' Luke asked, not really listening to the answer. 'We should be able to meet the king's forces here.'

Sri shot him a look of alarm.

The men in black moved closer trying to see the map. Luke started to stretch his arms and all of a sudden, he raised his hand in the air and clenched his fist. Two arrows came flying into the temple killing both men dressed in black at once.

'What the hell is happening?' the prince yelled just as Captain Voan rushed to join them.

'These men were spies, their leader is holding the town's children,' Luke said quickly.

'They have our families,' Sonisay said desperately. 'They've threatened to kill them if we didn't lie to you. Please help us and save our children. You've only a short time to act before these men are missed.'

She reached into one of their pockets and pulled out a mirror they had been using to signal.

'There's a woman with a baby with them, it could be Chantrea and Johan,' Luke looked at Marcus.

'They have the new prince,' Arun whispered in disbelief.

'I'm so sorry Your Majesty, honestly we were just going to send you in a different direction. We needed to protect our families,' he said desperately. 'I didn't know they had one of the royal children, the king will never forgive us.'

He dropped to his knees.

'Get up man, I know why you've done what you have, but I need to get your children and the prince back, do you understand me?' Sri pulled the frightened man to his feet.

'Yes Your Majesty,' Arun replied, still trying to compose himself.

Sonisay pulled a map out from under all the papers on the table.

'The Cham are here,' she pointed at the forest on the map. 'Go quickly and attack them before they realise the deception.'

Sri nodded and they rushed out of the temple into the makeshift camp.

As they ran Voan spoke, 'On Luke's instructions I've sent our scouts into the forest and they have located the Cham. I've positioned a few of our best archers in the trees and they are ready to attack on your command. The rest of the men are prepared'

He pointed to the men who had mounted their horses.

Sri, Luke and Marcus organised themselves and rode to the officers.

'Here's my plan, Voan tell ten of your best men to stay behind. I want them to be a decoy. On my command

I need them to make loud noises to cause a distraction, it will pull the Cham forces out into the market. You'll join me in the jungle, we'll instruct the remaining men to start the attack by firing a flaming arrow into the sky. Until then get them to hide, I want the Cham to think we've left town.'

'Yes Your Majesty,' Voan replied and raced off to instruct his men.

'The rest of us will join the scouts in the forest, Myan take half our force to the left of them. Voan and I will lead the remaining forces to the right and we'll surround them. Do I make myself clear?

All the commanders acknowledged the prince's orders. Once Voan re-joined them, they began to ride loudly out of town.

The road out of the town bent slightly right, obscuring the view of them from the marketplace. When Sri was sure they were out of sight Sri instructed his men to dismount their horses and enter the jungle. Myan and Sri split their forces and headed to their respective positions.

The men Voan had sent into the Jungle were experts at covert missions, it wasn't long until one of them spotted the prince's forces. He managed to signal to Sri and climbed down to join him.

'They're over there Your Majesty, we have many of them in our sights.'

Sri noticed that the Cham were positioned on a small knoll. He could see them pacing around the children who had been tied up in the middle of a clearing.

'Voan when I give the signal, fire the arrow to alert the men, but first where's Chantrea and Johan? He asked.

'Over there,' the soldier pointed.

He could see Chantrea holding baby Johan, her feet were tied and her mouth was gagged. Sri looked closer and he could see her gently rocking the little prince.

'We go on my order, make it clear no one fires anywhere near the woman. Is Myan in position?'

The soldier climbed back up the tree scouring the forest, after a little while later there was a strange bird call.

Voan smiled as the man in the tree signalled that everyone was in place.

'We're ready, on your order we'll fire,' he instructed.

'Luke, go after the town's children and take a number of men with you, Voan you'll come with Marcus and I, we'll go for Chantrea.' Sri held his breath for a few moments, 'Voan, signal your men.'

Voan tied a small rag soaked in flammable liquid around an arrowhead and struck two flints together to light it. He mounted the arrow on his bow and pulled it back, releasing it towards the town.

After what seemed like ages, loud noises came from the market and the men in the clearing moved forward.

Sri composed his thoughts, he looked down at the Cham camp once more and said, 'Go.'

Captain Voan let out a strange bird call, he began to slowly count down.

'Five, four, three, two, one.'

As he spoke a barrage of arrows fired into the camp, a number of the Cham guards fell down dead instantly. There were screams and shouts of panic coming from the children.

Sri shouted, 'Charge,' and his men swarmed into the clearing.

They outnumbered the assassins nearly three to one. Luke headed to the town's children, a few of the Cham soldiers had regrouped and it was clear they were going to attack them. Luke ran as fast as he could to get to them before the Cham could, he was closely followed by a number of his own force. Luke got there just in time to stop one of the Cham from impaling a frightened girl with a spear. His sword shattered the spear and he threw himself in front of her. Another Cham charged at him with his sword swinging wildly, Luke dodged the man and their swords clashed together with a chilling metallic clang. Luke fought the man face to face, and a volley of arrows from Colonel Myan's force shot past him straight into the remaining Cham. Luke hadn't realised that the enemy was charging at him from behind, a few further arrows shot passed him killing another Cham running towards the children.

Luke continued to fight his assailant. He had practised his sword skill with the prince's elite guard. But this was the first time he'd been fighting in anger or fighting for his life. Luke dodged the Cham's attack and he managed to trip the man over. It was a move Luke had learnt from the late Major Keo. Luke seized the opportunity to knock his opponents' sword aside and held his blade at the crazed man's throat. The Cham's eyes were wild and he was flailing all over the place. Luke pressed his foot hard on the man's chest stopping him from moving.

'Kill him,' one of the prince's guard shouted.

Luke held firm.

'We need answers, we need intelligence about our enemy,' he shouted.

'No Khmer scum will get anything from me.'

The man pulled a dagger out from his boot and lunged for Luke, but he managed to swerve the blade. Luke plunged the sword deep into the man's chest. His mind erupted with guilt as the man screamed in pain. Luke could feel every bone, muscle and organ that the sword penetrated. He knew he'd never feel the same again.

Marcus, Sri, and Captain Voan had charged for Chantrea. They met stiff resistance. It seemed a number of the Cham had hidden in the undergrowth and were fighting hard. Captain Voan swung his sword and managed to sever one of the Cham's arm, the man yelled out in pain and fell to the floor and Voan dispatched him quickly. Sri was fighting a large man who was skilful with a blade, he dodged his assailant's lunge, missing the blade by inches. He dropped to the floor and punched the Cham in the chest causing him to fall to his knees. Sri elbowed him in the head and the man tumbled backwards. He rushed over and plunged his sword deep into the man's throat. Sri breathed heavily, resting for a moment on his sword which was still impaled in the dead man. It was then he looked around and notice that Marcus was struggling against his attacker. Marcus's arm had been cut and blood was pouring out, he had crouched down holding his sword up to protect himself. The Cham blade crashed down hard onto the metal causing Marcus to drop his sword, he was now vulnerable. Marcus looked up at the Cham who was smiling with pleasure when all of a sudden, he let out a terrifying howl. Sri's blade burst through the man's chest inches from Marcus's face. He pushed the dead Cham to the floor and pulled his sword out. Sri reached down pulling Marcus to his feet.

Suddenly a cry came from behind them, they turned and saw Chantrea being dragged on to a horse by what seemed to be the Cham leader. Chantrea was still holding Baby Johan who was now screaming.

'Don't worry about me, get my son,' Marcus yelled out.

Sri ran as fast has he could towards Chantrea, she was being carried away but he was determined to catch them. Out of the foliage a Cham jumped on Sri, causing him to fall and drop his sword, he quickly got up and they began to fight, his eye ever on the disappearing Chantrea. He managed to dodge another lunge then he stamped on the attacker's leg causing it to break, the man screamed out in pain as Sri pulled a small dagger hidden in his robes and slit the man's throat.

'What about Johan?' Marcus shouted, running hard to join him.

'I need my horse, they're already on the move, we need to get to…' Sri suddenly stopped speaking and as in slow motion, Marcus saw an arrow bursting through his chest.

Sri looked down at the protruding object, putting his hands around the arrowhead. He looked back at Marcus giving him a frightened stare and then fell to the jungle floor.

CHAPTER TWENTY-FOUR

Revelations

Luke with help from Colonel Myan, dispatched the remaining men who had been surrounding the children. The colonel ordered his men to take the hostages back to Rovieng and reunite them with their parents. A few soldiers escorted the terrified youngsters back, while Luke and the colonel search the battlefield for the others. It was then Luke heard Marcus shouting frantically. It didn't take long for Myan to locate them, he called for Luke and they both ran towards Marcus who was sitting in the middle of a small clearing. As they got closer, Marcus was still clutching the prince and calling for help. Luke crouched down seeing the arrow protruding out of his chest. Sri tried to talk but as he did dark red blood began to seep out of his mouth.

'Go after Johan, don't let him escape,' Sri forced out.

Voan had heard Marcus shouting and reached them all just as Sri coughed up more blood.

Marcus heard something.. Unexpectedly he put his bloodied hand up to catch their attention. They all paused and without warning he shouted, 'Archers in the trees.'

As he called out, one of the men next to the colonel was hit by an arrow and crumpled to the floor. They all dived for cover. Another arrow suddenly struck Myan in the arm, who let out a painful yell.

The soldiers continued to scan the trees looking for the Cham sniper, Myan spotted something and shouted, 'Voan, over there.'

He pointed to a large tree to the left of where Marcus was crouching.

Luke got his bow out and scanned the trees. He felt anger building in him but also terror. He was not afraid of the danger they were in, but for the possibility he may lose the man he loved. Luke's mind began to rage with thoughts he couldn't control. Then suddenly he felt the vibrations return.

'No, no not now,' he said, causing the colonel and Voan to look at him.

Luke closed his eyes trying to regain control of his emotions and it was then something clicked. He took a deep breath and calmed his mind to listen, he noticed he could hear everything. From Voan's beating heart to the singing of the birds in the distant trees.

Without warning Luke stood up, his eyes still closed. He pointed his bow up into the trees and fired. There was a sudden scream as his arrow hit the Cham archer. The man fell from the tree hitting the jungle floor with a loud thud.

Myan, Voan and a number of others stood up in amazement and looked at Luke. Luke still had his eyes closed, before the colonel could speak he held his hand up for silence. He pulled his bow back and shot to the right of Sri, and another Cham archer fell from the trees with an arrow embedded in his forehead. Voan and Myan looked at each other in astonishment, but they remained silent waiting for Luke's instructions. Luke sensed the danger had passed and he finally opened his eyes.

'All the Cham are dead, except for those that have fled. We're safe here, well for now anyway.'

Suddenly the magnitude of their situation hit him. Luke rushed to help his friend, partner, and lover who laid dying on the jungle floor.

***

Major Yom rode as fast as he could out of Rovieng, while Chantrea struggled to keep hold of Johan. Yom had managed to pull her up into a sitting position on the horse. He held her tightly while she gripped onto Johan who continued to scream.

'We ride for Vijaya and to my King. I've got enough supplies for a few days at least. We'll take the route through the deep jungle to avoid the main road and any Khmer forces that maybe patrolling it. I need you to listen and follow my orders without question, your only responsibility is to keep the brat alive.'

Chantrea nodded.

'He's warm, I think it's a fever, I need fresh water and some more milk,' she said hesitantly.

'I know a place to hide and someone who can help. There is a tribe of people who are sympathetic to Champa. I'll arrange for milk from surrogates when we get there, but the baby will have to wait for now.'

He galloped off the main road onto a small track which headed deep into the jungle.

'Why does the Champa king want Johan so much?' Chantrea asked.

'He wants to punish Jayavarman and raise a legitimate heir under his roof. The king needs someone with Khmer royal blood in their veins to legitimise his rule over the people.'

'But how can we, I mean how can the Cham defeat Jayavarman? The Khmer forces are too strong,' she said shakily.

'That's none of your concern, all I'll say is he has allies who look at the Khmer empire with jealous eyes. We'll take back the kingdom, or die trying,' Yom spat.

***

Luke carried Prince Srindra back to Rovieng, he was in a bad way. The arrow was embedded deep within Sri's chest. Luke refused to let the colonel remove it, he was fearful it could lead to greater blood loss. The town was cheering as the soldiers rushed back to the temple, they were grateful that their children had been freed. However, as they approached the crowd could see something was wrong.

Voan rushed ahead to the town elders. Luke had instructed him to get supplies ready so he could treat Sri. The streets were now silent as Luke hurriedly carried the dying prince through them. They soon arrived back at the temple where monks had already laid out fresh water and clean cloth. They were eager to tend to the prince's wounds as was their culture.

Luke placed Sri down, holding him in a sitting position. Sri was unconscious, his head rolled backwards as Luke held him tightly.

'Marcus, I need your help.'

Marcus was clutching his arm trying to stop his own bleeding. However he rushed over as fast as he could.

'I'm going to remove the arrow, press this cloth on his chest, I'll do the same on his back.'

Marcus nodded as Luke snapped the tail of the arrow. On the count of three Luke gripped at the metal head, he pulled at the wooden shaft until it was fully removed.

Instantly dark blood started to ooze out of Sri's wounds, just as Luke feared.

'I said press,' Luke shouted at Marcus as the blood continued to seep out.

'I want everyone out of here except for Myan and Voan,' Luke shouted again.

'But my lord, we've healers who can help,' Sonisay said kindly.

'I'll tend to the prince myself,' Luke said in a gentler tone. 'Please Sonisay, I know what I'm doing.'

He looked at the colonel who understood what he wanted.

'Out, let's give the prince privacy,' Myan said, ushering everyone out.

'Please ask the people to prey for the prince,' Voan called out.

'Yes of course,' Arun said as they left.

Myan ordered his men to prevent anyone from entering without his permission. It was now just the five of them and Luke turned to Marcus.

'Give it here, I know you've brought it with you.'

Marcus sighed. 'But what about the timeline?'

'What do you mean,' Luke shouted. 'Do you think anything we've done in the last year won't have had an effect. I'm not going to let him die, just like you wouldn't let Bo or Johan die.'

Marcus pulled the medical kit out of his bag. He hadn't had chance to return it to their hiding place since the babies had been born. It was a good thing too. Marcus took it with him, just encase Johan needed medical attention.

'You'll both need to Help me,' Luke said to Voan and Myan. 'This technology needs to stay between us. Give me your word you'll not tell anyone about it.'

'We do,' they both replied without hesitation.

Luke opened the medical kit, taking out the hyper-spray and medical scanner. He tapped a few buttons on the hyper-spray and pressed it against Sri's neck.

'Antibiotics, a sedative and an anticoagulant, this will help stop the bleeding,' he said to Marcus.

He then picked up the medical scanner and pressed a few buttons. A holographic screen appeared within the room which made Voan and Myan gasp. Luke ignored their reactions and studied the images of Sri's body. He focused on the wound and the screen zoomed into the affected area. Luke turned back to the group.

'This will take me a while to assess. I need to see how badly his organs have been damaged. Marcus, sort yours and Myan's wounds out.'

He threw the hyper-spray and the dermal regenerator at him.

Luke then turned and spoke to the colonel, 'Once you're fixed up, get our forces ready to leave. You need to keep searching for Johan, if you can't find him head to Stung Treng and join the king's invasion.'

The colonel looked at Luke in amazement, only six months ago this boy was fearful and cowardly. Now he was showing signs of a great leader.

'Yes Luke, whatever you need, you'll have,' Myan bowed. He walked over to Marcus who attended to his arm. Once the wound was sealed Myan left quickly.

'Captain Voan, I want you to ready the prince's men, get supplies and be prepared to move in thirty minutes,' Voan nodded and left without speaking.

Luke turned to Marcus, 'You'll need to carry on the search without us for now. But you must not stop, whatever happens find Johan.'

Marcus's guilt and fear were beginning to overwhelm him. 'What have we done Luke. I'm not sure we should continue on this path. The damage could be too great.'

'It's a bit late for that. Who's to say this isn't meant to happen, even if we do change the future, you can't leave your child to this fate,' Luke responded angrily.

'No, I can't, I need to get him back,' Marcus said coming to his senses.

'Get those wounds tended to, then ride out to search for Johan. I'll look after Sri and we will meet you in Stung Treng.' Luke paused and took a deep breath. 'Colonel Myan will need to lead the hunt now. I promise that once I've stabilised Sri, we'll catch you up.'

'It sounds like the best course of action,' Marcus said pacing the room. He was about to leave when he suddenly turned back. 'Thank you Luke, I don't know what I would've done without you.'

'It's OK, just make sure you see me before you leave.'

'I will, I'm sorry for even questioning you about using our technology, I'm such a hypocrite,' he paused. 'The worst kind, as I would've done exactly the same as you.'

He looked at Luke, giving him a strained smile and left.

***

It was night by the time Yom and Chantrea reached the secluded village, it was located in the deep jungle. The sky was dark but the stars sparkled brightly as Yom rode straight to the village elders' house. It was a large hut and the residence of someone important. Yom knocked hard.

'Bian, I need shelter for the night,' he called out.

There was the sound of locks being unfastened and the door swung open. A small woman looked at them, the woman was Bian Lac the village elder of Spóng, a small settlement high in the mountains which had a dubious past.

'What are you doing here Yom. You know they're searching for you and the village can't be seen collaborating with the enemy.'

'I had no choice, its only me left, the rest of my men are dead. Will you shelter us here,' he said pausing for a moment. 'Both my travelling companions are in need of your help.'

Bian stared closely at the young woman and the little baby, they both looked like they wouldn't make it through the night.

'You had better come in.'

Bian guided them into her secluded garden.

'You, sit here,' she said to Chantrea, I'll get you some food and water. This little one doesn't look well, I've some medicine that will help, would you like that?'

All Chantrea could do was nod, she was too exhausted to speak. 'Yom help me. Go get some water from the well that these two can wash with.'

'Yes Aunty,' Yom replied.

Just as they were out of ear shot Bian asked, 'Is this your child?'

'No not at all, I'm on a mission for the king of Champa. I'm not sure you want to know anymore. I've already put you in great danger.'

'Oh Yom, when will you learn these kings care nothing for us,' she shook her head.

'Tell me. who are these people in my house?'

Yom had always feared his aunt, but he also respected her. She was seen as the great matriarch of his family. 'I'll tell you if you help me leave the village before sunrise, I need to get back to Champa.'

'Okay I'll assist you. I know secret routes through the jungle and over the fields, I have contacts from the old days who can help, but first tell me.'

'Very well, the child is Prince Johan and the woman is Princess Bopha's lady in waiting. She stole the baby away from the court and we're travelling back to Vijaya, to present him to the king as a gift.'

There was stunned silence. 'You're in a lot of trouble.'

She reached out and grabbed his head, 'whatever possessed you to do this, you stupid boy.'

Bian slapped him across the face and shook her head, 'Everyone in the empire's looking for him, do you know how much danger you've put our village in?'

She paused, 'Has anyone seen you?'

'No,' he said quietly. 'I was careful, no one saw us as we rode to the village. All I know is that my men are dead, killed by Srindra.'

He sighed, but a smile soon crossed his face.

'However, the last I saw of Prince Srindra, he had my arrow sticking out of his chest. It's about time that bastard got what was coming to him,' he said, smiling at his aunt.

Bian ignored her nephew's boast.

'Come, let's go and help your guests before they both die in my house,' Bian said angrily. They walked back to the small garden to see Chantrea in tears holding a yelling Johan.

'I don't know what to do,' Chantrea said starting to panic. 'He's got a temperature. I know nothing about babies.'

'Give him here my dear,' Bian requested kindly. 'You look exhausted, go freshen up and get some rest, I'll care for this little one.'

Chantrea held onto Johan tightly, 'You have my word I'll protect him.'

She reluctantly handed Johan over to the elderly woman.

'Hello little man let's get you changed, bathed and fed shall we?' Bian carried him into the house turning just in time to see Chantrea collapse on the floor.

***

Luke had just finished another scan on Prince Srindra when Marcus and Voan entered. The temple had been sealed off to everyone except the prince's inner circle.

'Luke, Captain Voan and I have been speaking, he'll stay with you along with twenty men to protect the prince.'

'No, you need all the men to find Johan, go now before it gets dark.'

'We can't leave the prince unprotected, I won't allow it,' Voan said stepping forward. 'Colonel Myan and Marcus will ride to find the young prince. He'll take the queen's soldiers and half our force. I'll remain with my closest men, to protect the prince and to protect you. Luke, understand this isn't up for discussion.'

'The prince needs to be protected, he is the future king,' Marcus said. 'Voan can't in all good conscious leave him when he's most vulnerable.'

'Very well,' Luke replied.

He turned to Marcus. 'Go now, you need to make up time before it gets dark. How do you propose to track this Cham anyway?'

'I managed to scan him as he rode off, I've got a faint signal on him. My implant should be able to guide us in the right direction at least, unless he gets too far away,' Marcus replied.

'Don't use technology,' Luke muttered under his breath frustratedly. 'Well, what are you waiting for, Go.'

Marcus turned to leave.

Luke realised he may not see his friend and mentor again, so spoke tenderly, 'Look after yourself.'

He couldn't stop himself from embracing his friend, or in reality his father. Marcus hugged Luke back, knowing this was the first time they would truly be separated since they'd met. They broke apart and Marcus gave Luke a withered smile, he then turned and left.

'Captain Voan if you're remaining behind, I'll need more water and fresh bandages,' Luke requested. 'Please make sure no one except you enters, for now at least.'

'Very well,' Voan replied walking out of the temple to find the villagers.

As he walked to the town centre, he saw Marcus and Colonel Myan riding out of town fast. Voan's remaining men were split, a few were resting at the makeshift camp while ten guarded the small temple where the prince was being treated. Others were positioned as lookouts around the town. Voan found fresh water and more bandages. Sonisay had been very efficient, ensuring they had everything they needed. He thanked her once more and headed back to the temple, however as he approached, he heard Luke shouting.

'No, no it can't be happening,' Luke cried out.

Voan rushed in and asked, 'What is it?'

'Sri's gone into shock, I don't know what to do, I'm not a medic,' Luke said desperately.

'I don't know what shock is,' Voan responded confused.

'Of course you don't,' Luke snapped.

The scanner he was holding sounded an alarm and Luke focused all his attention on it. He pressed a few more buttons then realised Sri's pulse had stopped.

'Oh no, I don't know what to do. Arrrgh,' he yelled, gripping his head as the scanner dropped to the ground and the room began to spin.

Voan managed to catch Luke before he fell to the floor. Luke breathed heavily clutching his head as a magnetic pulse burst out of him. It caused metal objects including the medical equipment to fly in all directions.

A moment later Luke managed to gain control, his nerves began to calm, and clarity of thought struck him. Without thinking he broke free of Voan's grip and placed both his hands on Sri's chest. A few moments later a pulse erupted from him, but this time it was directed towards Sri. The temple shook, causing a number of stone carvings to fall to the ground smashing loudly. Luke's eyes remained focused on Sri, despite the commotion happening all around him. A little while later the noise began to settle. Luke's mind felt free, he could hear a reassuring beep coming from the medical scanner, which was now under a pile of rubble. He could hear Sri's heartbeat and it was beating clearly again. Luke's hands were still on Sri's chest. It was moving and he could feel Sri breathing. Luke removed his hands and as he did a weakness hit him, it caused him to stumble back. He turned slowly towards Voan who was visibly shocked by what he'd just witnessed. Luke tried to speak but no words came, then everything went dark.

CHAPTER TWENTY-FIVE

Reflections

Chantrea woke with a startle, the first thing she could think of was where's Johan. Her mind began to clear and she realised she was laying on a makeshift bed. She'd been covered by a blanket, her head propped up by a number of cushions. Chantrea pulled the blanket off quickly and rushed into the next room.

'I see you're awake,' Bian said, holding a sleeping and contented Johan.

Seeing the sleeping baby caused her to sigh with relief. The child had become her responsibility and she felt deeply connected to him.

'Will he be alright?' she asked hesitantly.

'Yes my dear, for now anyway,' Bian replied kindly. 'Can I ask you a question?'

'Umm sure,' Chantrea replied, not really knowing if she had a choice or not.

'Why did you take this little one from his mother?' Bian asked pointedly.

A surge of guilt hit Chantrea and her emotions began to rise.

'I had to, I had no choice,' she said through tears.

'We always have choices. Some are just easier than others.'

'Do you think this was easy, to betray the princess, to put Johan in danger and to denounce my people. I'd do anything to go back and change my decision, even though I'm certain it would mean my death.'

Bian looked at her, carefully choosing her words.

'You still have choices my dear. My nephew may be taking you to Champa, but remember there are always options,' Bian said wisely. 'You need to do everything to protect this innocent child.'

'I will, I promise,' Chantrea replied.

As she finished speaking Yom entered the room.

'I've packed supplies and readied the horse. We should leave now before dawn. I don't want anyone to know we've been here.'

'Very well nephew, but remember Kings care nothing for us. They use people for their own selfish desires, so tread carefully and don't risk the lives of innocents.'

'How can you say that Aunty. After all the Khmers have done to our family and all we've lost. I need to put my faith in a leader who'll help me get revenge. The only people that can do that are the Cham,' Yom said angrily.

'We make our own paths nephew.' She stood up and walked over to Chantrea.

'Take him,' Bian said giving Johan to her.

She walked to a nearby table to collect a scroll. 'Take this, I've written down a few things you'll need to remember when looking after a baby.'

Bian reached for a small bag. 'I've also prepared these herbs. They'll help control his temperature.'

She took Chantrea's hand. 'Remember what I said, believe in yourself and what you can do.'

Come let's go, I want to be out of this part of the jungle before sunrise' Yom ordered, ushering Chantrea out of the house.

Bian followed.

'Nephew, I fear I may never see you again,'

'That may be so Aunty. Or you'll see me as the great General who brought the Khmer empire to its knees,' he replied smiling. He galloped off with Chantrea gripping onto Johan tightly.

***

King Jayavarman was able to mobilise a force of thirty thousand men in Angkor. The Lavo ambassador confirmed that five thousand troops were to join the king's invasion, they would meet him at Stung Treng with the other reinforcements. The king expected fifteen thousand men from his forces based in the east to join them. General Thorn had declared that all forces would join up at the strategic crossing in Stung Treng and push east into Champa.

Under the king's orders, General Thorn mobilised the men quickly. It was announced that the king's force would be ready to march two days after Prince Srindra left in search of Johan. The Khmer empire placed all forces on high alert and was readying themselves for war. The commanders had standing orders to protect the borders from any foreign aggressors, who could take advantage while the king was away fighting in Champa.

The queen had deployed a number of her trusted spies across the Khmer lands and sent many into bordering countries. She had ordered them to watch for unusual troop movements. The queen was also keen for reports on what their neighbours thought about the abduction of the prince. The spies knew to send urgent information back to the palace at once, all of which would be collated and reviewed in the newly constructed war room. Indradevi had convinced her husband that while he was away, she would oversee all intelligence and rapidly redeploy any urgent forces if needed.

The king had always trusted his wife with such things. It was her plans and insight that helped him retake Angkor all those years ago. The queen, like Thorn, had worked fast. She set up intelligence installations at strategic points throughout the country, they would relay important news between them. Indradevi's mandate from the king stretched further than just redeploying the reserve troops to areas of concern. He approved her plans to recruit mercenaries. She would work with Nakry to use the empires financial resources to support the invasion. The queen had already taken the opportunity to hire mercenaries from trusted allies. These units were already on route to the capital, to fight under her command for whatever she needed.

The main invasion force was ordered to congregate at the parade ground in the morning, the king was to address them all personally. He awoke early and dressed in his finest robes, then walked to his favourite room in the palace which looked over the city. The king stared for a moment. He had always tried to avoid violence, but as he watched the mist rise off the water surrounding the great temple, he knew that confrontation with the Cham was inevitable. His mind seemed to connect with the surroundings just as the increasing mist caused an eerie light to envelop the city.

He walked down the hall and entered the war room where he saw Indradevi. She hadn't been to bed. She'd been up all-night planning with Nakry. They'd both been reviewing General Thorn's invasion plans, making sure the finance was in place for supplying such a large force.

Their other focus had been on how to protect the rest of the empire while the war was waged. Indradevi had taken time to familiarise herself with the units across the empire. She was identifying areas of military weakness keen to know where she would need to send the mercenaries. Indradevi looked up when she noticed the king had entered.

'My dear, are you prepared for today?' she asked gently, knowing the conflict raging in his mind. 'Is there anything else I can do to support you?'

He turned and looked at her. 'Evi I'm ready, I still have doubts about this invasion and the cost to our people, but the actions of the Cham have made this day unavoidable.'

He sighed. 'I need you to know that whatever happens to myself, Sri, or any of our family. You're to do everything to protect our people, I mean everything.'

'Don't think that way, you'll going to teach the Cham the consequences that their vile behaviour brings. I have faith in you and so do the people.'

She put her arms around him, and they embraced.

'I've had the servants polish your armour, so you'll shine like the leader you are,' she replied.

Indradevi then took her husband by the hand and guided him back to a room next to their bed-chamber. She helped him dress into his gleaming golden armour.

'I want you to have this.' Indradevi took off her large sapphire necklace and placed it around her husband's neck, she positioned it gently underneath his armour.

'Do you remember giving this to me?'

The king nodded.

'You'll give it back to me when you return,' she said lovingly.

The king stood up and paced around the room one last time, 'I'm ready Evi, let's get this over with.'

She smiled back and took his hand. They walked confidently together through the palace and out onto the parade ground. The vast Khmer army was waiting patiently for their king, the soldiers erupted with cheers when they saw him.

General Thorn, Princess Bopha, Prince Virak, and the rest of the council greeted them. They all stood together looking down at the colourful force before them, showing the unity of the court and the unity of the empire.

The king stepped forward onto the podium to speak. 'Today we embark on a great battle to help the innocent and punish the guilty. You strong men and women before me, join in our honourable fight to protect our lands, protect our people, and protect our way of life. The Cham attacks over the last few years have cost many lives. The abduction of Prince Johan is just their latest vile attack, showing the contempt the Cham have for our society. From today they'll pay for their deceit, they'll pay for their betrayal and they'll pay for their murderous acts. I ask you to join with me and fight for our people. To fight for what's right, to fight for honour and to liberate the Cham from their tyrannical king. Our victory will ensure they'll become part of our empire and we'll teach them the true meaning of respect. Are you with me?'

The army erupted with cheers and horns began to blow, the king kissed his wife, embraced his daughter and thanked each of his king's counsel for their support.

Finally, he reached Prince Virak and spoke gently, 'I know we've had differences, but I need you to step up and support our family, protect your mother, sister, and our interests?'

'Yes Father, all I've ever wanted to do is to defend our people. I'll keep our city safe from all threats either domestic or international, whatever the cost.'

'Good, I need you to live up to your responsibilities while I'm gone.'

'You can trust me,' Virak replied as the king smiled back proud of the man his son was becoming.

Little did he know of the deception and betrayal that Virak had been undertaking over the last few years.

***

The sun rose slowly over Rovieng and a warm morning breeze blew through the unsettled town. On the surface, the town seemed calm, much calmer than it was last night when the ground began to shake. Luke had been unconscious all night. Captain Voan sort help from the villagers after he collapsed, not sure what to do. It had been a long night and the captain was exhausted, he had ordered his men to secure the town while he kept guard over the prince and Luke. Voan didn't know what caused the room to shake. All he knew was that both men still breathed, however, he didn't know if either of them would wake again. Something strange had happened, something he couldn't explain and something he wouldn't speak about, not yet anyway.

After the ground had shaken Arun and Sonisay had rushed to the temple. Voan stumbled out shouting for help. He told the village elders that Luke had been hit by debris. Everyone thought they had experienced an earthquake. He didn't dare tell them the truth. In the short time between Luke passing out and the townspeople arriving, Voan managed to carry Luke to a nearby bed. He had also hidden the medical kit. He knew better than to risk exposing Luke's abilities. Sonisay arranged for the town's healers to tend to them, while Voan watched on protectively.

It was a little after nine in the morning when Prince Srindra woke, it caused the young woman wiping his forehead to jump. Voan heard the noise and went straight to his side.

'Where am I? What's happening?' Sri asked groggily waving the young woman away.

Voan dismissed everyone and the prince looked at him. Voan looked strange, it was like he was frightened, something the prince had never seen before.

The young captain cleared his throat, 'Your Majesty you were hit by an arrow and brought here to recover.'

Voan took a deep breath and continued. 'Colonel Myan and Marcus have gone in search of Prince Johan, while Luke remained to look after you.'

'Where is Luke?' Sri began to look around the room with concern.

Voan paused, unsure of what to say. 'He's over there, I think he's passed out but I'm not sure. The healers have been tending to him.'

The prince tried to get up but as he moved he felt a deep pain in his abdomen. 'Careful, Luke was very insistent that you don't move or it could break something called stitches, but I don't really know what that means. I saw him use this, Voan pulled the device out of his bag, he used it over your chest and on your back which seemed to help heal your wounds.'

'But why did he collapse, what happened?' Sri looked at Voan, he was acting strange. 'I can tell there's something you're not telling me, I want to know immediately, Captain.'

'I don't really know what happened,' Voan sighed. 'Since you've been injured Luke has shown some unusual abilities, he managed to shoot two Cham archers out of the trees without looking. And last night, I, um, something strange happened…'

Captain Voan hesitated.

'Tell me,' Sri ordered.

'It looked like you were going to die, this device showed Luke that your heart had stopped beating and he began to panic, we both did.'

Voan was extremely uncomfortable but continued. 'All I can tell you is a force erupted out of him which shook the whole town. But he managed to control it somehow, then he used this force on you.'

Voan paused and thought for a moment, then pulled out the medical scanner. 'This device sounded showing your heart was beating again, Luke looked at me relieved, then collapsed.'

'Are you serious?' the prince asked.

'Very, he used some of these tools on you,' Voan showed Sri the medical devices. 'You're alive because he helped mend you, I don't know how or why but I thank Buddha he did, you should be dead.'

Sri tried to get to his feet again, he wobbled as Voan rushed to help him. He managed to stand and he hobbled over to Luke. Sri reached out and put his hand on Luke's chest.

'His heart's still beating.'

Sri stood over him and watched as Luke's chest rose and fell with every breath he took. 'I'm going to tell you something. Only a few people know this and its restricted information, you're to tell no one, is that clear?'

'Yes Your Majesty,' Voan replied.

'Luke and Marcus are from the future. The four strangers came here in an accident, we've known about their strange technology for some time. The king has forbidden us to use it. You mentioned a power inside him, that's something none of them have ever discussed with us,' Sri said concerned.

As he finished speaking Luke's eyes began to open and he sat up quickly. The sudden movement made him grip is head in pain.

'Are you ok?' Sri asked.

'You're alive,' Luke said ignoring the question.

He jumped out of the makeshift bed and hugged him.

'Ouch,' Sri said smiling at Luke's affection. 'I'm a little tender but I think I'll mend, Voan tells me I'm alive thanks to you.'

It suddenly hit Luke, he remembered what had happened and the energy that had come out of him. Luke backed away, concerned he could hurt them.

His mind raged, *What was that power that came out of me and how did I harness it?*

He turned to Sri and Voan and spoke with concern, 'Something strange is happening to me, I don't know what it is, but it frightens me.'

***

Marcus and Myan had made slow progress, stopping often to check the direction of the rider. It had been a long night of riding and around lunchtime they reached a small turning in the road. The midday sun was beating down and the men seemed exhausted, but they needed to keep searching. If it hadn't been for Marcus stopping suddenly, they would have missed the discrete path into the jungle. Marcus jumped off his horse and began to pace, he looked up the steep track and called to Myan. He subtly activated his implant and looked at the fading red line.

'It's this way' he whispered, showing Myan the small screen highlighting a red line. 'He's heading into the hills.'

'I know where this path leads,' Myan responded. 'That village has never been loyal to the king, we need to be careful, this is a dangerous trail for us to follow.'

Marcus acknowledged the warning and they mounted their horses to ride up the winding track. It became increasingly narrow until the men had to ride in single file. Marcus was becoming increasingly impatient as it seemed to be taking them ages to navigate the jungle path. About an hour later they finally came into a small clearing. Marcus rode to join the colonel where he saw the stunning sight in front of him. His eyes were awash with green foliage and he could hear the tranquil sound of water. He scanned further seeing pools of water feeding into terraced rice paddies. The glistening water caused Marcus to squint at the afternoon sun.

'Don't be fooled by this place, the clan here is treacherous.'

They rode further into the clearing eventually entering a small settlement. The group passed a number of small wooden huts and people began to flee in terror. Myan pressed on towards the centre of the village. It was clear the villagers were watching them, Marcus noticed several frightened men, women and children looking at them from behind closed windows, while others ran from the fields into the jungle.

'Raise your swords men,' Myan ordered as the sound of steal being unsheathed echoed through the clearing.

The men rode slowly into the village square where more frightened locals let out screams and ran for shelter.

These people are no threat, Marcus thought to himself as the force came to a stop.

Before the colonel could say anything, a woman stepped forward.

'What do you want here,' the village elder said forcefully.

'I think you already know,' Myan replied looking down at the elderly woman before him.

Marcus gave Myan a look of fury. He dismounted his horse and walked over to the woman greeting her kindly. 'Forgive my companion, we're searching for my son, he's been stolen and I must find him.'

She looked at him then back at the colonel, without warning she placed her hands on Marcus's head and stared into his eyes. The colonel and his men jumped off their horses rushing to Marcus's aid. The woman released his head and held her hand up to the approaching soldiers, it stoped them in their tracks. She continued looking into Marcus's eyes.

'I've never seen a man like you before, of course I've heard the rumours about the white men that arrived in Angkor.' She paused still holding her hand up stopping the colonel.

'I assume you are Princess Bopha's husband,' she said kindly to Marcus.

'I, umm, yes I am, but there's no time.'

The woman interrupted him before he could finish, 'You're looking for your son, you've already said that. My name's Bian and what's yours.'

'Marcus,' he replied hesitantly. Colonel Myan began to walk forward ignoring the woman's raised hand.

'Why do you think your son's here?' she asked gently, keeping an eye on the soldiers.

'We've followed tracks which led to this village,' Myan jumped in. 'The king's left you in peace since we retook Angkor, he's respected your village now you need to tell us what you know.'

'Respected us has he, how many of my family have I lost in his wars, let's see, my husband, my brother, my sons and of course my nephew,' she replied sarcastically.

'Well, you chose to side with the Chams,' Myan said through gritted teeth. 'The king has forgiven that betrayal, but I'm much less forgiving.'

'Enough of this, I don't want to hear about your arguments. I don't care about your history and who wronged who, I want to find my son.' Marcus's emotions were breaking, and he walked away staring out at the rice paddies.

This took Bian by surprise and she followed him. As she approached, he turned to her.

'Please help us, he's so young, I fear for him,' Marcus said, unable to control himself. 'Bian please tell me where he is, I'll do anything.'

She looked at him trying to gage the man, she reached out and gripped his hand. 'I'll help you.'

Bian shouted over his shoulder, 'Stand down.'

Marcus looked up and saw a great number of villagers in the trees and on top of the buildings, all pointing arrows directly at them.

'You colonel will wait here, I'll speak with Marcus alone, I suggest you keep your men under control.' Myan's eyes fumed with fury, but he said nothing and Bian led Marcus into her home.

She gestured for him to sit and poured him a cup of her special tea. 'Drink this, it will help with your nerves.'

'Bian, I really don't have the time, I need to keep searching. I don't even know he's alive or if we're searching in the right location,' he responded desperately.

'I said drink,' He took a mouthful of her tea and instantly his mind calmed. 'Marcus, I have no quarrel with you, but I do with the king and his family.'

Marcus tried to speak but Bian stopped him. 'That being said, I don't approve of abducting children, nor do my people support the Cham, despite what the colonel may think.'

She paused and poured some tea for herself, she took a small sip and continued. 'I've seen your son. He's with a man called Yom.'

She paused, carefully considering her words as Marcus listened intently.

She finally spoke, 'He's my nephew, I want you to promise me that my village will not receive reprisals for my nephew's lone actions. His allegiance is with the Cham, we didn't ask him to come here, nor do we support him.'

'I promise, please tell me where they are?' he asked desperately.

'Yom came to me last night with a woman and a young baby. Both the woman and boy were not well,' Marcus tried to stand but Bian held her hand up. 'I helped them, I tended to the boy while the young woman rested. It's important you know I helped them both recover. I need you to understand if I hadn't it's likely the boy would've died.'

Bian sighed.

Marcus gasped. 'Where are they now?'

'They left this morning and are making their way back to the Capital of Champa, Vijaya. They're heading for the crossing at Stung Treng.'

Bian got to her feet and walked to a nearby table, she began rummaging around, Marcus was afraid to move.

'Here it is,' she said to herself and called him over.

Bian pointed at a map on the table, 'I sent him down this road,' Marcus started to head to the door.

'Wait,' Bian called out to him. 'If you and the colonel take this road, you'll have time to catch him before he reaches the river.'

She handed him the map.

'Thank you so much,' Marcus said, hugging her.

'You're welcome, babies should never be used as a weapon and I'll not support it, even if that means betraying my nephew,' she replied sadly.

'I promise your village will be safe. I'll return with my son one day to thank you for your help, as long as I get him back.'

'Go, find your boy and help make this Kingdom better,' she replied.

Marcus raced out the hut to join the colonel and they soon left the village. They took the path Bian recommended and in no time were racing towards the river.

CHAPTER TWENTY-SIX

Rapid Rivals

It had been a long ride from the capital, the king was grateful when they eventually reached the base in Stung Treng. He seldom enjoyed travelling and riding on that elephant was never a pleasurable experience. However, the people had come to expect to see their king riding the magnificent animal, it exuded power and status. General Thorn had already sent units ahead to Stung Treng. Ensuring they had all the supplies they needed and that the encampment was secure.

As the king rode through the city, he was reminded why he had always hated Stung Treng. It was a ragtag town full of traders who would sell their own mother for profit. He knew that the city's loyalty was equally split between the Khmer and Champa empires. This regularly caused conflict in the population. This divided loyalty meant that he never really trusted the local officials. The town itself was split across the great Mekong River. It was built to withstand the frequent flooding that occurred, which was due to the spring thaws way upstream. Although the king hated the city he also found Stung Treng to be a place of purpose. It was a place where people could cross the fast-flowing water with safety.

Stung Treng itself lacked the grandeur of Angkor, which reflected its status within the empire. It was a place people passed through, not a place where respectable families made their homes.

It was late afternoon when they finally reached the base, General Thorn had set up a large military camp on the eastern side of the river. From his high vantage, the king saw a sea of tents stretching endlessly across the eastern side of the riverbank. Thorn guided the king through the soldiers to an impressive command tent, where his personal servants were waiting to tend to him. The elephant came to a halt and the king was helped off the beast, as his feet touched the ground he stretched widely. After the long march, he was in dire need of rest. It had been some time since he'd needed to travel this far from Angkor, and he wasn't used to it.

The king entered the grand tent and his servants were waiting patiently. They washed and changed him into a fresh set of robes. Once the dirt of the journey had been washed away and with a drink in hand, he called for the general to return.

Thorn arrived a short while later with a number of his commanding officers.

'General, have you heard from my son?' the king asked.

'Not yet Your Majesty, I'm sure they'll be here soon,' he replied cautiously.

‘What about our Lavo allies or the eastern king’s guard, I expected them to be here when we arrived?’ the king asked rather impatiently.

‘To be honest so did I Your Majesty, I’ve sent out scouts to search for them. I’m sure they’ll be here soon, try not to worry.’ Thorn paused.

‘May I suggest you get some rest while I prepare our forces,’ he recommended gently. Thorn wanted the king out of the way, he knew his constant worrying would only become more of a distraction.

‘Very well,’ he replied reluctantly and dismissed the general to get some rest.

***

Captain Voan’s men had been waiting patiently, they’d been ready to leave for over an hour. Prince Srindra had ordered Voan to be prepared to ride to Stung Treng at pace to join up with the king. In a rather heated discussion earlier, the prince made it clear to Luke that it wasn’t possible for them to re-join the search for Prince Johan. They had no idea where Marcus and Colonel Myan had headed. Sri insisted their best course of action was to head to Stung Treng. Voan had readied his men soon after and was getting impatient to leave, he never was one to sit still. However, he never showed any impatience to his men, he waited as ordered for Prince Srindra to exit the temple.

There had been little conversation between Luke and Sri since the discussion about where to go next. After Voan left the temple, neither of them spoke much, they didn't know what to say. Both of them didn't really know what had happened the night before and the disagreement about where to go next, only made things worse. All Luke knew, was that he could think clearly for the first time in ages, and he felt less fearful.

Luke insisted on giving Sri one more medical check before they left. Sri flinched as Luke scanned him which seemed to break the tension. Although Sri had become accustomed to the device he was using, it was still very disconcerting. Luke declared he was satisfied that Sri's internal injuries were healing well, however, he insisted on using the dermal regenerator one more time on Sri's wounds. He was keen to make sure the they were healed sufficiently for them to ride. Luke waved the device over Sri's skin, further knitting the wounds together and making the scars from the arrow fade. This made Sri gasp, he was amazed by what he was seeing. The last time Luke used this device Sri was unconscious, he was unaware of what it could do.

'This technology of yours is truly amazing, it seems like witchcraft,' Sri said, looking at Luke, who remained silent. 'Luke what's going on, tell me what happened last night and why do you have these powers?'

Sri's curiosity finally got the better of him and he couldn't control himself from asking.

Luke ignored the question.

'I really think we should wait a bit longer before leaving, it'll take time for all your internal injuries to heal,' he replied.

'Luke we can't, our family is out there fighting for our people, and I asked you a question.'

'You asked me a number of questions,' Luke replied curtly. 'Let me answer them, yes the technology is amazing and no it's not witchcraft, it's just a tool we developed like you have developed countless of your own, it's just taken another thousand years to get to this level. As for the other questions, I don't know what's going on with me, I'm just a man as you are. Nothing like this has ever happened to me, or in fact anyone from my time.'

His head dropped and he paused. 'I don't know what these powers are, all I can tell you is that something happened when Kalani's re-polarised beam hit me, when we were pulled here.'

He sighed. 'Since then, when I get emotional, I seemed to lose control. I can feel an energy force building up in me. Lately I seem to be able to control it, something I couldn't do a few months ago.'

Sri just looked at him not saying a word. Under the pressure of these questions, Luke's emotions started to get the better of him and he broke down. Sri pulled him close and kissed his forehead.

'I'm here for you no matter what, do you get that, I love you,' he said tenderly.

Luke looked up. 'You mean it, even if I am turning into a floating ball of light?'

Sri laughed. 'That would be a sight, but yes I mean it. I know how difficult this must be, but we can't stay hiding here, we're not safe and we need to get to Stung Treng.'

‘I know, like I could stop you anyway Your Majesty,’ Luke said mockingly.

Sri laughed which changed the atmosphere. They packed the remaining medical equipment and a few last supplies, then headed out to join Captain Voan.

It wasn’t long before they were riding through the town, as they rode cheers erupted from the townspeople who were holding up their children showing their appreciation. Once they had cleared the town Captain Voan instructed the men to ride as fast as they could. They would ride north onto the jungle road towards the river city. Sri knew this was going to be a long hard journey. He ordered his men to ride like their lives depended on it.

It was dusk when the prince’s small force approached the village of Kdoeung. Without warning the sound of horns erupted followed by panicked screams, which were heard by all.

‘Ready yourself,’ Prince Srindra shouted and his men drew their swords.

Voan, Luke and Sri rode side by side as they entered the village confidently. It was the Lavo forces, they were dressed in bright red and golden robes. This was very much the colour of that province and their men were easy to see. A volley of arrows were unleashed from the trees and a number of Lavo fell to the ground, screams of terror filled the village as the sounds of metal clashed furiously. Sri stared into the melee trying to understand what was happening, it was at that point he could see the familiar attire of his hated enemy. It was another Cham assassin unit, but this one was bigger, much bigger. He looked closer and saw a number of Lavo soldiers cut down by the Cham fighters in front of him.

Sri then raised his sword and without wavering shouted, 'Charge!' and they all rode into the chaos before them.

***

It was late night when Yom finally stopped. Chantrea had been complaining for hours she needed a break to change Johan, who was now screaming. Yom only agreed to stop when they finally emerged from the claustrophobic jungle. They entered a large valley and Yom stopped at the edge of the tree line, he helped Chantrea off the horse and she breathed deeply taking a good look at the scene before her. She realised that they had arrived at the river Mekong. Chantrea scanned the picturesque valley before her seeing fast-flowing waters battering the riverbank, which made her increasingly anxious.

'We can stop here for a few hours,' Yom said. 'Then we'll follow the river north until we get to the crossing at Stung Treng. Now sort that brat out, I can't be doing with all this noise.'

'I'm doing my best,' Chantrea replied emotionally, placing Johan on the ground. 'Babies aren't supposed to travel like this, I'm doing everything I can to keep this child alive.'

'Well you better, or I would've lost my men for nothing,' he replied jumping forward and forcing her against a nearby tree.

He gripped her neck firmly so she couldn't move as Johan continued to scream on the floor. 'I don't know what Virak promised you but you're in the service of the Cham now, we don't accept failure.'

Yom held her tightly until he saw enough panic in her face, then let her go smiling.

Chantrea fell to the floor, she put her hands around her neck massaging where he had gripped her. Silent tears began to fall down her face. Without saying another word, she got up and began to tend to Johan, changing and feeding him while Yom made a fire.

A little while later once the fire was crackling, Chantrea sat next to it rocking Johan gently. She wanted to get the little guy back to sleep, so she could rest. Once Johan was settled, she raised her head slowly and stared with hatred at the man she was travelling with. Chantrea took in a few inhales of breath trying to compose her emotions and calm her inner voice. It was then she smelt the sweet scent of jasmine that was growing nearby, it seemed to relax her.

Yom sat staring deep into the burning fire, he rummaged through his bag pulling out some bread that Bian had given him, he tore it in half and threw it at her.

'Eat, I need you alive, for now anyway.'

Chantrea just stared at him, however before she could reply there was a sudden crackle in the undergrowth which startled her, and she looked around. Yom was already on his feet, he put his finger to his lips signalling her to be silent and walked into the undergrowth. He moved close to the trees blending into the background. As he looked deeper into the foliage he saw the purple robe from one of the prince's men. Yom scanned the trees further and saw flashes of purple and blue material, it looked like they were surrounding them. Yom crept undetected behind the closest soldier and in a flash slit his throat. The soldier slumped to the floor while Yom rushed quickly out of the jungle.

He pulled Chantrea up and stamped on the fire. 'Come, I've no idea how they've found us so quickly, we must leave now. Our plans need to change, we won't be able to ride north without being captured, we must cross the river here.'

'But how, it's too fast, we'll drown,' Chantrea said a little too loudly.

'We've got no choice. We must go and go now.'

As he spoke, a horn sounded behind them, the dead soldier had been discovered. Chantrea gave Johan to Yom while she pulled herself onto the horse, Yom handed the sleeping child back. He grabbed his weapons and mounted the horse. They began to ride towards the river as fast as they could. As they approached the river bank General Thorn and Marcus appeared at the edge of the jungle. They looked down into the expansive valley before them, spotting the man they had been searching for trapped by the fast-flowing river.

***

The division from Lavo was in complete disarray, their forces were about five thousand strong, which vastly outnumbered the Cham attackers. Arrows flew from the surrounding trees, cutting down more of the Lavo men while a small Cham-mounted force attacked the Lavo cavalry, causing horses to bolt in all directions.

'Luke, you take half our men into the forest and find those snipers. Voan and I will firm up the Lavo's crumbling line.'

'Be careful, you're still healing,' Luke shouted at Sri who was already riding to the centre of the Lavo force.

Luke turned to the remaining men and yelled, 'Come with me,' and they rode into the thick jungle.

Sri got to the centre of the Lavo force and the disorder was clear to see.

'Who's in charge here?' he shouted.

'It was Major Lek, but these bastards took him out with the first volley of arrows. The enemy surprised us, they took out most of our commanding officers before we knew what had happened,' a young captain shouted back.

'Who's left?'

'I think it's just me and Captain Thahan Sar, he's fighting over there,' the officer said and pointed to where the Cham were attacking the cavalry.

'What's your name and rank soldier?' Voan ordered.

'I am Captain Chatri Moa,' he replied. 'I look after a unit of five hundred men.'

'Rally the men,' Sri shouted. 'Get them to use their shields to protect themselves from the incoming arrows while we seek out the attackers. Voan, help Moa to secure this flank. I will get to Sar.'

Voan acknowledged the order, dismounted his horse and rushed towards Chatri, barking orders as Sri rode to join Sar.

Back in the Jungle Luke and his men were clearing the archers from the trees, Luke's ability to sense where the enemy was positioned was incredible. Time after time, he pointed to the trees and one by one the Cham fell to the floor, making a loud *thud* as they hit the ground dead. Large trees surrounded the village, which the Cham took advantage of to attack the Lavo. However Luke and his men were ruthlessly clearing the archers from the trees.

After a while he felt sure they had killed all the Cham, he called the men back smiling at their success. His mind began to wander and a strange feeling was bothering him, he couldn't explain what it was. In his distraction, a Cham archer jumped out of a nearby tree and began to run furiously towards Luke with his sword raised. Luke went to raise his bow, but it was too late, the man reached him before he could fire. A yell came from behind the attacker and just as the Cham began to launch himself at Luke, the head of a spear broke through the man's neck splattering blood all over his face.

'We can't all be perfect,' one of Captain Voan's men shouted back in jest and they both returned to searching for the enemy.

Sri arrived just in time to help Captain Sar, he had been knocked off his horse and was fighting hand-to-hand with a large Cham. Sar was holding his own against the muscled giant, the Cham's sword beat down hard onto the shield Sar clutched to. The Lavo captain was under pressure, but he kept fighting as the furious sound of metal clashing echoed through the village. Sri rode towards them, he pulled his bow back and shot an arrow into the head of the attacking Cham, who fell to the floor dead.

'Get up and get on your horse, we need to save your cavalry!' Sri shouted.

Sar did as he was ordered. He clambered onto his frightened horse and joined the man who had saved him.

'Who are you?' he yelled.

'Prince Srindra from Angkor, what's going on here?'

'It was a complete surprise Your Majesty, the Cham attacked us while we were resting, the major thought we were safe in Khmer lands,' Sar replied.

'These assassin squads have a very unwelcome habit of turning up where they're not wanted. Come, let's clear the bastards out, rally the men,' Sri ordered.

Sar reached for a horn on his belt and the sound rang out across the village and he shouted, 'Rally to me, rally to me.'

The men who were still fighting broke off and rode to Captain Sar.

'On my orders we charge, are you ready,' Sri shouted to the men that had joined them, they looked to Sar.

'This is Prince Srindra, we'll follow his orders,' Sar demanded.

'I said are you with me?'

The men shouted back in acknowledgement.

Sri began to ride. Sar joined him at the front as the rest of the cavalry rode behind them. Sri was leading the front of the wedge.

'Charge,' he shouted, and the men rode as fast as they could, cutting down any of the Cham infantry that were on the ground.

They quickly reached a small Cham cavalry line and Sri smashed into it head-on, swinging his sword wildly cutting down man after man. Finally, the large numbers of the Lavo cavalry turned the fight, crushing the remaining enemy and the battle was won.

***

'I can see them,' Marcus shouted at the horse riding fast towards the river.

Colonel Myan blew his horn, and his men exited the forest.

'After them' he shouted, and they began to charge.

Chantrea looked over her shoulder and her eyes grew wild. 'They're getting closer!' she screamed, gripping on to Johan and Yom tightly.

'I don't know how they found us so quickly, but we'll get out of this,' Yom raced towards the river.

'Look, a boat,' he pointed at a small fishing vessel being buffeted by the fast-flowing river. He jumped of the horse, grabbed his bag then forced Chantrea down. Yom smacked the horse hard, it reared in pain and galloped off.

'Are you sure we should do this?' Chantrea said desperately, her eyes pleading for any answer other than yes.

'In now,' he forced Chantrea onto the boat and Johan was back screaming. Yom picked up an oar and untied the mooring rope, instantly the boat was buffeted by the fast-flowing waters, and it shot downriver. Yom tried frantically to row but the currents were too strong, the boat was forced further and further backwards.

Marcus, Myan and the men had reached the river and were riding fast trying to keep up with the boat.

'Give me my son!' he shouted.

'Never,' Yom replied as Chantrea held Johan close to her.

Suddenly there was a loud splitting sound as the boat crashed into rocks. They were thrown closer to the eastern bank. Chantrea screamed and the boat crashed into more and more rocks until finally it broke apart, flinging them all into the river.

Marcus yelled as he saw Chantrea's head go under water, he and the rest of the men searched frantically for any signs of life. The noise of the river was deafening and the frenzied flow of the water relentless. Marcus feared he had lost Johan for good. A deep sickening feeling began to fill his stomach. He couldn't help himself. Marcus activated his palm implant and the screen appeared in front of all the colonel's men. He rode downriver following the red spot on his screen.

Finally, he shouted, 'Over there.'

The colonel searched the river bank and he saw what Marcus had located. Chantrea had managed to pull herself out of the water and onto the eastern bank, and to all their surprise she was still holding Johan.

'He's okay,' she shouted to Marcus over the deafening roar of the water.

He could see his child was safe and his deepest fears lifted. Chantrea smiled back at him. She was away from that awful man. She didn't care what had happened to him, she wanted to return Johan to his father.

'I'm so sorry Marcus, take him…'

She stopped mid-sentence as Yom put a dagger to her throat.

'Time to go, isn't it my dear?' he said menacingly. 'And keep your words to yourself.'

'Give him back,' Marcus yelled desperately as they disappeared into the jungle.

He turned to Myan.

'We must get across,' he shouted desperately.

'Marcus we can't it's too dangerous, we'll be swept down river, we must ride for the crossing at Stung Treng. I'm sorry I know we're so close, but there is no way across,' Myan replied sympathetically. 'Even if we find another boat, I can't risk the men, the water's too fast.'

Marcus let out a frustrated scream and began to ride north, knowing that he could have just lost his son forever.

CHAPTER TWENTY-SEVEN

The Battle for Stung Treng

The night had set in by the time the Lavo forces had chased off the remaining Cham. Prince Srindra sounded the horn, ordering all forces to return and regroup. The Cham had inflicted immense damage to the Lavo. Out of the original force of five thousand, over five hundred were dead and over a thousand were wounded. Most of the commanders had died, leaving the unit broken. The prince ordered the exhausted Lavo men to burn their dead and rest, while he sent scouts ahead to check for any more unwelcome guests.

Sri gathered all the remaining officers in the main village temple.

'We need to get to Stung Treng as soon as we can, we have seen multiple incursions into our lands by the Cham. We need to attack deep into Champa to draw them back.'

'Your Majesty, the Lavo are leaderless, my advice is for our forces to retreat back home,' Captain Moa replied hesitantly. His bright red robes were soaked in blood and his hand shook while he gripped his sheathed sword.

'Go home? The battle hasn't even started and you're ready to retreat. Pull yourself together, your men need stronger leadership.' Sri bashed his hand on the table. 'Are you ready to let your men die for nothing?'

He stared at the young Captain who didn't respond.

'Captain Voan, I'm promoting you to major. You'll command the Lavo while they are supporting us in the campaign against the Cham.'

The prince then turned to Sar and Chatri. 'Your men need you to step up and lead by example. Voan, work with the captains to understand who in the men has leadership skills that can replace the fallen commanders.'

Sri paused and took a breath, then said calmly, 'We need more commanders to help with this fight, be ready to leave at first light, is that clear?'

'Yes Your Majesty,' both Captain's replied and bowed before leaving.

Around the table remained Luke, Sri, and Voan.

'Your Majesty, what about my unit?' Voan asked.

'Luke will lead them for now, I need you to support our Lavo allies, they need a strong leader and that's you. I expect you to make them the best fighting force they can be in the limited time we have, is that clear?'

'Yes Your Majesty,' he replied bowing.

Sri gripped Voan's arm. 'You deserve this promotion, prove to the others you're worthy of becoming my top commander. I know Keo would've chosen you to replace him.'

'Thank you Your Majesty, those words mean a great deal,' he bowed again and turned to leave, just before he did, he spoke again. 'You have and will always have my sword and my bow,' then left to take up his new command.

'Luke, I know what you're going to say, you can't command but I need you. Whatever you promised long ago you've already broken,' Sri said without looking up. 'My men trust you and so do I, so step up and become the man I need you to be.'

Sri lifted his head.

'I know what I need to do and I know what's best for my family.' He reached his hand out placing it on Sri's chest. 'You have my sword, my bow and my heart. I'll ready the men for dawn and we'll ride on your order.'

Luke kissed the man he loved, then left leaving Sri contemplating his next move.

***

Chantrea was exhausted. Yom dragged her to a nearby farmstead, he ordered the frighten villagers to bring him dry clothes, food and fresh water. The terrified farmers did as they were told. Chantrea was soaked through, but she continued to tend to Johan who for the moment had stopped crying, unaware of the journey they had both been on over the last few days.

'Drink this,' Yom said giving Chantrea a flask of rice wine. 'We have time, they can't cross the river. We were very lucky to make it over ourselves.'

He paused for a moment.

'I expect they'll head for Stung Treng,' he said smiling.

Chantrea sipped the wine. It warmed her insides and she reached for the bowl of warm stew that the locals had prepared for her.

'What happens now?' she asked hesitantly.

'We join up with King Indravarman's forces and give the little brat to him, he'll use his bloodline to cement his claim on the Khmer throne.'

'You, do you have any horses?' Yom asked the terrified farmer who was cowering in the corner with his family.

'Yes sir,' he replied with fear.

'Take this and bring me your best horse,' Yom threw a pouch of money at the man. 'Fetch it now, we need to leave.'

The man bowed his head and scurried off, a few minutes later he returned.

Yom ordered Chantrea to move, she stood up carefully holding Johan who for some unknown reason was sleeping soundly. Yom forced Chantrea outside followed by the farmer who led them to the animal.

'You call *that* a horse?' Yom raged at the man. 'It won't make it further than a few miles.'

'It's the best horse I have sir,' the farmer replied fearfully.

Yom looked at him with contempt. 'It'll have to do.'

He helped Chantrea onto it and turned once more to the frightened man who'd helped them both so much. Yom grabbed the man by the neck and pulled him close.

'Best horse indeed,' he said sarcastically pulling a dagger out of his robes. He stabbed it deep into the man's stomach.

Chantrea let out a little scream as Yom pushed the man to the floor, still gripping tightly to his dagger. The farmer looked up at Chantrea in fear. As every breath became more painful, his life slowly left his body.

'I'll take that, this nag isn't worth the money I gave you. Plus you have no use for it now,' he said smiling sadistically as he retrieved his pouch.

He gave the dying man one last scornful look, smiled and rode north to join the eastern road to Champa.

***

The king had been in Stung Treng for over a day now and his worrying had reached fever pitch. He had not seen or heard from either the Lavo force, the eastern king's guard, or his son. General Thorn on the other hand, was more positive, the Khmer forces continued to arrive in larger numbers than expected. The abduction of prince Johan had mobilised the people, it was galvanising the country to fight against the Cham. To the king's great surprise, the feared tribe from Bakan had pledged their support. The Bakan were notoriously fierce fighters, they chose what and who they fought based on their strict codes. Their mysterious ways often led to claims they used magic to overcome their enemies. The people believed this legend due to the many victories these skilled female warriors achieved. Yet the Bakan hadn't come to the king's aid when he retook Angkor, they declared it was not their fight. So for them to travel so far from home and aid him in battle was a huge surprise.

The general spent the morning hurriedly preparing for the invasion, the army needed weapons, armour, food, water and supplies for the long and difficult journey. However the higher numbers of recruits that continued to arrive though welcome, presented a logistical challenge and left the army's supplies very delicately balanced. With the support of the queen, General Thorn had recruited the best foreign mercenaries. They had travelled to Stung Treng and were to be paid generously for their services. He had also employed a legion of blacksmiths to work in the foundries, so the war machine was fully mobilised. The general had used all his contacts from across the empire to arrange for weapons, armour and military reserves to be sent ahead to Stung Treng, resulting in wagons continually arriving. The city was awash with activity and with every hour the king's army looked more and more impressive. General Thorn was confident that his invasion force would be powerful enough to put an end to the Champa threat for good, and slay his old enemy.

The sun had not been up long when Thorn requested a meeting with the king. As the general entered the tent the king was closely studying a map of Champa.

Thorn walked to his side and said calmly, 'Your Majesty I say we go now. The Lavo can follow us when they get here, our forces are strong enough without them. There's no need to wait.'

The king didn't respond, he was still reviewing the map.

'I say we march here.' he pointed to the barracks at Lumphat, it was where the eastern guard were based. 'We'll meet those forces on the road rather than wait for them here.

'General, are you sure about this? I've not heard a single message from them and the scouts we sent out are still yet to return,' he replied worriedly.

'We have to take that chance, Indravarman will know you're moving against him. The longer we wait the more time he has to fortify his position and launch a counterattack.' Thorn began to pace the tent.

'I've been by your side on all our major battles, trust me we have to go,' he insisted.

'I trust you totally,' the king paused for a moment. 'Alright let's start moving our forces across the river, once we've secured that position, we will begin the march to Lumphat. It'll take time to get our people across and I hope by then our allies will have arrived to march with us.'

'I'll do as you order Your Majesty,' Thorn bowed and set off to mobilise the troops.

Over the next few hours, the men were readied. The Khmer officers were ordered to arranged their forces into different groups. Each group would cross the river and meet up at the eastern barracks of the city. Provisions were made for the horses, elephants, weapons and supplies to cross. The animals would follow once the general was sure the majority of men were safely in position. He wanted to be sure that they were protected against any attack or sabotage. Twelve large ferries had been commandeered to support this mammoth undertaking, each ferry could carry about a hundred people, or twenty horses, or four elephants. The ferries were sturdy wooden barges, each had a rope linked to a structure on either side of the river. The ferries were pulled across by ferry men on both the western and eastern shores. It would take about ten minutes to pull the barges each way and with loading time each trip would take about thirty minutes. The force now numbered forty thousand men, a hundred war elephants, four thousand horses along with five hundred waggons full of weapons and supplies. The general calculated it would take over a thousand crossings and in the region of two days to move everyone across.

Around lunchtime, Thorn signalled to start the ferry crossings and the mammoth task began. The transportation across the river continued all night with more and more soldiers and equipment safely reaching the eastern side of Stung Treng. General Thorn was overseeing the whole operation, however at around two in the morning he finally decided to get some rest. He left command in the hands of his trusted officers who were ordered to wake him if anything urgently needed his attention.

As dawn broke the general rose. He pulled on his robes and heard the gentle patter of rain bouncing off the canvas of his tent.

This is the last thing we need. He thought and strode quickly to the river.

Things seemed calm and under control, the ferries were moving as expected loaded with soldiers, equipment, and animals. The rain didn't seem to be hindering the operation, well for now at least. General Thorn decided to walk back to the river moorings to check how things were going, he knew this was when his men were most vulnerable. To his surprise he was met by the king, who had been up since the early hours, watching intently the impressive scene before him. The king also knew how vulnerable his army was as they crossed.

'What do you think Your Majesty?' Thorn asked.

'Very impressive,' he replied, and they began to walk along the western shore.

'How are the barges holding up,' the king asked one of Thorn's officers.

'Very well Your Majesty,' the officer said with pride.

However, as he spoke warning horns sounded and smoke began to rise from the eastern shore.

The general climbed onto a nearby lookout post followed closely by the king, he raised to his eye a rudimentary-looking device and peered through. To his shock he could see men dressed in black, which was the colour of the Cham forces. Fire was blazing in a number of buildings and ever-increasing smoke was rising from the settlement.

The general said forcefully, 'It's the Cham, how did they break through our defences?'

Thorn handed the king the looking device and rushed down to join his men, this was Thorn's biggest fear. The crossing had split his force, *how did the Cham get so close without the scouts spotting them*, he thought furiously. Thorn was far from the frontline and had no idea what was happening which made him rage.

The king descended the lookout post and joined the general who was already issuing orders to his officers. He turned to the king, 'I have to get over there, Your Majesty you're to remain here until I know it's safe. Take the king back to our camp and ensure he's protected.'

The major in charge of the king security began to escort him away, 'Wait I want to come too, I want to help,' the king shouted back.

Suddenly one of the lookouts yelled, 'In coming!'

Thorn grabbed the king and forced him under a nearby cart just as a number of objects landed around them. The general looked at what had just missed them. It was severed heads. He pulled a helmet off one of the heads and looked at the golden markings. He understood instantly and knew what this display was designed to do. The heads belonged to the men from the eastern battalion.

'In coming,' another lookout yelled, as yet further severed heads hit the eastern shore.

Thorn turned to the king. 'I can't win this battle while I'm worrying about your safety. Listen to me, the people need you here, you may rule the kingdom but I rule the army.'

The general then reached for the king's arm and they locked together. 'Do you trust me?'

'Yes,' the king replied instantly.

'Well do as I say.'

The king bowed his head and the major escorted him back to camp surrounded by guards.

Thorn now rushed to the shore and shouted at the soldiers who were controlling the barges, 'They stop for nothing, we must get our soldiers and supplies across.'

They acknowledged the order and the general jumped onto the nearest barge with some of his most loyal officers. It was soon being pulled to the eastern shore. The crossing seemed to take forever which only made the general more frustrated. Finally, they approached the river bank as a barrage of arrows rained down. The men who were not quick enough to raise their shields were cut down and fell into the fast-flowing water.

The barge hit the shore and the general shouted, 'Shields!' just as they were hit by a further volley of arrows.

As on the western shore, the general shouted to the ferrymen responsible for the barges.

'Don't stop at any cost,' he said before charging off to find his commanders.

He rushed through the streets where buildings were ablaze, the intense fires lit up the morning sky. The Cham set fire to the city to cause as much chaos as possible, they wanted to drive fear into the hearts of the men. The general continued to push forward, he could see death everywhere, bodies of Khmer soldiers and civilians laden with arrows. At that moment there was a loud whistling sound and an arrow shot past him, it missed him by inches however it found one of his junior officers. A

Khmer soldier managed to fire an arrow back hitting the Cham sniper who fell from the roof. Thorn drew his sword and charged down the main street where hand-to-hand fighting was intense. He battled his way through slicing down Cham after Cham desperate to find what remained of his commanders. The Cham and Khmer forces fought in doorways, on rooftops and in the streets all under constant arrow fire from each side. It took the general a good hour to reach the command post they had set up. The streets were a full-on battlefield, nowhere was safe.

Thorn finally reached the main command point, on the floor lying dead were most of the general's commanders, however, a few men remained to shout orders. To the general's surprise Captain Nisey had taken command, he was another of Prince Srindra's excellently trained officers who the general had huge faith in.

'Captain, tell me our situation,' he ordered.

Nisey stepped forward nursing a deep cut on his arm but continued without showing any signs of pain.

He pointed at the map in front of them. 'It was a complete ambush General. They knew what we were going to do before we did it, they know our plans. When dawn broke they attacked, all our horses on this side of the river are dead. From what the men have reported, the Cham forces have about twenty thousand men. We've managed to hold this line here.' Nisey pointed to a small ridge south of the city.

'They're attacking from the west.' He pointed at the map again. 'They have also taken the headland to the north of the Sekong tributary, you see where the river splits. We only had a small force garrisoned there which were easily overcome, the Cham are using it to pin us down. What are you orders general?'

'Focus to the west, we must break their lines before they turn our flank here.'

The general pointed at the map to the south of the city, he turned to one of his officers who had fought his way through the streets with the general.

'Suan, bring your forces here, do whatever to maintain our line.'

'Yes sir,' Captain Suan said before leaving to arrange his men.

The general spoke to another young commander, 'Captain Brak whatever the cost we keep the ferries running, we need more men and horses.'

'Yes sir,' Captain Brak replied then left.

'Captain Nisey you take your men west, I'll join you once I'm sure the city is secure. Captain, needless to say, I need you to break their lines. So find me away through.'

'Yes sir, I'll do whatever I can,' he replied and rushed off.

To the remaining commanders, the general issued a number of orders all focused on holding the city.

At that moment, a lookout yelled, 'incoming' and another volley of arrows came down.

The officers raised their shields to shelter but for one young junior commander it was too late, he was hit by multiple arrows and fell down dead.

The general threw down his shield and looked over the besieged city in anger, death now surrounded him everywhere. The rain fell hard and thunder could be heard in the distance. The streets were quickly turning into swamps. Thorn looked out from his vantage point observing the battle, it was then he saw three of the ferries drifting down the Mekong laden with men, the ropes had been severed by arrows. The ferries were disappearing out of sight, he yelled in anger.

At least there are still nine others working, he thought to himself. *Captain Brak will hold them I know he will.*

Over the next few hours, Thorn constantly barked orders, his command comforted the men and his strategy was paying off, they were holding the city. However, it came at a high cost. The bodies of Khmer and Cham fighters filled the streets. The river ran thick with the dead, the bodies floating down stream like autumn leaves. The Cham force based on the Phum Hangkhoban headway continually hampered the Khmer, continually firing volleys of arrows at them. It made it impossible to fight in the open, the Cham didn't seem to care who they were killing, and many of their own men fell to their own arrows. This just drove the Khmer to fight harder while the Cham morale seemed to be faltering. The general knew his men were ready to fight to the bitter end, this couldn't be said for the Cham.

***

It was early evening when Prince Srindra arrived at Stung Treng with the Lavo, the battle had been raging all day and there was a sense of panic in the air. Sri rode quickly with Major Voan, Luke and the Lavo Captain's to the king's command tent. Where he was embraced emotionally by his father.

'Sri, I'm so glad to see you on this horrid day, I feared I had lost you too,' he said emotionally.

'Father, sorry it took so long to get here, we had a few problems with more Cham assassin squads. Tell me what's happening with the battle, there's no time to waste,' he replied, knowing the pressure his father was under.

'What about my grandson, where's Marcus and Myan?' he asked, ignoring Sri's questions.

'They're still searching, we were split up but there's no time for that now. Father, tell me about the battle,' Sri insisted.

'Our messengers have confirmed we are holding the eastern part of the city, we're down to seven ferries now and we have lost countless men and horses.'

The king's guilt was clear to see, it was he who had made the decision to invade and the weight of the empire seemed to be pulling him down.

'We don't seem to be able to break out of the city, the army is pinned down due to a force to the north. The enemy are holding the Phum Hangkhoban headway and every time we try to break west, they are met by a barrage of arrows. My spies tell me King Indravarman is to the west near Ban Bung, I can't believe he is already this far into our lands,' the king dropped his head. 'The eastern guard is no more. The Cham have slaughtered our garrison of five thousand men. My aids also tell me that our Lavo allies have abandoned us.'

'The Lavo are with me, they were attacked by the Cham. Most of their officers were killed but the men that survived are here with you,' he gestured to the two captains. 'Major Voan will be commanding their force for now.'

'At least that's some good news, well not that they were attacked.' He looked at the Lavo Captains, he reached out his hand in friendship and they gladly took it.

'Where's General Thorn?' Sri asked.

The king turned back to his son. 'He's leading our forces on the eastern bank and thank Buddha he has. But as I've told you, they're pinned down and it's getting dark. I fear if we don't get out of this situation, they'll be crushed, and our forces wiped out.'

Just as he did another horn sounded.

'What is it now?' the king said rushing out of the tent.

Thankfully it was more good news, Marcus and Colonel Myan had just arrived. They dismounted their horses and rushed up to the king, who embraced them both. Luke looked at Marcus, he had known this man all his life and he knew something was wrong, the man looked shattered.

'Your Majesty, I was so close to Johan, but they escaped,' Marcus said darkly. 'These people will do anything. They have no honour and shame.'

'They're keeping Johan alive Marcus, that is a good sign trust me,' the king said kindly and reached out to him once more.

A soldier then ran into the room and gave Colonel Myan a message. 'Good news, we've managed to salvage two of the ferries, we have nine working and our forces continue to cross.'

'That's no good if we can't break through, how bad are these waters by Kaoh Sralau?' Prince Srindra asked, pointing at the rapids to the north.

Major Kiri Nau one of General Thorn's commanders in charge of the western shore stepped forward. 'They can be crossed. But it's dangerous to attempt it when we've had strong rains like today.'

He paused, noticing everyone was looking at him.

'I grew up in this province, if we want to break out of the city we need to crush these Cham archers on the headway. I know it will be dangerous to cross, but I believe it's possible if you're willing to take the risk,' the major declared.

'If what you say is true and we can cross, we'll be in your dept,' Sri replied. 'Father, I say take the risk, Major Voan and I will lead a force to capture it.'

Sri turned to Myan. 'Colonel, you get our remaining forces across the river. If we succeed, you'll have the opportunity you need to break through and drive them out of the city.'

'Wait, I can't send you on such a dangerous mission Sri, what if the major is wrong and I lose you,' the king replied.

'If you lose this fight, the kingdom will lose much more than me,' he responded.

Before the king could speak, Sri turned back to the commanders. 'I'll take the Lavo unit and my men, Colonel Myan, you take the rest of the queen's battalion and re-join the main forces.'

Myan nodded.

'It's a good plan Your Majesty, listen to Sri,' Myan interjected.

The king looked at the colonel and then back to Sri.

'It's very dangerous my son, are you sure it can work?' he asked.

'I'm sure Father. I've already survived a number of attempts on my life over the last few years, the water won't take me. The Cham have this coming and I'd like to pay them back with vengeance,' he replied angrily.

'Very well, you have my support, go now before I change my mind.'

'Just before I do, I hear that the feared Bakan tribe have come to our aid, is it right they've pledged to fight with us?'

'Yes, that's correct,' one of the king's aids answered.

'Do you know if they've crossed yet?' Sri asked intently.

'No, not yet,' the aid replied again.

'Then I request they join us, if you allow Father?'

'Yes take who you need, but why do you want them?'

'When we crush the Cham archers, I want to take them behind enemy lines to Ban Bung, with their help maybe we can get to Johan. This is exactly the right mission for the Bakan. I know they'll help us get Johan back,' he replied.

Marcus who had been listening to them stepped in, 'I want to come. If there is any option of getting to Ban Bung and to my son, I'm coming.'

'Very well Marcus you have my permission also, but make sure you return,' the king replied. 'All I seem to do is lose family in these never-ending wars, I'm not going back to Bo without you.'

'Father we'll return, I've faith we'll win this war and crush the Cham whatever the cost. Captain Voan, can you inform the leader of the Bakan tribe to join me in my tent before we leave. I believe her name is Rotha Aem, I'm keen to speak with her privately.'

Voan nodded and left the tent immediately.

'Myan will you advise General Thorn of our plans?' the king requested.

'Of course Your Majesty.'

'May Buddha bless you all with good fortune. But for the kingdom's sake please come back alive.'

One by one they embraced the king and left.

CHAPTER TWENTY-EIGHT

The Bakan

Rotha was taken by surprise when she was summoned by the king. She was led to his command tent by Captain Voan, this was unusual as he wore the prince's colours. Rotha had not expected the Bakan fighters to be welcomed so warmly by the king and his men. The Bakan had never shown much support for him in the past and she expected the king to distrust their motives. However, the abduction of Johan had been a turning point for the tribe. Rotha spent many hours convincing the village elders to join the fight against the disgraceful Cham, eventually they agreed.

It was common knowledge that warriors from the Bakan tribe rarely got involved in the wars of Kings. They were focused on honour, protecting their village and ensuring their unique culture survived. It was widely known that many invaders had tried to conquer the small Bakan settlement over the years, however, they all met the same fate of defeat. The Bakan grounds were sacred and attackers, trespassers or thieves that entered never returned. The legend of their ferocious female warriors and the secretive culture had gained the tribe quite a reputation.

It was Rotha who succeeded in convincing the tribe to support the Khmer. Her impassioned speech about the violation of nature committed by the Cham gained much backing. She argued if they were willing to abduct a child to meet their own selfish desires, what would they do to the kingdom if they won the war?

It was this realisation that convinced the elders and they voted overwhelmingly to support the Khmer, in particular Princess Bopha. The queen and her daughter were already greatly respected by the Bakan. Both women had sent aid and support to help the tribe and promote female education. This generosity of spirit served to foster warm relations between the empire and the tribe. It resulted in the Khmer army having an ally they didn't know they had. Rotha declared that the abomination of the Cham King must be dealt with. She convinced the tribe that the return of Johan to Princess Bopha was of the upmost importance. With the support of her tribe, she gathered her skilled band of female warriors and left to join the war.

Voan guided Rotha to the king's tent. If she was completely honest with herself she was nervous, not that she'd show it. However instead of the king, Prince Srindra sat in his place, he gestured for Rotha to sit and poured her a drink.

'I guess you're wondering why I've asked you to join me,' he said.

'Yes,' she replied forcefully. 'I'm not sure what to call you, we don't tend to stand on ceremony where I come from.'

'Why don't you just call me Sri, all my friends do and I hate all that "*Your Majesty*" rubbish'

'Fine, Sri why have you called me here? My warriors were getting ready to cross the river and join the battle.'

He smiled at her, he knew already he liked this woman and recalled his sister's description, it was very accurate. Bo had met Rotha on one of the few aid missions she'd taken part in.

'Straight to the point. Very well, I'm arranging a surprise attack to destroy the archers on the Hangkhoban headland. I want to wipe out the Cham force before heading after Indravarman, where I'll rescue my nephew and avenge the Cham atrocities.'

Rotha stared back deep into his eyes, saying nothing which made him uneasy. 'I was surprised to see your tribe come and fight with us. My sister's told me a little about your culture, but her information was limited. I believe you have a strong honour code, is that right?'

'Honour is everything to us.'

'I want you to fight with me, to help rescue Johan and to make the Cham pay for this betrayal, what say you?'

Rotha smiled at him, her sharp-edged teeth caught his eye, he noticed she'd filed them down. 'My tribe believe that the gods put us here for a reason. We're here to protect the innocent and prevent wrongdoings against the natural world, anyone who doesn't live by that code isn't worthy. Your sister has shown great kindness and respect to my people. When we heard of the abduction of her son, my tribe committed to help fight this war.'

'I thank you greatly for your loyalty to my sister, will you join us in our plans tonight?'

'Yes Sri, on one condition,' Rotha replied.

'What's that?' he asked.

'I command my warriors, I will follow your orders, but they follow mine, is that acceptable?'

'Yes certainly, I'm not sure your tribe would follow anyone else,' Sri grinned at Rotha causing her to smile back.

'I do have one other task for you and your warriors. I can't explain everything, so you'll need to trust me.' She looked at him intrigued. 'I need you to protect my sister's husband Marcus, he's not used to our way of life. He'll do anything to get his son back, but I fear for his abilities. Can you do that for me and for my sister?'

'My warriors and I will protect this Marcus, you have my word,' she replied.

'Thank you again, I can't lead this attack while worrying about protecting Marcus,' Sri said bleakly.

'What about this Luke, does he need protecting too?' Rotha asked. 'I hear he's different also.'

Sri smiled at her, 'Luke has special skills, he looks after me as well as himself, he needs no extra protection. These strangers have brought a fresh perspective to court, something I hope you've started to see.'

'When do we leave?' Rotha asked.

'Soon, be ready to leave in two hours,' he replied.

She got up to leave and bowed to him. He was thankful this mighty leader was joining him on his mission.

***

Yom reach Ban Bung just before night fall, the sun had set but there was still a dusk light in the air. The sound of the fierce battle at Stung Treng vibrated through the wind as he rode into the Cham camp. The ride had been long and hard. Chantrea and the child had managed it well, but he knew they were both struggling. Yom passed the heavily guarded makeshift walls of the camp and made his way up to Indravarman. However, before he could get close, he was stopped by Indravarman's guards who force them all to dismount.

'I'm Major Yom, I've been on a mission for the king and I've brought him a present. Lead me to him now,' Yom said, pushing past the guard who was taken by surprise.

'You.' He pointed at a frightened servant. 'I need food, water and milk for the baby. Clean them both up, they need to be respectable before being presented.'

The servant bowed, leading Chantrea and Johan away. Yom on the other hand raced up to the command post keen to share his victory. He had been away far too long and couldn't wait to be welcomed back. Yom entered the farmhouse that the Cham leaders had taken over, however, he was met by more guards who blocked his way.

'Let me in, I'm here to see the king,' he demanded.

'Who are you?' one of the guards replied not moving.

'I've already explained that, Major Yom, now let me in,' he demanded again.

The man didn't move and Yom knew better than to force himself passed. He had noticed the guard's hand on his sword.

'Speak to the king he'll want to see me I'm Major Yom.'

The guard called a fellow soldier over and whispered in his ear, the soldier nodded and left.

He turned back to Yom.

'You'll wait here,' he ordered the frustrated major.

The soldier returned and whispered into the large guard's ear, who smiled.

'What are you smiling about? I demand to see the king,' Yom shouted again.

'The king has ordered you to wait, he will call for you when he's ready, now leave,' he demanded.

Yom stood there, his mouth a gasp for a moment then without a word turned and left. He headed back to where he'd left Chantrea, searching for the servant that had led them away. He quickly found a small house where Chantrea was being washed, other servants tended to Johan.

Chantrea looked at him, her exhaustion plain to see and asked, 'does he want to see us?'

'You are to wait,' he snapped back. 'The king is busy.'

Over the next hour they waited to be summoned, servants brought them food and drink while Johan slept in a makeshift cot.

After what seemed like hours the large guard entered the small hut.

'The king will see you now, all of you.'

He looked at Chantrea and the sleeping child.

'Follow me.'

Chantrea picked up Johan. They were led out of the hut and into the farmhouse the king had made his command post.

Chantrea had never met the king of Champa and as they entered the room, he had his back to them. He was focused on the map of the battlefield in front of him. Indravarman turned around slowly and Chantrea couldn't help but stare. The king was a small skinny man and he looked young despite his aging years. Chantrea looked closely and despite his youthful appearance she noticed he had a hard look about him. She thought he looked like he was used to hardship, but he had a face which seemed fearless. Indravarman's eyes were dark brown and sunken deep into his face. He wore dark blue robes adorned with golden jewellery and wore a golden crown studied with sapphires.

'So, you've returned,' the king walked up to Chantrea and placed his hand on Johan.

'This is the son of Princess Bopha, I'm still astonished you managed to steal him away,' Indravarman said with a smile, staring at Chantrea which made her extremely uncomfortable.

'Yes Your Majesty,' Yom responded keenly. 'We've ridden relentlessly to bring him to you and to fulfil my promise.'

'Fulfil your promise? Where are the men I sent out with you, where are the additional troops you promised to rally from your homeland?' The king moved towards Yom. His eyes looked furiously at him waiting for an answer.

'We were attacked Your Majesty,' Yom's voice had a sense of panic in it. 'I prioritised bringing the child to you and the men sacrificed themselves so I could do that. As for my people, they're ready to rebel. We just need to show them we're in control when we march deep into Khmer territory.'

'Liar, my spies tell me your family has betrayed you. This plot you worked out with Virak has united the Khmer, not turn them against Jayavarman.'

'But I was only following your or…'

'Silence,' Indravarman shouted.

The king knew only so well it was his own plot that had backfired. However, he wouldn't be taking the blame for it.

'Girl, bring me the baby,' he ordered.

Chantrea walked forward nervously with Johan who was still sleeping.

'Such a strange-looking child, his pale skin is so unusual,' Indravarman observed. 'He still may yet have value to me, girl keep this child safe.'

Indravarman turned back to Yom, 'I trusted you to protect my men, I trusted you to rally your people and you have done neither of these things.'

'Your Majesty, I've only ever wanted to serve,' Yom desperately replied.

'Prove it, go back to Stung Treng and help our forces. The enemy has regrouped and are making up ground, you're no use to me here so go back to the battle and prove you're worthy,' Indravarman said dismissively.

'Yes, at once,' Yom replied completely crestfallen.

The king turned his back on the Major. Yom was escorted out of the house by guards, leaving Chantrea on her own and unsure what to do with the king of Champa.

***

The heavy rain had stopped, the clouds had cleared and the moonless night sparkled with distant stars. Prince Srindra's force soon reached the river crossing at Kaoh Sralau, its fast-flowing water shimmered in the dim lights. He looked back at Stung Treng noticing a red glow rising from the eastern shores as the city burned. The commanders soon joined the prince and stared nervously at the fierce rapids in front of them.

'This way,' Major Nau ordered.

The commanders followed him a little further upstream. He reached a part of the river filled with huge rocks and boulders.

'We'll cross here, one by one, I'll lead the way with this,' Nau held up a wooden bucket filled with a red paint-like mixture.

He pulled out a large brush, 'I'll mark a path for us all to follow.'

Nau then took a number of wooden stakes from one of his men and hammered one into the ground.

'This rope will guide our forces across,' he said tying the rope to the stake.

'Go tell our warriors, we will cross unit by unit,' Sri ordered.

They bowed.

The Lavo commanders and Rotha returned to arrange each of their forces.

'Major Voan wait,' Sri said waiting for the rest of the commanders to leave. 'Luke, Marcus and I will go first with Major Nau, then Rotha and her warriors.'

He gripped Voan shoulder. 'I need you to lead the attack on the Cham with just my men and the Lavo. I'll head for Ban Bung over the other rivers with the Bakan. I've faith in you my friend. Take down the Cham and link up with Thorn in readiness for the invasion into Champa.'

Voan acknowledged the order, they gripped arms before Voan left to plot his attack.

'If that's the plan there's no time to waste,' Nau replied. 'I'll come with you all the way. You'll need my help to cross the other rivers.'

'Very well Major,' Sri replied. 'We're in your hands.'

Rotha arrived back first with her impressive warriors. Nau started to cross, followed closely by Sri, Luke, Marcus, and the rest of the company. The crossing was hard, but Nau managed to paint a marker on the rocks and attach more stakes in strategic positions. He wedged them tightly between the boulders and the rocks, tying guide ropes for the force to follow. It required great strength to push against the fast-flowing currents of the river and on multiple occasions they slipped, tripped, and dropped supplies. Rotha followed with her unit, she was directly behind Marcus, often helping him back to his feet when he stumbled and struggled against the river. After a good twenty minutes, Nau managed to get them across. He stood watching as each of Rotha's warriors arrived at the western bank, followed in quick succession by the Lavo forces. Once a good number of the main group were across and a bridgehead was secure, Sri said his farewells to Major Voan and they headed through the jungle and onwards to Ban Bung.

***

Colonel Myan paced impatiently on the barge as he made his way across the river. The crossing itself was calm, the Cham didn't seem to be attacking the eastern shore anymore, allowing more and more of the Khmer forces to cross unhindered. As soon as he arrived, he ordered a soldier to take him to General Thorn. When he reached the command point Myan spoke loudly.

'We need to attack now, let's drive our advantage home.'

'Don't lecture me on what we should do Myan, you've just got here. I'm in command of our forces not you,' Thorn replied and paused, letting out a loud sigh.

He had a complex relationship with Myan, he knew only too well the colonel's exceptional capability, but also his volatile personality.

Thorn spoke calmly, 'We've cleared this part of the city, but we're pinned down in the northeast region and can't break through. We need to clear a path towards the northern road to help us breakout of the city. Myan we need to make sure it's clear of Cham, before I order our men to march. I can't do that with those bastards shooting at us across the river.'

'Prince Srindra will clear the way,' Myan stated with complete confidence.

'Yes, I've heard of his plan, but we'll have to wait until he does. Myan now you've arrived take command of the cavalry, their commander is dead. Organise what we have left from the king's battalion, queen's battalion and the prince's elite guard and get them ready to ride. I need you to crush their remaining positions on my command. You'll need to charge here,' Thorn pointed at the map, 'Just where the Sekong bends.'

'Yes General,' Myan bowed turning to leave.

'We've worked together for years, I trust you and your skills, do as I ask and we'll prevail today,' Thorn said firmly stamping his authority.

Myan had always respected Thorn despite his young age. The support the general had just shown him was very welcome. Myan nodded and left to undertake his orders.

Over the next hour, the cavalry was prepared. Myan worked tirelessly to make sure each unit was equipped and ready to ride. He also made sure horse crossings on the barges were prioritised, making sure as many riders as possible were available to bolster his forces. Just as it reached midnight he completed his task and the cavalry were mobilised with two thousand riders ready. Satisfied with his force he returned to the command point. To his surprise, General Thorn was standing exposed atop the ruins of an old stone building looking north. In the last hour a bright full moon had risen, and the moon light exposed the embattled city.

'Myan come,' Thorn whispered.

'What do you think you're doing, you're totally unprotected,' he said, clambering up to join the general.

'Look, do you see,' Thorn whispered again, ignoring Myan's words and pointing across the river.

There was a sudden flash of light coming from the northern shore.

'Signal back,' he said quietly to one of his officers below and turned to Myan. 'Looks like the prince made it, now get ready to ride on my orders, I want you to take all your men and charge along the main road. The infantry will follow and clear the remaining Cham out of the city. This is our chance, if we're successful, we'll have a clear path to capture Ban Bung.'

Myan acknowledged his orders and returned to his riders, it was a nervous wait as a series of torches were waved to different units across the city, signalling instructions. In the early hours of the morning, horns began to sound and the colonel's men charged.

Across the river, Major Voan's force had managed to surround the Cham without being seen. It had surprised Voan greatly that the Cham had such confidence that the Mekong was uncrossable, they had only placed a few lookouts to guard their northern flank. Voan's men made quick work dispatching them and he was now looking down on the Cham encampment. As horns sounded from across the river, the Lavo forces unleashed a barrage of arrows into the camp below. The Cham archers were taken by complete surprise and as arrows continued to fall, they cut down the Cham relentlessly. The brave Cham commander tried to rally his men however it was too late, Voan's forces charged into the clearing with swords raised high and the battle was won.

***

Prince Srindra had set a relentless pace since leaving the headland. The Bakan and Luke were keeping up well but Marcus was clearly struggling. They reached the islands at Kaoh Dan Man in the Srepok River and Marcus collapsed into a heap retching.

'I'm doing my best, but if I'm slowing you down go on without me,' he said throwing up again.

'You're coming with us,' Rotha said firmly, 'I'll help you get there. Your child needs you.'

She looked at him with a strange sense of pity.

Luke pulled him to his feet. 'You can do this, drink.' He gave Marcus some water which he gulped down and it instantly made him feel better.

'Ready,' Sri said to him sternly and Marcus nodded.

Sri gave Rotha a knowing look and they set off to cross the final stretch of water. The Bakan women had covered themselves in mud and tied foliage to their robes and hair. They paced the island banks until Major Nau found a slower flowing part of the river. They began to cross disguised as floating bits of debris.

After swimming for ten minutes they made it across the river unscathed. Marcus was helped out of the water and they were back racing towards Ban Bung. Every now and again they would come upon a Cham soldier keeping watch. As if by magic the Bakan would locate them expertly and dispatch them quickly causing no alarms to be raised. Within the hour they had reached the edge of Indravarman's encampment. Prince Srindra raised his hand signalling to hold position. Sri stared into the camp waiting for the right moment to attack and rescue Johan.

***

King Indravarman's encampment itself was frantic, a number of messengers had returned supplying updates on how the battle was progressing. In the command hut Indravarman had called his generals together for an urgent meeting.

'You say they've broken through all our lines and the force we deployed to pin them down has fallen?' he shouted.

'Yes Your Majesty,' the grave-looking general replied. 'We need to get you out of here, you're exposed, and our forces are in full retreat. The Khmer have now taken the eastern road and will be here soon.'

'How far are they from us?' Indravarman asked.

'At best, a couple of hours, but at worst, who knows.'

There was a sudden sound of horns as a number of Cham fighters approached the camp at great speed, riding with them was Yom. The king rushed out to see what was happening and a scene of injured and broken men greeted him.

Yom rode up and dismounted his horse.

'Your Majesty it was a complete rout, our force has fallen, the Khmer cavalry crushed us. They had so many men, I don't know how they've mustered such a large force,' he said shaking his head. 'They're riding on the camp. You need to leave now.'

Indravarman was visibly shaken, it was not supposed to go like this, he was going to crush Jayavarman. He was going to rule over Champa and Khmer, just like he did in the years earlier.

'Bring me Chantrea,' Indravarman ordered, and his servants scurried away to fetch her. 'If I can't take back Angkor then Jayavarman will pay in blood, he'll pay for every piece of land he tries to take from us.'

Chantrea was brought before the king, 'You girl, give me the baby.'

Indravarman drew his sword, it was clear what he was about to do.

Chantrea screamed and clutched Johan tightly, 'No, I didn't bring him here for this, he was to bring our people together.'

Her eyes went crazy. She looked desperately between the king and Yom, seeing not a shred of humanity in either of them.

'Stupid girl,' Indravarman said walking towards her. 'Give me the child now or you'll face the same fate.'

Just has he said those words there was a loud *thud* and the king's guards fell to the floor. Indravarman looked up in horror as the Bakan fighters descended on the camp from every direction. Soon every Cham soldier was fighting and the camp had descended into chaos. Yom grabbed Indravarman and forced the king to his horse. He ordered the remaining men to fight to give them a chance to escape.

Chantrea on the other hand had taken the opportunity to flee, she was running as fast as she could to the fighting women before her.

She could see Prince Srindra, then she saw Marcus and called out, 'over here, Mar…'

Before she could finish her words, she felt an intense pain consume her. An arrow began to pierce through her back and she could feel it forcing itself through her body and towards her chest, where she was grasping Johan tightly. Somehow, she managed to move him to one side just as the arrow burst through her chest. Chantrea dropped to her knees slowly. Suddenly the taste of blood hit her mouth. Chantrea looked over her shoulder seeing Yom laughing cruelly. He reared his horse and fled the camp with King Indravarman clutching him tightly from behind.

Chantrea looked down slowly, she could see the arrow sticking out of her chest. Her mind collapsed into a haze of confusion as blinding pain filled every part of her body.

'Johan' she mumbled, then everything fell into darkness.

CHAPTER TWENTY-NINE

Vijaya

Marcus had seen Chantrea running towards him holding his baby, she was calling to him as she fell.

'Sri it's Johan, he's over here,' he shouted as loud as he could and without thinking ran towards Chantrea.

As he approached, three of Yom's men charged toward him, he raised his sword shakily ready to fight. However, before he could wield it Rotha jumped in front of him, she cut down the men in three short strikes. Not thinking he pushed her aside and raced to Chantrea, where Johan was lying on the grass screaming. He was safe despite the chaos that surrounded them. Marcus picked him up and gave him a loving embrace. Holding his child tightly his attention turned to Chantrea, she coughed dark blood which began to trickle down her cheek.

With deep sadness in his eyes, he asked the dying woman in front of him one word. 'Why?'

It took all her remaining strength to reply, 'I didn't mean,' she took another breath as Marcus held her hand. 'No, choice.'

More blood splattered out from her mouth. 'Beware, Vi.'

She couldn't speak any more and her frightened eyes looked at Marcus. He couldn't help but feel deep pity. He continued to hold her hand as Chantrea's final tears fell from her eyes, still gripping the hand tightly of the man she had betrayed.

Marcus's emotions began to crumble, he pried his hand from hers and got up still clutching his son. Johan was now quiet and he turned to Rotha. She had been watching him and was astounded by the behaviour of this man. He had offered sympathy and great comfort to the woman who had taken his child. Marcus's eyes were full of tears, his face stricken by the horrors he had experienced. Rotha put her arm around him and led them both back to the protection of her warriors. They soon reached their makeshift base in the jungle and called for Prince Srindra who arrived with Luke quickly. Marcus showed them Johan who was safe in his arms. They erupted with smiles and both hugged Marcus joyfully. However, Marcus pointed towards Chantrea's dead body lying a few meters away and broke down.

'She saved him, she gave her life to bring him to me,' Marcus forced out.

'She had some honour after all,' Sri replied, turning to look at the dead woman with pity.

***

The next few hours were a bit of a blur, Marcus stayed with his son protected by Rotha. Sri and the rest of the Bakan ensured that any remaining Cham were dispatched. The Bakan warriors were exceptional, they fought fiercely and the Cham didn't stand a chance. Once the village was secured, a number of the Bakan fighters returned back to the clearing along with Sri. He was accompanied by Sophal Hem, Rotha's second in command. She was as ferocious as Rotha although Sri knew she had a gentle temperament.

'How is he?' Sri asked rushing back to Marcus.

'Okay I think, he's a little hot.'

'May I?' asked Sophal.

Marcus nodded, he got up and handed the sleeping baby to her.

Sophal examined Johan carefully, 'This little one seems fine, his weak, hungry and needs rest, but I am confident he'll be fine.' Sophal was about to hand Johan back to Marcus when unexpectedly he bent over and threw up.

'But I'm not so sure about his father,' Sophal said looking at Sri as Marcus slumped to the floor in exhaustion.

Both Luke and Rotha rushed to assist him.

While the others tended to Marcus, Sri spoke quietly to Sophal, 'Luke will want to check Johan over privately. He has a talent for healing. Please could you take my nephew to him once he's finished helping Marcus?'

'Yes Your Majesty,' Sophal replied.

Sri walked over to them, he put his hand on Luke's shoulder who was kneeling next to Marcus. He was trying to give him more water, but he seemed unresponsive. Luke looked up at Sri who gave him a worried smile and then spoke directly to Marcus.

'Johan seems fine, he's a little bruised and battered but considering what could've happened we're lucky.'

Marcus didn't respond, he was in shock about the events that had just happened. Sri spoke again, 'Marcus, drink we need you stronger, I'm sure my sister would want you and Luke to check Johan over properly.'

He paused.

Marcus looked up at Sri with glazed eyes, he wiped his brow and tried to pull himself up.

'You're right she would. I'm sorry, I'm just not as strong as all of you.'

'Yes, you are,' Luke interrupted. 'You've been like a father to me, through the good and bad. We never thought we would ever have to experience violence and hatred like this. As much as we've studied past battles, it's very different to being in one.'

Rotha shot Sri a strange look, while Luke helped Marcus to his feet.

'Come, let's go and check on your son,' Luke instructed. He led Marcus away to examine Johan in private with the medical scanner.

'That was a strange comment, what was it all about?' Rotha asked Sri after they'd left.

'They're strange people, I'm afraid I can't tell you the whole story, not yet anyway. What I can say is that they're very different to us, despite their best efforts to fit into our society. Please ask no more about it, I do however need your council on another matter.'

'Of course Your Majesty,' she replied.

'I've heard word that General Thorn has set off for Vijaya to crush Indravarman for good,' Sri sighed showing his weariness of fighting. 'I know your warriors have achieved their goal by rescuing the prince, I expect you'll want to return home now.'

He paused, thinking carefully about how to phrase his question. 'However I'd like you to come with me to Champa, I value your strength, insight and loyalty. I expect I'll need them in the days to come. What do you say?'

'You have it, the cruelness of Indravarman needs to come to an end and I pledge my sword to help you achieve that,' Rotha replied and they locked arms together. 'But I can't ask my warriors to continue to fight, as you say they've achieved their mission, which was the rescue of the prince. It's all the village elders approved and I have no authority to take them further.'

She looked towards Sophal who had been listening carefully, 'Sophal will guide them home, but as for me, my path is with you.'

Sri gave her a withered smiled slightly disappointed that the Bakan force would be leaving them, but he was still thankful for her support.

'Rotha your continued assistance honours me and my family,' he replied kindly.

***

Yom and Indravarman had been riding for hours. Yom had been fearful to stop since they left Ban Bung in case Khmer riders had been able to follow them. Late into the night, they reached a secluded village on the outskirts of Lumphat, where the Cham had garrisoned a small reserved force. Yom was greeted by the commander who helped them both dismount. Indravarman seemed a broken man, his gamble hadn't paid off and now he was facing an invasion from his hated enemy. The commander brought them food and water, Yom took a large drink.

'Bring me a map,' he ordered.

The commander rushed off to collect one and returned quickly. The three of them studied it closely.

'Have you heard from any of our forces along the road?' King Indravarman asked shakily.

'No Your Majesty, we—' he paused. '—feared you were killed in the battle, that is the rumour spreading through our men.'

There was another long pause before the Champa king spoke, 'This is what I want you to do, send riders to all our positions, tell them to fall back to Champa territory and head for Vijaya. Leave a skeleton force behind to distract the Khmer. Ask them to be creative in slowing their advance. The main priority is to get what forces we have back to Vijaya.'

'Are you sure Your Majesty? You'll be trapped if we head for the city,' Yom said, concerned.

'I'll not run from my home, our invasion may have failed but Jayavarman will pay a heavy price for every piece of Champa land he takes,' Indravarman replied and turned back to the commander.

'Spare no man, I want all of our forces to know I'm alive and to know we have a plan,' he ordered.

'Yes Your Majesty,' the commander responded.

He bowed and set off to fulfil his orders.

***

'No Marcus, you should go home with Johan, I can't protect you when we go into Champa,' Sri said forcefully. 'It's going to take us weeks to get there and we'll have to fight all the way, I expect hard resistance.'

'Sri, I don't care what you say, I'm coming. I'm going to find the man who took my son and well, I don't know what,' he replied.

'Luke, say something, this is madness,' Sri said, shaking his head. 'Bo would never forgive me if something happened to you, plus you're not exactly built for war.'

'Marcus, Sri's right, let us fight this battle,' Luke said gently. 'I'm not sure your nerves can take another fight.'

'I'm coming, these people killed Maya, killed Kalani and abducted my son, I want to know why,' he replied adamantly.

'I'm telling you the king won't allow it, we'll re-join him in the next few hours and I know he'll order you to take Johan home,' Sri said plainly.

'Well, I'll just have to convince him. The Cham's wronged me and my family as much as the king's and I have a right to know why.'

Sri threw his hands up in the air in frustration and left the clearing. 'Luke I'm telling you I'm coming, there's something very wrong here and I want to know what it is. I also know I need to be by your side, I can feel it.'

'Marcus, I'll support you no matter what you decide, but what about your son, who's going to take him back to Bo, who can we trust to do that?' Luke asked.

'I know Rotha has agreed to accompany Sri to Champa but the Bakan warriors are heading back home, I trust them. I've asked Sophal to take him under the protection of the Bakan, they'll return to Angkor with our injured soldiers.'

'If you're sure then I won't stop you, but as Sri says this will be dangerous, mark my words,' he replied.

Over the next hour the Bakan readied themselves to leave, Marcus met with Sophal, he cuddled his son one more time before giving him to the strong warrior before him.

'You promise to protect him?' he asked again.

'I do as I've said many times,' she replied kindly.

'Marcus why go on with this invasion? you have your son back and you should head home,' Sophal asked.

He looked at her, 'I know I'm needed. I don't know why but I can feel it, all I know is my heart is telling me I have to go.'

Sophal reached out putting her hand on his chest, 'The gods speak to us in different ways, if your heart is telling you to go, then you must follow it.'

He looked at her and smiled, *finally someone who understood*, he thought. Marcus said his goodbyes and walked back to Luke, Sri, and Rotha who were waiting on horses they had captured from the Cham.

'You mean to go through with this then?' Sri asked.

'Yes, I follow my heart.' He looked at Luke and said, 'Like always.'

***

Prince Johan's abduction was the main topic of discussion across the empire and beyond. Huge sympathy for the princess had roused much support for the Khmer cause, it seemed the horror of having a child abducted resonated. The news of Johan's rescue caused great celebration amongst the men fighting. The rumour of the rescue began to spread quickly across the provinces, to great celebration. Reports that Prince Srindra, the Bakan, Marcus, and Luke had won a spectacular battle inspired the army to press on. It was the abduction of a child that continued to unite the people against the Champa King, despite any cultural differences they may have had with the Khmer. Indravarman had become hated and ridiculed across the empire, in Lavo, and even in Champa. Indravarman was now known as the baby snatcher, someone who would sneak into your home and steal your children, someone to fear. The more the story spread the more people were horrified. As the Khmer army marched towards Champa, the force swelled with new recruits eager to fight.

It took Sri, Luke, Rotha and Marcus a few hours to catch up with the marching army. King Jayavarman was riding his familiar regal elephant at the centre of the force. Riding alongside him was General Thorn and Colonel Myan in their splendid golden and blue uniforms. All Khmer forces had managed to cross at Stung Treng, General Thorn had organised all units to march towards Champa except for a small reserve force he left in Stung Treng. The marching army now numbered forty thousand strong, it had been walking since dawn and stretched far along the road with colours of the king, queen, prince, and Lavo blazing brightly. It was a true sight to behold.

To everyone's surprise, the king agreed that Marcus could join the fight against Vijaya. It was Marcus's passionate plea to understand why and how the abduction had happened, that convinced him. Once all units were reunited, they began to march east, it took three days for them to reach Lumphat constantly fighting of attacks from the Cham. To Jayavarman surprise, these attacks were easily dealt with and the Khmer lost very few men. When they finally reached Lumphat what the Khmer army found was nothing short of horrific. The eastern king's guard had been decimated, a force of five thousand men had been slaughtered. The barracks itself had been burnt to the ground and the surrounding areas were littered with decaying headless bodies. The jungle seemed to have reclaim the men as wild animals feasted on the decomposing remains.

The king ordered for pyres to be constructed and that the men be given a respectful burial. This slowed the army down considerably but the king insisted, despite Thorn's protests. This action only strengthened the army's resolve and morale due to the respect the king showed to the fallen. It took the army a further week to reach the Champa border, resistance had become non-existent as the Khmer force swelled to over forty-five thousand infantry, and eight thousand cavalry as more and more allies joined the campaign. Champa was now isolated and its people ridiculed. They stood alone as every ally abandoned them, fearful of supporting the baby snatching King.

The first major resistance in Champa came at Kon Don. The Khmer were navigating a steep mountain path as the Champa attacked. The damage was light, the Khmer infantry quickly managed to locate the attacking archers, dispatching them with Luke's remarkable intuition. A few days later the main Khmer force approached the walls of Vijaya. The city itself was large and well-fortified and its red brick buildings loomed imposingly over its surroundings. As the sunlight hit the city a red glow reflected back towards the Khmer army, as if shouting danger. The king sent emissaries to negotiate and prevent a full-scale attack, but Indravarman fired the heads of the men back at the waiting force. The king ordered that no further negotiations would take place and he began to besiege the city.

It was two weeks since the king had ordered the siege and it was clear that Indravarman had gambled everything on winning against the Khmer. Vijaya was not ready for a long and protracted blockade and its people began to starve. The loss of their soldiers, the loss of their pride and the conduct of their King hurt deep. The proud citizens of Vijaya, were now broken people who stood alone.

As the siege entered its third week horns blew from the city and the gates opened, to the Khmer commander's surprise. Out rode three men with white flags trailing behind them and they headed for the king's command. Khmer archers pulled back their bows as the men approached.

The rider shouted, 'Indravarman is under arrest, Vijaya surrenders.'

A cheer erupted from the soldiers as the riders approached. The men dismounted their horses and General Thorn ordered their weapons removed, and the men searched.

Thorn said, 'It's agreeable to see you again Gia, it's been some time.'

'Welcome home General,' the man responded.

Gia Nguyen was the son of a powerful lord the day Prince Vidyanandana, as the general was once known, was sentenced to exile. It was after his exile that Thorn came and fought with King Jayavarman against his Champa enemies.

'Do you surrender unconditionally?' Thorn asked, looking closely at the man before him.

'We do,' he replied.

The king approached the three men flanked by Prince Srindra, Luke, Marcus, Rotha, and Colonel Myan.

Fire blazed within the king's eyes, 'Where's your treacherous baby snatching King?'

'He's in the dungeons along with his foul commanders, our people have rebelled against him. We don't support a king who steals babies for his political ambitions,' Gia replied hesitantly.

'If we can avoid bloodshed all the better,' the king said, turning to Thorn. 'Go, take a large force into the gates to prove what these men are saying, I'll not risk any more of my soldiers' heads without protection. If these men are lying, kill them and burn the city to the ground, if they tell the truth then we'll welcome Champa into our empire.'

'Yes Your Majesty, Myan take command over our forces here, while I go into my old city,' General Thorn ordered.

He shouted a few more orders and then rode out with a force of five thousand infantry. Prince Srindra, Marcus, Rotha, and Luke accompanied them, despite the king's initial objections.

They reached the gates and entered the city cautiously. White flags waved from every building just as the Cham lords had confirmed. Gia led them to the main hall where the city's great treasures were proudly on display.

'Take what you want, all we ask is that you spare our people,' Gia replied genuinely frightened.

Marcus looked at him. 'We're not murderers and we didn't come here to steal your treasures. We'll not kill your people in revenge and nor will we kidnap your children.'

Prince Srindra interrupted, 'Long has your king tried to kill me, bring him and his treacherous dogs to us, I want to speak with them. If I'm satisfied that you and your city are innocent of the crimes against my family then we will spare your people. If not, your city will burn.'

Sri's eyes were glazed and focused on Gia, who squirmed under the pressure. Luke had seen Sri's anger in the past, however, he had never seen the ruthlessness that was on display and it frightened him. Luke loved the man in front of him, but Sri's anger burned fiercely and despite Marcus's comments, he didn't know what Sri had planned for the city.

'Yes Your Majesty,' Gia replied, he issued orders and Champa soldiers hurried away.

They brought back ten commanders one being Yom along with their former king, Indravarman.

'The people of Vijaya beg forgiveness for our treacherous leaders, they do not speak for us' Gia said, shaking.

The commanders were chained, gagged, and forced to the floor. King Indravarman was then pushed to the front, he, like the others, was chained and gagged but also blindfolded.

General Thorn walked over to Indravarman and lifted his blindfold, he turned and nodded to Prince Srindra.

'You will order your forces to lay down their weapons, leave the city and surrender to Colonel Myan. After our interrogation of your soldiers, we will decide their fate. My men will then search each house to check for traitors, weapons, or anything else we deem a violation. If you do this then your people will not be harmed, you have my word.'

'Yes General,' Gia replied and turned to leave.

However, before he could Marcus interrupted. 'There will be no massacre of soldiers in my family's name, do I make myself clear General Thorn?'

Thorn looked at him uncomfortably and replied, 'If they are innocent, they will not be harmed you have my word Marcus,' who nodded in acknowledgement.

'Gia, leave us, I want to have a discussion with the baby snatcher and his commanders.'

Nervously the Vijaya lords left the hall escorted by the general's guards, who shut the door behind them.

Prince Srindra turned his attention to Indravarman and spoke, 'You'll tell me how and why you abducted my nephew.'

He pulled down the gag causing Indravarman to gasp for air.

'I'll tell you nothing scum,' he replied.

Prince Srindra slapped him hard across his face and drew his sword.

'No!' Luke shouted.

Sri gave him a penetrating stare. It was clear he was not to intervene.

'I think we should ask him,' Marcus said pointing at Yom. 'This man kidnapped my son and murdered countless of your people. He killed Chantrea in front of my eyes as she ran towards me, Johan only survived thanks to her sacrifice.'

'It's a fair point Marcus,' Sri replied. He walked over to Yom and pulled the chains around his neck forcing him to the floor beside Indravarman. His gag was pulled from his mouth.

'Speak now before I make you,' Srindra said threateningly, holding his sharp sword against Yom's neck, which caused a trickle of blood to appear on his skin.

'You don't scare me,' he replied. 'You've no idea how many traitors are in your court and who are loyal to the Cham.'

Sri punched him in the stomach and Yom fell back gasping for breath. He was forced onto his back where Sri pushed his foot hard onto Yom's chest.

Sri spat at Yom. 'Loyalty you don't know the meaning of the word, your own people have betrayed you due to the despicable acts you and your former king have committed. Your vile attacks have united our people and our allies against you.'

Sri then pressed his blade against Yom's neck again, 'Tell me who the traitors are, or you will wish for death many times before I'm finished with you.'

'Wait!' Marcus shouted. 'Sri you can't, I know this is your way but it's not mine. Interrogate him, lock him up for all I care, but no torture.'

'Marcus this man is responsible for the murder of Maya, the murder of Kalani and the kidnap of your son. He tried to kill Johan and us all on numerous occasions, what right does he have for mercy,' Sri replied angrily.

Marcus walked forward and put his hand on Sri's shoulder. 'We're better than them, that's why. We don't do the despicable deeds they do, that's what's important and it's how my son and daughter will be brought up.'

Marcus reached out and forced Sri to lower his sword.

There was a moment of silence which was only broken by Yom, in the confusion he had managed to pull Marcus to the floor. He searched Marcus's body, quickly finding a dagger in his belt that Bo had given him many months ago. Yom pulled Marcus close and held the dagger to his throat.

Rotha jumped forward her sword raised ready to strike along with Sri's.

'Stay where you are or this fool dies,' Yom spat, holding the dagger at Marcus's throat. 'The crap this idiot spouts, it shows your weakness. You'll untie the king and the rest of us, or he dies.'

Sri and Rotha looked at each other, however it was Luke who stepped forward. He emitted a powerful force which pushed then both aside with such might they were thrown to the floor.

'The people you have murdered, the pain you have caused all in the name of this pathetic king.'

Luke waved his hand at Indravarman and a pulse erupted from him, the Champa King flew hard against the wall. He fell to the floor in agony as Luke turned his attention back to Yom.

'This man pleads for your life and you call him weak for doing so. It takes more courage than you'll ever know to stand up to your friends, to plead forgiveness for those who have wronged you. Commander your wicked nature and that of your king has no bounds. You respect no laws, no sense of morality and have no honour.'

Luke's eyes started to glow, and a whirlwind began to form in the hall. Luke raised his hand and the dagger Yom was holding against Marcus's neck flung to the floor with a clatter. Luke's attention was firmly focused on Yom, he raised his hand and Yom was forced into the air until his feet were dangling a foot from the floor. Marcus scrambled back to Sri as Luke raised his other hand, the dagger that had been cast aside flew into the air and headed directly to Yom. It stopped suddenly with the blade touching Yom's throat. He couldn't move, he just hung there in mid-air. Yom's eyes flickered around the room. He had no idea what was happening. Somehow he managed to raise his hand and grip the dagger's hilt.

'You have a choice, which is more than I can say for the people you've murdered. You can choose, if you let go of the dagger I'll spare you, if you continue to hold onto it, you will seal your own fate.'

Yom looked at Indravarman who was cowering on the floor, 'I'll not abandon my king,' he said wildly.

'Very well, I gave you a choice,' Luke said as Yom gave him a panicked look.

Luke stared directly into his eyes with fury.

Marcus approached his mentee's side.

'Luke, you don't have to do this,' he said softly into his ear, trying not to enrage him further.

Luke continued to stare at Yom. 'Marcus, we all have choices and I've given him a fair one. People make good and bad ones every day, but it's what we do after we make a mistake that matters. This man has made so many bad choices, but he continues to see no shame in those acts and he has no desire to change. Please don't judge me.'

He turned and looked at Marcus as the dagger sunk deep into Yom's throat.

There was a cry of pain as blood sprayed out of his mouth, Yom still hung in mid-air from the force emanating from Luke. His hand gripped tightly around the golden dagger hilt which now protruded from his throat. Dark red blood oozed out from the wound as the struggling man became still. The room was silent, nobody dared say anything. Luke finally pulled his hand back which released Yom's floating body which crashed to the ground, the dagger making a metallic screech as it connected with the stone floor.

'You reap what you sow,' Luke said coldly.

CHAPTER THIRTY

Repercussions

A strange sombre silence filled the room, Sri and Rotha had managed to pull themselves to their feet while Marcus just hugged his former apprentice.

'Luke, I don't know what's happening to you, but you can't become judge, jury, and executioner,' he cried.

'Marcus I won't, as I said he had a choice, he would have happily slit your throat.'

Luke pushed him away, 'Now go and retrieve the gift your wife gave you.'

He gestured to the dagger sticking out of Yom's throat.

General Thorn had been watching intently, he hadn't said a word since Luke stepped forward.

'Do any of the prisoners have anything further to say?' he asked.

None of them replied.

The general turned to Indravarman. 'Are you sure you don't want to tell us who the traitors are in the Khmer court?'

Indravarman remained silent.

'Very well, take them back to our camp, they'll come back to Angkor with us in the chains their own people placed them in. The king will decide what to do with them next. One last matter, if any of you discuss what you have seen here today, Luke will find you, do I make myself clear?'

There were mutters of yes from the frightened Cham commanders. The general then turned to Sri, Marcus, Rotha, and Luke.

'That goes for you as well, I advise we not discuss this with the king,' he gave Luke a very uncomfortable smile.

Thorn then led them out of the hall, ordering the waiting guards to take Indravarman and his commanders back to the Khmer camp. Many of Vijaya's residents had come out onto the streets, they watched their leaders be paraded through the city in chains. A few even threw what little rotten food they had at them.

General Thorn ordered that Sri, Luke, Marcus and Rotha take the prisoners to the king while he oversaw the city's formal surrender. He asked them to inform the king that the city was now liberated. It didn't take them long to ride back. They soon updated the king about the Cham surrender, the spies at Angkor and the lack of cooperation from Indravarman. It was this that prompted the king to agree to transport the enemy commanders back to Angkor. They would only leave once Vijaya had been made safe of course. No mention was made of the events that had happened in the hall. When it was possible for Luke to leave he slipped away. Sri noticed of course, he always did, he knew how Luke would react to the events of the day. Although this new power was frightening and Luke seemed to be changing. Since they had both met Sri had felt very drawn to the sensitive and vulnerable Luke, both had a connection like nothing either of them had experienced. However, what was happening to Luke was remarkable and scary at the same time.

Luke reached his tent quickly and slumped onto his bed. A few minutes later Sri entered and he looked up.

'How did I know you'd notice me leave,' Luke said smiling wearily.

'You expect me not to have my eyes on you after today,' Sri sat next to him. 'Do you want to talk about what happened?'

'No, not really, I'm tired of saying I don't know what's happening to me. But for the first time, I'm not worried about it.'

He took Sri's hand. 'For now let's just rest, I'm shattered.'

He rolled over facing the canvas of the tent, Sri lay beside him holding tightly. A few moments later Luke's exhaustion took hold and he fell into a deep sleep.

***

For the rest of the afternoon, Luke slept with Sri watching him constantly. He was only woken as the king had requested his presence at the large celebratory feast, which was to be held to rejoice at the Cham's surrender. The king had ordered that the army's food and drink be shared with the citizens of Vijaya.

The stars were sparkling brightly off the calm sea as the king stepped up to speak. The feasting was well underway by now and the king hoped his words would foster a new relationship with the Cham.

'I welcome the citizens of Vijaya to the Khmer empire and we celebrate your liberation day. Champa will be protected under Khmer rule, you will share in our great social and cultural advancements of the last decade. We know that the usurper Indravarman, has dishonoured your people and caused great suffering. We'll help you to rebuild the reputation of Champa and to become enlightened once again.'

The king sat back down next to General Thorn, his commanders and the frightened lords of Vijaya. The mood on the table was tense, but they feasted together all the same.

It was a very different atmosphere on Prince Srindra's table, Major Voan had joined them along with the Lavo commanders who were in full celebratory mode. Marcus, Rotha and Luke on the other hand all remained quiet, while Sri put on a show roaring with laughter hiding his real concerns. A little while later Luke decided he needed a break, he wanted to take in some air. He was keen to be alone and he began to explore the city, away from all the noise. Sri noticed Luke leave and gave Rotha a look, which She picked up on instantly. She nodded back at Sri and rose while he continued to entertain his men. Rotha caught up with Luke as he walked the city walls. She gave him a strained smile, making an excuse about being tired of the macho behaviour of the men, but it was obvious why she wanted to walk with him.

'Look Rotha I know you want to asked something, so do it,' he said rather frustratedly.

'Is that so,' she replied coldly. 'Are you sure?'

'Well, you can't be here to ask me out,' he said with a smirk.

'No, I'm not blind Luke,' she said responding a little warmer. 'So how long have you had these powers?'

'They've been growing in me for the last year.'

He paused to reflect.

'I've felt different since we arrived in Angkor, something's been happening to me, a powers been building. But I've never been able to do anything like I did today,' he replied honestly.

'Will you walk with me?' she asked. For some unknown reason, he really wanted to.

They walked up to the highest point on the city walls and sat down. The high vantage point gave them a great view of the ocean and the large Khmer camp which sprawled around the city.

'You know you're not the first person I've seen with powers like these,' she said gently.

'Really,' he said sarcastically. 'People can be fooled in many ways. But my powers aren't a trick, I've never wanted them and I don't know how to get rid of them.

'I speak the truth, if you're willing to listen I'll explain. But first let me speak plainly, I don't believe you come from Europe,' she said casually. 'I may not know your history but it's clear there's something's strange about you, and it's not just your powers.'

'Well, where do you think we've come from?' he said sharply, his temper rising at being called a liar.

'I don't know, but as I say I've seen powers like these before,' she replied.

'Rotha I speak the truth, I am from Europe, a place called England and Marcus is from a place called Sweden,' he said frustratedly.

'If you say so,' she replied and spoke no more.

After a long silence Luke spoke, 'Okay I'll bite, where have you seen powers like these?'

'Some people have gifts, gifts that they can share with the world. My grandmother had such a gift, she was able to see things and move objects, very much like you did today. However, her power wasn't as strong as yours.' Rotha stopped for a moment thinking carefully on what to share. 'The Bakan have always been seen as strong and powerful, why do you think that is?'

'I don't know,' Luke said generally interested.

'Many of our people descend from a great female warrior, she had many gifts similar to the ones you have shown. In particular, I noticed how you located the enemies in the trees. It's a true gift to hear the beating heart of another. The way you've located the Cham is the same way I locate my people, and how I locate our enemies—'

There was a long pause.

'It might interest you to know that a number of my warriors also have this ability. This power is found in most of the Bakan, however only a few know how to harness it and its mostly the woman.'

'I find it hard to believe your people have this gift. You don't know where I've come from and what I've been through, you're very different to me,' Luke replied gently.

'That I am, but it doesn't stop us from having the same gifts in common, how about we try something?' Rotha asked.

Luke agreed.

'Close your eyes, focus your mind, tell me what you can hear down in our camp.'

He agreed to Rotha's request. Luke began to listen and his mind wandered down to the camp, picking out one particular voice. It must've been a mile away and the tone was soft. Luke calmed himself and focused, suddenly he heard a Khmer soldier speaking to another.

'He's a great man that General Thorn, always looking after us. I just wish he would give us more rice wine.'

The other man laughed. 'Well he likes to keep a private stock for himself, do you know the rumour about the woman he has back in Angkor? Apparently, she lives out by the western baray.'

Luke opened his eyes.

'Actually, the general has three women scattered around the city, he visits them on different nights. These men only seem to know about the woman out by the western baray,' Rotha said smiling at him.

'You heard that too?' Luke asked in shock.

'Yes, I heard it, but let's not discuss it further here, it's not safe.'

She paused for a moment.

'When you get back to Angkor, I'd like you to visit my village, to understand more about your gifts. However, I'll need to seek approval before you do, our rules strictly forbid outsiders. But I think they'll make an exception in your case. I'll speak to the elders on your behalf and contact you once they approve.'

Luke wanted to know more but Rotha brushed off his questions.

'Come, lets head back to the feast, I believe the king is going to announce something important.' She guided them both back just as the king was making another toast.

'I'm pleased that our fight with Champa has finally ended. I hope we can build on our similarities rather than our differences, to unite as one people under the same rule of law. As part of my commitment to you, I'm appointing my closest aid General Thorn, as Prince protectorate of Champa. He has been a loyal friend over these long years and as a former prince of these lands, I know he'll help to bring us together.

The crowd gave a muted response, no one actually believed that Thorn could bring them together. After all, he had lived most of his life in the Khmer empire not in Champa. The king's decree had been set into law, so no one wasted time objecting to the new ruler. Finally, the crowd toasted the king's announcement. The drinking, feasting, and partying went on into the early hours whether the citizens of Vijaya wanted it or not

***

Over the next few weeks arrangements were made to station troops across Champa. After the victory in Vijaya, the king made it clear that Champa was to be a province in the Khmer empire. He declared that a new union of provinces would be formed along with a governing council. Each province would select representatives to help guide the empire. This new decree was met by much celebration across the land.

A month passed since Champa had surrendered, Prince Thorn was now secure in his position and it was time for the king to head home. He felt confident knowing his closest ally would run Champa and control the Cham. Departing with the king would be the majority of his forces, only a small experience unit would remain to support Thorn while he rebuilt the Champa army. During the month after the surrender new alliances and compromises had been reached. Deep distrust still existed between the two peoples, however King Jayavarman guided by Sri had made some rather enlightened appointments. He had selected many local lords to help, focusing on ones who were particularly loyal to Indravarman. These appointments, although seen as risky, seemed to help secure Thorn's rule, well for now anyway.

Colonel Myan had been promoted to general and would take up the role as commander in chief of the

Khmer forces. It was declared he would move from the queen's Battalion to the king's guard to replace Thorn. The king decided to formally recognise a number of his key soldiers, he promoted men who fought well in the Champa campaign. Prince Srindra was promoted to the colonel of the queen's Battalion while he remained in command of his own elite guard. Major Voan's battlefield promotion was confirmed, and he would move to serve the king's Battalion. Rotha and Luke were both given the freedom of Angkor as a thanks from the king for their service. The news of the appointments and the now famous battles spread through the empire, their names were celebrated through great stories and songs.

It had been five weeks since Thorn took over the Cham and the Khmer forces were finally ready to depart. However, the king had one last task to do before they left. Prince Thorn had requested a private audience with him and of course, the king agreed. He was guided to the main hall where his former commander in chief was looking regal sitting on the Champa throne. Thorn ordered the lords and servants in the hall to leave, he asked that the doors be secured tightly to give them privacy.

'I see you're getting used to your new role,' the king said with a slight chuckle as the sounds of locks echoed through the room.

'Yes Your Majesty, I didn't know what I was missing,' Thorn replied with a mischievous wink.

'It's good to have you here, I know that in your hands the Cham could one day become enlightened. Just watch you're back, the alliances I've struck are new and I still don't trust these people, not yet anyway.'

'I will, it's about trust why I wanted to speak to you,' Thorn said cautiously. 'I know that our friends from the future have proven their loyalty to you, but how well do you really know them?'

This was a strange question the king thought. Luke and Marcus were so integrated within his family that they'd become like sons to him. He paused for a moment also remembering that Maya and Kalani had died in service to him.

'I know enough to trust them. They've saved my family on many occasions.'

'That maybe so, but how much do you know about their strange behaviour?' Thorn asked.

'What do you mean,' the king replied. 'I know they have technology which could be a danger to us, but they've sworn not to use it. From what I've seen this technology is remarkable, but I respect their decision not to use it further.'

'It's not the technology I'm talking about,' Thorn paused. 'I'm sure you've heard rumours of Luke's abilities, his strange ways of finding the enemy.'

'Yes,' the king answered. 'It's just rumours, or you would've told me?'

Thorn moved uncomfortably. 'It's not that easy, at first I thought he was using technology to find the enemy. I was fine with that. He was helping us win. But there's more to it.'

There was a silent pause as the king's mind rolled with confusion. 'Your Majesty, as your commander I need to warn you. Luke has some abilities where he can control earthly forces. It's like he has a power from the gods, I've seen this with my own eyes to devastating effect.'

Thorn sighed as the king looked at his friend suspiciously. 'I've only seen Luke use his powers to protect your son and to protect our people, but his powers are growing. My spies believe he doesn't know what these powers are and I've no reason to doubt that. Prince Srindra knows about them and is protecting his partner. I didn't tell you as I don't know what to say. However as I'm not going to be by your side protecting you, I need you to be aware.'

He paused again.

'These powers are remarkable and Luke could be a danger to you, and to the kingdom. Watch them both closely.'

Prince Thorn got up from his throne and walked over to the king.

He took the arm of his friend and said, 'I'll always be here if you need me, all you need to do is ask.'

***

The king left the great hall of Vijaya feeling sick and uneasy, he headed back to his forces in silence pondering what Thorn had told him. He was greeted by Prince Srindra, newly promoted General Myan, Marcus, and Luke, he couldn't help but give Luke a concerned look but said nothing. General Myan gave the signal to move out, horns sounded, and the Khmer forces began to move. To their surprise the large horns and drums from Vijaya sounded, filling the air with noise. The sounds were to send the troops on their way with good wishes for their long journey home.

The Khmer army marched through Champa to the sound of cheers from the people. Gone were the attacking enemy, replaced by people throwing flowers. It was a very strange response to receive from a conquered people but the king was delighted at the reaction. Boos sounded at the carts carrying the prisoners of the former King Indravarman and his remaining commanders. The people pelted them with rotten fruit and vegetables, it was clear many felt that they had betrayed their people.

The army crossed the border back into Khmer territory and soon reached Lumphat. General Myan rearranged the Khmer forces, he created a new eastern King's Guard and stationed experienced troops there under the command of Major Voan. The Lavo forces would be returning home and the kings battalion needed some experienced commanders. The Major said a fond farewell to the Lavo captains he had become so close to during the campaign. He would miss them dearly, Voan had worked hard to train them to become the fighting force they were today.

A day later the Khmer forces pressed on heading for home, within a few days they arrived at Stung Treng. Myan began to transport the force across the Mekong. The city had already begun to rebuild after the battle a few months ago. The king ordered that the men rest there for a few days. It would take a while to cross and resupply, so it would be a perfect place for a few days of rest.

Once the full force had crossed, the march back to Angkor continued. Myan had arranged the Khmer forces into a ceremonial parade, it was an impressive sight. It showed off all the colours and loyalties of the men, he wanted the people to see the power of the army as they marched through the heart of the empire. The cavalry was split, it led the procession while also guarding the rear, the infantry marched between the horses and in the middle was the king riding on his elephant, flanked by the other war elephants.

Behind him was Prince Srindra's elite guard who secured the prisoners. The Champa King and his commanders all remained obedient. They were fearful of Luke, although none were willing to share any knowledge about the traitors in the Khmer court. It took just under three days to make the full journey from Stung Treng to Angkor. All the way they were met by cheering crowds and admiration. The reactions of the people made the king beam with happiness and pride.

The response on the road was nothing to the reception that they received when they finally entered Angkor. Golden banners flew from every building and the people flowed onto the street, cheers and screams came from the crowd and more flowers were thrown. The temple bells rang out joyously over the city. As they rode through the gleaming streets the sun began to set and a bright orange glow seemed to welcome them home. The army arrived at the large parade ground where the king's council were waiting, including the queen, Princess Bopha, and Prince Virak. People scrambled to get a view of the king and the spectacular army. The grounds were packed with cheers and music filled the air. The king descended his elephant rather ungracefully and climbed the podium where he was greeted lovingly by his wife. It had been over three months since he left Queen Indradevi and being back at her side, was deeply comforting to him. Beside the queen was the princess with two cradles containing Princess Jorani and Prince Johan, she smiled widely when she spotted Marcus. He couldn't contain his joy and rushed up to embrace his wife with such passion, the crowd erupted with more cheers which made him jump in surprise as Bo laughed. He smiled shyly and began to dote on his children who had grown considerably since he'd last seen them, particularly little Jorani.

Prince Srindra, Myan, Rotha and Luke joined the king who held their hands up in triumph. Yet more cheers erupted, and the crowd shouted in jubilation. The king took a deep breath and then spoke loudly.

'My friends after the horror of the last few years with our lands under constant attack, our struggle has finally come to an end. The despicable Indravarman was betrayed by his own people for the crimes he committed, he will remain in our dungeons until we put him on trial.'

The crowd broke out in applause.

'Our forces, along with our Lavo allies,' the king nodded to the Lavo ambassador who was standing with the council. 'Fought bravely, we both suffered many losses in the invasion, I commit to you that we will help the families and loved ones of all our fallen heroes. It was with such strength that Prince Srindra, Rotha, Luke, and Marcus were able to free Prince Johan from the vile abductors. We owe them our thanks and respect.'

The king paused to let more cheers subside. 'Now we need to build friendships across our lands, to prevent further bloodshed and protect the peace we've fought so hard for. My hope is that never again, will I need to send our people to invade another country in anger. But for now, enjoy our victory and the great celebrations. I ask you to do one last task as a people, raise a drink to those who didn't return.'

The king took a cup from a nearby servant, he raised it to the crowd and those that could, joined him. As the cup was raised fully, the sky suddenly burst into bright pinks and purples. It was like the heavens were speaking to them and saying farewell to the soldiers that hadn't return.

***

It had been a week since the great celebration feast and the city had returned to some sense of normality. Rotha said farewell a few days later and returned to her people. She made Luke promise he would visit her tribe in the coming days. It was clear this wasn't a request and that he was to visit once she sent word. Marcus reunited with Bo and seemed as happy as could be, they moved into their new home just as they were planning to do before the abduction. The king increased their protection and granted Marcus a seat on the King's council.

Myan had been busy rearranging the Khmer forces, he ordered that the prince's Elite guard be enlarged. The Elite guard would become his specialist force responsible for training the army, in a new military academy that was to be built.

Sri and Luke had retreated to his compound for some well-needed rest. They both wanted to spend time together away from prying eyes and constant gossiping. The campaign against the Cham had brought out brutal sides to both their personalities and they wanted to reconnect and reflect. They spent a solid week alone together, no servants, no bureaucrats, no family, just the two of them and the peace was bliss.

It was early morning when Luke took a swim in the cool secluded lake within the compound. The spring sun was yet to rise, Luke breathed in deeply closing his eyes and he could smell the familiar scent of the nearby jasmine. It had been two weeks since they arrived home and a few days ago he received word from Rotha, the elders had agreed that the Bakan would see him. He'd been reflecting on the words she spoke to him at Vijaya, and his mind had become fixated on understanding more. Luke swam to the lakeside pulling himself out of the water, he took a robe to cover his naked body and joined Sri on the veranda, who had been watching him closely.

'What's wrong? You only go this quiet when something's on your mind,' Sri said playfully.

Luke didn't respond and he paced for a moment before speaking, 'There's something I haven't told you.'

'Oh, what's that?' Sri asked sitting up.

Luke sighed, not sure what he should say. 'While we were in Vijaya, Rotha spoke to me, it was after.'

He paused, 'You know, the events in the hall.'

Luke looked down in shame.

'What did she say?' Sri asked impatiently, annoyed Luke hadn't told him.

'It was strange and took me by surprise, I wasn't sure I believed her,' he replied. 'She mentioned that her grandmother had powers like mine, I thought she was just being fanciful. But then she mentioned that her people had powers a little like mine and she proved it.'

Sri got up and walked over to him putting his arms around him.

'What did she do?' he asked, looking at Luke while putting a hand to his face.

'She proved she can hear and feel things like I can, you know the way I sense people. I've no doubt about her claims.'

Sri was taken aback by this revelation.

'Why didn't you tell me and what does she want?' he asked, trying to remain calm.

'I don't know,' he said sadly. 'Sri, I don't know what's happening to me and I don't know what it means. Before we travelled here all I did was study, these powers I have don't make scientific sense. However, look at me now, I'm a commander in the Khmer army. I see and feel things that I know shouldn't be possible. Rotha knows something about it and she's willing to tell me more, to let me see the secrets of the Bakan tribe.'

'She really said that?'

'Yes, well I think so anyway.'

'The Bakan fighters are legend. No one has ever been granted such an honour to visit their village. Many have tried to find out more about them, some by force but those people have all ended up dead.'

'Sri I want to go and see Rotha. I want to understand what she knows about whatever's happening to me.'

'I'll come with you, Luke I'm not letting you go alone and that's an order.'

'I'm not sure that's wise, Rotha made it clear it was an invitation for me only.'

'Luke I'm not letting you go alone and that's that, when do you want to leave?'

'Today, I need to know more, it's all I can think about, but I don't want anyone else to know.'

'I'll arrange for us to go out riding and say we're paying a visit to our new allies. My guards will want to come but I'll order them not to enter the Bakan village. I'm not sure they would anyway, the fear of that tribe is engrained deep within our people. Be ready in two hours and Luke remember this,' Sri said kissing him deeply. 'I love you no matter what's happening to you, and no matter who you turn out to be.'

CHAPTER THIRTY-ONE

Evolution

Before they left Angkor, Sri sent out his most trusted riders ahead to advise the Bakan that they were coming. It was imperative that the tribe didn't see them as a threat. They set off just after breakfast and made it to the Great Lake by early afternoon. They were met by a Khmer attack boat. The impressive red ship could seat twenty men and its hull was adorned with golden serpent carvings. The soldiers rowed across the lake which took most of the afternoon, they reached the shores by Chuor Nom just as night fell. Sri had arranged for them to ride to Bakan the following day. They would stay in a hut overlooking the Great Lake for the night.

The moon seemed to be following them, however there was something about the red moon that worried Sri. He had never really been a spiritual man but even to him this had meaning, he felt that something dark was coming. Sri ensured they had enough protection. His elite guards patrolled the area and the attack boat watched over them from the lake. Sri had become paranoid that another assassin squad would attack, his anxiety had multiplied since losing his best friends at the jungle retreat a year ago. Even though the war had now been won, he didn't trust the Cham to honour the peace. Luke, on the other hand, seemed unconcerned about an attack, he was more worried about the danger he posed. Luke feared that if he lost control, he'd hurt those he loved.

It was late when they finished a dinner of fresh fish from the lake. They sat in silence looking out over the water which sparkled red from the light of the moon. Sri took Luke's hand and although there was nothing he could do to ease his partners worry, he would at least try to make him feel safe and loved.

He pulled Luke into his lap and they kissed bumping noses, causing them both to laugh. No further words were needed, Sri just held Luke and they stared out over the water. It wasn't long before they fell asleep safe in each other's company.

***

Early the next morning Sri woke with a jolt. Luke wasn't beside him and a sudden fear gripped him. He jumped to his feet and raced out the hut. After a quick scan of the area he saw Luke swimming in the lake and let out a huge sigh. Water seemed to calm Luke's mind. The sound of a trickling brook, or waves hitting a rocky beach comforted him.

The elite guard continue to watch over them both. It was no secret to the prince's men, or to the people of

Angkor about the relationship they had, nor did Sri feel the need to hide it.

After a quick breakfast they were ready to set off to Bakan. It would take a couple of hours for them to reach the village over challenging terrain. It would be a difficult ride, but the journey didn't faze them, they were used to long trips now.

It was just after midday when they reached the Bakan village, the sun beat down strongly on the riders' backs and the temperature sizzled. They approached the edge of the settlement and warning horns rang out. The village was surrounded by a ten-meter wooden wall and in the centre of those walls was a large gate. It began to open slowly. Rotha accompanied by a number of her warriors including Sophal, walked out to meet them.

She smiled at Luke as he approached, but turned to Sri giving him a rather disapproving look.

'We would've rather you came alone,' Rotha said.

'Do you think I'd let him come on his own, without my men's protection and without my support?' Sri responded rather angrily. Rotha was an ally, she knew about their relationship and after all, he was the prince of the empire and her future king.

'I meant no offence Your Majesty,' Rotha replied. 'However, you know our laws.'

'I do, it's why I sent my men ahead to advise you of our intent,' Rotha bowed acknowledging his actions.

'You and your men will need to remain here. The leader of our clan, Maly Lon has only granted Luke passage into our village,' she said firmly.

'Rotha I'm coming with Luke, do you think I'd leave him alone and unprotected,' he stared into her eyes.

Before she could reply Luke spoke, 'Sri comes with me or we leave, I trust him completely, as should you. If you're unwilling to extend your invite to him, after all we've been through together, then I guess my questions will have to go unanswered.'

'Very well, but your men will remain here. Anyone who approaches the gate or walls, will not survive.'

She gestured to the female archers in the trees.

'You know our strict rules.'

Sri nodded and ordered his men to stand down.

'While in our village, I insist you follow my instructions, however unusual they seem, is that clear?'

They both agreed. Rotha gestured for them to follow her, and she led them into the village. As they passed through the wooden gate it seemed like an energy force hit them both. It didn't affect them physically in any way, however they felt it. Rotha guided them through the village, wooden huts with thatched roofs were dotted about the hilly settlement and like most of the dwellings in Cambodia, they were linked by channels of water feeding into large pools. The village was situated within a particularly dense part of the jungle. There were dwellings in the trees as well as on the ground, which was very unusual. Rotha led them through a clearing where a number of small skinny men were working in the rice paddies. They were in stark contrast to the strong women who seemed to have all the power. She guided them up a hill until they reached some stone steps which led to a small ridge. Suddenly they noticed an incredible sight, it was a geological basin, which looked like that of an extinct volcano. However in the centre of the basin stood an elaborate thatched wooden hall. It was surrounded by what looked like water, with only one wooden rope bridge that could be crossed. Trees lined the ridges that surrounded the basin. Within those trees were a number of large platforms, each holding five female archers who were aiming arrows directly at them.

'Rotha, what's the meaning of this?' Sri asked.

'They'll not harm you if you do exactly as I instruct,' she replied calmly. 'Follow me.'

Rotha led them down the winding path towards the rope bridge. They cautiously followed her across, then for some reason Luke began to feel tense. He could sense something, a powerful force of some kind.

'You feel it don't you?' Rotha asked, sensing Luke's hesitation.

'What's happening to me?'

Sri began to reach for his weapon, but before he could Luke instinctively pulled his hand away from the sword.

'Do as Rotha orders, we're in no danger here, I can feel it,' Luke said.

All Sri could do was nod. He had no energy to speak, it was like something was draining him.

'Luke it's hard to explain, this place is not quite in our reality,' Rotha replied cryptically.

She led them into the hut where they were met by Maly. The village elder had her eyes closed and was crouching down meditating.

Maly spoke without opening her eyes. 'Like you said Rotha, he would not be separated from the prince.'

She opened them and smiled. 'There seems to be a strong bond between you both.'

Neither of them replied.

Maly rose slowly and began to circle them while Rotha leant against a wall in the hut. 'It was foretold many years ago that a white man would visit. I'm pleased our ancestor's vision has finally come to pass.'

Maly paused, then walked back into the middle of the room.

'Come sit, both of you,' she ordered.

They hesitantly stepped forward and sat on the cushions in the middle of the room.

'What is this place?' Luke couldn't help ask.

'It's a pocket in time, never changing within our universe. It was created a long while ago by our founding ancestor,' she replied.

'You mean Rotha's grandmother?' he asked.

'No, long before that. Come, I want to examine you.'

Luke cautiously moved closer. Without warning she grabbed his head pulling it close until their foreheads connected. A force erupted out of them, Sri was thrown back while Luke and Maly's heads remained locked together.

Sri struggled to his feet and he still couldn't speak, he turned to Rotha who held her hand up and said, 'Wait.'

He watched in amazement as the strange red beams seemed to bounce around Luke and Maly's heads. They weaved in and out of each other until a bright blue light began to grow around them. It got brighter and brighter until suddenly it exploded. A white light burst from them both, it pulsed through the hall and out into the basin where it continued through the jungle.

Suddenly a powerful force pushed Maly and Luke apart. Sri forced himself forward to catch Luke, who in all the commotion had fallen unconscious. Maly on the other hand was still awake but shaken. She tried to pull herself to her feet but stumbled. Rotha raced to her aid, Maly had never been affected like this, not the hundreds of times she had performed this ritual.

'He's a walker,' she said breathlessly struggling to speak. 'The *first* walker.'

Rotha looked at her in astonishment, then back at Luke who was lying unconscious in Sri's arms.

***

The king had just held his first council meeting since he returned to Angkor. Everyone was in attendance except for Prince Srindra, which seemed to irritate him. The council meeting itself went well, the queen announced her educational plans for Champa which were enthusiastically received. Nakry confirmed that the empires finances were healthy, despite the cost of funding the war. This was mainly due to the revenue they now received from the new province. The king also imposed reparations on Champa, which helped to compensate the families who'd lost loved ones.

However, something had bothered the king since his discussion with Thorn back in Vijaya. As the council left, he asked Prince Virak, to stay behind.

'Your mother tells me how much of a support you were to her while we were all away fighting,' the king said keen to praise his son. 'I know Chantrea's betrayal must've hit you hard, but I'm glad to see you live up to your potential.'

'Father, I've tried to help her many times. But when I challenged her about mixing with the wrong kind of people, she spread a web of lies that my family were only too keen to believe. I'm afraid the mistake of trusting Chantrea must weigh heavily on Bo and Marcus. I promise to do whatever to protect my niece and nephew, while living up to your high expectations,' he lied.

'Virak it makes me so happy to hear you say that, since returning from our campaign, I've had doubts about our foreign friends,' he replied carefully. 'I'll trust you with this information, however you're forbidden to share it. General Thorn told me about powers Luke's revealed, something he's seen with his own eyes. Thorn described that he has an ability to control earthly forces. I want you to interrogate Indravarman, you seem to have a skill in finding out information, so use it. Sri is planning to question him when he returns from his trip. I want you to get to Indravarman before he comes back. Find out what he knows, find the spy in our city and find out what happened in the hall at Vijaya. Then report back to me and me alone.'

'Yes Father, I will,' he paused.

'What if you don't like the things I find out?' Virak asked.

'All I care about is the truth, protecting this land and protecting my family. Whatever you find out I'll deal with it, by whatever means,' the king replied rather menacingly.

***

It was a good ten minutes before Luke awoke, he looked around and saw everyone staring at him.

'What was that? What did you do to me?' he desperately asked the village elder.

Maly was still recovering and responded breathlessly, 'Our cores connected, except the power of your Quantum core was much greater than I've ever experienced. I couldn't contain our energies.'

'Quantum core!' Luke said, shocked. 'How do you know about Quantum physics?'

'I don't know what physics is, but our ancestors told us that our special abilities come from something they called our Quantum Cores,' Rotha interjected.

Luke's mind was bursting with more questions, he turned to Sri.

'We connected, what does that mean?' he asked frustratedly. 'What happened?'

'It was just as Maly said, your foreheads touched, followed by a bright white light, which pulsed out of you. I've never seen anything like that before and well,' he smiled. 'I've lived with you for some time and I'm used to experiencing strange happenings.'

Luke didn't laugh or respond as Sri had expected. 'Tell me what this power is,' he said firmly to Maly, his temper starting to rise.

The ground began to vibrate and the wooden hall shook violently. The sound of cracking wood filled the air, as pots crashed all around them.

'He shouldn't be able to use his powers like this, where's it coming from?' Rotha asked Maly urgently.

Maly ignored her and reached her hand out gripping Luke's.

'You need to calm down, I know this is strange and you don't understand what's happening to you, but you need to calm your mind. Rotha, fetch water now,' Maly said without breaking eye contact. 'Luke, I'll explain everything, but drink this.'

Rotha handed him a ceramic cup. Instinctively he took a sip and as the cold water flowed down his throat. The tremors began to subside, a calmness returned to Luke and to the hall.

Both Rotha and Sri were on their feet not knowing what was happening, or what to do. Maly breathed a sigh of relief.

'Now for me to truly understand what's happening to you, you'll need to tell me all about your life and how these powers started.'

'You wouldn't believe me,' Luke replied sombrely.

'Have we not shown you our secret place, shared our history and let you see our powers,' she stared at him. 'You need to trust us, like you do your prince.'

She broke into a smile.

This reaction helped him feel more at ease. He took another sip of water and began to tell them about his life, where he grew up and importantly when. He talked about Quantology, the technology Maya invented and how they found themselves in Angkor. He told them about the loss of his friends and when he started to feel his powers rise. Luke explained about how he had saved Sri and the day he killed Yom. When he'd finished opening up, it was like a huge weight had been lifted from his mind and he could see clearly for the first time since Vijaya.

'Thanks for your honesty, it's quite a journey you've been on, the technology you created seems very enlightened and insightful. However you mentioned you were the only person to be able to create the stable wormhole, is that correct?' Maly asked.

'Yes, no one has been able to create a portal like I can.'

'That's interesting,' Maly paused, 'Luke I believe you're a Quantum Walker. It was not your technology that opened the wormhole through time, but you.'

'No, that can't be right, Maya did all the calculations, we used antimatter which created the portal,' he argued.

Maly raised her hand to stop his protests. 'It may have helped, but like I said, you're a Quantum walker.

Someone who can bend time, can walk between subspace and travel between dimensions. Luke you're someone with a great gift. There have been others, including the founder of our tribe. Her female descendants have inherited some of her abilities, although none of us have the ability to time walk.'

'A Quantum walker, I don't even know what that means. Maly, how can you know the words I'm using and how can you understand about science?' Luke asked with disbelief.

'I can't give you all the answers you seek. All I can tell you is the truth about what and who you are.'

Maly gripped Luke's hands. 'Your powers will continue to grow and you'll understand more in time. Remember this, you're extremely special and can guide humanity down the right path. You can help us to become more than our petty wars and more than our selfish desires. I'll leave you with one last word of caution, learn to control your emotions. They create great instability within your core which could be your undoing. Listen to my experience, if you ever feel out of control turn to water. Think about the touch, the movement, the smell and the sound. Use it to calm those ever-expanding thoughts and to relaxed the waves in your mind.'

***

It was dark and dank as Prince Virak descended into the dungeons, there was a smell of rotting flesh and the sounds of rats gnawing bones. He walked confidently as he approached the cell that Indravarman was being held in. He stopped and looked down at the pathetic former Cham king before him. Virak waved a piece of paper containing the king's orders at the guards. He instructed them to leave as he was to interrogate the prisoner alone. The guards were under Sri's orders and didn't like being dismissed, but the king's commands were clear and they had to follow them. There was a long silence before Virak spoke.

'That didn't go to plan did it, my father and brother still live and you're in this cell,' he spat with contempt.

'How was I to know the people would turn against us and that your father had an enchanter in his service. My men didn't stand a chance against him,' Indravarman replied with equal disdain.

'What do you mean an enchanter?' Virak laughed. 'You've lost your mind old man.

Indravarman looked at him strangely. 'You really have no idea about your brother's whore.'

He smiled.

'Tell me what I need to know before my brother comes to finish the interrogation,' Virak demanded angrily.

Indravarman laughed hard, his manic face contorted with both terror and amusement.

'You, my young prince, are royally fucked. If your scum brother brings his whore with him, then all my secrets will be spilt.'

'I don't understand, you'd never break,' he replied.

'This Luke has powers. I saw him lift up one of my men with his mind and thrust a dagger deep into his throat, with just a wave of his hand. From what I've seen this was a simple task for him, if he can do that what will he do to me, to get to my secrets.'

Indravarman paused, staring at Virak.

'Your treachery will be discovered unless you kill your brother and his whore, I can guarantee you that. However there's still a chance we can turn our defeat into victory. But if you're going to do something you'll need to do it quickly and without this Luke expecting, otherwise you won't stand a chance.'

'Are you sure about his powers?' Virak pressed in disbelief. 'They claimed they were from the future, but I thought it was a trick to fool my stupid brother and sister. I've heard nothing about any powers, just the close relationship he has with my brother.'

'I'm sure, and so was Thorn. He ordered everyone to keep Luke's powers secret on pain of death. You must decide what you're going to do, you can run or fight, those are your only options now.'

A look of terror came over Virak, he'd always gotten men to fight for him and he was a coward at heart. He possessed very little fighting skills, but now he would need to fight. He would need to kill his brother and this enchanter.

'I still have men who are willing to fight with me, I'll come for you when the deed is done,' Virak said shakily.

He then turned sharply leaving Indravarman with a hope of redemption and a desire for revenge.

***

It had been hours when they finally left Maly's hut. Luke was exhausted by his ordeal and Sri had to help him up the banks of the basin. Rotha guided them through the village until they reached the gate, all the time with the Bakan archers still aiming their arrows at them.

'Luke, I advise you to tell no one about your talents, these powers put you at great risk. Sri you'll need to protect him against anyone who'd do him harm, he'll need your support. There are many out there who would come for him if his powers become widely known,' she said sadly.

'Rotha, I will protect Luke with every ounce of strength I have, you need not fear that,' Sri replied.

'The village of Bakan stands with you as an ally, if you need our support, guidance, or protection you'll have it,' she bowed and walked back into the village.

They mounted their horses and rode to join Sri's elite guard. They'd been waiting patiently for them at the outskirts of the village. Sri ordered that they ride back to the shores of Chuor Nom, they were to stay a further night as the sun had already begun to set. Much like the night before, they sat there looking over the great expanse of water bathed in the reddish moonlight, which only made Sri more nervous.

It was a restless night for them both, they rose early taking the ship back to the lake's northwest shores arriving just after mid-morning. They stayed for lunch at a local village, both a little worried about returning to Angkor. Finally Sri said they could wait no longer and they rode back to the city in the afternoon sun. The ride itself was uneventful and in truth, Luke had not spoken much since the revelations from Maly. The words 'Quantum walker' rolled over and over in his mind and his fear about his powers continued to grow.

When they reached the city the festival of enlightenment was in full flow and the citizens of Angkor were awash with delight. Luke and Sri navigated through the great crowds many of whom stopped to cheer the prince when they saw him. They reached the temple of Angkor Wat just as the sun set. The sparkling golden spires seemed to strike a thought within Luke.

'Sri, we need to go to the temple now, I need to find a piece of scripture Kalani showed me.'

Sri ordered his men to stop and they dismounted. The temple was packed. The festival of enlightenment was a great opportunity for the people to present offerings to Buddha. They passed many joyful people and headed directly to Tamal. He was enjoying the merriment of the occasion with his fellow priests.

'Brother, Luke what brings you here on this joyous night?' he asked.

Luke stepped forward and spoke fast, 'We need to see the scriptures that Kalani was studying the night he was murdered.'

Tamal's face fell, he missed his apprentice deeply and the memories of that horrid night still hit him hard.

'I've left the scriptures where he was last working on them. I couldn't quite bring myself to put them away, not yet anyway,' he said soberly. 'They're still in his quarters, feel free to seek what you need but I must ask that the manuscripts stay within the temple.'

'Of course brother,' Sri replied, gripping his hand and pulling him into a hug.

They headed down the tunnels towards Kalani's quarters which were deep beneath the temple chamber. They descended a number of stone steps, soon arriving in a dark room. Sri retrieved a torch and used a flint to light it and the room was illuminated. There were cobwebs everywhere, Luke brushed them aside and he approached the manuscript that was still lying on Kalani's desk.

'Sri this was the document he showed me, look it has strange calculations like the ones Maya used within her experiments.'

Luke put his hand on the parchment and without warning a green spark erupted from it, they both looked at each other and then a smile came over Luke's face. It was like the parchment was talking to him, he closed his eyes as waves of green light pulsed over him. After a few moments he looked up and smiled.

'I know what this means,' but as he finished the sentence, he noticed someone behind them, not just one person but many.

'Look out!' Luke shouted, and an arrow flew towards Sri.

Luke raised his hand and the arrow stopped in mid-air and dropped to the floor with a clatter. Sri raced to Luke's side pulling out his sword. More torches lit the corridor to the room and about ten men dressed in black entered, they were led by Prince Virak.

'So, what Indravarman said is true, you have powers,' he announced angrily.

'Brother what's this, who gives you the right.'

Virak interrupted Sri before he could finish, 'I give me the right, I'll end this unnatural relationship and kill you both.'

'What, you'll betray us, betray your brother?' Sri shouted back.

'I've been betraying you all my life, you with your elite guard, your victories, the way mother has doted on you and the expectation you will succeed Father. That comes to an end today.'

The ten men all raised their arrows.

'You may be able to stop one arrow Luke, but can you stop ten?'

The black assassins raised their bows and pulled them back, releasing a barrage of arrows. Luke held up his hand this time stopping all the arrows which again fell to the floor. However, his anger was building and the temple began to shake. A bright green light erupted from him which pulsed through the room and out into the temple. Suddenly the stone walls began to crack and fall all around them.

'What are you doing?' Virak shouted as one of the temple stones fell onto a black assassin crushing the man, then another was hit by falling debris, then another.

'Luke, stop you'll bring the temple down, you'll hurt our people,' Sri shouted but it was no use Luke continued.

Sri then rushed up to him pulling at his face until they were looking directly at each other.

'Luke, the ceiling, it's collapsing,' Sri shouted. 'You need to calm down, think of the calm waters of the lake, the smell, the touch, the taste.'

Virak was glued to the spot. It was like the energy that came out of Luke had immobilised him.

'Luke the ceiling,' Sri shouted again causing Luke to look up.

As rocks fell into the room, Luke's attention focused on Sri, he grabbed him tightly which broke his hold on Virak.

Virak ran to escape the room, leaving the dead or injured assassins to rot. There was a sudden intense bright purple light which filled the room. The ceiling began to collapse in on itself, Virak looked back as he fled seeing Luke and his brother enveloped by the purple light. There was a sudden flash. Virak's eyes adjusted just in time to see them both vanish. A few seconds later the ceiling came crashing down.

EPILOGUE

Return to the Future

It was a dark grey cloudy day in Cambridge, winter was beginning to turn to spring but the trees were still bare. The temperature was cool and the mist drifted over the river as a gentle breeze bristled through the trees. It was early morning on a deserted Midsummer Common when a sudden flash of purple light appeared. Out of the light stepped Luke and Sri.

They felt the cold immediately, both were dressed in their normal robes which weren't suitable for northern European weather. Sri had never experienced a temperature so cold, the climate in Angkor was always hot.

'What happened and where are we?' he asked, shaking uncontrollably.

'We're home, well what I used to call home,' Luke replied with a shiver.

A loud beep sounded, his palm reader had connected to the internet and updates began to pour in. Luke activated the holographic screen and the world news appeared, he read it carefully. Sri looked at the strange words, he didn't understand them and nothing made sense.

'It looks like I've brought us back a few days after the accident in the lab. The news is still reporting about it,' he pointed to the page.

Sri just nodded. He could see a picture of Marcus, Maya, Luke, and Kalani with strange words underneath.

'Come, let's get back to mine and change, we need to decide what to do next.'

Luke led Sri from the common and through the empty streets of Cambridge. They passed a few joggers as they walked and received some funny looks. However, no one stopped to ask about their clothing, assuming they must've been at some kind of university party.

Sri senses were in overload, the buildings, the cars and the people, it all seemed so different. Holographic screens lit up the shops, advertising everything from toothpaste to holidays. It was then he saw his home, the ruins of Angkor, on the screen in the shop window. He was scared, more scared than he'd ever been in his life.

Luke's apartment was situated on the top two floors of a large Victorian house on Hertford street, as they approached he noticed a policeman standing guard. With a wave of his hand the man collapsed and Luke walked over him.

'Don't worry he'll be fine, I've just put him to sleep,' he replied casually.

Luke placed his palm on the door, it opened and they headed up to his apartment.

As soon as he entered Luke knew his home had been searched. It was obviously someone trying to find out what had happened to them and who had sabotaged the Quantology dig. Luke walked straight into his bedroom and opened the wardrobe, he stared for a moment before pulling out some clothes.

'Put these on, we can't stay here for long my entry to the apartment has probably triggered an alarm.'

'Luke what's happening, how did we get here?' Sri pleaded, but Luke kept quiet.

'Get dressed,' he ordered. Sri did as he was asked, giving him an extremely worried look.

Luke pulled on some jeans and a jumper. He grabbed a couple of coats, scarfs and gloves and they left quickly.

'Don't look at me like that, I can't tell you anything until I'm sure we're not being listened too.'

They left the flat quickly, carefully passing the sleeping policemen, Luke guided Sri to the gardens next to the River Cam at Magdalene college. They sat on a park bench and Luke breathed deeply. He stared at the river trying to calm his mind, then turned to Sri.

'I know what a Quantum walker is, someone who can bend space and time with their mind. The equations on the parchment Kalani showed me now make sense, it made me realise that by thought alone I can open a window through time.'

'But why come here?' Sri asked desperately. 'We need to go home and save our family, they're in danger.'

‘I know.’ Luke put his head in his hands. ‘I didn’t mean for us to come here, for some reason I was pulled back to this time. I’ve tried to open a portal home, but I can’t.’

He breathed deeply again. ‘I don’t know why. I’ve run the calculations through my mind but I can’t open one. It should be working.’

‘But why here?’ Sri asked.

‘I don’t know, I wanted to get us somewhere safe and my mind flashed back to Cambridge. I knew I needed to save you. I don’t know why but I could feel how much Virak wanted to kill you, kill us both.’

Sri hugged him and gave Luke a kiss for reassurance. They held each other tightly for a few moments, both scared about their situation while trying to control their emotions. After a few minutes, Sri regained his composure and he noticed someone standing in the trees at the edge of the park. A young man was looking at them, he went to grab his sword but realised he had no weapon, he’d left it back at Luke’s apartment.

Luke noticed Sri’s reaction and he turned around. Charlie Evans was standing there watching them both intensely. He stared at them emotionless, not saying a word. Without warning he pulled out a small metallic device, pressed a few buttons and an orange gas enveloped them. Suddenly everything went dark.

ABOUT THE AUTHOR

This is the first novel by Kris Auld and he is extremely proud of his achievement.

Kris grew up in Hertfordshire, England, surrounded by beautiful countryside but also close to London. He began reading books at an early age where he found a passion for English literature, in particular Shakespeare. Kris found school difficult due to his Dyslexia but his passion to be creative led him to study media, drama and video production at university where he obtained a bachelor's degree. While studying Kris spent a semester in America which ignited his love of travel. His travels and love of history has inspired him to write this book.

After Kris completed his studies, he spent a short while working in the TV and film industry, however due to a lack of opportunities, Kris decided to move to Manchester where he began a career in finance. Over the last 15 years, Kris has continued to work in finance roles, supporting teams across the UK and around the world. While working Kris has continued his passion for studying, obtaining a number of professional qualifications.

Lockdown reignited Kris's love of reading and gave him the opportunity to write his first novel. He has big plans for the Quantology series with the aim to build it into a new genre of science fiction. Kris hopes that one day Quantology could eventually make the transition to film.

Printed in Great Britain
by Amazon

46786505R00310